Praise for

Little Monsters

A *New York Times* Editors' Choice

An Indie Next pick

An Apple Best of the Month Pick

A B&N Book Club Pick

An Amazon Best of the Month Pick

A Book of the Month Alternative Selection

A Harvard Bookstore Subscription Selection

A Boston.com Book Club Selection

"A juicy portrait of a wealthy family on the brink of disaster . . . *Little Monsters* simmers with tension as secrets explode out into the open . . . Tensely constructed and absorbing . . . A consummate summer read, which somehow evokes smooth beach glass and hot pink sunsets with nary a mention of either."

—***The Washington Post***

"*Little Monsters* is so alluring, with its sense of looming familial implosion within a cultural implosion . . . Brodeur is very deliberately examining a small family horror story within a larger political context."

—***The New York Times***

"Adrienne Brodeur knows her way around a family drama . . . [and she] weaves a story dense with stinging secrets and simmering resentments, rooted in another context that she knows well: the manicured towns and wild fringes of Cape Cod . . . Set against the island's rippling dune grasses and scrub pines, [the] narrative is as elegantly rendered as it is compulsively readable."

—***Vogue***

"A mesmerizing, modern day saga . . . The author's knowledge of Cape Cod, its environmental laws, the indigenous intricacies of land and sea and all that lives above or below the ocean or flies overhead makes *Little Monsters* a visceral, multisensorial feast woven into the perfectly paced story as each chapter builds by connecting the dots and ends with the lure of a page-turning cliff-hanger . . . It is an extraordinary story, unique while it informs even as it entertains."

—***New York Journal of Books***

"Written with a palpable love for this family and their Cape Cod home, *Little Monsters* tackles family trauma, forgiveness, and toxic masculinity."

—**Arianna Rebolini, *Bustle***

"Told in exquisite prose, this family drama shines a light on family, friendship, art, science, love, and loss."

—**Zibby Owens for Katie Couric Media**

"Filled with delicious secrets . . . One of the most heralded novels of the year."

—**Boston.com**

"[Adrienne Brodeur] is a deft and captivating storyteller."

—**Maggie Shipstead, *Condé Nast Traveler***

"Brodeur creates an evocative sense of place in a Cape Cod-set novel that's affecting and powerful."

—***The Guardian***

"Beautiful and heartbreaking . . . A compelling, earnest portrait of a family more fractured than its members realize."

—***Shelf Awareness***

"Compelling."

—**NPR's Mary Louise Kelly,**
All Things Considered

"My favorite theme [in *Little Monsters*] is the family skeleton, we've all got them—unless you're from a functioning family, which in that case, congratulations. Any dysfunctional family knows about the family skeleton

PRAISE FOR

LITTLE MONSTERS

"This smart, page-flipping novel has more secrets than you could successfully hide from your Sunday school teacher."
—**THE BOSTON GLOBE**

"A mesmerizing modern-day saga [and] a visceral, multisensorial feast . . . Extraordinary."
—**THE NEW YORK REVIEW OF BOOKS**

"The book is brilliantly written. . . . Each character's voice is vivid and strong, flawed, funny." —**JENNETTE McCURDY,**
#1 *New York Times* bestselling author of *I'm Glad My Mom Died*

"Brodeur's searing insight into character, motivations, and relationships will leave readers gasping in recognition and appreciation. Don't miss this masterpiece." —**LIBRARY JOURNAL** (starred review)

"A page-turner about the conspiracy of silence and corrosive nature of skeletons in the closet." —**FINANCIAL TIMES**

"Shimmering . . . With this intricate story, Brodeur distinguishes herself as a novelist of the first rank."
—**PUBLISHERS WEEKLY** (starred review)

"Gorgeously told . . . The work of a seasoned and wonderfully wise storyteller." —**PAULA McLAIN,**
#1 *New York Times* bestselling author of *The Paris Wife*

"Treat yourself to this novel's gorgeous writing and irresistible storyline." —**REAL SIMPLE**

"EVOCATIVE, AFFECTING, AND POWERFUL." —THE GUARDIAN

you grew up with and you pretended wasn't there, that you ignored, and some time it bubbles to the surface. That's what happens in this book. It's brilliant, and I hope you check it out!"

—**Jennette McCurdy, #1 *New York Times* bestselling author of *I'm Glad My Mom Died***

"Nobody describes the natural beauty of Cape Cod or the lovely, messy bonds of family better than Adrienne Brodeur. *Little Monsters* is an absolutely captivating read."

—**Elin Hilderbrand, *New York Times* bestselling author of *The Hotel Nantucket***

"Gorgeously told, with psychological nuance to spare, Adrienne Brodeur's latest fiction returns us to a world she knows by heart, wind-blown, wave-swept Cape Cod and the fraught, labyrinthine territory beneath the surface of family. This is the work of a seasoned and wonderfully wise storyteller. Brodeur is as masterfully attuned to the complex DNA of kindred secrets and high-risk loyalties as she is empathetic to the specifically tangled lives of the Gardner clan. We ultimately want for them what we want for ourselves, the freedom that comes with hard-won healing and truth telling, and the intimacy that waits if we're brave enough to look back down the loaded barrel of love."

—**Paula McLain, *New York Times* bestselling author of *The Paris Wife***

"*Little Monsters* is an elegant and ambitious novel, a family saga deeply rooted in the landscape of Cape Cod. Adrienne Brodeur writes about complicated, sometimes difficult people and the natural world they inhabit with lyrical precision and deep emotional intelligence."

—**Tom Perrotta, *New York Times* bestselling author of *Tracy Flick Can't Win* and *Mrs. Fletcher***

"Beautiful, lyrical and unvarnished, Adrienne Brodeur's *Little Monsters* delivers its powerful emotional punches so subtly that they sneak up on you and leave you floored."

—**Miranda Cowley Heller, *New York Times* bestselling author of *The Paper Palace***

"Who understands complicated family dynamics better than Adrienne Brodeur? *Little Monsters* is a gripping portrait of how we carry the past into the present, and how the boundaries of kinship blur and change over time."

—Mary Beth Keane, *New York Times* bestselling author of *Ask Again, Yes*

"Wrenching, psychologically complex, and emotionally satisfying, *Little Monsters* is an immersive pleasure. This sprawling, big-hearted family saga is about the lies we tell each other and ourselves that enable us to maintain alliances—and what happens when we start telling the truth."

—Christina Baker Kline, *New York Times* bestselling author of *The Orphan Train*

"Adrienne Brodeur brings to life, with her unerringly sharp eye, another complicated family, populated by brilliant, damaged characters who alternately love and drive each other crazy. Brodeur conveys an understanding of Cape Cod beyond the life of casual summer vacationers—a mysterious and beautiful coastal world where nature, not summer rentals, dominates in all its wonder—and of the demanding, infuriating patriarch who presides over the landscape. With rare compassion, she shows how it is possible to love the same people who may have hurt us most—and to forgive them their trespasses."

—Joyce Maynard, *New York Times* bestselling author

"In *Little Monsters*, Adrienne Brodeur plunges into a multicharactered family novel that is richly satisfying, like the best of meals, taking the reader into the heart of what Freud called 'the family romance,' with all its complexities, evasions, buried guilts, forbidden passions and sibling rivalry. As sharply observant about her characters as she is of the landscape and seascape of Cape Cod, where they live, her novel is that rarest of things: a truly great read."

—Michael Korda, *New York Times* bestselling author

"I so admire the layered complexity of this beautiful novel about a flawed yet unforgettable family—the interlocking ironies and wounds and strivings for love and clarity and accomplishment and growth, all so deeply embedded in the lush natural world that is the Cape. Every character in this mesmerizing story is distinct and real, and I found myself rooting for them all."

—Andre Dubus III, *New York Times* bestselling author of *House of Sand and Fog*

"Smart, funny, and beautifully written. Brodeur is a brilliant dissector of family relationships, a lyricist of the natural world, and an astute observer of our inner turmoils."

—Monica Ali, bestselling author of *Love Marriage*

"Engrossing . . . Brodeur writes knowingly and lyrically of both the coastal area and the casual privilege of its denizens . . . Prepare for an emotional gut punch."

—Zoomer Magazine

"Brodeur offers a nuanced and thoughtful portrait of Cape Cod and its culture . . . *Little Monsters* is a perceptive novel about a complicated family that will both infuriate and fascinate readers."

—BookReporter

"A sophisticated page-turner with both heart and brains."

—Hannah Harlow, *The Cricket*

"The ultimate beach read and then some!"

—The Colorado Sun

"Thoughtful . . . Brodeur effectively juggles these interlocking perspectives in chapters that shift seamlessly . . . [She] makes effective use of her familiarity with the captivating qualities of that setting, its natural beauty and wildlife, to lend texture to the story. [A] quietly engaging novel."

—BookPage

"Brodeur brings the Cape to life . . . a beautiful tribute to a beautiful place . . . I was reminded of both Ann Tyler's and Barbara Kingsolver's work . . . A very enjoyable read."

—WAMC's Book Picks from Bennington Bookshop's Phil Lewis

ALSO BY ADRIENNE BRODEUR

Wild Game

Little Monsters

a novel

Adrienne Brodeur

Avid Reader Press

New York London Toronto Sydney New Delhi

Avid Reader Press
An Imprint of Simon & Schuster, LLC
1230 Avenue of the Americas
New York, NY 10020

First Avid Reader Press trade paperback edition May 2024

AVID READER PRESS and colophon are trademarks of Simon & Schuster, LLC

Simon & Schuster: Celebrating 100 Years of Publishing in 2024

For information about special discounts for bulk purchases, please contact Simon & Schuster Special Sales at 1-866-506-1949 or business@simonandschuster.com.

The Simon & Schuster Speakers Bureau can bring authors to your live event. For more information or to book an event, contact the Simon & Schuster Speakers Bureau at 1-866-248-3049 or visit our website at www.simonspeakers.com.

Manufactured in the United States of America

1 3 5 7 9 10 8 6 4 2

Library of Congress Cataloging-in-Publication Data

Names: Brodeur, Adrienne, author.
Title: Little monsters : a novel / Adrienne Brodeur.
Description: First Avid Reader Press hardcover edition. | New York : Avid Reader Press, 2023. |
Identifiers: LCCN 2023005845 (print) | LCCN 2023005846 (ebook) | ISBN 9781982198107 (hardcover) | ISBN 9781982198121 (ebook)
Subjects: LCSH: Cape Cod Bay (Mass.)—Fiction. | BISAC: FICTION / Family Life / Siblings | FICTION / Literary | LCGFT: Domestic fiction. | Novels.
Classification: LCC PS3602.R6346 L58 2023 (print) | LCC PS3602.R6346 (ebook) | DDC 813/.6 [B]—dc23/eng/20230306
LC record available at https://lccn.loc.gov/2023005845
LC ebook record available at https://lccn.loc.gov/2023005846

ISBN 978-1-9821-9810-7
ISBN 978-1-9821-9811-4 (pbk)
ISBN 978-1-9821-9812-1 (ebook)

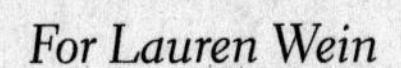
For Lauren Wein

If you cannot get rid of the family skeleton,
you may as well make it dance.

—GEORGE BERNARD SHAW

April

Adam

Adam Gardner hadn't slept well in weeks. He awoke daily to random words, incoherent thoughts, and fleeting images, convinced that their meaning, though not yet clear, would develop in the gelatin silver process of his mind. Each morning, buzzing, he slung his legs off the bed and sat bolt upright, naked, allowing his male parts to hang over the edge of the mattress, and did his best to capture these jangled dreams, recording what details he could remember in a spiral-bound notebook kept by his bedside. His daytime musings spread onto legal pads, Post-it Notes, and the backs of envelopes and receipts, mostly in the form of unedited bullet-point lists. His house, located deep in the Wellfleet Woods, was littered with scraps of paper covered with his fastidious penmanship.

- *Deepening pitch of whale vocalizations*
- *Ocean spirals: shells, whirlpools, waves, bubble nets, seahorse tails*
- *Sound's relationship to the inner-ear labyrinth (another spiral?)*
- *Mystery of infinity: 1 = .99999999 . . .*

Adam tried to decipher the clues his mind was depositing. He had one big discovery left in him, he felt sure of that. This thing, whatever it was—an idea? a theory?—was taking its own sweet time to make itself known. He knew he needed to trust the process. If he could practice patience and maintain equilibrium, Adam felt certain that every book he'd ever read, every piece of art that had ever moved him, every conversation, creature, curiosity, and concept he'd encountered in his lifetime would align like cherries in the slot machine of his mind.

For now, the anticipation of it, the pre-buzz of impending discovery, was as mouthwatering as the squeak of a wine cork before dinner.

He basked in an exquisite sensation of déjà vu, feeling a comradeship with other great discoverers: James Cook, Charles Darwin, Jacques Cousteau . . .

To his credit, at the onset of this latest bout of insomnia, Adam followed protocol and made an appointment at the clinic in Hyannis knowing full well what to expect: a blood draw, a barrage of questions, an adjustment of medication. What he hadn't expected was that the doctor who'd been treating him for the last three decades had retired. Why Dr. Peabody hadn't bothered to inform him directly was beyond him. Thirty years was . . . well, a very long time. Adam pointed out the oversight to the front desk clerk, a busty young woman with blue fingernails, who assured him an email had been sent to patients the previous month. Had he thought to check his junk folder? she asked, clicking together her talons. Adam started to answer but held his tongue. (Who, but an idiot, would bother to check a "junk" folder?) He followed her down the hall to the exam room, still puzzling over why his longtime doctor, at least five years his junior, would have retired. To do what?

In Peabody's place, a kid half Adam's age, outfitted in tight pants and alarmingly bright orange socks, strode into the exam room. Was it too much to ask that the person evaluating his mental state have at least one gray hair on his head? The new doctor acknowledged Adam only cursorily, opting to study his electronic patient chart first—mistake number one. Mistake number two was the doctor's lecture on "sleep hygiene." For the love of God! Why not just call a thing a thing? "Passed away," "big-boned"—what was so wrong with "dead" and "fat"? Euphemisms were tools of the feeble-minded. "Hygiene" brought to mind feminine products, something Adam did not wish to contemplate. But that led him to think about parts of the female anatomy he *did* like to contemplate.

Stay focused, Adam reminded himself. He took notice of the boy's weak chin.

"I don't think we've had the pleasure of a proper introduction," Adam said, cutting the lecture short. "I'm Dr. Gardner."

In his lifetime, Adam Gardner, Ph.D., had had an acclaimed career as a research scientist for the Cape Cod Institute of Oceanography,

CCIO to those in the know. His glory days were in the late 1970s when, as a young scientist, he was part of a team that disproved once and for all the notion that life could be sustained only by a photosynthesis-based food chain. In the pitch-black depths of the Pacific Ocean north of the Galápagos Islands, they'd encountered evidence—in the form of foot-long clams, giant red tube worms, and spiny white crabs—that even in darkness, there was life. Adam and his team discovered and named more than two dozen species. In the decades since those early successes, he'd become one of the foremost experts on cetacean biology, studying the population dynamics and communication of humpback whales. Beyond these professional accomplishments, he was a Vietnam veteran who had single-handedly raised his two children after his beloved first wife, Emily, died suddenly at the age of thirty. In short: he wasn't about to let some kid outrank him.

Adam looked his so-called doctor in the eye and delivered a formidable handshake. He'd teach this generation proper conduct, one millennial at a time.

"It's a real pleasure, Dr. Gardner," the doctor replied, accepting the rebuke with bemused resignation.

"I believe the word you're after is 'habit,'" Adam said.

The doctor regarded him blankly.

"Sleep *habit*," Adam repeated. "Not 'hygiene.'"

At this, the doctor plastered on the kind of smile a kindergarten teacher might offer an unruly child at the end of a long day. He exhaled audibly and resumed his list of banal recommendations: limit stress, exercise daily, eat a balanced diet. The doctor reviewed Adam's long history of episodes, noting that he generally cycled once a year, typically in the late spring, with symptoms lasting anywhere from ten to fourteen weeks. "Looks like you're not too far off your normal schedule," he said. "We should be able to manage this pharmacologically, no problem. That said, many of my patients benefit from group therapy. Have you considered this option, Dr. Gardner?"

Adam regarded the doctor's garish orange socks, a pathetic attempt at nonconformity. Back in his day, socks like those indicated only one thing:

a pansy. Not that he had anything against gays, but when had it become so hard to tell them from normal guys? And when had doctors stopped wearing white coats? No one gave a damn about appearances anymore, as far as he could tell—full arm tattoos on white-collar professionals, women in their "comfortable" shoes, blue jeans as the pant of choice.

It was the first day of April 2016, and the world was a white-hot mess. Adam was willing to put money down that soon the presidential choice would be between a boorish billionaire and an unscrupulous woman. Hard to say which was worse. He'd vote for the woman, maybe, but he couldn't stand either of them—the pronouncements, promises, platitudes. But really, how was the billionaire still standing? The things that man said about women, Blacks, Mexicans, Muslims! Adam's mistakes were never so easily ignored. If he so much as glanced at a woman the wrong way—or, God forbid, commented on her appearance—he'd get an indignant earful from someone, most likely his granddaughter, Tessa, or his daughter, Abby. When had it become a crime to appreciate an attractive woman?

One thing was for sure: he'd be damned if he would abide by the half-baked blather of a child doctor. As far as he was concerned, this young man could take a long swim in shark-infested waters before he'd consent to any of his quack remedies. Adam closed his eyes and massaged his temples with his thumbs as his mind raced.

"Dr. Gardner?"

The voices in his head, which had been passing through for several weeks, seemed to have taken up permanent residency. "Right here, Doctor," Adam replied, blinking his eyes open and smiling. He tried to focus. What was the question? Oh yes, if he'd considered group therapy. Adam rearranged his features to look as if he was contemplating sound advice. "I get all the support I need from my children. From my family."

"Okay, then. Is the CVS in Orleans still your primary pharmacy?" the doctor asked, concluding their visit as he'd started it, hunched over his computer.

Adam confirmed that it was.

"Great. I'm emailing in the prescription now."

• • •

Determined to conduct himself as a model patient, Adam drove himself straight to the pharmacy to pick up his medications.

He waited in line behind a lumpy woman in leggings, an unfortunate fashion choice. Once she waddled off, it was his turn. Adam handed over the prescription slips—although the doctor had emailed them, he insisted on a paper copy—and smiled patiently at the bespectacled man who moved like molasses behind the counter. When the pharmacist finally presented him with his two bags of bottles, Adam could practically hear his doctor's computer pinging from twenty miles away, alerting the good man that his new patient, Adam Gardner, Ph.D., had picked up his lithium and Seroquel prescriptions and was in medical compliance.

If Adam was serious about his plan, he had to stay in control. He'd had slipups before—too many to count, really—but this time would be different. For the first time, Adam intended to succumb knowingly to the allure of mania. He would enter the state with intention and leverage it to his advantage. *Perhaps with careful planning*, he thought, rattling the pills in their containers, *he could extend his mania beyond its usual course, buying himself enough time to solve the puzzle of cetacean language.* His goal was to announce his breakthrough by his seventieth birthday, August 18. To think, so many people were desperate to get their hands on a bottle of Ritalin or Adderall, and Adam was lucky enough to have a built-in supply. He'd been around this block enough times to know how to read the signals. The trick would be to monitor his moods and avoid spiraling out of control. (Ha! Another spiral.) What did he have to lose? He lived alone: no wife to worry about, no children to neglect. Hell, the simple fact that he was weighing the pros and cons of the decision was evidence enough that he was behaving rationally. That others found his ingenuity threatening was not his problem; perhaps they should be the ones consuming mood-regulating drugs. Soon his brain would be making the types of cosmic connections only possible once liberated from its narcotic anesthetization. He realized now that lithium, the magical salt that had stabilized his moods for years, had also been sapping his energy and brainpower. The lithium rationing would start today. He'd drop his dose by half—maybe three-quarters—and tweak as necessary.

Exiting the pharmacy, white prescription bags tucked under his arm, Adam felt giddy at having outmaneuvered his odiously smug new doctor. So much so that when he saw the overhead camera suspended in the corner, he flipped it the bird. *I wasn't born yesterday, Socks.* With a spring in his step, he climbed into his beloved 2002 Subaru, patted the steering wheel, and noted with satisfaction that the odometer had just passed 208,000 miles.

Route 6 was chock-full of incompetent drivers, as usual, people who had no business being on the road. Adam swore under his breath at an old lady driving forty in the fast lane and raised his arm out the window at a lunatic in a convertible cutting in and out of traffic. It would only get worse in the coming months when knuckleheads from around the country descended on Cape Cod for their summer vacations, cars loaded down with bikes, surfboards, and diapered toddlers.

At home, Adam tossed the pharmacy bags on the kitchen counter and made himself a cup of tea, which he took outside. He wrapped his teabag around a spoon and set it aside so he could use it again later. Pine needles had gathered between the slats of his large wooden deck, and Adam contemplated giving it a sweep but instead sank into the Adirondack chair facing the pond. A gentle breeze stirred the budding leaves in the topmost branches of the trees, but the air was still at ground level, the pond water glassy. It was a mild day that signaled spring was arriving on schedule: cattails rising, waterfowl returning to nest, frogs croaking lusty songs. But the evenings were still cool enough that he'd pull the extra blanket at his footboard over himself as he went to bed. Time was passing. The end of another decade loomed. If he was lucky, he figured he might have five—maybe ten—good years of brilliance left in him. The only thing that mattered now was coaxing this new idea out of hiding. An overhead movement caught his attention, an osprey being driven over the tree line by a group of smaller birds. Adam could relate—those aggressive, young scientists at CCIO clearly wanted him gone.

Adam willed his gaze to soften. The pond and the woods blurred, and he turned his concentration inward, hovering over the dazzling presence of his idea, which was still just out of reach. It was like swimming beyond the coral reefs and snorkeling out to where the shelf dropped off. One moment, you're studying the white-pink sand below; the next, you're over a blue-black abyss and staring into darkness. The only way to proceed is to steady your nerves, take a breath, and plunge into the depths, trusting that the darkness will hold you. Like birth. Or death.

Ken

When the call with his lawyer concluded, Ken Gardner bowed his head, placed his hands together in prayer, and pressed his thumbs to his forehead, absorbing the magnitude of what had just happened: the deal was inked.

"Thank you," he whispered. "Thank you, Brian." (His business partner.) "Thank you, Phil." (His lawyer.) "Thank you, Stefan." (His lender.) "Thank you, God." He noted the date, April 7, and committed it to memory. Ken would make more money in 2016 than he'd expected to earn in his lifetime. The thought of the tax implications sickened him, but Phil would figure out the loopholes. That's what he was paid to do. He was a genius at it.

For now, Ken would focus on the positive. At this very moment, money was being whisked electronically out of one account and into another. To be precise, money was flying into the account of a shell company Phil had created for just this purpose. Ken could practically hear the delightful percussive sound of flipping bills, like an ATM delivering cash. He was sitting behind his large and tidy desk, alone in what his twin daughters had dubbed "Command Central," a high-tech workspace set off from their home overlooking Stage Harbor in Chatham.

"Thank you," he said again.

Having married into an old Boston Brahmin family—one that took pride in tracing its ancestry back to the original seventeenth-century clergy of the colonial ruling class—Ken already had social status and access to money, plenty of it. But this deal changed the balance of things. For starters, he'd no longer feel beholden to his wife. He'd be pulling his own weight; this money was all his. Well, technically not *all* his. His father-in-law had been the angel investor who'd put up the dough in the first place, but that's what Theodore Lowell did: invest the family money. Ken would take enormous pleasure in paying the old man back. The Lowell family stood to make lots off this deal, perhaps even enough to feel indebted to Ken for a change. Probably not. But the bottom line was, this windfall was his.

A surge of electricity shot through his limbs, a tingling sensation that made him feel like he was having an out-of-body experience, watching himself from above both as the quarterback and the fan. One minute, he was on the field; the next, he was in the bleachers. On the field. In the bleachers. Field. Bleachers. Even though Ken had known for months now that it was all systems go—the deal was going to happen—the gulf between anticipation and realization was more profound than he'd imagined. This was what power felt like. There was something else in the mix, too: relief. Huge. Fucking. Relief. All these years of planning, effort, and discipline weren't for naught. No one would be laughing at him now.

Ken said a quick prayer. He'd converted to Episcopalianism—if going from nothing to something counted as "converting"—when he and Jenny had married. His father-in-law had encouraged it, pointing out the advantages: country club memberships, a wealthy network, political connections. "If you haven't heard, son, God is an Episcopalian from Boston," Theo had joked.

But to his surprise, Ken took his conversion and vows seriously and, over the years, developed a solid personal relationship with God. He prayed nightly, attended services on Sundays, and created rules to make sure he stayed in line. He could look but not touch, for example. Ken felt sure God understood the baser male inclinations, having created man in his image and all, so he negotiated a fair deal, a deal he could live with, a deal in which he would not cheat on his wife. Ken allowed himself regular use of porn—what red-blooded American male did not?—but limited visits to strip clubs to out-of-state business trips. Lap dances were for special occasions only.

Ken pumped the air with his fists. "Yes. Yes. Yes," he repeated until the words blended into a serpentine hiss, a sound that transported him back to his sixth-grade biology lab and a room full of reptiles and amphibians.

He stood holding a scalpel over his frog, but instead of diving in like the other kids, he paused, bile rising in the back of his throat. It took him only a second or two to regain his composure, steady his breath, and drag the knife down the two inches of body. But in those two seconds, all was lost. Danny McCormick, the most popular kid in his class, had seen his hesitation, and Ken's reputation as a loser was sealed in middle school as it had been in elementary, where he'd been teased for not having a mother and crying easily, but most of all, for being fat.

Well, who's crying now, Danny McCormick?

Ken had kept an eye on that dickhead's net worth, and from now on, it would be from his rearview mirror. Adrenaline coursed through his bloodstream, and he stood up. The experience felt physical, as if his body was expanding in tandem with his financial portfolio. He'd just joined the ranks of men who owned the world and could buy whatever they pleased: a $2,000 bottle of wine, a Ferrari, a box at Fenway.

Ken had always wanted to be rich, but, like most people, he didn't know how to get there other than to keep running faster on the treadmill. After college, he'd made a better-than-average living by flipping houses, but still, it was real estate development with a lowercase "r." It wasn't until Jenny came into his life and her father encouraged him to broaden his horizons that the playing field changed.

"To quote Yogi Berra, son," Theo said, "'A nickel ain't worth a dime anymore.'" At Ken's blank stare, he added, "If you're going to be part of the family, you need to start thinking like a Lowell. And that means *big*. Don't build residences, Ken, build communities. What's the next housing trend? That's the question you should be asking yourself."

At those words, something clicked. The next big trend was obvious. Ken had studied the census figures and knew that there were close to fifty million people in the country older than sixty-five. In another twenty years, that number would increase again by half. *Cha-ching*. He'd been only thirty-one when he bought—albeit with a seven-figure leg up from his father-in-law—a tract of land with a singular vision: to create a state-of-the-art retirement facility for discerning and exceedingly wealthy seniors. These would not be your grandmother's cookie-cutter assisted-living apartments.

From the start, Ken had zeroed in on the 1 percent of that senior population, betting that if he spared no expense in creating stunning prototype designs for homes and communities that not only were Green but also took advantage of all the latest technology—integrating exterior-space planning with health-focused and ergonomically thoughtful interiors—wealthy seniors would line up to pay top dollar. Ken's mother had been an architect, and Ken liked to think that he'd inherited her sense of proportion, space, and light.

Ten long years of negotiating, financing, designing, and marketing later, his gamble paid off. Not only had his designs won every "silver" architecture award out there, but they'd also garnered accolades in mainstream architectural journals for their "innovative and purposeful aesthetics" and "seamless attention to form and function." Yes, his mother would have been proud. Most remarkably—and what his lawyer had just confirmed—Ken had been able to translate and leverage his original vision for a blue-ribbon senior community on Cape Cod into a viable business model that could be duplicated in tony zip codes across the country. What Melvin Simon did for the American mall in the 1980s was what Ken Gardner would do for retirement communities nationwide today. Best of all, the money he made would pave the way for his political aspirations. He had plans to run for the House of Representatives in 2018. Then the Senate. And after that . . . Well, he didn't allow himself to say it aloud.

"Alexa, call Jenny," Ken said.

His wife's voicemail picked up.

"Babe, where are you? Call me as soon as you get this. I just closed. Everything's real now. I want to celebrate." Unexpectedly, Ken felt turned on, some conspiracy of adrenaline, nerves, and blood vessels. Already, the power dynamic in his marriage was shifting. "I'd like to meet in Boston. Tell the babysitter we need her to spend the night with the girls. Don't take *no* for an answer. Pay her triple time, whatever. Reserve a room at the Ritz. Meet me at the bar at seven p.m." He loved the way it felt to talk to Jenny this way.

"Alexa, call Abby."

Voicemail again. Ken hung up without leaving a message. *Probably for the best*, he thought. Abby wouldn't quite get the significance and, if they spoke, she would likely say something annoying. Something sanctimonious. Something emasculating, like, "Oh, that's wonderful, Ken. If it makes you happy, that's all that matters." And then he'd want to kill her. Abby competed with Ken by pretending not to care, which he had to admit was a fucking brilliant strategy. No way to win. She was just like their father, two peas in a pod with their moral superiority and talk of purposeful work. They never put it exactly that way, of course, but they both acted as if the pursuit of money was somehow vulgar, beneath them. But guess who they ran to whenever they needed help? He'd been bankrolling his sister for years, allowing her free use of their mother's studio space (technically his), and he'd loaned his father money on occasion.

Ken decided then and there that he would sit on the news until he figured out the best way to share it. But what would that be? He could show up for the next family dinner in a Lamborghini (not really his style). Or treat the whole gang to a first-class trip to Tahiti. Or—now here was a good idea—he could give his father an extravagant gift for his upcoming seventieth birthday, a gift so over-the-top that the old leftie might think twice about his condemnations of capitalism, religion, and freedom.

Ken stood, reached into his pants pocket, and pulled out his lucky golf ball, placing it carefully on his putting mat, a long and narrow rectangle of green that ran almost the length of Command Central. He waggled his club, which had a sweet spot the size of a nickel at best, and squared off. *Concentrate*, he told himself. "Listen to me, you dimpled son of a bitch," he told the ball. "You were put on this earth to do only one thing: go into that hole." Ken focused, drew the club back a few inches, and gave it the restrained tap that sent the ball rolling in a perfectly straight line, up the tiny slope, and into the hole. *Yes!*

"Alexa, turn off computer. Turn off lights. Shades up."

As the blinds lifted, Ken blinked against the morning sunlight, glinting off the scalloped waves of the inlet. Then he noticed the exposed root system of a shrub that had gone over the edge of the embankment. Despite the fortune he'd spent shoring up his property line, nature seemed to be winning.

"Alexa, play 'Like a Rolling Stone' by Bob Dylan."

His mother's favorite song. He flashed back to his childhood, him swaying on her feet, and felt a stab of longing.

"Alexa, louder," he said. His mother had been dead for thirty-eight years—since he was three and a half years old. He had no idea why she was suddenly on his mind all the time. He needed to fire that damn shrink of his. Vulnerability was overrated. But then Ken felt his mother's presence, along with a swelling in his heart that he read as her approval of his success. Emily Gardner wanted this for him. She was proud of his accomplishments, and he could feel it. Ken recalled how she used to kiss the top of his head and say, "I love you more than anything in the whole wide world." She'd inscribed those words into his copy of *Where the Wild Things Are*, which he kept hidden at the back of the bottom-left drawer of his desk, so he could pull it out from time to time and run his fingers across the words she'd written just for him. Sometimes, knowing that his mother had loved him the most felt like all he had.

When the song ended, Ken opened the door to Command Central and took in the smells of the harbor—the brine, the seaweed, the distant fumes sputtering from the stern of a fishing boat. The tide had turned and was starting to come in, slowly at first with a deceptively thin membrane of water gently licking the shore. But soon it would gather strength, stopping at nothing until the harbor was filled to the brim. Then, after a moment of slack, it would reverse itself, rushing back through the channel, dragging bits of his precious shoreline along with it. Today, Ken would try not to let thoughts of erosion ruin his good mood.

Overhead, the wind pushed ivory clouds into silver-edged mountains and, looking at them, Ken felt transported, as if for one moment, he understood everything important in life. But when he tried to zero in on the sensation, it was as elusive as a dream. No matter. He tossed a balled-up to-do list into his wastebasket—score!—and redirected his thoughts back to the tangible: planting more vegetation to stabilize his embankment, determining locations for the next three Gardner retirement communities, and raising capital for his congressional campaign. With this deal, Ken had created a path for himself. He punched the air. He was untouchable.

Abby

By the time Abby pulled into the small parking lot above Coast Guard Beach in North Truro, she was fifteen minutes late and annoyed with herself. It was an interview, for God's sake. She'd been the one who suggested they meet here and start with a beach walk, and she couldn't even arrive on time. This profile, national coverage in a prestigious art magazine, was a huge deal for her. As was her upcoming group exhibition at the Institute of Contemporary Art in October, where her work would be included in a show called "Identity and Self-Portraiture."

The contemporary art world was more localized than people realized, and it was rare to succeed if you didn't live in a major art center—New York, Los Angeles, Miami. People who were part of the art scene understood this. But from the outside—where her father and brother stood—it seemed ludicrous. Paint. Brushes. Canvas. Couldn't that be done anywhere? But how to explain to two men who didn't know how to listen that to get traction in the art world—with dealers, critics, buyers, and other artists—convenience and accessibility were key? The public needed to be able to visit your studio and experience your work, not easy on this sandbar with its single main highway. But remote as her location was, Abby did have an advantage that most artists didn't and that was the Arcadia, her glorious and free studio space in the dunes, designed and built by her mother. It was also Abby's home, having a small bedroom and bathroom off the back, everything she needed.

Abby glanced at herself in the rearview mirror. She put on a knit cap, sliding a forefinger along each side to smooth down her hair. Better.

Frida's tail pounded maniacally against the passenger seat and door. "Hold on, girl," Abby said, reaching under the seat for the leash only to realize she'd forgotten it on the peg beside her front door. Her fingers found a poop bag among the detritus of the passenger-side floor. Hopefully, the reporter from *Art Observer* magazine wouldn't notice she was a total mess.

Rachel Draper was easy to spot, propped against the only car with New York plates, staring out at the vast ocean and looking more stylish than any local. She wore dark jeans and a gray turtleneck, and was huddled into a lightweight, fitted down jacket. Her delicate scarf, the color of blood, fluttered on the breeze like a living thing.

When Abby opened the driver's side door, she was smacked by a brisk ocean wind. Frida bounded over her lap and sprang down the sloping dune to the shoreline, where a flock of gulls lifted lazily to avoid her. Abby pulled the tab on her jacket's zipper, knitting its teeth, and stepped out of the car.

Rachel's gaze went from the dog to Abby, and she pushed her sunglasses onto her head. "Abigail?"

"Yes. Hi, Rachel," Abby said, reaching for Rachel's outstretched hand. "I'm so sorry I'm late. And please, call me Abby."

"It's so nice to finally meet you, Abby. I'm a big fan. And who's that?" she asked, her eyes following Frida as she raced along the water's edge.

"That's Frida," Abby said.

"Frida," she repeated and smiled. "Such a great name. I love goldens. I have two at home."

A dog person. Rachel looked to be in her late fifties with blue-gray eyes and a kind, open face. Abby liked her immediately.

From where they stood, the beach below seemed to stretch indefinitely in both directions. The Atlantic was unseasonably calm, sending in waves that didn't so much break as dissolve when they came ashore, depositing thin lines of lacy foam as the water retreated. The sandbars were submerged, visible only as green patches beneath the dark water, and the tide was still going out, which meant that walking conditions would be excellent for the next several hours.

At the edge of the parking lot, a smocked artist in fingerless gloves stood behind an easel facing the dunes to the north. This was the stereotype that Abby was up against, that Cape Cod artists painted the visual equivalent of romance novels: sunsets over marshes, plovers scurrying along the wave line, lobster boats followed by flocks of gulls. Pleasing vistas to hang over a mantel. This artist was putting the finishing touches on a cumulus cloud, and to Abby's dismay, she'd missed everything unique about it: the gradations of illumination, the hidden colors, and the curving layers that gave it dimension. Abby had stopped painting seascapes in high school.

"My God, talk about breathtaking," Rachel said, one hand on her brow to shield her eyes from the late-morning sun. "Is this where you walk every day?"

"Oh, no, not every day. I'm an equal opportunist when it comes to beaches," Abby said, smiling. "I also love Race Point and Cahoon Hollow, but I walk on the bay side, too. It all depends on tide, wind, and mood."

Rachel strapped her iPhone high up on her arm, explaining that she would be taping the interview.

A familiar dread beat its wings inside Abby's chest. Talking about her art, about herself, had never been easy, and her new paintings were personal, a departure from the sculptures that had brought her into the public eye. Those pieces, life-size replicas of sea creatures made from garbage collected from Cape beaches—a humpback whale skeleton assembled out of discarded bleach containers, a great white shark composed of flip-flops fastened together with strips of deflated Mylar balloons, enormous starfish made from beer bottles, tampon applicators, golf balls, and the like—told a straightforward narrative, calling attention to ocean dumping. From a distance, they were appealing and inviting; up close, they packed a punch. Abby's big break came when Jeff Koons—who'd seen her work while vacationing in Provincetown—mentioned her giant loggerhead sea turtle in an interview when answering a question about young artists to watch. Overnight, it seemed, she had fans and an exhibit in a local gallery. The loggerhead sold for $12,000, a life-altering sum of money to her at the time. But that was a decade ago and the frenzy was short-lived. Her follow-up show didn't yield any sales, and her gallery dropped her.

Abby's new work was far more intimate. She wasn't sure how to talk about it, let alone to a reporter on the record. *A bit late for regrets now*, she thought, and popped a piece of cinnamon gum into her mouth, chewing until her mouth tingled. A profile in *Art Observer* was only a good thing, she reminded herself. A great thing. Hard-earned.

There was a chance, albeit a slim one, that her work would be featured on the cover. A photographer was scheduled to shoot her at her studio in the summer. Even if the cover didn't happen, a profile in *Art Observer* was still the type of exposure that could move the needle, allowing her to quit her teaching job at Nauset High School and support herself with her art. It wasn't that she didn't like to teach; she did. She loved her students, and they loved her. But teaching meant less time painting, and she found herself counting the days until the end of the school year. The issue would hit the stands in October.

"All set," Rachel said. "Ready?"

On the shoreline, they fell into an easy banter as Frida ran ahead and looped back, again and again, chasing sandpipers that pecked along the waterline for worms and sand fleas. Abby recited her basic biographical information: born and raised on Cape Cod; highly regarded marine biologist father; architect mother who'd died young; successful real estate–developer brother; graduate of RISD, 1999; had been making art on Cape Cod ever since.

"I read an article about your father in the *Cape Cod Times*. That must have been challenging for him—pulling it together after your mother's death, maintaining prominence in his field while raising you two mostly single-handedly. Not every man could do that. And look at you both now, thriving in your respective spheres. Amazing," Rachel said.

Abby smiled. Yep, that was the official family.

"Let's talk about your art. Do you paint with a goal in mind?" Rachel asked.

"Storytelling," Abby said. "My goal is narrative, to tell a story that strikes a nerve. Whenever I paint the truth, no matter how strange, people see themselves in it. Life is in the details."

"How do you know when it's working?" Rachel asked.

Abby kicked the sand ahead of her with the toe of her sneaker. Making art felt dangerous and exhilarating. "It's like how you feel when you let go of the rope as you swing out over a dark pond."

As they walked, Abby collected things that caught her eye: elegantly spiraled whelks, worn bits of driftwood, the brittle, black egg case of a skate with sinister prongs on both ends. In these items, she found shadows, curves, and patterns invisible to most people. Thanks to winter storms and a lack of tourists, April was a great month for beachcombing. But not everything she picked up was from the natural world; she also gathered marine debris that had floated in from gyres and discarded or forgotten junk left by beachgoers from seasons past: a knot of frayed rope, a rusted lure, the head of a Barbie doll. She always walked with a mesh bag slung over her shoulder for hauling treasures.

About a mile into their walk, Abby saw a distant spray that she thought might be a whale spouting. Hoping to see another, she and Rachel plunked down onto the sand and squinted into the water's glare. Rachel sat cross-legged with an erect spine, her shoulders pulled down and back, like a yogi. Abby was hunched forward, arms wrapped around her knees.

"This is when they come back to the Cape to feed," Abby said, unfolding herself and straightening her back, willing herself to blossom.

They stared at the horizon, the point where sky and sea melted into each other, but saw no whales. Frida, meanwhile, played an interspecies game of hide-and-seek with a seal, barking frantically each time it bobbed under the surface, only to pop up a minute later.

"So, should we talk about your new work?" Rachel suggested. "I'm curious what precipitated the departure from sculpture."

All at once, Abby couldn't wait to get Rachel to the Arcadia. "Let's head to my place." She hoped the work would speak for itself.

The wind pushed them along as they walked back to Coast Guard Beach. A half-mile from the parking lot, a broken bit of ceramic, periwinkle blue with a distinctive orange serpentine pattern, softened and rounded by the ocean, caught Abby's eye. Goose bumps rose like constellations on her forearms. She hadn't found a specimen like this in over a year. It was a rare pattern—one she knew from research was not mass-produced—and yet, she had a full bowl of these fragments on a table in her studio. Over the years, she'd found pieces in such far-flung places as Turks and Caicos, Corsica, Montauk, and right here on Cape Cod.

"What an unusual pattern," Rachel observed.

"Isn't it?" Abby ran a finger across the raised glaze of the snake as if she were reading Braille. However foolish it sounded, she'd always believed that these ceramic chunks were gifts—messages, really—from her mother. She'd confided this secret on only one occasion: to her brother when she was eight and he was eleven. It had not gone well. Kenny had become enraged and accused her of lying, insisting she stop pretending she had some special connection to their mother. "You don't. And you never will," he told her. When she protested, her brother said, "You know you're the reason she's dead, don't you, Abby?" That silenced her.

Later that night, Kenny slipped into her bed to apologize, distraught. "I didn't mean it," he said. But Abby knew he had. "I'm sorry," he said. "I just miss her." Overwhelmed by guilt and confusion, Abby comforted him, heartbroken to know that she was responsible for their mother's death and her brother's loss. She vowed to do everything she could to make things right with him, holding him as he wept, embracing him until his tense body relaxed beside her and he was overtaken by sleep. From that day forward, she kept her communications with her mother to herself.

Abby had been a collector for as long as she could remember. When she was little, her father would leave her on the beach for long stretches of time while he took Kenny sailing. In hindsight, those solitary days were formative for her as an artist. For hours, she would build neighborhoods out of seaweed, driftwood, shells, and whatever flotsam and jetsam she came across. But she was never truly alone. Her mother was always right there on the beach with her, tossing treasures a few feet ahead for her to discover. She'd wonder where each object came from, and stories would drop into her head: an iron nail had been part of a Viking ship; a barnacle-covered pebble had traveled the ocean in a striped bass's stomach; a piece of sea glass—the lip of a perfume bottle—had been hurled into the ocean by a jealous sister. Some people would consider these daydreams childhood fantasies, but to Abby, they were memories.

She pocketed the piece of ceramic and whistled to Frida. What were the chances? An interview with *Art Observer* and communication from her mother on the same day.

Abby's studio was a short drive from Coast Guard Beach, and Rachel followed in her rental car. They wended up a steep dirt drive and parked in front of a simple rectangular structure made of cinder blocks, barn planks, and glass, bathed in sunlight. Abby steered Rachel around a loose stair board, hoping she wouldn't notice the chipped paint on the door. The Arcadia needed care. But that meant asking Ken if she could dip into the maintenance fund he kept, a conversation she avoided.

Stepping inside, Rachel Draper was struck silent. Abby tried to imagine what it must be like to take in the space for the first time. The funk of oil paint and wet dog; the floor gritty with sand; peeling painted cabinets lining the far wall; decades-old appliances in the kitchen—a refrigerator with rounded edges, PHILCO embossed in chrome above the handle; a stocky cream-colored gas stove; a cast-iron sink with yellowing enamel. Crap everywhere: dried-out tubes of paint, old paperbacks, abandoned canvases, ghostly drop cloths, a desiccated bouquet of wildflowers. *Would it have killed her to pick up a bit?* she wondered. At least the high ceilings worked against feelings of claustrophobia.

"This place is paradise," Rachel whispered.

Abby exhaled at those kindred words and followed Rachel's eyes as they scanned the studio. First, to walls covered in imagery: thirties porn magazines, anatomical illustrations, photographs of surgeries. Next, to windowsills where collections of starfish, sea glass, periwinkle shells, and lucky stones overflowed from mason jars. Then on to three canvases leaning along the back wall, which she had titled *Id*, *Ego*, and *Superego*. Abby had taken to giving her paintings psychoanalytical terms as titles, in part because it amused her, but also because the labels were poetic and fitting. Then, the moment Abby had been waiting for: when the journalist's gaze followed a slanted shaft of sunlight and landed on her work in progress.

Rachel approached the painting, bending close to scrutinize it. Her eyes darted across the canvas and its vivid, fluid lines, the result of Abby's vigorous brushwork and layering technique. "Jesus," she whispered, squinting. "This is incredible." Then she stepped back to take in the whole, her index finger tracing a trajectory in the air in front of the piece. "The implied lines are kinetic, just tugging the eye from scene to scene." Her mouth twitched, and she was quiet for a minute. "It's a lot to process, but I see what you mean about storytelling. There's turmoil but also hope." She reached for her iPhone. "Do you mind?"

"Go right ahead," Abby said, blushing as she kissed the top of Frida's head.

"Does it have a title?" Rachel asked, clicking photos.

"Not yet," Abby said. She had a list of contenders, but none seemed quite right.

As the dunes outside slowly shifted from green to gold with the sun's changing angle, Rachel studied the paintings on the walls, flipped through canvases organized haphazardly in oversized storage racks, and returned again and again to the work in progress. Speaking staccato style into her iPhone, Rachel dictated a one-way conversation that left Abby feeling lightheaded. "Comp: Lucian Freud, unidealized female form. Comp: Chaïm Soutine, portrayals of carcasses, damaged flesh. Comp: Tracey Emin, autobiographical, confessional. Comp: Twombly, energetic use of lines, color."

When Rachel finally tucked her phone into her pocket, Abby suggested they go up to the roof-deck. She tossed a tin of almonds, a Granny Smith apple, and a paring knife into one of the tote bags hanging off the back of her chair and filled two large glasses with water. Hands full, she kicked open the studio's back door and led Rachel up a delicate, spiral staircase—too steep for Frida to manage. The metal structure was all but encased in a tangle of wisteria, whose gnarled cables grew every which way, wrapping around the railing, snaking under the roof of the cabin, and lifting rain gutters.

A month from now, in mid-May, the behemoth would blossom, and a thousand fragrant flowers would purple the side of the studio, attracting trembling monarch butterflies in need of a break from their arduous trip from Central America. Ken was always after her to trim it back; he liked things clean and orderly. The wisteria had been a birthday gift from his wife, Jenny, who'd warned Abby that she'd need to tame the beast or risk havoc. Wisteria required planning and training, Jenny had explained, advice Abby ignored, neglecting to twine the young shoots around each other as instructed, and always forgetting to cut the vines back at the end of summer. Now, the task was beyond her. The wisteria was a beautiful mess.

The views from the studio's rooftop deck were expansive: straight ahead, there was Pilgrim Lake; to the east, dunes that gave way to the Atlantic; to the northwest, the sweet curve of Provincetown, the last part of the Cape to form, created by littoral drift ten thousand years earlier, the blink of an eye, geologically speaking.

"Wow!" Rachel exclaimed, leaning against the railing and looking at the moonscape of dunes that rolled into the ocean and the distant horizon line beyond, gradations of blue.

"I know, I'm so lucky. It was my mother's studio first," Abby said, placing the water glasses on a square table, unpacking the haphazard snacks from her bag, and slicing the apple into wedges. "I mentioned she was an architect, right? She built this herself."

"You did. What a meaningful legacy to leave to you. Your mother must have known you had an artistic spirit like she did."

"Oh, no, well, not really." Abby walked over to where Rachel stood. "My mother's death was . . ." She paused, reaching for the words. They'd always been difficult for her to say. "Well, it was sudden. She died within hours of my birth."

"Oh, I'm so sorry," Rachel said, putting a hand on Abby's arm. "How devastating for your whole family."

"It was. It was terrible. My parents were deeply in love and were great partners. And, of course, my brother Kenny was just a little guy when it happened," Abby said. It always pained her to imagine her brother's grief. "Anyway, it's complicated. My mother hadn't updated her will. You know, trusts and so on. Long story short, her two most beloved possessions, this studio and her sailboat, were both left to my brother for when he turned eighteen. My father tried to do the right thing and divvy things up fairly as he knew she'd have wanted—giving me the Arcadia and Ken the *Francesca*. But technically, by law, my brother still owns both."

"And what about your stepmother?" Rachel asked. "I read an article about her bioluminescence research. Were you close?"

The woman did her homework. Yes, Abby had adored her stepmother. The day Gretchen finally called it quits, leaving after an epic fight with her father—one where both accusations and dishes flew—Abby had been devastated. Gretchen had been her ally and the only mother figure she'd ever known. And since visitation rights weren't a thing when it came to stepparents, Abby had no way to stay in touch. Gretchen had been deemed the enemy. *Crazy. Unhinged.* End of discussion. But unbeknownst to her father and brother, with the advent of the Internet, Abby had found Gretchen, and ever since, they checked in on each other a couple of times a year—birthdays and holidays.

"Talk about ancient history," Abby said, wondering how much Rachel knew about her former stepmother. "But yes, Gretchen was amazing. It wasn't her fault. My mother left some pretty big shoes to fill . . ." Abby motioned toward the chairs. "Let's sit."

Rachel took the hint and pivoted back to the Arcadia. "So, why doesn't your brother just sign over the deed to you?"

Another sore subject. But it was Abby's fault for going there in the first place. She wasn't thinking clearly—why would she air all this dirty laundry in front of a reporter? She bit down on a chunk of apple and the sourness made her salivate. "Can this part about my brother be off the record, please?" she asked. "I'd be very grateful. I'm sorry. You're just . . . Well, it's very easy to talk with you."

"Of course," Rachel said. "Absolutely. But now I'm curious."

"I think it's a matter of control. It's how he keeps me in line and beholden to him, I guess," Abby said, shrugging. "He'd tell you he's doing it to be a good guy, you know, taking care of the taxes and maintenance and stuff. Helping me out. But there's more to it. Do you have siblings?"

"Ah! Say no more. I totally get it."

Rachel and Abby got comfortable, sitting in wicker chairs on either side of a small table, nibbling on the snacks, and looking out over rolling dunes illuminated by the late-afternoon light. Frida whined from below.

"Quiet!" Abby called down, and for once, the dog obeyed. "Good girl," she said. "I'm so sorry. She's not used to company or having to share me."

"Just a few more questions and I promise to leave." Rachel scrolled through notes on her phone, whispering to herself—"Arcadia, family background, monthly open houses, RISD"—until she landed on ground she hadn't covered. "How do you like teaching at Nauset High?"

"Oh, I love it. There's nothing like connecting with kids and watching them develop creatively. I mean, it doesn't happen with every student, for sure. A lot of them don't look up from their phones. But when it does, it's the best." Abby shrugged. "Plus, it pays the bills."

"Who do you show your work to first?"

"My best friend, Jenny. Always Jenny. We were roommates our freshman year at RISD," Abby said. "Now she's married to my brother. I introduced them."

"Interesting, wow," Rachel said. "So, your sister-in-law is an artist, too?"

"*Was*," Abby said. "A ceramicist. But Jenny changed paths long ago."

The understatement of the century, Abby thought. Jenny Lowell came from a totally different background and was the friend Abby didn't know she could hope for. The two had bonded the very first night of college, minutes after Jenny's parents, Theodore and Isabel, had left, when Jenny handed Abby a pair of scissors and invited her to help shred the Frette bed linens her parents had left as a "dorm-warming" gift.

"Won't they be furious?" Abby had asked, wondering if she should be talking Jenny out of the plan, or if they'd somehow blame Abby for being a bad influence.

Jenny's smile let her know that her parents' wrath—her mother's, in particular—was part of the pleasure. "Craft is my rebellion of choice," she said and taught Abby how to braid scraps of sheets into a rag rug, which they later placed on the floor between their beds.

Over time, Abby learned that destroying and reassembling fancy gifts from her parents was Jenny's favorite pastime. She broke heirloom teacups to make mosaics, turned the arms of cashmere sweaters into fingerless gloves, and melted jewelry to use as lacquer in her ceramic work. They told each other everything.

All these years later, Abby was still sad that Jenny had abandoned her dreams of being an artist, but her friend was figuring things out. "Despite getting into one of the best art schools in the country and possessing an insane amount of talent, her parents never took her work seriously. They considered it a hobby, not a real career," Abby said. "And their doubts took a toll."

"How so?" Rachel asked.

"It's hard to explain. Despite the outward bravado, Jenny lacked confidence. Her parents wanted her to find a suitable husband with, you know, the right connections, and art school wasn't where they thought this would happen. Then, when her mother got sick—breast cancer—Jenny left school and never came back. But we stayed close. She spent a summer here with me when we were in our early twenties, and that's when she fell in love with Ken." Abby found herself editing the story to protect her friend—the wildness, the stints in rehab. Then, when it became clear that Isabel Lowell was not going to survive the cancer, something seemed to shift. Jenny wanted to make sure that her mother knew she was on the right path.

"But she did find a suitable husband at art school—through you," Rachel said. "Your best friend and your brother. You must admit, it's kind of sweet."

"I guess," Abby said, thinking of the compromises they'd had to make to their friendship in service of Jenny's marriage. She wanted to move off the subject of her family. "Can we talk about something else?"

"Okay," Rachel agreed. "Tell me about your literary influences."

"How long do you have?" Abby joked. "*Frankenstein* comes to mind first. It covers everything: ambition, revenge, loss, a body's impermanence . . ."

Abby had first read *Frankenstein* as a teenager, where it awakened something dormant in her, kindling a lifelong fascination with bodily transformation. For years afterward, she had a daily practice of making watercolor sketches of such metamorphoses—blood coagulating, a penis engorging, color rising on a cheek—works she completed loosely and quickly with the goal of capturing the kinetic energy of change itself.

"Plus, Mary Shelley's mother died in childbirth, so we have a kinship."

Abby considered the shifts occurring in her own body at that very moment: veins surfacing along the sides of newly tender breasts, insistent pressure on her bladder, an inner blossoming. She was seven weeks pregnant. She had yet to tell a soul.

Before Abby or Rachel knew it, a "few more questions" turned into a lengthy discussion of literary heroes—Adrienne Rich, Toni Morrison, Nadine Gordimer—turned into a glowing orange sunset, turned into a conversation about the thrilling prospect of a woman in the White House, turned into stars pricking through a velvet blanket of night sky, turned back to her painting in progress.

"Oh gosh, it's getting late," Rachel said. "Thank you so much for your time, Abby. You've been so generous. I have one final question about the painting, if you're game."

"Of course," Abby said.

"Can you tell me about that circular gesture, the viewing frame—it's an eye, right? An observer?"

"Um, something like that," Abby responded, giving a warm smile. She'd already revealed more than she'd planned to. Rachel Draper didn't need to know whose eye it was. Abby could keep some things private. As for the body parts, they were all hers. Every figure she'd ever painted, whether it resembled her or not, was somehow her—the same way every person in a dream represented the dreamer and every character in a novel was the author. Abby could fictionalize the flesh—change skin or hair color, add pounds—but the work came from her.

Abby planned to give the painting to her father for his seventieth birthday; it would also be how she announced her pregnancy. She could picture his eyes on the canvas, taking it in, and then making the connection between artist and subject. There was a body inside her body, as there was a body inside the central torso of the painting. A baby boy. Don't ask her how she knew, but she did. Her father—a classic male chauvinist blind to his chauvinism—would finally get the grandson he'd always wanted. Normally, Jenny was the first person Abby would tell news of this magnitude, but something was off between them lately, a chilliness that seemed to have blown in with the new year. They hadn't fought, but Jenny had been avoiding her for a while now, rarely answering her calls and claiming to be too busy for their weekly lunch date. Abby was trying to give Jenny space, but she felt confused by the runaround. They'd always been direct with each other. If Abby had said or done something to offend Jenny, why not just say so?

Abby felt sure she wasn't the first woman to be terrified of giving birth—hell, she had more reason than most—so why didn't women talk about it more? For as long as Abby could remember, she was scared by her body's powers. As early as middle school, when all her friends were excited to get their periods, the prospect horrified her. What her body would be capable of. When Abby finally went through puberty at twelve, she coped by withdrawing and all but stopping eating, which had the desired effect of deflating her breasts, making her period irregular, and giving her a false sense of control. Her father didn't seem to notice, but Ken did, and he pestered her to tell him what was wrong. She couldn't explain. She just didn't want him anywhere near her anymore—not on the sofa, not in the woods, not in her room. She needed space.

At first, Abby doubted she'd go through with the pregnancy. She'd never been interested in marriage, so she hadn't thought too much about motherhood. But she was thirty-eight and decided to sit with the pregnancy for a couple of weeks before making a final decision. If she was going to be a mother, it was now or never. She worried about what motherhood would mean for her work and whether she wanted to raise a child on her own. To her great surprise, with each passing day, she felt more connected to the being inside her. She felt a power gathering within her that made her feel invincible and visible. For the first time in decades, she was hungry. Instead of wanting to disappear, Abby wanted to be seen.

Steph

Steph stared at her newborn through the clear hospital bassinet, his little chest moving up and down, lips pursed as if ready to be kissed. She waited for revelation, for her son's birth to bring clarity to recent events. Nothing. Instead, the miracle of the life she'd created took a back seat to her existential crisis: Michael Murphy wasn't her father, and she had no idea how to process this bombshell. Her whole life had been based upon a lie.

She took deep breaths and concentrated on what she knew for sure: she was a loyal friend, a loving if sometimes impatient partner to her wife Toni, and an excellent police officer. Scratch that. How could she consider herself anything but mediocre at her job given all the clues she'd overlooked? Her parents were light and freckled; she was olive-skinned and smooth. They were soft edges; she was angular. They were sweet; she was sharp—the only person in her family to swear. Still, Steph had never once thought to question her heritage. Hers was an unremarkable childhood in a stable home with loving parents and a supportive extended family in a close-knit Irish Catholic community. When she felt like she didn't fit in, she assumed it was because she was queer.

Had it not been for her difficult pregnancy, she might never have stumbled upon the truth. She'd become klutzy in her second trimester, sloshing coffee and dropping things. Everyone reassured her that clumsiness was normal in pregnancy, but Steph sensed that there was more to it. At around the six-month mark, her lack of coordination moved from her hands to her feet, and she had a fall.

After many tests—including one in which needles were inserted deep into her muscles to gauge their responsiveness—Steph was diagnosed with a rare but mild case of a genetic disorder called myotonic dystrophy, a condition that affected its carriers differently, causing problems that ranged from the muscular sluggishness she was experiencing to heart abnormalities. Turned out, she'd always been a carrier, but something about the hormonal cocktail of pregnancy had made her more symptomatic. Her obstetrician scheduled a C-section, quashing their hopes for a home birth.

With the diagnosis, Steph went straight into detective mode, investigating everything she could about the disease. One fact gnawed at her: myotonic dystrophy was an inherited genetic disorder, yet none of her relatives exhibited symptoms or had the telltale musculature. The disease was most common in families of French Canadian descent and Ashkenazi Jews. Her family hailed from County Kerry, Ireland, on both sides.

At one of their regular Sunday-night suppers at her parents' row house in South Boston, Steph grilled them. "Do you ever grip onto something and then have trouble letting go?" she asked. "Like when you try to unlock the car door on a cold day and it's hard to un-pinch your fingers from the key?"

Michael and Mary Beth shook their heads; they had not.

"Okay, try this," Steph said. "Squeeze your hands into fists—tight, tight, tight."

Toni touched Steph's leg beneath the table, but she was too worked up to stop.

Her parents balled their hands into fists and squeezed hard as instructed. Steph did the same, counting to ten as the broiled salmon grew tepid on their plates.

"Okay, release," she said.

Her parents' hands unfolded easily, but hers responded in slow motion. Steph had lived with this condition her whole life and thought nothing of it, assuming everyone had trouble ungripping. No one talked about it because it was a simple fact of being human, like getting goose bumps or sneezing.

"What about other relatives? Grandma or Grandpa? Or Nana or Papa? Did anyone ever complain about muscle fatigue?"

Her parents looked as baffled as she felt.

Even as a child, Steph's muscles had always been well-defined. She had mounds of biceps big enough to impress the boys, even a slight flare of Popeye forearms. A lifelong tomboy, Steph had been proud of her athletic build, taking credit for her muscles' definition, although she'd never done much to earn them. Now she understood that her physique was the result of a disease that caused her muscles to get stuck in a flexed position for a nanosecond longer than normal, resulting in an unintentional workout.

Now the baby made a soft cooing noise. Could he be dreaming? Steph had read that babies collected stray bits of their mothers during the birth process—blood and cells and such—and that parts of the baby were left in her, too. She liked to think that bits of them would live on in the other. She rolled away from the bassinet to face Toni, who was propped at an improbable angle on a recliner against the wall, a hospital blanket wrapped around her shoulders, sleeping soundly. *Sleep when the baby sleeps*—the most basic parenting advice of all, and Toni was crushing it. Adding to her wife's peace of mind, Steph knew, was that their son had squeaked in under the midnight cutoff of April 19—officially an Aries, the first sign of the zodiac. Don't ask. It mattered to Toni, a third-grade teacher by day and an amateur astrologer, Tarot card reader, and intuitive by night.

Moments later a freckle-faced nurse wearing pink scrubs, matching lipstick, and hoop earrings pushed in a medical cart.

"Good morning," the nurse said, writing "Judy" on the whiteboard at the foot of the hospital bed, using the curved part of the "y" to make a smiley face. It was 6:30 a.m.

"How are the moms today?" Judy asked.

"Swell," Steph said, put off by the woman's cheery disposition.

"Tired," Toni said, stirring at the intrusion.

"Give it eighteen years," Judy said.

Steph wondered how many times Judy had used that line.

The nurse peered inside the bassinet. "And who's this big boy? Do we have a name yet, mister?"

Steph wished Judy would fuck off.

"Not yet, but we're working on it," Toni said.

The nurse frowned and took Steph's vitals, giving the webbed bandages across her lower abdomen a cursory glance. All normal. "Shall we try to breastfeed again?" she asked.

Toni gave Steph the thumbs-up, but Steph felt unsure. With the anesthesia now out of her system, her abdominal wound prickled and stung when she moved. She felt an odd fluttering beneath her clavicle; her breasts were engorged and felt as hard as melons.

Toni unwrapped their swaddled son, checked his diaper, and placed him on Steph's chest. His skin felt silky and warm, and his blue-gray eyes looked like he was trying to blink her into focus. Then Steph felt a tingle high in her chest, electric but not unpleasant. She aimed a nipple at the baby's slack mouth, but it slid out, causing his tiny legs to jerk. Steph repeated this effort without success.

Then Judy took hold of Steph's breast, as casually as she might have shaken her hand, and squeezed until yellow droplets formed, which she brushed back and forth across the baby's lips until he opened his mouth wide. Then in one swift motion, the nurse shoved Steph's whole nipple into the baby's mouth. With a stab of pain, Steph understood what the term "latch" meant. She watched her son's fist curl against her breast. What followed was a wet suckling, louder and sweeter than Steph thought possible.

"Would you look at that," Toni said. "The dairy's in."

Days before her son's birth, Steph had accompanied her parents to Sunday mass at St. Joseph's, where they'd attended services her entire life. From the outside, the church was an unimposing brick structure with arched wooden doors and a single, high, stained-glass window. But inside, it was dizzyingly ornate—carved pulpit, gilded crucifix, draped statues, votive candles, the works. Her mother wanted Father Mulligan to bless the pregnancy, and although Steph was no longer a practicing Catholic, she could give this to her mother.

The sermon that morning was about truth, and Father Mulligan seemed unusually fired up, preaching from the Gospel of John, reading aloud, and gesticulating as he went. "And Jesus said, 'If you abide in my word, you are truly my disciples, and you shall know the truth, and the truth shall set you free.' "

Her mother loved the Gospel of John. She reached for Steph's hand and squeezed. "John is a terrific name, don't you think?"

"Mom—"

Steph didn't understand why Catholics seemed to stick to the same dozen or so names—John, Peter, Michael, Joseph, Thomas. She had her heart set on something unique: Denzel or maybe Tegan. She only hoped she'd be able to convince Toni, also a lapsed Catholic, but one who clung more to tradition.

Steph shifted uncomfortably on the wooden pew. The weight of the baby on her bladder was killing her.

"Do I have your attention, my friends?" Father Mulligan preached. "I'll say it again: the truth shall set you free. I'm talking to you." His finger appeared to be pointing directly at the Murphys.

Where was all this fire and brimstone coming from? Normally, Father Mulligan wasn't much of an orator. What endeared him to his congregation was his speed. His nickname was "Fast-Mass Mulligan." Soon enough, Father Mulligan invited the congregation up for the sacrament.

Hallelujah. A quick blessing for the baby and Steph could pee. Only then did she notice the streak of tears trailing down her mother's cheeks.

Her parents had been high school sweethearts who'd married young and found themselves pregnant immediately. Steph was born when they were both eighteen and although they'd wanted more children, it never came to pass, a fact that evoked pity within their community where large families were the norm. Steph never particularly minded being an only child. In her neighborhood, she'd been the *only* only child, which made her feel special.

With the genetic mystery of the disease consuming her, Steph went home with her parents after church to root through family records and see what she could dig up. Her father, an avid Red Sox fan, retreated to the den, while she and her mother flipped through old photo albums, letters, and medical files at the dining room table. It had never bothered Steph that she didn't resemble her classically Irish-looking parents. She'd always taken her own good looks for granted, never wearing much makeup or struggling with her weight. "Black Irish" was what dark-haired, olive-skinned members of their community were called, mixed-blood descendants of Spanish traders who'd settled in Ireland centuries ago. It was considered a compliment.

"Honey, what exactly are we looking for?" Mary Beth asked.

"Unsure," Steph said, examining a baby picture of herself taken the day she was born. She looked like a troll doll with that shock of black hair. "I have a feeling I'm missing something obvious."

Her mother touched the photo. "Honey, you need to stop worrying about this. In a few days, you're going to be a mother. Babies have a way of putting things in perspective."

"There's a fifty percent chance that my son will have this disease," Steph said, annoyed by her mother's platitudes. "And either you or Dad is a carrier. Asymptomatic, obviously, but still . . ." Steph flipped through a medical file. "It's just odd that we can't identify anyone in the family with symptoms."

"Well, that's a good thing, right?" her mother said.

"I guess," Steph said. "But it leaves a mystery. And the only explanation I can come up with is that someone in our family wasn't as God-fearing as you. Someone had an affair, no two ways about it." There, she'd said it. "I'm just trying to figure out who. Grandma Maria, maybe? She was kind of a flirt."

"Really, Steph," her mother snapped. "That's hardly your business. And Grandma Maria would never."

Her mother rarely spoke sharply. "Are you okay?" Steph asked.

"Steph, *please*," her mother implored, and then her eyes got glassy again. "Just let go of this."

Steph felt a pang of guilt, imagining that she was dredging up a horrible memory, some long-buried family secret that pained her mother to think about—rape or sexual abuse. She'd seen it all working on the force and knew that such violations were common. Had something awful happened to her grandmother? Steph didn't know how to be anything other than direct, though she tried to soften her voice. "I can't, Mom. It's too important. Please, tell me what you know."

Her mother shook her head.

"If not for me, for your grandson."

Mary Beth stared at her hands, which were folded in her lap. "It happened such a long time ago."

The truth had never occurred to Steph. Not once, not in her wildest dreams. It hadn't been rape. Or sexual abuse. And it hadn't happened in the distant past to a relative in the old country. It had happened to her mother right here in Boston, close to four decades earlier. A familiar story of alcohol and ignorance. The details that her mother shared were cliché: a handsome stranger, too much to drink, getting in over her head in the back of his car. Mary Beth couldn't remember big chunks of the night and had been naïve enough to be unaware that she'd lost her virginity until she missed her period.

Long story short, Steph and her father were not biologically related.

"Who am I, then?" Steph stammered, unable to process the information.

"Why, you're you, of course," her mother said. "Our Steph. Nothing's changed."

"Are you kidding?" Her mother's parental jujitsu left Steph dumbfounded. "Who's my real father?"

"Don't be ridiculous, Stephanie. Your dad is your real father," her mother said, having the gall to sound irritated. "He raised you, taught you how to throw a baseball, helped you get onto the force. Your father will always be your father. Your *only* father." Her mother reached out a hand, and Steph slapped it hard, shocking them both.

"Don't touch me," Steph said, wrapping her cardigan tightly around herself. "What the hell, Mom? What the hell? I'm fifty percent someone I don't know and I'm walking around with his genetic disorder."

Steph hadn't realized she'd been shouting until her mother shushed her and glanced toward the den. And then it hit Steph. "Oh my God," she whispered. Her father didn't know.

"Steph, I'm sorry. I'm so, so sorry," Mary Beth whispered, making the sign of the cross. "You have to remember, I was barely eighteen when I got pregnant. A child, really. I'd lived a sheltered life. I was terrified."

"Mom, you haven't been eighteen for a very long time," said Steph. She didn't have space for anything but the stripped-down truth. "You've had decades to make this right."

Her mother was silent.

Cheers exploded from the next room. A Red Sox home run, no doubt. Her father would be pulling his clenched fist into himself, saying, *Yesss.* How would Michael Murphy, the gentlest and most trusting man she knew, take this news? Would he still feel the same about her? Steph felt bereft, then suddenly, she was enraged at him, too. The obliviousness. He could count, couldn't he? Nine months was nine months. Had it never struck him as strange that his wife gave birth to an eight-pound baby six and a half months after their wedding? Was it possible that he hadn't done the simple math?

But the worst part of all of it, the unforgivable part, was how the lie had become enmeshed into Steph's narrative. For as long as she could remember, her parents had used her premature birth to explain everything from her quick temper to her ambitious nature. Steph was their "early bird," their "line cutter," their "eager beaver." And she'd internalized all of it. Compared to them, Steph was anxious, self-centered, impatient. Now, the truth made her want to scream. She hadn't been premature. She'd been a full-term baby, happily swimming in her amniotic bath until her appointed due date. The reason she wasn't *like* her parents was that she wasn't *of* her parents. Her differences—and there were many—were written into her DNA by an anonymous author. It was all too much. Not only did she have to contend with having a new father, but Steph also had to wrap her head around this new mother—one who lied and kept secrets.

"Do you even know who my biological father is?" Steph asked.

"Of course I know who he is," her mother said, sounding offended. She reached for her rosary and worried the beads.

Steph wasn't getting anywhere. "Please, Mom, tell me everything you remember," she said softly.

Her mother had been invited to a gala at the New England Aquarium by her best friend, Nancy, whose father served on the board and had a table to fill. There had been a champagne fountain, passed hors d'oeuvres, music, and dancing. Mary Beth had never seen such glamour in her life. Each table had a guest of honor, and she'd been seated beside the one at hers, a dashing young marine biologist who traveled the world.

"The words he used. The way he carried himself . . ." Her mother's voice took on a dreamy quality.

"Mom."

Mary Beth cleared her throat. "One moment, we were drinking champagne and the next—" Apparently, that's where the details became blurry. "Well, the next thing I knew, we were in the back of his car making out. I didn't know how I got there. My dress was up, and everything was spinning. I needed to vomit."

Steph nodded for her to go on.

"There's nothing else. We were both embarrassed. I think he'd had too much to drink, too. When he saw that I was scared and sick, he apologized and drove me home. Honestly, he looked horrified by what had happened. He kept apologizing."

"Does he . . . know about me?"

Mary Beth closed Steph's baby album. "When I realized I was pregnant, I asked Nancy about him, pretending to have a crush." She shut her eyes. "Nancy knew only that he was married, which meant I was on my own."

Abortion would not have been an option for a Catholic girl like her mother; Steph knew that much. "What's his name?"

Her mother pressed her lips together. "No good will come of it."

"Tell me," Steph said. "You know I'll be able to track him down. Save me the time and humiliation. You owe me that much."

Later that night, gripping Toni's hand as if it was the only thing that tethered her to the earth, Steph Googled Adam Gardner. Her biological father's Wikipedia entry made him sound important: a marine biologist who'd discovered all sorts of species and researched humpback whales. Then Steph's eyes landed on his birth year: 1946. The man had been in his early thirties when he'd gotten her eighteen-year-old mother pregnant.

And the photos. *My God.* There were dozens and dozens of them: Adam Gardner getting out of a submersible; Adam Gardner standing on the bow of a boat; Adam Gardner bobbing in the ocean with a mask propped on his forehead; Adam Gardner accepting an award in black tie. The shiny dark hair, high cheekbones, Y-shaped chin cleft—their likeness left no doubt. Steph was looking at her biological father. Then, another photo that made her breath catch: Adam Gardner embracing two beautiful children, a son and a daughter. Steph touched the screen. She had siblings.

May

Adam

Since going down on his meds, Adam was hyperaware of the effect he was having on people, women especially. His brain was as nimble as a ballerina, able to stretch and contort into places he'd had no idea were within his reach. Just this morning, for example, he'd regaled Betty, the pretty barista at his local coffee shop, the Plover, with his knowledge of yeast. Yeast!

"It's a powerhouse of an organism," Adam said, picking up the white baker's bag that held his cinnamon bun. "It's hard to believe that a single-celled beast can flavor beer, raise bread, and make electricity."

"You don't say," said Betty, giving him a big smile. "Anything else for you today, Adam?"

"That'll be it," Adam said.

"A large cappuccino and cinnamon roll. That'll be $8.45, please."

Adam dug into his pocket and handed her a twenty-dollar bill. "Over fifteen hundred different yeast species."

"You don't say," Betty said again, taking the bill.

Adam leaned over the counter toward her. "They reproduce asexually in a process called budding," he whispered, feeling bold. "Mother yeast cells can divide into two equal daughter cells."

Betty grinned and cocked her head at Adam as if taking him in for the first time. Over the years, Betty had smiled at Adam countless times, but this one was different. It was a curious, closed-mouth, little Mona Lisa of a smile. The word *sfumato* popped into Adam's head. What? Would he be speaking Italian next? What his mind was capable of! He wondered if it would impress Betty more to continue down the path of science or if he should pivot to history. Or he could kill two birds with one stone with Louis Pasteur's fermentation studies of the 1850s. Where the yeast facts were coming from, he had no idea. To his knowledge, he'd never kneaded dough in his life, and yet, at this moment, he could teach a graduate seminar on the subject. Perhaps there was truth to the adage that you only use 10 percent of your gray matter.

When Betty handed him his change, her finger grazed the side of his palm, leaving in its wake an electric trail that made him feel like a schoolboy. Adam placed the change—all $11.55 of it—into Betty's tip jar. If it wasn't for the line of customers behind him, he'd have invited her to join him at one of the outdoor tables. Instead, he tipped an imaginary hat and made his exit. He had more to say but this morning he'd heed his son Ken's advice and "not talk past the close."

The takeaway was clear—now that Adam was unburdened by the mind-numbing effect of his meds, he had a remarkable facility with a broad and unexpected range of topics: Shaker furniture, Tibetan culture, black holes, Homer, string theory, you name it. It was as if every fact he'd ever stumbled across in his life was newly accessible. No exaggeration. But it wasn't witty banter and brainpower alone that was exciting the pheromones of the fairer sex. Adam had lost weight—maybe eight pounds of paunch—and looked damn good, if he said so himself. Clint Eastwood at around fifty, only with better hair, darker and more of it. And Betty had noticed, hence the eye lingering. He couldn't understand why women took such offense at being admired. He rather enjoyed it.

At home, Adam took a long, hot shower. He hadn't slept in days and even through a condensation-covered mirror, he could see dark half-moons shining beneath his eyes. With his children coming to dinner later in the week, Adam knew he had to bring himself down lest they notice and stage an intervention. Abby, in particular, had a radar for his early signs of mania. Even as a little girl, she was always the first to notice. "You're getting bouncy again, Dad," she'd say, her face etched with concern. When Abby was eleven, Adam had left her and her brother alone for a weekend, which he did from time to time, telling himself it was good for their independence. Only this time, he forgot to return on the appointed day, and for the next four days, as well. When he finally arrived home, they were gone. He ended up spending time in a psychiatric ward while his children stayed with his parents. Young Abby had made him swear on a photo of her dead mother, his dear Emily, that he would never stop taking his medication again.

Recalling this long-ago promise made to his distraught little girl, Adam felt unsettled. *He was doing the right thing, wasn't he?* He regarded himself in the mirror, noticing the loose skin at the base of his neck. Clint Eastwood, hell. Time was running out. He couldn't afford to wait a moment longer. Adam tapped his index finger against his reflection and quoted his hero, Charles Darwin: "A man who dares to waste one hour of time has not discovered the value of life." What was a promise, anyway? Just a string of words. Scientific advancement trumped that any day of the week.

Adam cracked the bathroom door to let the steam out and allow the music in. He hummed along to the love song that was blasting from speakers placed throughout the house, applying shaving cream in circular motions. The piece was building to its crescendo. He tilted his head, placed the razor on the clean line of his sideburn, and drew it through the lather and around the bend of his jawline, again and again, until his face was clean of whiskers and cream. Five handfuls of frigid water and the job was done. He thought of all the times Kenny had stood beside him as a boy, mock-shaving, just as Adam had done with his old man. Too bad Ken didn't have a son. No grandson to carry on the family name. Only granddaughters, two of them. They were smart and capable, but still . . . it was a shame that this father-son ritual would die with Ken.

As would splitting wood, Adam thought despairingly. He considered wood chopping the most satisfying of the masculine arts. The sense of provision. The meditative rhythm—place, stand, breathe, whack. The arc of the ax as precise as the cast of a fishing line. The pleasing sound of metal against wood. The way the split radiated out and revealed a secret topography. The faint poof of scent, as ancient as the smell of earth itself. And how, with each reverberating *thunk*, his thoughts rearranged themselves like a kaleidoscope, providing a magical new way of looking at the same problem. When Ken was little, he liked to help Adam stack the split wood. They made quite the team.

The music streaming into the bathroom had hit a curious bridge, a series of trills and groans that made Adam's heart swell, just as thinking about Ken and Abby as children did. He used to call them his "little monsters." Yes, there'd been women in his life, but he'd prioritized his children. Not every father could say that. Sure, mistakes were made. He'd traveled frequently, often taking research trips for weeks at a time, leaving them in the care of his parents. And when he was home, he was consumed by his important work. But unsupervised time was good for young people, right? It made them creative and resourceful. Resilient. And, yes, he'd had slipups with his medication over the years, but on balance, he'd managed his mood swings well. When his children were old enough to understand, Adam had sat them down and told them the facts: bipolar disorder was a mood affliction that he managed with medication. End of story.

Adam's immediate concern was that he might already be past the point of no return. How long had he been awake? Two days? Three? He couldn't quite remember. He wished he could "log" as whales did, envying their ability to rest and remain conscious at the same time, necessary so they could surface and breathe. Alas, humans weren't built that way. Adam needed to rein himself in and get some sleep. He couldn't afford time in a psychiatric hospital, not when he was this close to putting it all together. If only he didn't feel so damn good, so full of insight and energy. He didn't want that to end. As he brushed his teeth, he opened the bathroom door a bit wider, listening to a playful back-and-forth duet—the guy proclaiming his love, the girl playing hard to get.

The music he'd been listening to—that had been piping through the house 24/7 for weeks now—was a loop of whale songs. Humpbacks or *Megaptera novaeangliae*—translation: "big winged New Englander"—so named for their giant pectoral fins. Adam's obsession. He'd memorized every verse, bridge, and chorus. He'd taped the vocalizations himself using an undersea glider to roam the depths of the Stellwagen Bank National Marine Sanctuary, 842 square miles of protected ocean off Provincetown.

At the start of this project, Adam's goal had been to compare these relatively new recordings to ones made twenty-five years ago, in the hopes of solving the mystery of the deepening pitch of whale songs. But in the last few weeks of listening, something else began happening, something miraculous. Just as Pfizer tested a drug to treat angina only to discover that it promoted erections (Viagra) and the inventor Dr. Silver tried to create a strong adhesive only to produce a weak one (the Post-it Note), so, too, had Adam encountered an unexpected outcome. While attempting to solve a small piece of the puzzle—and emboldened by his newly uninhibited mind—Adam was on the verge of cracking the whole code. Without meaning to, he'd created an immersion language program for himself. He was the Rosetta stone—no, the Doctor fucking Dolittle—of whale songs, on the brink of understanding the language, the meaning of each soulful utterance.

For weeks, Adam had been mapping the phonetic structure of each whale song unit, assigning numbers to every pitch, frequency, and wavelength, and creating spectrograms that used mathematical modeling to see the patterns beneath the calls. He'd created hand-drawn chart after hand-drawn chart, some of which plotted harmonic frequencies in X-Y coordinates, others of which assigned numbers to pitches and phrases to calculate the information content of each song. He'd analyzed more than one hundred song units. And, no surprise, just as visual patterns in nature found explanations in chaos theory and other mathematical patterns, so, too, he knew would the audio vibrations of whale songs. Adam had heard it with his own ears and seen it with his own eyes. The walls of his office were covered with diagrams—graphs, tables, plots. Each time he taped up a new one, Adam thought of da Vinci's *Vitruvian Man*, that perfect rendering of human proportion within a circle and square. In that simple drawing, da Vinci had demonstrated that the human form could be broken down into a series of golden ratios. Discovering golden ratios was what Adam planned to do with whale songs, which he thought might just provide clues to the origins of the universe.

But first, Adam needed rest. He'd figured out that he had, indeed, been awake for a full seventy-two hours. There was no way he could maintain this level of concentration without some sleep, and he needed to bring himself down enough so as not to raise his children's suspicions at dinner on Friday. With that in mind, he consumed the first full dose of his medical cocktail in over three weeks, washing it down with the dregs of his cold cappuccino, which made him think again of Betty's bewitching smile.

Even though Adam reacted more quickly to lithium than most, results by Friday were unlikely. He would need to supplement. He opened his medicine cabinet to see what else he had on hand: Dramamine, Benadryl, some expired clonazepam, Advil, three muscle relaxants (also expired), Seroquel (the ultimate mellower), Ambien, and NyQuil. A treasure trove. Adam tossed back three pills—a Seroquel, a clonazepam, and a muscle relaxant—with a shot of Benadryl. That should do the trick for now. He closed the cabinet door, noticing a spray of white toothpaste dots on the mirror that formed the shape of a whale. He was onto something for sure.

Adam grabbed a legal pad and a black felt-tip pen from the Maxwell House coffee can on his desk. He turned off the music and lumbered outside, letting the screen door thwack shut behind him. He plopped into his Adirondack chair and looked out at the pond where the water was still and glassy. A lone female cardinal with drab feathers and a candy-corn beak startled away three chickadees gorging at his feeder. As the pills got to work slowing him down, Adam regretted taking them. His theory about whale language was drifting from him like floating debris after a ship has gone down. *Did his gorgeous charts and graphs add up to anything? Had the whales really been communicating in full phrases?* he wondered as he drifted off to sleep.

Adam had fallen in love with the Wellfleet Woods in the late 1960s when his mentor, a free-spirited older scientist named Davison, invited him to a party at this very house. Newly married at the time, Adam and Emily showed up with a mason jar full of daisies and a bottle of cheap burgundy, feeling immediately at home in the gathering of bohemian intellectuals—artists, writers, and scientists—many of whom occupied other cabins in the same woods. After an evening of guitar strumming, joint smoking, and swallowing oysters from their shells, he and Emily undressed and marched down to the pond to enjoy a midnight skinny dip. She was a vision, his bride, and he could still picture the billow of her strawberry-blonde hair floating briefly on the surface before she dove into the darkness. Later, they would joke that they never really left the party. Adam had been living in the house for over forty years.

The house, a mid-century modern classic designed by one of the original émigré architects of the post-war era, was a low-slung assemblage of rectangles and glass and featured a large deck supported by stilts. Emily, an architect herself, admired the use of salvaged materials, the exposed structure, flowing open-floor plan, and, most of all, the seamless transition between indoors and out. They loved everything about the place, from the streamlined building to the kettle pond it faced to the industrious carpenter ants that scurried across the countertops and floors. When Davison had a debilitating stroke the following year, Adam and Emily bought his house and the adjacent lot, about seven acres of pond, woodlands, and dunes. A short time later, when Emily came into a small inheritance, she bought some acres in the dunes of North Truro and built a studio. A room of her own, she used to like to tell Adam, something every woman needed. A slice of heaven on earth; she called it the Arcadia.

Hours into his nap, the staccato of a woodpecker roused Adam. He kept his eyes closed, allowing the soundscape of the pitch pine and scrub oak forest and its denizens to envelop him. He heard spring leaves rustling, ravens flying overhead, wings *whishing* rhythmically, and woodland creatures scampering underneath the brush, disturbing twigs. As a scientist, Adam understood sound not as an ephemeral phenomenon that disappeared once heard, but as waves capable of pulsing through air, water, and solid objects. He understood that by the time he heard a sound, it was physically touching him—it had winded its way into his ear and was playing on its drum. Eyes still closed, Adam zipped up his jacket and enjoyed the orchestra: peepers starting their evening chorus, bullfrogs *kerplopping* into the pond, and birds calling. Then he turned his attention to the dimming light visible through his shut eyelids. The sun's angle, now filtered through the trees at a slant, revealed that it was late afternoon. He'd been asleep for longer than he thought. When, finally, he allowed his eyes to flutter open, they landed on a creature marching on sturdy legs along the shoreline. From the look of it, his former pet now weighed over twenty pounds, its carapace painted in algae and mud.

"Charon," Adam whispered, marveling that the Testudines line likely had occupied his kettle pond for some thirteen thousand years when huge chunks of ice detached from moving glaciers and formed depressions in the sandy soil. "Greetings, old friend."

Thirty-some years ago when he and Kenny, almost four at the time, had discovered the turtle in the grass beneath the deck, it was the size of a half-dollar, all legs and tail and neck. On its lower shell had been the vestiges of a yolk sac and umbilical connection, scant evidence of a mother's investment in her offspring. The sight of the yellow smudge had undone Adam, who couldn't help but compare the fledgling creature to his boy, both with so little of their mothers to sustain them. Emily had been dead just over three weeks at the time, her ashes recently scattered into the pond before them.

"Can we keep him?" Kenny asked, touching the row of tiny spikes running down the center of the carapace like an archipelago. "Please."

"I don't see why not," Adam said, though caging a wild creature went against everything he believed. Emerson's words, "First, be a good animal," came to mind. But this boy, his son, needed something to love.

Adam held the baby turtle between his thumb and forefinger and turned it over so Kenny could examine it from every angle, identifying the various parts as he went: the carapace (the top shell), the plastron (the lower plate that protected the stomach), the head, arms, legs, and tail. Adam pressed his pinkie finger beneath one tiny foot to splay it, revealing webbing and sharp claws.

"Why do you think they're called snapping turtles?" he asked.

"Because they bite?"

"Clever boy," he said, ruffling Kenny's hair.

Adam showed his son how little room there was for the hatchling to tuck its extremities into its shell, a morphological difference that explained the snapper's irascible disposition.

"What should we name him, Dad?" asked Kenny.

"How about Charon?" Adam said, picturing the turtle as ferryman, ushering his wife's ashes to the bottom of the pond. Then, as happened so frequently in those early weeks and months of grief, he was transported abruptly back to the hospital room, to the instant when Emily had collapsed before him, standing one second, crumpled in a heap the next, a pulmonary embolism having traveled from her leg to her lungs in a matter of seconds. Adam ran down the familiar maze of useless scenarios of what he might have done differently to change the outcome.

"But that's a girl's name," Kenny said.

"Not when it starts with a C."

When the tiny reptile whipped around its surprisingly long neck and struck Adam's thumb, they both flinched and then laughed. Adam embraced his son.

"'Snappy' is better," Kenny said.

But the name Charon stuck. For the next decade, taking care of the turtle was a central activity in the Gardner household. He was kept in a large glass tank and fed worms or insects or tiny balls of raw hamburger meat every day. The children loved to watch him approach the meat, which he would attack with gusto as if competing with an invisible hawk or bass.

Ken and Abby were devoted to Charon, cleaning his tank without having to be asked, dutifully washing the slime off every stone and twig. They liked to create elaborate habitat installations—log boats, stone pyramids, mazes, and more. His children liked to build things, a trait they inherited from their mother.

When Ken and Abby first proposed a big seventieth birthday/retirement celebration earlier in the year, Adam balked.

"Why flaunt something my good genes enable me to hide?" he joked. There was no question that Adam looked at least a decade younger than his years. He was energetic and sharp as a tack. But what lay behind his reticence about being feted was a gnawing fear. The very idea of retirement, the notion of becoming irrelevant, terrified him.

Recently, however, Adam had started to warm to the idea. A party in his honor—with its requisite tributes made before a well-curated guest list—could serve him well. He pictured heartfelt toasts given by friends, family, and colleagues, outlining the magnitude of his achievements. And then, under the guise of humble thanks to his guests, he could hint at his impending discovery, whetting the public's appetite for what was to come, this brilliant final chapter of his life. Relevance was everything in the world of marine biology, where you were only as good as your latest discovery. This event was the PR opportunity of a lifetime.

Adam tapped his pen against the yellow legal pad on his lap. He wouldn't go so far as to dictate his children's toasts, but surely Ken and Abby would appreciate some facts to pepper into their remarks. Later, they could repurpose them for his obituary.

- b. August 18, 1946, Watertown, MA
- Dartmouth, BA
- Boston University, Ph.D., marine biology
- Wife #1: Emily Reid. Married in 1972.

Emily. His heart. Mother of his children. Love of his life. Adam thought of her every single day. Emily had been gone for almost four decades, dead for longer now than she'd been alive. What a thought. Adam knew it took time to get over the people you loved, but he would never get over Emily. It still surprised him how, out of nowhere, something unexpected could shatter him anew—most recently, it was the iridescent inside of a mussel shell, that softest shade of blue purple, Emily's favorite color. It scared him how those feelings, stored deep inside, were just waiting to escape.

- ~~Wife #2: Elizabeth Swan. Married in 1979, divorced in 1980.~~

Was it necessary to count Beth? The marriage had been a "rebound," as they say, only lasting a few months. Adam had been in mourning. And

Beth, sweet and young, had been willing to mother baby Abigail and was already bonded to Kenny, who she'd seen through those first terrible months of loss as his preschool teacher. Abby was most likely unaware of her first stepmother's existence. And if Ken did remember Beth, he hadn't mentioned her since the day she left, his second mother to vanish. Adam scribbled through the name again. This marriage didn't need to go on his permanent record.

- ~~Wife #3: Gretchen Wingfield. United in 1983, splitsville in 1990.~~

Technically, this one didn't need to count, either. They'd had a "unity ceremony," not a legit marriage. He made a mental note to instruct Abby to fight back if the *New York Times* obit editor argued the common-law angle. But whatever they ended up calling Gretchen—wife, partner, girlfriend—there was no denying her existence. Opinionated. Headstrong. Great in bed. A nightmare to live with. She had a taste for confrontation, and their fights were legendary. Gretchen was career-minded, which was attractive at first. But Adam had assumed those urges would settle as she devoted herself to him and the children. No such luck. She was uninterested in parenting and, as it turned out, two scientists in one house was one scientist too many. When Gretchen left in an unpleasant storm after seven contentious years—accusing Adam of negligence and worse—Adam swore off marriage (of any sort), once and for all. He'd been a bachelor ever since.

- Fatherhood

Despite his inability to secure a surrogate mother for his children, Adam felt sure he'd been an excellent father. Sure, Ken and Abby had their complaints—what kids didn't?—but Adam had provided them with a rigorous education, plenty of freedom, and an idyllic home in the woods. Plus, unlike parents today, Adam hadn't let them rot their brains in front of screens. They'd turned out just fine.

Yet while he loved his children dearly, Adam would be the first to admit he didn't understand them. How had they ended up so unlike him? Ken actively aspired to a conventional life as part of the New England establishment. He wore polo shirts, golfed, took vacations at all-inclusive resorts, and—perhaps most preposterously—upgraded his car every single year. At least his son had found a good match for himself in his daughter-in-law, Jenny, whose mother had been a card-carrying member of the Daughters of the American Revolution. Jenny had happily relinquished her career as a fund manager in her family's business to become a stay-at-home mom, serving on the boards of numerous prestigious nonprofits. Ken was dutiful, Adam would give him that, but his son also treated him like an archeological relic.

As for Abby, when was that girl going to figure out her life? No husband. Limited income. Talented, for sure, but all too content to putter around in artistic obscurity. Adam wondered if his daughter wanted children. She wasn't getting any younger. She was a special snowflake of the highest order, unable to commit, even to an art form. First, she built sculptures made of ocean debris. A replica of a whale held together by tampon applicators. Good God! You didn't need to be Freud to see the daddy complex there. At least now she was putting her talents to good use by *painting*—a big improvement. But still, her subject matter left something to be desired. In his opinion, Abby was overly focused on her message, which often came at the cost of creating something beautiful. Make no mistake, Adam was sophisticated in terms of his taste in art, but when it came to portraying the female form, beauty was what mattered. And yes, he knew better than to say as much to Abby. He'd heard all he ever needed to about the male gaze.

One thing was for sure, neither of his children could be counted on to get the facts of his life right, especially the professional details, so Adam returned to the yellow legal pad on his lap to begin listing his impressive scientific accomplishments.

Abby

Abby parked a couple of miles from her childhood home so that she could forage on her way to dinner. Her father had caught three bluefish earlier in the day, which he planned to grill, and Ken had promised to pick up a decadent tart at his favorite bakery in Chatham. Abby would gather mushrooms for a savory side dish. The musky smell of damp soil encouraged her. It was early in the season, but she felt confident that the previous week's rain would provide good conditions.

Their family dinners, which for years had been monthly occasions, happened less and less frequently these days. For a while, Abby attributed the steady demise of this ritual to practical matters: everyone was busy with their careers, and now that the twins were tweens, there was a lot of social activity to juggle. But other factors were at play, too. Abby couldn't pinpoint a date, but over the last few years, the distance between the three of them had turned into something more palpable, a liquid congealing into a solid. Ken was nursing old grievances, their father's fuse was growing ever shorter, and Abby felt herself pulling away from them both. At this very moment—with Frida loping along beside her, twigs snapping underfoot, birds fluttering away—she was figuring out which white lie to tell as an excuse for not drinking wine with dinner later: *I'm fighting a cold. I had too much to drink last night. I have to get up early tomorrow to help one of my students.*

Abby was almost at the end of her first trimester, past the stage of worrying about miscarriage, but she didn't feel ready to divulge her pregnancy to her family. She'd also decided against telling them about her upcoming exhibit and the profile in *Art Observer* magazine. She wasn't sure why she was keeping secrets, except for an underlying feeling that her success might derail the men in her life, who were accustomed to getting the lion's share of attention. The last thing she needed right now was to have to manage their egos. Her success might stir something in Jenny, too, reminding her of the artistic career she'd given up. Their family dynamic was fragile, this much Abby knew, and she took care not to disrupt the established order. Especially when it came to Ken. She never knew what might set him off.

Abby meandered through the familiar forest, the ground dappled with sunlight, following trails that were the maze of her childhood—tracks from summer homes to backshore beaches, worn paths to long-abandoned lifesaving stations, and shortcuts to cherished blueberry patches. She watched tiny birds flit and flutter in the low limbs, crossing the path ahead of her in short bursts of flight. There was a special clearing in the woods about half a mile from her home that she'd stumbled upon as a child, a small patch of open space that glowed with yellow light. This glade was where Abby came to understand that she saw things in a special way: how sunshine showered through leaves, wrinkled tree knots were flecked with brightness, and moss was inlaid with a thousand colors. It was Abby's secret place, a spot where the eyes of unseen birds and woodland creatures—or perhaps even her mother—watched her. Time was suspended here, not metaphorically, but actually. As a child, she lingered in this clearing for as long as she liked, and when she left it, no time had passed. Inexplicable but true.

May was a bit early for boletes, but Abby knew where she could find morels. She had a sixth sense for mushrooms, often becoming aware of their subterranean presence before seeing them. She would be walking along one minute, and then feel a prickle at the base of her hairline, alerting her to a vast network of billions of organisms, neither plant nor animal, beneath the forest floor. She'd stop, allow her eyes to adjust, and suddenly the fruit of the mysterious ecosystem wondrously popped into view, peeking out from beneath a carpet of pine needles, blossoming from rotting stumps, gathering in clumps of moist soil. It always happened this way, and today was no different. Abby knelt, brushed away the dirt, examined wrinkled caps and spongy undersides, and placed mushroom after mushroom into her wicker basket.

With the dog close behind, Abby emerged from the woods and into the clearing of her childhood home, where from a distance, the house looked camouflaged, like part of the environment. Her father was shirtless, laying a good-size fish on a sheet of plywood he'd built for just this purpose. He'd lost some weight since she had last seen him a few weeks ago, quite a bit from the look of him.

"Hey there," she called, not wanting to startle him with a knife in hand.

"Abigail," her father called back. "You should have seen the ocean today. Gentle swells. No mung. The bluefish were going nuts, churning the water, driving up the baitfish." A sun-browned arm pushed up his visor so she could see his eyes. "It was my kind of mayhem: birds diving, fish leaping." He placed a palm behind the bluefish's pectoral fin, slipped the filet knife into the soft belly, and pulled it up to the gills. Out slid satiny guts and a pink purse of stomach. "How was your walk?"

Frida bounded over to Adam and pressed the warm leather of her snout into Adam's fishy hand.

"Lovely. Peaceful," she said.

Adam patted the dog's side. "Good girl."

"I found a great morel patch to the south of the old fire road," Abby said, raising her basket to show him her bounty.

Her father had sparked her interest in fungi as a child when she'd accompanied him on long walks and he explained the metabolic wizardry of decomposition. Mushrooms could digest anything from wood to rock to chemicals, he told her. "It's simple: composers make, and decomposers unmake. No fungi, no us." She recalled her father stomping on a log to make his point and watching it disintegrate into soil. The process amazed her.

"I know of an even better spot than that one," Adam said, his eyes lighting up like lanterns flickering in the wind.

Of course he did. Her father always knew the better spot. As Abby approached the house, the thrum emanating from the pond grew louder and louder. "Wow, the peepers are out in force," she said.

"They started last week. Soon, they'll reach their crescendo, and then"—Adam snapped his fingers—"it'll all be done."

They turned in the direction of the pond, listening to the rising trill.

"You have to admire their efficiency when it comes to romance," he added, smiling. "They announce their desire, get down to business, and wrap things up quickly."

"A commitment-phobe's idea of perfection," Abby said.

"Pot calling the kettle black," he shot back.

"Fair enough," she admitted.

Adam went back to work on the bluefish. With a few more deft strokes of the blade, he had six perfect fillets. He wiped his hands on his shorts and removed the basket from Abby's arm. "You'll never guess who made an appearance this afternoon."

"Who?"

But Adam got sidetracked inspecting the morels, giving each mushroom the once-over. "Just making sure you don't unintentionally off me."

"Don't give me ideas," Abby said. "Who?" she asked again. At her father's blank stare, she steered him back to the topic he'd initiated. "Who made an appearance?"

At this, Adam dropped the basket and grabbed Abby's hand, tugging her toward the pond. "Right there!" he said, pointing to a patch of shoreline. "He was right there."

"Who?"

"Charon," he said, as if it was Abby who was slow on the uptake. "The old bastard had the nerve to look surprised to see me."

Charon? Abby scanned the reeds along the pond's edge, hoping to glimpse her old friend. April and May were the months when snapping turtles awoke from their long sleep, so maybe her father had seen him. Charon. Something splashed in the middle of the pond, releasing ripples that undulated outward. It had been years since she'd glimpsed him. She slipped off her shoes, rolled up her jeans, and dipped her toes into the bracing water. Out of her peripheral vision, she saw the S-shape of a black water snake slide across the pewter surface and instinctively leaped back. It turned out to be a twig, and she had to endure her father's snicker.

Charon had been less than an inch long when her father and brother found him and made him the family pet. When the turtle measured ten inches, her dad decided to release him back into the pond. She and Ken had protested, but to no avail. Adam had made up his mind.

"Our Charon? Are you sure it was him?" Abby asked.

"Well, it's not like I'm a renowned biologist or anything," her father said. "Of course I'm sure. I'm positive."

She waited, watching the water, thrilled to think Charon was close by.

"Fucker thinks he's going to outlast me, but I'll show him," Adam said, raising a fist in salute. That her father was swearing with abandon was not unusual, but his frenetic gestures gave Abby pause. Or maybe he just seemed energetic compared with how she felt, lethargic. She'd almost fallen asleep during her seniors' portrait class earlier in the day.

"Did you hear me, Charon?" her father yelled at the pond, saliva gathering in the corners of his mouth.

Okay, something was definitely not right. Abby's chest tightened. "Looks like you've lost weight, Dad," she said, trying to maneuver the conversation. "Have you been eating enough?"

Adam flexed his muscles and slapped a palm on his flat belly. "You bet I have. Looks good, right? I've had to fend off the ladies," he said, giving Abby a wink. "They can't keep their hands off me."

"Gross," she said, rolling her eyes.

"Oh please, don't tell me I raised a prude."

Abby changed the subject. "How about I start preparing the mushrooms and make a salad, and you"—she sniffed the air—"take a shower?"

"Subtle as a tidal wave, kid," her father said.

About twenty minutes later, Ken pulled into the driveway in an unfamiliar new car, metallic silver and sleek. To Abby's surprise and delight, Jenny was in the passenger seat. She wouldn't be outnumbered by men tonight. It had been a while since Jenny had shown up to one of these dinners. Kenny got out of the car first, tart box in hand, wearing a blue polo shirt, khaki pants, and a Vineyard Vines whale belt, the uniform of the Chatham prepster.

Her brother had come out the winner when it came to their parents' DNA. They both took after their strawberry-blonde, brown-eyed mother—and anyone who saw them together could tell they were siblings—but Ken got the better version of every feature. Underweight and flat-chested with small, dark eyes, Abby wasn't unattractive, just easy to overlook, which was how she preferred it. Since she and David split as a couple, years ago now, she chose not to seek out male attention. Ken, on the other hand, was so handsome that he was hard to look away from.

Her brother hadn't always been the alpha male he was today. The older and more powerful he became, the more often Abby thought back to the plump, pimply boy Ken had once been—crooked teeth, unruly hair, and husky (to be kind about it). A growth spurt at eighteen had resolved his height/weight conundrum and, with that same hormonal burst, his acne dried up. These days, her brother maintained his physique with daily personal training sessions, leaving no trace of that soft-bellied boy.

The passenger door opened and out popped Jenny, dressed in a simple, sand-colored sundress made glamorous with a chunky, turquoise necklace that brought out her blue eyes. Jenny always looked fresh and sun-kissed, like a day at the beach minus the wind—her long arms tan and fit, never a hair out of place. Abby smiled and waved to her friend through the kitchen window. The Jenny of today was unrecognizable from the girl Abby had roomed with during her freshman year. Back then, Jenny played the rebel card hard: dirty hair, ripped jeans, a $200-a-week cocaine habit. She was the enfant terrible of RISD, and Abby adored her. They remained inseparable even as Jenny whiplashed into a different version of herself when her mother got sick and died in a matter of months. Abruptly, her friend quit art school and transferred to NYU to study finance, recreating herself as the responsible eldest child her parents had always wanted her to be. After graduating, she joined her family's firm.

A few years later, when Jenny fell hard for Ken and moved to the Cape, Abby felt certain her old friend would resurface. But at their wedding, Jenny gave a heartfelt toast in memory of her mother, thanking her for being the best role model a daughter could have. Champagne rose unpleasantly in Abby's nostrils. Maybe the old Jenny was gone for good. At art school, Isabel Lowell had been Jenny's anti-muse, representing everything Jenny found abhorrent about the role of women in society. Neither Jenny nor Abby had anticipated how the new terrain of sisterhood would complicate their friendship, requiring boundaries and rules. Abby understood that she was not to tell Ken about the wildest parts of his wife's wild-child days, and Ken made it clear that the topic of his past was off-limits in her conversations with Jenny. Her brother had worked hard to become the striking, successful man that Jenny had fallen in love with, and he did not want his bride to know that he'd ever been anything less than that.

As Abby stepped out onto the deck, Frida shot past her, greeting the arrivals with unbridled enthusiasm, nosing Jenny's hand onto her head. Her sister-in-law patted Frida politely but tried to keep the dog at arm's length, away from her dress.

"Down, Frida! Heel. Sorry about that, Jenny," Abby said. "It's so good to see you. You look fab; I love your necklace."

Jenny's eyes landed on Abby's frayed tank top, and Abby reflexively folded her arms across her chest.

"Where are Frannie and Tessa?" Abby asked. "I haven't seen them in a while."

"Join the club," Jenny said, softening as she always did whenever she spoke of her daughters. "They have a birthday party. I swear, their social schedule is out of control." Jenny bent down, retrieving a Tiffany-blue eggshell that lay in the grass at her feet, and handed it to Abby. "Pretty. That would be a good color for you. Pink kind of washes you out."

The eggshell was weightless in her hand. Abby tried not to take offense. It was just Jenny being Jenny, always trying to get Abby to up her fashion game.

"How's the work coming?" Jenny asked.

"It's going well. Really well," Abby said. "I'm working on something new and I'm in that crazy, obsessed phase. Any chance you can come by and see it? I could use your help. This piece is . . . Well, you'll see. It's different." She handed back the eggshell.

"I'd love to. I mean, things are pretty busy right now, though," Jenny said. "I'll try?"

Abby studied the ground, not wanting Jenny to see that she felt hurt. It was probably just the hormones.

"For you," Ken said, handing Abby the bakery box.

"Thanks, Kenny," Abby said, giving her brother a peck on the cheek.

"Is it really so hard?" he asked.

Ken hated being called *Kenny*. He squeezed his key fob, locking his car with a beep and a flash of headlights.

"Sorry. Sorry," Abby said. "Old habits die hard." She changed the subject. "Is that new? It looks a bit eco-friendly for a Republican."

"It's a Tesla Model S. Over four hundred miles with a single charge," Ken said, giving her a closed-lipped smile. "And, in case you haven't heard, we're an eco-friendly party."

"Oh, really? Try telling that to your presumptive nominee," Abby said brightly.

Overhead, a hawk slipped levels, eyeing something on the ground.

"Please, guys, please, no politics tonight," Jenny said, stepping in. She looked at Ken, asking a question with her eyes, which he answered with a nod. "Abby, I wanted to talk to you about your dad's party. We'd like to host it at our house. If that's okay with you, of course . . ." Jenny's voice trailed off.

A pity offer, to be sure, but relief flooded through Abby. "Oh my God, that would be amazing. Are you sure?" she asked.

Jenny nodded.

The thought of planning her father's seventieth birthday party had filled Abby with dread—all those details, all that cleaning. By contrast, it was a task Jenny could do in her sleep. Jenny had learned her way around a seating chart, dealt with caterers all the time, and seemed to enjoy matching flowers with table linens and votive candles. Besides, their well-manicured Chatham home was designed with entertaining in mind; it seemed as if they threw parties multiple times a week. True, Adam might prefer to be feted right here in his own home and no doubt he'd find fault with his daughter-in-law's blue-and-white nautical decor and fussy passed hors d'oeuvres. But the decision was easy for Abby.

"Well, if you're both sure you don't mind?" Abby said, her relief palpable. "I'd be over the moon. Thank you."

"Of course," Jenny said. "It's our pleasure."

At the sound of the shower turning off inside, Abby knew they had only a few more minutes before their father joined them. "There's something else," she said, lowering her voice. "I'm a little worried about Dad. He's pretty"—she paused, searching for the right word—"energetic."

"Abby, he's fine. You're always so dramatic," Ken said, dismissively. "I talked to Dad yesterday. He's just worked up about some new whale research."

Adam

Energetic? Had Adam heard his daughter correctly? He toweled himself dry beside the open bathroom window, straining to hear more of the conversation. To think, his children had the nerve to be discussing him in the third person. On the deck of his own house. Standing on planks he'd hammered down with his own two hands. Damn straight, he was energetic. He was on fire. If Ken and Abby had any inkling of the precipice he was on, the magnitude of his impending discovery, they'd be full of pride. Instead, they were planning to thwart him. *Sharper than serpent's teeth, both of them.*

A sudden dizziness forced Adam to grab the sides of the sink before lowering himself onto the closed toilet. He bent over and placed his head between his knees, feeling his pulse thumping in his temple. The sound in his head was not unlike the time when, during a deep-sea dive, he'd encountered a humpback at least fifty feet long and weighing well over fifty thousand pounds. He and the whale floated, staring unblinkingly at each other, seemingly sharing a thought: *Please don't harm me, fellow sentient being afloat in the vast ocean.* Only the whale took the examination a step further, sending out echolocation sonar that moved through Adam's body like an MRI scanner, causing a tingling sensation that reverberated through his skeleton and ricocheted in his skull.

Adam rose shakily from the toilet and peered out the bathroom window. His children's voices had receded, and the deck was empty. *Paranoia is part of bipolar disorder*, he reminded himself, knowing it would be in his best interest to fight the feeling and give his children the benefit of the doubt. Adam hung up his bath towel, poked his feet through his boxers, yanked up a pair of jeans, and put on a faded Hawaiian shirt. He checked himself in the mirror and patted his hair into place. He looked good.

Try as he might, though, Adam couldn't shake the feeling that Ken and Abby were plotting against him. Little monsters, indeed! Adam thought of every splinter he'd ever painstakingly removed from their feet. He calculated the number of meals he'd prepared for them in their lifetimes: three times a day, seven days a week, fifty-two weeks a year, eighteen years. About twenty thousand meals, give or take. He was loath to think of all the miles he'd driven, schlepping them here and there. And what about the nightmares he'd soothed? Or the idyllic home he'd provided? This one right here, looking out over a pond full of white egrets and electric-blue dragonflies. Did either of his children appreciate any of the sacrifices he'd made?

Adam tiptoed into the kitchen where the sautéed morels smelled earthy and buttery. The cutting board and knife were in the dish rack, the mushroom stems in the compost bowl, the counter wiped. Everything seemed to be in its proper place—cast-iron skillets suspended from a pot rack overhead, spatulas and wooden spoons in a terracotta planter beside the stove—but something was amiss. He felt sure of it.

He stepped onto the deck and saw that Ken, Jenny, and Abby were down by the pond now, no doubt so they could talk about him out of earshot. The way they stood. The hand-wringing. The weight of their big heads tilted toward one another. His children looked tiny in the distance. Then, it was as if there was a sudden tear in space and time, and suddenly Adam saw Ken and Abby as they were when they were young, running wild through the Wellfleet Woods on swift feet. His sweet, unruly, little monsters. Back then, Adam was their king, ruler of all they could see. God, how his children used to worship him.

A memory surfaced, unbidden. Ken and Abby wrestling playfully behind a canoe in the boat shed. What game were they playing? At the time, he'd pushed down the uneasy feeling in his gut. *Kids will be kids*, Adam had thought as he stepped back and closed the door to the shed. He'd always subscribed to a laissez-faire parental philosophy, letting his children sort out their differences on their own. But now he wondered if he should have intervened more. The image of his young children blurred, and Adam couldn't bring it back into focus.

Deep breaths. Inhale. Exhale. Adam took five and willed himself to return to the present. He shook his head and studied grown-up Ken and Abby. They were okay. He'd been an excellent father, he reminded himself, no matter what Gretchen had to say about his parenting skills. God, that woman was full of vitriol. He studied the pond. His pond. Somewhere in the muddy bottom, Charon lurked. On clusters of lily pads, bullfrogs blew their insides out. And swarms of water striders zipped across the surface. Everything was okay. *He* was okay. Now, he just needed to convince his children of that.

Dinner. Dinner would take about two hours. All he had to do was get through the meal without sounding bombastic—not easy when you were on the brink of the biggest breakthrough in marine biology ever. He also needed to convey his expectations for his upcoming birthday party. To be precise, this soiree needed to be a well-orchestrated affair, one where each toast built upon the preceding one, leading to the inevitable moment when he, the man of the hour, took to the stage and made an announcement that would forever change the perception of the animal kingdom.

Grandiosity, he knew, was a telltale sign of mania and one that his daughter was always on the lookout for. Adam reminded himself that he'd been outsmarting his children for decades. He took five more breaths. There was no reason for alarm. He would be humble and calm tonight, avoiding topics that agitated him, namely politics or the unctuous young scientists at CCIO who were after his corner office. The only thing that mattered was getting everyone on the same page regarding his birthday party. That, and being the opposite of "energetic." Tonight, mellow would be his superpower.

As he watched his children scheming at the edge of the pond, Adam chipped wax drippings off his wine bottle candlesticks and replaced the candles. *Divide and conquer*, he thought as he unrolled four place mats, flipping them over to determine which side had fewer stains. It was Abby who was fueling this fire, calling him "energetic" and stoking havoc. So, he'd take Ken aside and set the record straight, man-to-man. An eye roll. A back pat. It wouldn't be hard to get his son to see it from his perspective.

Forks on the left, knives on the right, napkins under the forks. They both knew that women tended to be dramatic. Abby was overreacting. Simple as that. A bud vase with three daisies. *Take that, Martha Stewart*. With this plan in mind, Adam summoned an authoritative and detached calm. He opened the screen door and released it, the hinges screeching as it swung shut. Three faces snapped around to look in his direction.

"Greetings, family," Adam said, raising a hand and smiling benignly. He could do this. "It warms my heart to have you here tonight. Enjoy the nature symphony down there. Dinner will be ready in fifteen minutes."

Ken

"Good morning, George," Ken said, taking his usual spot on the middle of the sofa and stretching his arms long across the top of the cushions. "I've been giving it a great deal of thought, and"—here, he allowed for a meaningful pause—"I don't think therapy is working for me." He liked the idea of putting it out there right away. He wasn't going to be one of those save-the-big-reveal-for-the-last-five-minutes type of patient.

On the chair catty-corner to Ken sat Dr. George Kunar, his shaggy-haired therapist. Ken's comment elicited a slight twitch at the corner of George's mouth and a recrossing of his legs, right ankle over left knee.

"As I see it, I've been coming in for, what, close to three months now?" Ken continued, clearing his throat, realizing he'd been rehearsing this monologue the entire drive from Chatham to Boston. "I've been open. I've done my best to be 'vulnerable' "—air-quoting the word—"I've prayed about my problems. But the fact is, talk doesn't change much. I schedule my week around our meetings. And you know what? Most Thursday afternoons, I leave this office thinking a hot stone massage would do more at one-third the price."

At this, his therapist's face softened into a smile. "That's hard logic to argue, Ken. Not much competes with a hot stone massage," George said. "But even with a massage, the goal is to go deeper, right? Working through the knots can be painful, but you leave feeling better."

Apparently, George could turn anything into a metaphor. *Nope, not taking the bait today, buddy.* Ken sank further into the cushions, taking in George's deliberately neutral office. The room was a basic rectangle with George's chair on the far end and Ken's sofa along one of the longer walls. The couch and chair were part of a set, beige and neither antique nor modern. A couple of paisley throw pillows. The sofa was comfortable, he'd give George that. A low walnut bookcase ran the full length of the wall opposite him and held no surprises: Jung, Freud, and other therapy classics alongside some more contemporary analysts. Three large windows filled the room with slanted columns of dust-permeated light. What else? A coffee table, an end table (the requisite box of tissues on both), and a couple of unremarkable glass-based lamps.

The only revealing items in the room were six primitive masks that dotted the wall above George's chair. They were unsettling, bordering on disturbing, and Ken avoided looking at them, focusing instead on his disheveled hippie of a shrink. Dr. Kunar might be billed as Boston's best psychoanalyst, but often Ken couldn't look past his need for a haircut. On more than one occasion, the bottom button on George's shirt was left undone, revealing a white slice of belly dappled with strands of curly black hair. Ken never felt sure that George was the right guy for him. Especially when he snacked on strips of seaweed during their sessions.

"What's up with the masks, George?" Ken asked. "And for the love of God, don't ask me what I think is up with them."

"Okay, Ken, I get it," George said, lifting his hands in surrender. He tore open a cellophane package and pulled out a square of nori, mulling over his next move.

The guy was so beta. How could Ken take life advice from a seaweed-eating pacifist?

"How about this," George said, puffing his cheeks frog-like as he exhaled.

What was with the lag time between questions and answers?

"If I promise to tell you about the masks, will you tell me why you suddenly want to leave therapy?"

En garde, Ken thought. "Nothing sudden about it. I'm not feeling much in the way of progress. I'm goal-oriented, George, and I pay you a fortune. For what exactly, I'm not sure. My marriage hasn't improved particularly. Jenny still can't seem to let go of"—he searched for the word—"that incident. And for that matter, nothing's changed with my sister or father." Ken needed to make his point. He leaned forward and tapped the coffee table between them. "It's as simple as this, George: I need things to move along at a faster clip. I need a plan, and for there to be an end in sight. This 'trust the process' mumbo jumbo isn't working for me." Ken found George's eyes and didn't blink. "Explain the process, please."

George showed his palms. "The therapeutic process?"

"What else are we talking about here?" Ken said. "I've been doing my part. I come, I unload, I leave. And I'm not saying that you've never connected any dots or offered interesting insights. You have. But the clock is ticking. I have a congressional run on the horizon. I can't afford cracks in my marriage. I need to keep my family in line."

"Ken, you know therapy only works on the self," George said. "The goal is to understand yourself. There's no streamlining the process. It doesn't work that way."

"Come on, George. Are you suggesting there's no way to speed things up? In business, I set goals—for the day, the week, the year. You know, one foot in front of the other. I get that therapy is more touchy-feely, but it certainly can be done more efficiently."

George took off his glasses and cleaned them on his shirttail. More belly. "The work happens in three phases," he said, replacing his glasses. "Phase one, you tell me why you think you're here, and I mirror that story back to you, and in doing so, try to help you understand the unique circumstances of your experiences. And, of course, I root for you."

"So, phase one . . . check?"

"Not so fast. The phases are ongoing. In every session, the idea is to dig deeper," George said. "But that requires trust, and trust takes time. Would you agree that you're still a bit guarded with me?"

Ken chose to ignore the question. "Okay, phase one gets a partial check. Phase two?"

"The next step is for me to show you the underlying patterns, so that together, we can solve the jigsaw puzzle of your life. Again, I try to hold a mirror up for you to see how your behavior affects you. And I still root for you."

"What's with all the 'rooting'?" Ken said. "I'm not a kid in a soccer match. I don't need a cheerleader."

"All I mean is, I want you to succeed. Phase two is a kind of loving confrontation." George paused. "And it's the most difficult stage in therapy. It's perfectly normal for you to want to leave during this phase. You wouldn't be the first."

Ken did not like the insinuation that he was behaving as expected, like all of George's other patients. But the truth was, he did want to leave. Bolt out the door right now. Why the hell had he come back to explain himself when he could've just not shown up for the appointment?

"Again, it would be helpful to know exactly what Jenny walked in on that drove you here in the first place."

"I told you at our first session what brought me here," Ken said, hating to think about what Jenny might have seen or heard that day when she'd walked in on him in Command Central. Why had he thought wearing noise-canceling headphones was a good idea?

"Try me again," George said.

Ken crossed his arms. "It's not what you think." He had nothing to feel guilty about. "I've never touched a woman other than my wife since I got married." This was true, and he felt proud of it. He should get a damn medal for all the opportunities he hadn't pursued in sixteen years of marriage.

"So, what is it you're seeking online that you can't get at home?" George asked.

None of your business is what. Ken sighed. His shrink didn't need to know every detail. Ken leaned forward, angling for a man-to-man moment. "George, would it be possible to simply acknowledge that no one woman can meet a man's every need and no amount of therapy is going to change that?"

"Hmm."

Ken threw up his hands. He was paying $350 an hour for one-syllable grunts? "For Christ's sake, George, I don't want to end therapy because it's difficult, I want to end therapy because it's going nowhere. We're just not a good fit. I need more reaction."

"Okay," George said, nodding. "Here's some reaction for you: three months ago, you walked through my door because Jenny gave you an ultimatum and you didn't want your marriage to end. But you still haven't let me in on exactly what disturbed her. If you want our therapy to be successful, the ball is in your court."

Touché, thought Ken. "I've already told you. Jenny walked in on me role-playing in a chat room. I can't undo what she saw." Ken shifted uncomfortably. He liked to watch people cuddle was all, not something he planned to admit to George. "This is an inane line of questioning," he said, getting up as if to leave. "I'm tired of feeling I'm to blame for everything. Why is this all on me?"

"It's not all on you. Please sit down. Please stay. These feelings are difficult and part of the work," George said. "Marriage is a dance between two people, but you and I can only work on your moves. Jenny is in therapy, too. We must trust she's working on her issues."

Ken sat back down reluctantly. This was not going as planned. A redirect was in order. "Okay, George, I'll admit I was careless. But can you admit this has gotten a bit overblown?"

George's face was inscrutable. "The goal is to help resolve your intimacy issues."

Ken let his head fall back onto the cushions and allowed his eyes to follow a crack in the ceiling that ran the width of the room. "Am I really such a bad guy?" he asked. "I go to church on Sundays. I get home in time to have dinner with my family most nights. I'm self-made. My mother died when I was just a kid. I had to deal with dozens of my father's girlfriends as they came and went." Ken took pleasure in lumping his stepmother, Gretchen, into a mass of nameless women who'd consorted with his father over the years. He lifted his head and jerked his chin once to the side, cracking his neck. "For as long as I can remember, my father's been on some monomaniacal mission around whales. You have no idea how much oxygen one man can suck out of a room. And my sister—" Why was it always so difficult to describe Abby? As children, they'd been best friends, but now they barely spoke. She was a painter who specialized in weird, quasi-abstract portraiture. She'd had a brief moment of fame a decade earlier but failed to exploit her success. He'd been supporting her ever since. What other people perceived in her as shyness, Ken knew was her sense of moral superiority. And there was this way in which she held the secrets of their childhood against him like a noose around his neck. "Let's put it this way: my sister is one of those people who thinks she's the only person on the planet who composts," he said, realizing he sounded ridiculous. He thought about how Abby had withdrawn from him abruptly when she was twelve or so, the memory still filling him with shame. She'd stolen his best friend in the process. More shame. "Abby's never done anything remarkable, and yet everyone seems to think she walks on water. My father, especially. His patent favoritism used to hurt, now I'm just numb to it."

"Let's talk about your father and the numbness," George said.

When it came to his father, Ken was more concerned with the here and now. Seventy was far too old to live alone in a drafty house in the middle of the woods, having to drive fifteen miles to get to the nearest supermarket. He needed to get his father into a safer living situation. Ken shook his head. At $350 an hour, once again, George had missed the point.

"Children experience loneliness like shame, and that might explain why you feel numb," George droned on.

Not a path Ken wanted to go down. "Jesus, George, this is the problem: you want to dive down every rabbit hole. Phase three, please."

As George started to speak again, Ken stared out the windows into tree branches and the sky overhead, allowing his vision to soften and blur, a technique of leaving a room; he'd perfected it long ago. It drove Abby crazy.

"Phase three is where you start to connect current feelings and reactions to your past and understand how they relate. For example, when Jenny distances herself, you might experience that as abandonment, which is familiar to you. Maybe it reminds you of when your mother died. Or when your stepmother left. Or when Abby pulled away. And those are unpleasant feelings, so your subconscious tells you to try to avoid or escape them."

Ken was too far away for the words to sink in.

"And that, my friend, is where the healing lies. When you can understand how you react to stressors and what's going on inside yourself, you can make different choices. Hopefully, ones that will draw you to your wife. Does that make sense?"

Sunlight from the windows appeared a yellowish pink behind Ken's closed eyelids, and he lost himself in the patterns of light and shadow. Then he was with his mother on the bay sailing on the *Francesca,* her thirty-five-foot Hinckley Pilot Yawl. It was their favorite pastime. He felt this memory with his whole body. The way his mother stood close behind him at the wheel, and how snugly he fit against her warm torso. She'd built a box for him to stand on so he could see over the steering wheel. Her hands were clasped over his, helping him steer, both of them drenched in ocean spray. "You're going to be a great captain someday," she told him. His mother's voice, so musical and full of love.

"But the more you resist, the longer it takes," George continued, his words disembodied in the room.

Now his mother was reading a bedtime story to him, her hair hanging down near his face. One memory bled into the next. But was that what they were, really? Did Ken actually remember his mother? Or had he created this mental montage out of photos and nostalgic stories? He'd been so young when she died. The one thing he remembered with certainty was the day his father brought Abby home wrapped in a blue-and-pink hospital blanket.

"Where's Momma?" he'd asked. And although he'd been too young to understand death, his brain formed a permanent wrinkle connecting his sister's arrival and his mother's departure.

By the time Ken realized that George had stopped talking and the room was silent, he was unsure how long he'd been lost in thought. Was it seconds or minutes? He worried that he might have called out to his mother. Or worse, Abby. Had he said her name? He might have. Yeah, he was pretty sure he did. He didn't understand why these bittersweet memories were suddenly surfacing. Thirty-eight years, and still, just a finger snap from grief. When Ken blinked open his eyes, his cheeks were wet and George was leaning toward him, regarding him with compassion.

"It's okay," George said. "Stay with it, Ken. This *is* the process. The numbness you feel isn't the absence of feeling, it's the opposite. You're overwhelmed by so many feelings."

Ken wished George would just shut up. Was the goal of self-knowledge to experience pain more lucidly? He felt a rising pressure in his belly, a feeling so intense he thought he might vomit. He tried to swallow the saliva pooling in his mouth, but the sensation continued to build. He pulled a sofa pillow onto his lap and pressed his face into it. Then it erupted, a wail so loud and long it sounded like an animal was being murdered inside him.

Ken took the long route home, needing to put distance between himself and his session with George. Miles of road vanished under his tires as he meandered through the picturesque seaside villages of the northeast part of the ninth congressional district: Humarock, Ocean Bluff, and Green Harbor. Over the past year, he'd had coffee in every diner, flirting with the waitresses, many of whom he knew by name, and stopped in at every hardware store, chatting up men as they browsed shelves for the right screw or drill bit. He knew it was early for this type of grassroots campaigning. His manager liked to remind him to focus on the "grass-tops" at this stage, meeting with influencers, and party and community leaders. Ken was doing that, too, but above all, he enjoyed winning over the regular Joes. He lived for the moment when he saw their faces transform, when whatever suspicion or doubt gave way to trust, and their look said, *What a great guy*. That was when Ken would flash a Kennedyesque smile to seal the deal, knowing his work was done.

He'd already opened a small office for his campaign in Plymouth. Again, it was early for this step—his planned run wasn't for two years—but Ken was nothing if not prepared. He'd filed with the FEC, had a manager in place, and had already raised some serious money. Although the ninth district had been in Democratic hands for fifty years—it had supported Obama in both elections and would most certainly go with Hillary in November—it was the palest blue congressional district in Massachusetts, and Ken would use this to his advantage. The constituents of this district were not Elizabeth Warren–style Democrats. They were prosperous individuals who'd worked hard to accumulate wealth and didn't care for or share her semi-socialistic ideals. Ken considered himself a left-leaning Republican, fiscally conservative, and socially progressive—exactly what the ninth district needed.

The guy who currently held the office was unobjectionable but lackluster. In his mid-sixties, he was a political lifer who was out of fresh ideas and low on energy. Ken knew he was the sitting congressman's high-octane opposite. He'd been blessed with good looks, a sharp mind, wealth, and killer political instincts. But his other great assets were the three beautiful women in his life: Jenny and their fiery, green-eyed twin daughters, Frannie and Tessa, twelve going on twenty.

A few miles from the Sagamore Bridge, where seagulls soared on invisible currents of air, Ken realized that George had never answered his question about the masks. A *deal was a deal,* he thought, and wondered what the hell had happened to him in there today, anyway. He lowered the windows, inhaling the briny air. Therapy. What a racket. Ken did not enjoy mucking around in his subconscious and reminded himself he didn't have to return. But when and if he did, he was sure as hell going to get to the bottom of those ugly masks.

Chatham, the town where Ken and Jenny moved once they determined that the long game included a run for Congress, was more civilized than where he'd grown up. Located at the elbow of the long arm of Cape Cod, Chatham was the perfect combination of quaint charm—climbing roses along picket fences, cedar shake–sided cottages, beach plum bushes that gave way to low-lying wooded hills—and rugged wilderness—barrier beaches, harbors, estuaries, and salt- and freshwater ponds. It also offered more creature comforts than most other Cape towns: excellent restaurants, private golf courses, marinas, even an airport. Jenny sometimes missed city life and worried about the girls' education at the local public school, but Ken didn't share her concerns.

Unlike where he grew up in the lawless Wellfleet Woods, where people thought nothing of trespassing across one another's property to get from one kettle pond to the next, and dinner parties migrated from home to home, private property was respected in Chatham. Things were too unruly on the outer Cape, if you asked Ken, as he recalled a childhood with little adult supervision—nights spent by bonfires with older kids, days exploring the woods or beach where he and Abby would run down giant dunes together, arms wheeling, the surf crashing nearby. When their father disappeared, which Adam did from time to time, they were inseparable, taking refuge in Ken's room, where they felt safe.

The early evening light was soft when Ken reached Stage Island and pulled into his white clamshell driveway, culminating in a hand-carved sign, THE GARDNERS. The sprinklers were on, greening his already green carpet of lawn and creating mini-rainbows in the process. The property was a marvel this time of year, buds blossoming, resurrecting the land with the reliable annual miracle of new growth and color. The dogwoods and cherry trees were in bloom, as were the forsythia and lilacs, so many fresh smells welcoming him home. From the honeysuckle bushes that lined the driveway to a border of tulips and daffodils that ran along the bluestone paver path leading to the front door to the humble daisies that sprouted from the grasses along their beach trail—all this was Jenny's domain. She'd been an investor at the family firm when they first met but had shifted her boundless energy to domestic pursuits once they married. She made it seem effortless, throwing parties, overseeing their daughters' education and extracurriculars, and keeping their grounds pristine. Long ago, Jenny had wanted to be an artist, but the garden seemed to satisfy that itch. She was fanatical about color and shape, and how they changed over time, referring to her blossoms as nature's paints.

In the distance, lobstermen and fishermen worked on their boats, readying them for the season. Ken could hardly wait to get the *Francesca* out of dry dock and back into Stage Harbor. He longed to get out on the open waters and take Jenny and the girls to the Vineyard or Nantucket. He loved the sound of the ground tackle scuttling across the deck as the wind shifted and the feel of the wheel tugging against his grip. Of course, he'd need to relearn the harbor. Every winter, storms shifted the sand and changed the channel, creating a new configuration to the cut that led to the Nantucket Sound. Even without global warming and the resulting sea-level rise, erosion was inevitable on the glacial spit of Cape Cod, where the loose sand had no resistance to wave attack. In a few thousand years, the entire sixty-five-mile arm would be reduced to low-lying islands before eventually being swallowed whole.

To Ken, the erosion felt personal, an epic battle against natural forces that he knew he was destined to lose. Still, he wouldn't go down without a fight. Each year, the Atlantic robbed sand from his beach and sucked pebbles and stones from the rock revetment that protected his property. He went so far as to pay his daughters and their friends $20 an hour to collect rocks and stuff them back into the holes. He also constantly measured the loss of land. Jenny joked that he was like someone obsessed with their weight. But that didn't stop Ken from using his foot, exactly twelve inches, to heel-toe his way from each structure—the main house, Command Central, a tool shed—to the bank's edge, recording his findings on a spreadsheet. Typically, he'd lose an inch or two annually, but in the first five months of 2016, he'd already lost two inches. Unacceptable.

His father-in-law had presented them with this beautiful parcel of land as a wedding gift, and right away they decided to build their primary residence there. Once the plans were drawn, the house took three years to complete—six months to clear the land, dig the foundation, and bury all the pipes and cables; a full year for construction; and another eighteen months for interior work and landscaping. The house had six bedrooms, marble bathrooms, vaulted ceilings, a kitchen suited for a world-class chef, a detached garage and office, an infinity pool, and a jacuzzi—all of it wired to the nines.

The house was empty when he entered, a rarity Ken planned to enjoy. Jenny and the girls must be on a walk. He poured himself a bourbon and sat in his favorite chair on the screened-in porch, watching the sunlight glinting off the water. The air was soft in the spring heat. Soon, the *Francesca* would be back on her mooring, and the thought delighted him. He pictured himself in front of the polished mahogany wheel, flag waving from the stern—a campaign photo-op if ever there was one.

Ken heard his daughters' laughter before he saw them. Soon his family would be around the table, voices bubbling with excitement. He shut his eyes. The bourbon was good. The light was extraordinary. He'd created all of it. And this was only the beginning.

Steph

Naming a baby should not be this hard and it certainly shouldn't take a month, Steph thought, outstretched on the sofa. Her head rested on Toni's lap and her foot idly rocked the Moses basket that held their son. They were at an impasse: Toni refused to consider unconventional names on the grounds that their son might get beaten up on the playground.

"Having two moms is going to be hard enough for the kid," she argued.

And Steph had vetoed every run-of-the-mill Catholic name Toni suggested.

"So, where's the compromise?" Toni asked, running her fingernails through the length of Steph's black hair.

"We're not that far off," Steph said, her scalp tingling with pleasure. "So long as it's simple and strong, I can handle biblical. It just has to be a name that sets him apart. The world doesn't need another Michael, no offense to my dad."

"And no world has ever needed a Regis or Finley."

The argument looped endlessly like this; a Spirograph drawing gone rogue. One of them was bound to give in soon, if for no other reason than the tedium of it. They'd barely moved from the sofa all day.

The afternoon was gray with a mackerel sky and air that smelled of rain. A crack of lightning cut through the gloom and let loose a downpour that lifted the curtains. Toni got up, replacing her lap with a throw pillow for Steph's head, and rushed to close the upstairs windows, leaving Steph alone on the sofa to contemplate their dilemma. A boom of thunder erupted overhead, unleashing a single thought: *God is angry*. How embarrassing that this was what still surfaced when Steph heard thunderclaps. It was how her father used to explain it to her when she was a child.

"God's angry," he'd say, shaking his head. "Not at you in particular," he'd always add reassuringly before enveloping her in one of his bear hugs. "Just at all the dopey things people do."

Steph wondered how her biological father, a man of science, would have explained meteorological events to his children. She'd bet that there was talk of superheated air and charging precipitation particles. But she would never know that other life. Her parents hadn't gone to college, and she hadn't grown up with siblings. How different might her life have been with a brother and sister? Not to mention a famous father. Turned out, Steph's new relatives had professions, not jobs—a scientist, an artist, and a real estate mogul with political aspirations. These were people who followed their dreams. They probably never worried about things like job security or uniform allowances. How might they have advised her when she'd wanted to go to the Culinary Institute? She might be a world-famous chef by now.

Steph adjusted the pillow under her head, comforted by the familiar sounds of Toni's footsteps overhead. She picked up her iPad. She'd been Google-stalking her half-siblings like a starstruck teenager, curious to learn how the genes that made her had expressed themselves in these two. Ken and Abigail were as exotic as seahorses. Don't even ask her how many times she'd watched Ken's Facebook video announcing his plans to run for Congress with his silky voice promising to fight for her in Washington. Or, for that matter, how often Steph studied Abby's odd paintings, which, even when viewed on a small screen, elicited peculiar sensations. Two extremes on a continuum of professional opportunities that had never occurred to Steph. How quick she'd been to give up on her dream of becoming a chef, which now seemed indicative of her narrow worldview and working-class roots.

But here was something strange: whenever Steph looked at pictures of the Gardners, she had a strong sense of déjà vu. As a child, she'd harbored fantasies not that far from this reality. That she'd been adopted or switched at birth. Did all children experience this?

Steph scrolled through photos of her brother and sister, screenshots she'd taken from Facebook, websites, and newspapers. She examined one of Ken golfing. Golden skin, short-cropped copper hair, summer-narrowed brown eyes. The golf club, gripped in both hands, was raised over his left shoulder, his body twisting as he finished a swing—a swing that, judging from the satisfied look on his face, had landed well. Steph had always envied the physical ease with which men like Ken carried themselves. She spread her thumb and forefinger over the screen, magnifying the image. The determination on his face was unnerving.

She swiped to the next photo, another one lifted from his wife Jenny's carefully curated Facebook page, a veritable gold mine of Gardner family information. In this one, Ken looked like a king, sitting on a wingback chair, flanked by a daughter on either side and his wife behind him, her manicured hand, weighted by a hefty diamond ring, draped over his shoulder. Jenny had the pleasantly attractive face of a morning talk-show host, simultaneously pretty and forgettable. Her hair—blonde, blown, and sprayed into a stiff, chin-length dome—told a different story. *Don't fuck with me*, that hair said.

The girls, Frannie and Tessa, were something else. Even posed as they were in their prim holiday dresses, there was something electric about them. These girls were going to give their parents a run for their money, no question about it. The thought made Steph smile. They looked about twelve or thirteen, the age when hormones began to change everything. To think, Steph was an aunt; she was *their* aunt. Her newborn son had cousins.

Steph swiped through more photos until she landed on one of Abby. Images of her half sister were harder to come by. Although she had a Facebook account, she wasn't active on it and her digital footprint was small. Steph had found this photo on the bio page of Abby's website. Taken at a three-quarters angle, her sister was sitting on a weathered deck, squinting into the afternoon sun, a skinny arm slung around a golden retriever. She wore jeans and a faded pink T-shirt and had freckles, shoulder-length strawberry-blonde hair, and brown eyes, darker and smaller than her brother's. Abigail resembled Ken, especially in the mouth and coloring, but she was not beautiful like him. She had slightly too-large teeth, which diminished her chin and jaw, making her look nervous, vulnerable, and—if Steph were to be brutally honest—a bit rodent-like.

Steph saw little of herself in either of her half-siblings. Nor, for that matter, did she see much of their father in either of them. Ken and Abigail must take after their mother, though Steph hadn't been able to track down any photographs to confirm this. According to an obituary in the *Cape Cod Times*, Emily Gardner died in 1978, the year both Steph and Abigail were born. It struck Steph as ironic that she, the illegitimate child, got the most of their father physically.

In fact, Steph looked so much like Adam Gardner that she worried her face might betray her plans to get to know these new relatives. She'd decided to infiltrate the Gardners' lives on the sly. She and Toni had been renting the same summer cottage in the West End of Provincetown for over a decade, but this year—between maternity leave and stockpiled vacation—they'd cobbled together three months of time off and would have the place from June through August. Toni thought Steph should be up front with the Gardners. But fifteen years of police training gave Steph an appreciation for having the upper hand and the element of surprise. For all she knew, these fancy relatives might look down on her or think she was after their money. They might be homophobic. Any which way, Steph's existence would come as a shock. At best, it would establish Adam Gardner as an adulterer—nothing pretty about that picture. And there was no upside to discovering an illegitimate half sister or daughter. Steph needed to stake out this family first before she blew up all their lives.

She would start with Abby, whose studio in North Truro was open to the public once a month, a fact that seemed too good to be true: an invitation to stomp around her sister's personal space and ask questions incognito. A detective's dream.

The baby started to fuss, and Steph got up and lifted him from his Moses basket. He couldn't be hungry again yet, so she sniffed his backside. Not that, either. He smelled like talcum powder and sour milk, and she pressed him to her chest, tucking his head beneath her chin, and thumping his back while swaying in place. When Toni finally returned to the living room, she was carrying a tray: lime slices, two rocks glasses, a bowl of ice, and a bottle of tequila. "Surprise!"

"Your mother's a goddess," Steph said to the baby, whose hand was spread out on her chest, a pink star.

"A goddess with a brilliant idea," Toni responded. "There's plenty of pumped milk in the fridge. Let's not put off naming this kiddo a moment longer. How about we get a little drunk and just do it? Then we can leave for Cape Cod tomorrow, burden-free."

"Why I married you," Steph said, limbs loosening in anticipation of the first sip. It had been months. She sat back down on the sofa, a movement that made her incision tingle, a flash of fire followed by itchiness. "Don't worry, buddy," she said to the baby. "If your mother thinks a little tequila is going to make me okay with 'Tom' or 'Tim,' she's got another thing coming."

"Ye of little faith," Toni said, filling their glasses: two rocks and two, three, four fingers of gold.

As the tequila unraveled in ice, Steph adjusted the baby, now asleep on her shoulder. Toni was right: there was no time like the present.

They lifted their glasses, softly clinking rims.

"To our family," Toni said.

"To us," said Steph.

"I've come prepared," Toni said, producing a list from her back pocket. "Biblical names with pizzazz." The first one she read was Silas. "Silas was chosen to go to Antioch in the Book of Acts. Thoughts?"

Steph made a face.

"Okay, how about Solomon? We could call him Solly, for short."

Nope.

"Enos?" Toni proposed. "Son of Seth, grandson of Adam and Eve."

Steph bobbled her head, considering it. She might be able to live with Enos; the name was unique.

"Or Noah? Of Noah's Ark fame?" suggested Toni.

There'd been an annoying Noah in grade school, which would be hard to get past.

"Okay, how about"—Toni paused for effect—"Jonah?"

"Jonah," Steph repeated. "Jonah." Did she know any Jonahs? She didn't think so. "Jonah," she said again.

"I *knew* you'd love it," Toni said, shoving her list toward Steph. "See?"

All the names were written in small, tidy, black print. All but Jonah, that was. Jonah was scrawled in big, loose letters that stretched across the page and doubled as waves holding a boy afloat over an open-mouthed whale swimming up from below to swallow him whole.

Steph waited for it. Toni was bound to say something about trusting the universe. Steph liked facts; she was someone who believed things once they were verifiable. Toni processed the world differently, trusting her gut and intuition. And although Steph teased her about it, it was hard to argue that Toni didn't have unusual abilities. How many times did someone need to pass you your phone before it rang to understand that she could just sense things?

"Okay, I'll bite," Steph said, mellow from the tequila. "How'd you know I'd like Jonah?"

"You're a Pisces," Toni said, pouring a splash more booze into each of their glasses, "Latin for fish. Your ruling body is Neptune, your element is water, your birthstone is aquamarine, your color is turquoise . . . Need I go on?"

Maybe astrology wasn't complete bunk after all.

"Jonah," Steph whispered, her lips touching the silky tip of her son's ear. "Jonah."

Abby

Memorial Day. The smell of freshly cut grass and honeysuckle. An American flag snapping against a sapphire sky. Seagulls rising and falling, treading air in the wind. The sun reflecting brightly on the white clamshell driveway, dimming intermittently when clouds floated past, dragging bloated shadows. The spread at Ken and Jenny's annual summer opener was impressive: a margarita machine churned out slushies, bowls of chips, salsa, and guacamole dotted the deck's bench railings, and carne asada crackled on the grill, releasing spicy aromas into the clear day. Framing the scene were Jenny's well-orchestrated blossoms, where this week the azaleas were the showstoppers, blazing with frilly, trumpet-shaped blooms. Ken was omnipresent—one moment, steering cars clear of his strawberry patch; the next, skewering meat with a barbecue fork; the next, demonstrating his drone's capabilities, all while making small talk: Peyton Manning's retirement, traffic at the Sagamore Bridge, the uptick of great white sharks, and, of course, a reality TV host winning enough delegates to become the Republican nominee. No one knew what to make of that.

Abby admired the ease with which her brother toggled from one subject and conversation to the next. She was lousy at small talk, perplexed by discussions of weather and real estate, unknowledgeable when it came to sports and pop culture. She would have loved a frozen margarita, just one sip to ease her into the party, but declined when Jenny brought around the tray, opting for an iced tea instead, a perfect sprig of mint floating on the surface.

"What's up with you?" Jenny asked.

"Oh, nothing," Abby said, feeling conspicuous. "I'm not much of a daytime drinker these days."

"I was referring to the fact that you're wearing a dress," Jenny said, laughing. "You look great. And do I detect blush on your cheeks?"

Abby raised a hand to her face. This wasn't the first time someone had commented on her glow. As for the dress, she could no longer tolerate the feeling of a waistband. She felt awful for keeping her pregnancy from Jenny.

"Hey, is everything okay between us?" Abby asked tentatively. "Things have been feeling, well, a little off. I just wanted to put it out there."

Jenny placed the tray down on the counter and gave Abby a long look. "You're right. Things have been off. And yes, we do need to talk," Jenny said, looking uncomfortable as guests drifted by. "But now is really not the time. Can we pick this up later?"

"Sure. No problem. How about lunch next week?" Abby asked, relieved to have this thing, whatever it was, out in the open. "You could come to the studio."

"That works. Next week is good," Jenny said.

Abby would tell her about the pregnancy then. "By the way, who are all these people? I don't know half the crowd." The person she wanted to see was David.

"Me neither," Jenny said. "But Ken says they're all extremely important. You know, of the rich-prospective-donor variety. So do your best to be charming. Every party for the next two years is going to be about Ken's campaign."

"Ugh," Abby groaned.

"You'll thank me when I unveil an Abigail Gardner original in the rotunda of the Capitol," Jenny said.

"What? Not the White House?" Abby countered.

"One step at a time, my friend, one step at a time," Jenny said, floating off with the tray of drinks aloft once again.

Then Abby heard the voice she'd been waiting for: "Hey, Abs."

She looked up and smiled. There was David, sweet David. She hadn't seen him since their impromptu dinner in DC in March. She felt her breath catch at the thought. They'd gone their separate ways afterward, promising it would never happen again. Which was what they'd told themselves the last time, too. And the time before that.

"Hello, you," Abby said, embracing him and looking over his shoulder. When she saw that Rebecca was nowhere in sight, she held him an extra beat, feeling the warmth of his chest against hers. "I've missed you."

"Me, too," he whispered. Then he pulled back and took her in. "You look amazing."

Every summer, David, his wife, Rebecca, and their daughter moved from their home in DC into his parents' house, next to Adam's in the Wellfleet Woods. He and Rebecca, both journalists, had flexible work lives, able to write from anywhere.

And every summer, time would flatten, and David and Abby's relationship would pick up where it had left off. They'd been best friends since childhood, and each other's first loves.

"How's work?" she asked, giving them both some time to readjust.

David grinned whenever he spoke about his work. "The news cycle is nuts right now, and this election"—David was covering Hillary Clinton's campaign for *Politico*—"is unlike anything I've ever seen before."

Abby was happy for David. He'd been dreaming about covering a presidential election since they were young. "You'll give me the full scoop soon?"

"Yes, it's all good," David said. "Only downside is less Cape time for me this summer. I'll be going back and forth to DC probably every other week or so."

Abby tried not to show her disappointment.

"You looking forward to the end of school?" David said.

"Well, I'll miss the kids, for sure, but I'm looking forward to the break," Abby said. Graduation was in twelve short days and then, two and a half months of uninterrupted time to paint.

David took a moment to admire the galloping waves of Stage Harbor. "Where's Frida?"

"It's a 'no dog' party," Abby said, rolling her eyes. Frida had taken a giant shit on Ken's pristine lawn earlier that spring and had been banned ever since. Her brother had always disliked dogs and the mess they created, indoors and out. Frannie and Tessa had been working on their father on Frida's behalf, but thus far, no luck.

David squeezed her hand. "I'll come by the studio for a visit soon. I have something important to tell you."

They rarely texted or called between visits, an unspoken rule. It was everything Abby could do not to ask what the big news was, but this wasn't the place.

"Spotlight on you," David said. "What's your news?"

Abby's news? Only that she had an exhibition on the horizon, was about to be recognized in a preeminent art magazine, and was fifteen weeks pregnant with a baby boy, the gender having been recently confirmed by ultrasound. David's baby. They'd always confided in each other, but the simple truth was Abby wasn't ready to share this news.

She'd never forget the call from David all those years ago, letting her know he was finally moving on. Abby recalled everything about that moment, the details flash-frozen in her mind, how the sofa cushion had made a *pffst* sound as she fell back onto it. *I've met someone and it's getting serious.* Abby had pulled her T-shirt over her knees. She'd known this was possible. Who but Abby wouldn't want to marry David? He had it all: smarts, humor, and nerdy good looks. Deep down, Abby had always believed he'd come around and want to forge a nontraditional partnership with her. A bohemian life: an artist and a journalist. Either way, she hadn't expected him to rally from their breakup quite so quickly. Nor for it to be so painful.

But all that was ancient history. Abby was a grown woman, thirty-eight years old, and she'd never felt better, thrumming with energy, and fueled by the munificent feeling of hosting a life and the affirming sense of belonging to something larger than herself. Plus, she was creating as never before—on the canvas, in her body, the distinction between art and life a blur.

Oddly, now that they were face-to-face, the detail she most wanted to share with David was that she was ravenous, possibly for the first time in her life. David loved to cook and had always tried—and failed—to get her to eat with any real pleasure. These days, a simple bowl of linguine with chopped tomatoes, basil, and Parmesan shavings felt like a religious experience. Abby finally understood what all the fuss was about. But before any of these thoughts could assemble themselves into words, a young woman sidled up to them.

It took Abby a second to process that it was David's fifteen-year-old daughter. "Peony! Holy cow."

"Ta-da!" Peony did a twirl that raised her short skirt. She wore a sherbet orange crop top with cap sleeves and a scoop neck. Delicate blue bra straps peeked out and it was impossible—truly impossible—not to notice the buoyant breasts on display. Breasts that were not there a year ago.

She raised her eyebrows at David: *Are you seeing what I'm seeing?*

"C'mon, Abby, it was bound to happen sooner or later," Peony said and giggled.

Abby considered her own flat chest. "Not necessarily," she said, pulling her honorary niece in for a hug. "I've missed you, sweetie." She pushed Peony back to get another look. There was still a hint of baby fat beneath the girl's jaw, soft arms, and solid legs, and waves of honey-brown hair spilled from a loose bun. Abby placed her hand on top of her own head and wobbled it through the air, where it landed in the center of Peony's forehead. The girl was at least an inch taller than she, perhaps more. "You could have warned me."

Peony shrugged. "Where are Frannie and Tessa?"

"Down by the water, I think," Abby said.

And off Peony raced.

This Memorial Day gathering had been an annual tradition since she, David, and Ken were teenagers, and marked the beginning of summer. Back in the day, the party involved a bonfire on Longnook Beach and as much weed and alcohol as their core gang of eight friends could score. The group was a mix of year-rounders and summer residents. The locals lived on the bay side of Route 6, in and around the town of Wellfleet, and the summer residents had second homes in an enclave on the ocean side. Abby and Ken were the anomalies, year-rounders who lived on the ocean side in the Wellfleet Woods.

David had been part of their lives for as long as Abby could remember. His parents, permissive and wealthy New York analysts, provided the neighborhood kids with a flotilla of kayaks and canoes and a single sunfish. David was one year older than Abby, two years younger than Ken, and only around in August, which made his presence special.

Abby and David became true friends when she was eight and he was nine. They were playing flashlight tag in the woods between their houses, and Kenny was "it." Abby and David ran deep into the woods to escape the beam of Kenny's flashlight, and before they knew it, they were lost. They tried retracing their steps, just getting more and more turned around. Abby cried out for her brother, but he had already headed home, no doubt angry that his playmates had teamed up against him. The pitch pines, so familiar during the daytime, became menacing in the dark, craggy and arthritic. Abby sat down, hoping if they stayed put, the grown-ups would come looking for them. But even at her age, she knew better—the nightly transformation of the adults was well underway before their game of flashlight tag had even begun. Her father was probably already asleep on the sofa, wineglass balanced on his stomach, lips stained a ghastly red.

"It's okay," David said, taking her hand. "If we get to the beach, I can find my way back. We'll just follow the sound of the water."

Abby grasped David's hand tightly and they marched toward the hissing breath of the ocean. A fingernail clipping of a moon appeared, and after walking for what seemed like forever, they came to a familiar bend in the shoreline where the path from their houses spilled onto the sand. David slung an arm around Abby and produced a smashed baggie of Fig Newtons. "Everything's gonna be okay now," he said, and they tucked into the dune and munched on the gritty cookies. Huddled together, their fear subsided and their bond solidified. Abby and David fell in love as preteens and were an on-again, off-again couple for years, a shared past that never sat well with David's wife.

Now the whole gang was in their late thirties and early forties, their differences sharpened by time, opportunity, and fortune. Ken, originally the ugly duckling of the group, now had the biggest house, the fanciest cars, and the most attractive family. Even his twins were one more way of highlighting how he could do twice as much in half the time. Abby was the only member of the group who'd never married and didn't have children. *At least not yet*, she thought, placing a hand on the small swell beneath her dress.

David and Abby walked to the edge of the property to check out the *Francesca*, Ken's elegantly shaped thoroughbred of a boat. Twenty feet below them, Frannie and Tessa were playing with three younger children at the water's edge, hunched over and digging, the vertebra of their backs undulating beneath their skin.

"Hey, kids," David called.

The five glanced up, waved at David, and went right back to digging, absorbed in a game that involved "rescuing" recently caught minnows, hermit crabs, starfish, and periwinkles from unseen dangers—shorebirds, larger crabs, the incoming tide—and keeping them "safe" in a homemade maze of rivers and pools. Abby marveled at how the twins ping-ponged between child- and adulthood, one moment happily playing with much younger children, the next, sparring with grown-ups about the sorry state of the planet. They were twelve and a half, entering that borderless terrain of adolescence. At the end of Ken's dock, Peony sat beside another girl, their legs dangling over the edge.

"Can you please explain the hysteria around Hillary's emails?" Abby asked David. "Why's this story getting so much traction if everyone has private servers?"

"You really want to talk about Hillary?" he asked.

Abby felt foolish. "Not really. Want to tell me your big news?"

"Do I ever," David whispered. He looked around. "But not now, not here." His smile was enormous.

Abby's thoughts raced, wondering if it had to do with his marriage.

Then his phone quacked. Rebecca. The woman had a sixth sense when they were alone.

"Sorry," David said. "I'll be right back." And he headed up to the house.

Petty as it was, Abby felt gratified that Rebecca's notification sound was a quack. But that quickly gave way to jealousy: maybe the quack was an endearment, and Rebecca was his sweet duckling. Then shame: Abby *was* sleeping with the woman's husband, albeit very occasionally. *Stop*, she told herself, pushing away the guilt. David had been hers first. Rebecca was the interloper.

Abby meandered along the well-groomed perimeter of her brother's property in the direction of Peony and her friend. Out on the bay, a prehistoric cormorant was drying its wings on a slick rock. Gulls dropped crabs onto the rocky shore, swooping down to devour the succulent innards. A winding black trail of seaweed, left by the last high tide, snaked along the edge of the shore. When Abby came upon the girls, they were taking photos of each other. The late-afternoon light made their skin glow golden against the weathered boards of the dock. They made goofy faces—sticking out their tongues and looking startled—alternating at being the photographer and the model. They took breaks to examine the results, heads together staring at the screen, pealing into laughter. Then the poses changed, shifting from silly to artistic, and from artistic to straight-up provocative, the girls brazenly flouting the new real estate of their bodies: backs arched, skirts hiked. Abby smiled. Their attempts at sexy were so over-the-top as to be cartoonish, counterintuitively highlighting their innocence.

On the sloping lawn, in between the house and where Abby stood on the bank's edge, Ken and two guests, men she didn't recognize, stood in a semicircle drinking beer, fixated on the girls on the deck. There was something in their stance that made the hairs on Abby's arms rise. She didn't like to admit it, but men scared her. Men alone. Men in groups. She hated the power they had, remembering the times men had touched her without asking.

Abby forced herself closer, and their conversation became clearer.

"Some of that."

"Sweet Jesus."

And then, "Jailbait." Her brother's voice.

Chuckles.

Out on the dock, Peony was standing over her friend, who was resting on her elbows, head flung back, neck and chest lifted.

Abby blinked hard, wishing the scene away. As she stood frozen, Ken called out to her.

"Hey, Abby, get over here," he said. "I'd like to introduce you to some new friends."

"Hi, fellas," Abby said, approaching warily.

"Matt, Henry, this is my sister, Abby. Abby is a painter and teaches art at Nauset High School. Abby, Matt and Henry are supporting my campaign."

The men greeted her, but their eyes kept darting back to the dock.

Abby made a show of turning toward the water to check out what they were looking at: the girls. "Don't you guys think they're a little young for you?" she asked, keeping her voice light.

Ken gave a tight laugh. "As far as I know, there's no law against looking."

"Still," Abby continued, gaining courage, "it's a little gross."

"What's a little gross?" Jenny asked, appearing out of nowhere with a tray of crab quesadillas and cocktail napkins.

Abby could have kissed Jenny for her perfect timing. "Oh, you know, leering at teenage girls," Abby said, emboldened by her friend's presence.

But instead of agreeing, Jenny shot her an icy look. To the men, she smiled and said, "You boys are positively infantile."

Ken gave his wife's bottom a cheeky squeeze and Jenny sauntered back up the hill, swaying her hips.

"Your wife's awesome," one of them said.

"That she is," Ken said. He gave Abby a withering look. To his friends, he said, "I don't want you guys to miss the food and drinks. Why don't you head up to the house and I'll catch up with you in a bit."

As Matt and Henry headed toward the deck, Ken grabbed Abby's elbow. "What in God's name do you think you're doing?" he hissed.

"What the hell, Ken? Let go." Her brother's hands were large and powerful enough to easily palm a basketball or the top of her head. "You're hurting me."

"Do you have any idea who those men are? Do you? Do you even care about anything at all?"

"Well, I know I don't give a damn who they are," Abby said, trying to shake free. "They were obnoxious. And you should have been offended. You need to start thinking about Frannie and Tessa."

Ken looked confused. "How is any of this about Frannie and Tessa?"

"Are you kidding? In another year or two, they'll look just like those girls," Abby said, her heart galloping in her chest. "How will you feel about forty-year-old men ogling them?"

"Jesus, Abby," Ken said, keeping his voice low. "What's wrong with you?"

"I wasn't the one who brought up wanting to fuck teenagers. Jailbait? Please."

"For chrissakes, it's just an expression."

"It's hardly *just* an expression, Ken."

Her brother was silent for a moment, and Abby thought she caught a glimpse of contrition. But then his jaw tightened. "How about you save your high-and-mighty lecture for the girls putting on a soft-porn show on my dock?" Ken said angrily. "I was just standing on my lawn with my friends, minding my own business."

"Do you even realize that's Peony out there?"

Ken looked back toward the dock and squinted. Peony and her friend were giggling over their iPhones, looking like children again. A moment of recognition passed over her brother's face as if he'd swallowed sour milk.

"Now, let go of me," Abby managed through clenched teeth. "Control your temper."

Then a voice from above pierced the air. "Kenny-boy!" It was David, calling down to them from the deck. Abby hated that David knew her brother better than she did at this point. And why was it okay for David to call him Kenny? "I've been looking all over for you, man!"

In a single fluid motion, David leaped over the bench railing, somehow keeping his margarita upright, and strode down the hill toward them, grinning. "Nice spread," David said, raising his drink, oblivious to the tension. "To summer 2016!"

Abby jerked her arm at the same moment that Ken released it, reaching for his friend's extended hand as if nothing else mattered.

June

Steph

Steph cranked up the car radio to drown out her thoughts, then turned it down to hear herself think. Up, down. Up, down. It was just a short drive from their summer rental in Provincetown to Abigail Gardner's studio in North Truro. To think, she'd been within ten miles of her biological sister all these years. Bob Marley's "Three Little Birds" played. What on earth would she say to her half sister when they got there? Steph hadn't thought through this stakeout well. She didn't know the first thing about art. She hadn't set foot in a museum since a field trip in middle school, much less visited a gallery or artist's studio.

Toni lay a reassuring hand on Steph's thigh. "Seriously, you have nothing to worry about. I checked your chart. You've got good planetary energy ahead."

That Steph didn't shut down Toni's star babble immediately indicated how nervous she was. She'd take whatever shoring up she could get.

"Neptune is floodlit by the Gemini new moon," Toni continued, head bobbing to the hypnotic power of the Wailers, "and there's a four-way planetary showdown ahead, all good news for you. Today's the perfect day to make a connection."

"Absolutely no astrology talk when we get there," Steph snapped. "I mean it. The last thing I need is for Abigail Gardner to think we're flakes."

"Got it," Toni said lightly. If her feelings were hurt, she didn't let on.

They turned down a rutted drive with scraggy woods and thickets of poison ivy on either side and pulled into a cleared parking area beside an old white Jeep, which Steph knew from a public records search belonged to her half sister. She turned off the motor and tucked the keys into her pocket. The studio, a simple structure of wood and glass, sat on a forested hill, appearing to grow out of the landscape. The location was protected and secluded, but the building felt vulnerable with its large windows. From inside her vehicle, Steph could see a figure, presumably Abby, moving around the studio. How could a person paint—or do anything for that matter—knowing that a nutjob could be lurking outside? Steph had been trained to keep her back to the walls and her eyes forward.

As soon as she placed one foot on the ground, Steph's breathing became shallow, a panic attack brewing. If she did this, there would be no going back. She turned to look at Jonah, strapped in his infant seat. She was doing this for him. Toni was here with her. She could do this.

Toni helped fasten Jonah into the sling on Steph's chest. The air was salty and dense, and she could hear waves in the distance—music that never stopped. As they approached the stoop, a golden retriever rose to welcome them, tail wagging. Steph paused at the threshold and peered inside through the screen door. There was a vase of hydrangeas on a pedestal table, loose petals scattered on faded floorboards. Two stainless-steel dog bowls, one empty, the other full of water. A chipped mug. Canvases, completed and in progress, were everywhere—on the walls, stacked in racks, propped on easels. Abby stood in front of a large painting, hip slung out, skinny legs poking through cut-off denim shorts. She wore an oversized white Oxford shirt and paint-spattered work boots, and her hair was pulled back in a haphazard ponytail, hair sprouting out at odd angles. There was a familiarity to the posture, the musculature, the way she leaned back instead of forward to study her work.

A delicate bell chimed as Steph pushed open the screen door.

"Come in," Abby called over her shoulder. She put down her brush and interlaced her fingers behind her back, lifting her arms back and up, as Steph did frequently to stretch her own shoulders.

"Hi," Steph said tentatively as she and her family stepped inside, the retriever pushing past them.

"Welcome," Abby said, turning. "I see you've already met my guard dog, Frida. I'm Abby."

"Steph," Steph said with a little wave. "And this is Jonah and Toni."

"Toni. Jonah. Steph. Nice to meet you," she said. "Are you from South Boston?"

Toni flushed; already they'd made a bad impression. "That obvious, huh?"

Abby smiled warmly. "Well, have a look around and make yourselves at home. Let me know if I can answer any questions." Then Abby cocked her head at Steph. "We've met before, haven't we?"

Steph lifted her chin, welcoming her half sister's gaze. "I don't think so," Steph said. "But anything's possible, I suppose. We've been coming to the Cape—to P-town—for years." She gripped Jonah's socked feet to stop her hands from trembling.

Frida went to her water bowl, drinking in clumsy laps.

Abby stared without blinking. "I can't place you but I'm sure we've met. It'll come to me." Then she laughed, a breathy burst that lifted her cheeks. "I'm sorry, I'm being rude. What brings you to the Arcadia?"

"Steph read about you online and was intrigued," Toni said. "We thought it would be fun to have a look at your paintings."

"Well, I'm glad you stopped in."

"We're not really art people," added Steph.

"No worries," Abby said. "Don't be shy if you have questions."

Steph approached a large work that hung on the nearest wall, where a jumble of lines—red, black, tan—bled down the canvas. But as she studied the lines, a reclining body emerged, an apparition in the chaos. Then Steph understood the figure wasn't reclining, it was collapsing as if struck. Another blur of lines materialized into a figure behind it, and she saw the perpetrator.

"What's happening here?" Steph asked.

"What do *you* think is happening?" asked Abby.

"A crime," Steph guessed.

"Interesting," Abby said.

"Interesting, how?" Steph asked.

"Well, everyone has their own take," Abby said. "What do you see, Toni?"

"Heartbreak," Toni replied. "She trusted him, and he devastated her."

"Case in point," Abby said.

"Are you kidding?" Steph said to Toni in disbelief.

Toni shrugged. "That's what it looks like to me."

"It's all about perspective and interpretation," Abby explained. "Over the years, I've learned that what I paint is not necessarily what people see. Everyone interprets art through their own lens and creates a narrative to explain it."

"Okay, but which is it *really*?" Steph asked. "An act of crime or love?"

Abby regarded the painting. "A bit of both, I think."

Jonah let out a cry, redirecting Steph's attention. "Okay to feed him here?"

"Of course." Abby pointed to a faded blue sofa. "Sit. Make yourself at home."

Steph unstrapped Jonah and sank onto a love seat against the wall opposite the door, the perfect vantage point for surveying the space. She put the baby to her breast and noted a battered copy of *Frankenstein*, opened and lying flat on the cushion beside her. The book looked like it'd been read a thousand times. There was a photo on the end table, a young couple on the beach with their son, a boy of perhaps three, holding a bucket. From their jackets, Steph deduced that it was the off-season. The woman, visibly pregnant, lay in the sand, head resting on the man's lap. Finally, a picture of Emily. The man—unquestionably Adam Gardner—gazed at his wife tenderly. He didn't look like a sexual predator or a serial philanderer, and definitely not like the kind of guy who'd had drunken sex with a teenager in the back of his car a few months earlier.

"What a beautiful picture. Your parents?" asked Steph, focusing in on her father's muscular build and dark features, so like her own.

"Yes. My whole family," Abby replied. "The little boy is my older brother, Ken, and I'm in my mother's belly. It's the only photo I have of all of us. My mom died shortly after I was born."

"Oh. Sorry," Steph said.

"Don't be. It was a long, long time ago, and needless to say, I don't remember any of it," Abby said. "How old is Jonah?"

"Seven weeks," Toni said.

"He's beautiful," Abby said. "And I love the name. I've been trying to come up with boy names myself. I'm sixteen weeks."

A twist. Steph had not been expecting that bit of information and allowed her eyes to travel down to Abby's belly, invisible beneath the oversized shirt. "Congratulations," she said, wondering if Abby was even aware that myotonic dystrophy ran in her family.

"I know, it's hard to tell," Abby said. "Did you show at sixteen weeks?"

Toni laughed. "Steph showed at sixteen minutes."

"What can I say? Any excuse to gorge. Is this your first?" Steph asked, already knowing the answer.

"Yes," Abby said, placing a palm on either side of her mostly flat belly. "It wasn't exactly planned and I'm going it alone." Her voice lowered. "Is that completely nuts?"

"Not at all," and "Completely," answered Toni and Steph, simultaneously.

"I'm going with you," Abby said, pointing at Steph. "I know it's nuts. But I'm thirty-eight, and if not now, when? I just decided to go for it. I had no idea that I even wanted to be a mother until this happened."

"What's your due date?" Toni asked. "I'll make you a birth chart."

Steph cleared her throat to remind Toni of her no-astrology promise.

"I'd love that!" Abby said. "November 22."

"Hmm. Right on the cusp. He'll be one or the other, Scorpio or Sagittarius. Either way, he'll have both signs within him, which is good. Fire and ice," said Toni. "Scorpios are intense, but the Sagittarius in him will soften the sting."

Jonah slid off Steph's breast, slack-lipped and dozy. She tossed a burp cloth over her shoulder and gently patted the baby's back.

"What else can you tell me?" Abby asked Toni.

Steph shot her wife a look—was it so hard not to talk about astrology?—just as Jonah spit up on her shoulder. "Your future looks like this," she told Abby.

Abby tossed the copy of *Frankenstein* aside and slid onto the love seat beside Steph. She gazed at Jonah, touching a finger to his tiny hand.

"Would you like to hold him?" Steph asked.

Abby nodded.

At the sight of her half sister cradling Jonah, Steph felt an internal wall collapse. Jonah had an aunt. She had a sister. It was all too much. She could feel tears welling, and Steph never cried.

Intuiting Steph's overwhelm, Toni offered her a hand up and swapped places with her, sitting beside Abby and Jonah on the sofa.

Steph took the opportunity to wander about and study Abby's paintings, which were striking, atmospheric, and unsettling. And after a minute of staring, images would emerge and take shape. It reminded her of the way Shakespeare plays always sounded like gibberish at first, but if she gave it ten minutes, magically, she was able to understand Elizabethan English. On the far wall, there was a series of forlorn female figures, more girlish than womanly, surrounded by white space, their outlines fragile. Some were whole, but most were truncated figures that struggled to claim their place on the canvas. The paintings made Steph feel uneasy and lost, the way she felt when she learned her dad wasn't her real father.

On a canvas in an upright rack was the outline of a woman curled in a bathtub, the faucet morphing into a penis as Steph stared. The painting unlocked an old memory, a story a friend had told her long ago. As this friend recalled it to Steph, he was a young boy who knew nothing about sex. So, when his preadolescent fumbling resulted in orgasm, he thought the goo that spurted out of his penis was brain matter. Despite this, he stayed home from school for days, pretending to be sick so he could masturbate, unperturbed that he might be lobotomizing himself.

"I call that one *Active Imagination*," Abby said, explaining that the Jungian psychological term described the gap between the conscious and unconscious minds.

Steph recalled reading somewhere that Abby liked to use psychological terms for titles. *Active Imagination.* Well, the painting had indeed activated her imagination. Steph hadn't thought about that friend or his story in years.

She moved on and stood in front of the painting that Abby had been working on when they entered. It was a large canvas, perhaps six by nine, simultaneously disturbing and hopeful. It was full of Abby's signature chaotic lines, lines that kept rearranging themselves, morphing from tender to brutal and back, somehow compelling the viewer to create a story. Steph studied two figures tussling in the lower right, a favorite line of Father Mulligan's springing to mind: "Sin is crouching at the door." Steph shuddered. At the center of the canvas, the lines formed a pregnant torso, beatific somehow.

"This one's intense," she said. "What's its title?"

"Hmm, don't know yet," Abby said. "I'm painting it as a gift for my dad. For his seventieth birthday."

Steph snorted.

"What's funny?" asked Abby, looking up.

"Sorry," Steph said. But was Abby kidding? Among other things, there was nudity on the canvas. "Church laughter."

"Ignore her," Toni said. "Steph laughs at inappropriate stuff all of the time."

"Let's just say that the most personal gift I've ever given my dad is Old Spice," Steph explained.

Abby seemed to mull that over. "It *is* weird, I guess. I hadn't thought of it that way. I think some part of me wants my father to know the full story of who I am before it's too late." She rose from the sofa, still cradling baby Jonah, who'd fallen asleep in her arms, and stood beside Steph, staring at her painting.

There were things parents didn't need to know, Steph thought.

"Do you know what you're going to paint before you paint it?" Toni asked.

"Yes and no. I didn't set out to paint this particular painting. It kind of demanded to be painted. Most days, I feel trapped in the canvas, like I'm trying to scratch my way out," Abby said. "Oh my God, I sound crazy. Do I sound crazy?"

"Toni believes in birth charts. So no, not really," Steph said. "Are you always this open with strangers?"

Now it was Abby's turn to laugh. "Not at all, actually," she said, her cheeks pinking. "Normally, I'm shy. I honestly have no idea why I'm blathering on. Must be the pregnancy."

"Hey," Toni interrupted. "We should probably get going before you-know-who wakes up." This was all part of their plan to keep the first visit short. "I'm starving."

"Where in P-town are you staying?" asked Abby.

"West End," said Steph. "We've been staying at the same cottage for years. We get a deal."

"Have you tried Tzuco's yet? Great food. Great views. The high tide comes under the dining room twice daily and makes you feel like you're eating on a boat," Abby said. "My father swears on their calamari."

Steph knew that Toni was having a woo-woo field day with that one. Later, she'd get an earful about there being no such thing as coincidences. "If you can believe it, Tzuco's is where we met," Steph said. "Toni was a hostess. And I worked in the kitchen."

"What are the chances," Toni marveled, eyes gloating. "Steph was what Anthony Bourdain called the 'grill bitch.' She's an amazing chef."

"Really?" Abby said.

So, Adam Gardner was a regular at Tzuco's. "Small world," Steph said.

Abby adjusted Jonah as she prepared to transfer him back to his mother. "My father's name should be engraved on a barstool for all the time he spends there."

"Well, thanks for the recommendation. I guess it's time to return to the old stomping grounds," Steph said, glancing at Toni, whose back was turned as she gathered the infant paraphernalia from the sofa. "I'd love to come by again, maybe without the baby so I can look at your work more leisurely."

"Sure. Stop by anytime."

At that, Steph reached to collect Jonah from Abby's arms, and their fingers touched, sending an electric jolt up Steph's arm. Abby pulled her hand back, and Steph wondered if she felt it, too.

Jenny

The *Cape Cod Times*. A perfectly foamed cappuccino. Her laptop, a notebook, a pen. A tall glass of cold water and a couple of Advil, everything Jenny needed to jump-start the day. Plus, the ultimate mood enhancer: the view from her screened-in porch of her garden and Stage Harbor beyond. Jenny shut her eyes and massaged her temples. She felt flannel-mouthed and dull. How had one glass of wine turned into the whole bottle *again*? Through the screen, Jenny watched a coneflower sway, a bumblebee tiptoeing across its disk, rear legs coated with pollen.

In just two short weeks, Tessa and Frannie would be out of school. Normally, there was nothing Jenny looked forward to more than summer and its promise of unstructured time with her girls—beach picnics, lawn camping, a steady rotation of their favorite meals. But things were changing, and the girls were far more interested in hanging out with their friends than their mom. Also, one look at the color-coded spectacle of her Outlook calendar—yellow for the girls, green for Garden Club activities, and red for political events and fundraisers—and Jenny knew there wasn't a lot of relaxation on her horizon. So much effing red!

Jenny downed the pills with a gulp of water and reminded herself to keep her eyes on the prize: a future as a political wife who could make a difference. No offense to Laura Bush, Cindy McCain, or any of the rest of them, but Jenny had no intention of cheering from the sidelines. Ken might be in this for power, but she'd signed on for purpose. She'd given up on her own art years ago, but with Ken in office she could take on art as a cause. The thought that purpose was in her crosshairs filled her with hope. If she didn't blow it, that was. She massaged her temples, again.

And how could she? Soon their housekeeper would go up to a twice-weekly cleaning schedule and the babysitter would be on hand to drive

Frannie and Tessa wherever they needed to go. Jenny had even splurged and hired a landscaping team to tackle the weeding and deadheading she normally did. At the thought of help being on its way, a snide voice popped into her head—her younger self, eager to provide commentary on the person she'd become: a ridiculous and entitled housewife who relied on others to clean up her messes and take care of her children. Everything she'd sworn she'd never be. Her mother, right down to the blue vein that snaked over the back of her hand and slithered along her fourth finger into her diamond engagement ring.

Give it a rest, Jenny told her younger self. Had she really been that much of a self-righteous pain in the ass? Oh yes, indeed, she had. She cringed at the thought of what she'd put her parents through. No cause was too small for her; she'd march, rally, sit in—whatever it took to get arrested. During her sophomore year of college, she'd burned—yes, *burned*, as in literally put a match to—the money her father had wired into her account for tuition. The spectacle, an installation piece she called "Cash to Ash," was part of her commentary on capitalism. When her father informed her that he would no longer be supporting her, she capitalized on that, too. "Being disinherited was part of the vision," she told the student reporter, posing in front of the bursar's office, tin cup in one hand, silver spoon in the other.

It would be the last hurrah for that particular girl. That Jenny—the badass, the rebel, the destroyer of things—would disappear. The next time she saw her father, Jenny was in rehab again, her third stint. When Theodore Lowell entered her room, it was with none of his usual bluster. He folded his large frame into the chair beside her bed, and said simply, "No more nonsense, Jennifer. Your mother needs us." The words that followed included: "metastasized," "stage IV," "palliative care." Words that Jenny could hardly make sense of, fixated as she was on her father's Adam's apple, bobbing over the knot of a bow tie, blue with tiny butterflies, the cheeriness calling into question the reality of what her father was telling her.

Isabel Lowell lived just twelve brutal weeks longer. Jenny stayed at her mother's side, dabbing her mouth with a moist washcloth, applying Vaseline to her lips, and administering morphine. She made every promise she could think of to give her mother peace. She'd clean up her act. She'd go to a "real" college. She'd find a suitable partner, settle down, have children, and make a beautiful home. She'd do right by the Lowell family name and leave her mark on the world. She'd do all those things and more, if only . . .

Jenny had no regrets. Or did she? She certainly didn't regret marrying Ken or having children, but she wondered if she'd done the right thing by giving up on her art. Why had it seemed like an either-or? She shook her head. It was too late for second-guessing. The fact was, she was a card-carrying member of the 1 percent—always had been, always would be. She had to live with the demoralizing knowledge that she already had what everyone else was desperate to get. She wondered if her mother ever boomeranged as she did between feelings of shame and superiority, a discomfort Jenny tried to mask with philanthropy, Sancerre, and keeping a pristine home (truly a challenge for her). But there was no escaping the fraudulent feeling of living an unearned life. She hoped that things would change as Ken became a money-making machine in his own right—surely, earned money would feel better than inherited money. At the very least, she'd no longer have to engage in the daily gymnastics of shoring up her husband's ego when it came to living off her family's wealth. That would be a relief. That said, Ken's new swagger was already getting on her nerves. Jenny sighed, dismayed by her own negativity. She *was* happy for him. Ken had struck it big as he'd always told her he would. She just wished her own life felt less empty.

She looked back to the job at hand. For the moment, she'd need to find contentment with hostessing, her superpower. On the immediate horizon was an end-of-the-school-year PTA lawn party for sixth-grade families. Beyond that, she had weekly garden tours followed by teas and cocktail meet and greets to spread the word about Ken's political plans—events she could do blindfolded and with an arm tied behind her back. And then there was the biggie: Adam's seventieth birthday/retirement extravaganza, still two months away, but gathering force. You'd think it was a royal wedding for all the energy it was commanding.

When she'd volunteered to host the event, Jenny had imagined an informal and festive cocktail party, a free-flowing gathering with champagne and abundant passed hors d'oeuvres—mini lobster rolls, stuffed mushrooms, tomato crostini, etc. She imagined an intimate group composed of Adam's family and closest friends, mingling and meandering from the grand living room to the deck and onto the grounds, raising their flutes to make impromptu and heartfelt toasts. But oh no! Adam had a different vision for his party; he'd made that painfully clear at the family dinner last month. Adam thought it should be an indoor, sit-down affair. In August, no less. Who wanted to be inside in August? He'd gone so far as to present Ken and Abby with detailed notes for their toasts. The man was expecting *speeches*. And not just from his children, but from his friends and colleagues, too. When Jenny proposed a more spontaneous approach, Adam shot her down.

"A man doesn't turn seventy every day, Jenny," her father-in-law said, enunciating each word in that patronizing way of his. Jackass.

Jenny took a sip of her cappuccino. She'd been procrastinating long enough on this one. She'd sent out a save-the-date email, but that was it. All the basic decisions—theme, menu, flow—still needed to be made, followed by a million small details, the true backbone of any event. The coffee was the perfect temperature, and Jenny drank it down. She would do what she always did: rise to the challenge and throw a beautiful party that her guests would talk about for weeks to come, recalling some exquisite detail—the hint of cilantro in the lobster bisque, a whiff of honeysuckle on the breeze, or perhaps a single long sprig of curly willow in each centerpiece. If he wanted grand, Adam Gardner would get grand. A string quartet? Sure. A podium and mic? No problem. Jenny would deliver exactly what the old codger wanted with a smile. And no one would be the wiser as to how conflicted she felt about her role as model wife, always prioritizing the happiness of men.

Sorry, Mom, she thought.

Her phone vibrated. A text from Abby.

r we still on for lunch today?

Ugh. Jenny knew it was irrational to be mad at Abby. It was her husband's strange fantasy, after all, and had nothing to do with her best friend. But Jenny couldn't unsee or unhear what she'd walked in on: Ken online in a private chat room, telling a pajama-clad young woman how all he needed was "to be held." Had he called her Abby? Jenny had stood behind him for several seconds before clearing her throat to alert him of her presence. If only she'd interrupted standard-issue role-playing. She could have handled a Catholic schoolgirl or whip-wielding dominatrix, but what was she supposed to do with this? Her husband fixated on the screen, some woman promising never to leave him.

Of course! Jenny typed. Or was this Abby's way of telling her she wanted out? Texts were impossible to interpret. They still hadn't even talked about what happened at the Memorial Day party, and Jenny knew she'd been harsh. Abby had been right—Ken and his friends had behaved like cavemen, ogling those girls on the dock. But come on. Boys will be boys. *Not one word*, Jenny warned her younger inner critic. Did Abby have to air the grievance so publicly? There was just too much at stake for Ken. Abby needed to learn how to play the game.

Jenny sent a thumbs-up emoji.

Abby shot the same emoji back.

Jenny texted: **i'll pick up lunch on my way. what do u want?**

going to plover? Abby asked.

yes, Jenny pecked.

tomato basil mozzarella panini please, cran muffin, 2 brownies.

Was Abby kidding? That was more food than Jenny had ever seen Abby consume in a day. **WTF**, Jenny responded, adding a wide-eyed emoji.

Abby replied with a pig emoji, then: **starving don't judge!**

Jenny called out "hello" as she pushed open Abby's door, stepping over a jacket on the floor. Abby was curled up on her side on the love seat, one arm dangling down to pet Frida's head, her hind legs splayed out like a frog below her.

"Hey. Hard at work, I see," Jenny teased.

Abby stopped rubbing Frida's head, and the dog looked up at her ruefully before making her way to the bedroom for a long siesta, claws clicking against the hardwood floor. "Just a little catnap. I finished my painting at two a.m. last night." She sat up, stretched, smiled, and patted the cushion beside her. An invitation.

"Wait, you finished? You got unstuck without me?" Jenny asked.

The painting was on an easel in the corner, facing the wall.

"I did. I got unstuck without you," Abby repeated, marvel in her voice. "I'm excited to show it to you. Nervous, too."

"My girl's growing up," Jenny said. Even Abby didn't need her anymore. She mock sniffed and plunked down on the sofa, giving her friend a warm hug.

"But let's eat first. I'm famished," Abby said, grabbing a solvent-wet rag and working it along her nail beds and into the skin between her fingers. Then she washed her hands thoroughly. "Shall we head up to the deck?"

"Nah, too bright up there," Jenny said, pulling their sandwiches out of the Plover bag, artfully covering the coffee rings tattooed on Abby's table. "Besides, I didn't bring my hedge clippers and the sight of your wisteria will drive me mad."

"You should have known better than to give me a plant that requires that kind of care," Abby said. "And don't even think of cutting it back. I love that unruly monster just the way it is."

"You'll feel differently when it lifts off your roof."

"Not *my* roof," Abby said pointedly, taking a bite of her sandwich.

"*Not* going there," Jenny volleyed back. She hated being caught in the middle of Ken and Abby's battle.

"What did you get?" Abby asked, changing the subject.

"Roast beef grinder."

"Aw, your old hangover fix!" Abby gave her a big smile. "Do you remember that time when—"

Jenny raised her hand. Whatever college escapade Abby was about to remind her of—drunkenly dancing in the Shampoo Room at the Limelight club or getting caught skinny-dipping after hours at the pool at Brown—Jenny couldn't stomach it right now. She closed her eyes as a small wave of nausea passed. At the rate she was going, when Ken ran for office, she'd likely draw Kitty Dukakis or Betty Ford comparisons. She needed to get a grip. Better yet, she needed to hydrate. She took a sip of water.

"You okay?" Abby asked.

"Yes, fine," Jenny said, then admitted she was nursing a hangover.

"I don't know how you do it, Jenny." Abby sounded genuinely impressed. "I couldn't go to a cocktail party every night, let alone throw one."

But Jenny had neither gone to nor thrown a cocktail party. She'd been alone. Or almost alone. The girls ate early and were upstairs studying—or doing whatever twelve-year-olds did in their rooms. Ken was in Boston for two days, busy with meetings and hopefully seeing his therapist. She'd started with a tonic and lime, but when that wasn't doing it for her, she poured in a splash of gin, enjoying the sunset from the porch. Then, feeling blissed out, she decided to splurge on a bottle of Sancerre with dinner—only she hadn't bothered with dinner, just a couple of crackers and some Gouda to maintain the delightful buzz.

And now, here she was, taking small nibbles of her roast beef sandwich, hoping to keep it down. "Yes, I am amazing, aren't I?" she said and rolled her eyes.

"Hey, what's going on?" Abby scrunched up her panini wrapper and tossed it back into the bag. "What's wrong?"

Jenny yearned to tell Abby everything: her feelings of purposelessness, her drinking, Ken's disturbing online proclivities. *Sob, sob.* Even her thoughts seemed pathetic. But she couldn't. Going to Abby about a problem in their marriage was something she'd promised Ken she'd never do. Her husband expected loyalty and was territorial when it came to his sister. And Jenny got it. Sort of. It was complicated. Even she could appreciate the boundaries and compromises that made their adult lives work. Abby knew things about Jenny's wild past, stuff that no one else knew and that Jenny preferred to stay in the past. When they were roommates, they'd shared everything. But boy, had Jenny gotten it wrong when she thought that marrying Ken was a way to stay close to Abby and cling to their bohemian past. Instead, her marriage made everything about their friendship more difficult.

"Talk to me," Abby said. "Please, I'm worried about you."

"Oh, Abby," Jenny said dismally.

"Come on! Whatever it is, it will lose power in the open air."

Jenny doubted it. "Everything falls under the header of topics we've sworn to avoid."

Abby put down her sandwich and wiped the corners of her mouth. "Maybe it's time we changed the rules," she said. "What's a best friend for if not the safe storage of shameful secrets?"

Jenny let out a small laugh.

"Look, you've been married to my brother for sixteen years now. You're not in a witness protection program. Can't we still tell each other some things?" Abby's face brightened, an idea forming. "Maybe we could figure out a workaround. Do you remember when we made that rule that it was okay to smoke in foreign countries?"

Jenny nodded.

"What if we did something like that around our friendship? Our new rule: What's said in the Arcadia, stays in the Arcadia. What is shared in my home goes nowhere. Sealed in a bubble." Abby took her last bite, licked her fingers, and unwrapped one of the brownies.

"Do you have anything to drink?" Jenny asked. This hangover wasn't going to go down without a fight.

Abby gestured at the bottle of Poland Spring set out on the coffee table in front of her.

"A drink-drink," Jenny said, exhaling impatiently.

"Oh." Abby pointed to the cabinet. "Make yourself whatever you want. I'm going to stick with water."

Two strong rum and orange juices later and Jenny felt ready to unburden herself. Who the hell was Ken to tell her who she could and couldn't talk to? This was not the 1950s. She'd been best friends with Abby long before she'd ever met him. And of course Abby *should* have the deed to this place, but that was not her battle to fight. Reclined on one of two lounge chairs on the roof-deck, Jenny tilted down her floppy hat to protect her skin from the midday sun. Her thoughts swam loose, buoyed by the booze and the elusive aroma of the wisteria. She found herself liking the proposed rule about the Arcadia more and more.

"So, three things that the other person doesn't know, right?" Jenny asked.

"Yep," Abby replied.

"Fine, you first," Jenny said.

"Okay, but let's alternate," Abby suggested. "And maybe wait until all three are out before we dig deep."

"Deal," Jenny said. "And then . . . straight back into the vault." She zipped her mouth closed and threw away the key, laughing at her mixed-metaphor mime. She was drunk. She thought of Betty Ford again. Perhaps a clinic named in her honor would be purposeful enough.

"Here goes," said Abby. "I'm mad that you didn't have my back with Ken at the party."

"Hardly a secret," Jenny said.

"No commentary," Abby reminded her.

"Fair enough," Jenny said. "I know I was bitchy. I'm sorry. But I was mad at you for making an unnecessary scene in front of donors. It could've been handled differently." This was not going in the direction she wanted. Were they really going to waste their newfound freedom by picking over a stupid fight? "Don't you have any better secrets?"

"As a matter of fact, I do," Abby said.

Jenny waited.

"Really? You don't know?" Abby seemed incredulous.

"Know what?"

"I'm pregnant."

"Shut up!" Jenny gave her friend a long, hard look. Then all at once, Abby's enormous appetite, her not drinking, the shift to loose-fitting clothes, and the boobs—how had she possibly missed the boobs?—piled up like cars in a collision. This was not a joke. Abby was pregnant. Jenny felt surprisingly wistful at the news. She should have been hunched over the pregnancy test beside her best friend, waiting for the lines to emerge.

"Talk about burying the lede," Jenny said, draining the last of her drink, watery pulp. She reached for Abby's hand. "I'm so happy for you," she said, and she was. "This is wonderful, wonderful news. The best. And the girls will be over the moon! Just think, you'll have built-in babysitters."

"Thanks," Abby said, her eyes glassy. "I'm so sorry I didn't tell you sooner. I've felt guilty about that. It's taken me a while to wrap my head around the idea. I had to sit with it by myself for a few weeks."

"I get it, I do. Is it Eddie's?" Jenny asked, realizing she didn't know who Abby was seeing these days. Eddie, a lobsterman out of Provincetown, was someone Abby hooked up with from time to time. Abby never brought anyone home to meet the family.

"Nope," Abby said.

"Then who?"

Abby picked at a cuticle. "Do you swear not to breathe a word to anyone?"

Jenny drew an X across her heart.

"Seriously, you must swear-swear, like on a stack of Bibles. Even *he* doesn't know about the pregnancy yet," Abby whispered. "And I'm not 100 percent sure I'm going to tell him."

Jenny leaned in.

"David," Abby whispered.

"David?" Jenny repeated. "*Our* David?" Her chin dropped, turning her mouth into an O. Impossible. She'd been there with Abby through that painful breakup years ago—David wanting commitment of the old-fashioned sort, and Abby insisting that the institution of marriage, founded on ownership, was a raw deal for women, and one that he shouldn't ask of her. Heartbreak followed, months and months of it. At the time, Jenny thought Abby was making a mistake—if Abby knew she wanted to spend her life with David, why not just walk down the aisle? Despite Jenny's comparative bluster at RISD where she'd worn feminist T-shirts every day—*I Believe Anita, Girl Power, Smash the Patriarchy*—it was Abby who'd live out their ideals. Jenny had been the sellout. No sooner had Ken produced a diamond ring than she started planning a traditional wedding: complete with white gown, getting passed from father to husband, being announced at the reception as Mrs. Ken Gardner. She'd even allowed herself to be carried across the threshold, a custom that she knew from Abby had its roots in abduction and rape.

"Who else knows you're pregnant?" Jenny asked.

"Not a soul," Abby said. "Well, I mean, no one who counts. My OB, of course. Oh, and this random couple who came into the studio earlier in the week. Two women. They had a new baby, and for whatever reason, it all just sort of spilled out."

"Abigail Gardner, a mother," Jenny said, shaking her head. "What's your due date?"

"November 22."

Jenny tried to calculate exactly how far along Abby was, but she was tipsy enough that the math eluded her. Abby was well into the second trimester, that much Jenny knew for sure. "When are you planning on telling your dad and Ken?"

Abby's shoulders sank. "I don't know," she said. "I'm not eager to hear their opinions on the matter."

Jenny nodded sympathetically. Ken and Adam could be know-it-alls. But still, whether Abby admitted it or not, she was going to need help. This nonsense with Ken had to stop. Abby needed the security of owning her home, and Jenny needed to figure out how to make her husband do the right thing and hand over the Arcadia.

"Your turn," Abby prompted.

"Uh, pregnancy is a hard act to follow."

"It's not a competition," Abby said, "more like . . . a trust exercise."

"Well, to state the obvious," Jenny said with a grin, "I'm drinking too much again."

"Want to talk about it?" Abby asked.

"The drinking? Not really," Jenny said. "Back to you."

"I don't have anything else," Abby said, adjusting a cushion. "Besides, that was two: pregnancy and paternity."

"Oh, right," Jenny said. The secret she most wanted to confide was having walked in on Ken talking tenderly to some woman online. But no, she couldn't tell Abby—that would be the ultimate betrayal. Perhaps just a hint? Jenny said, "Here's another: your brother and I are in counseling. We've hit a rough patch."

"I'm so sorry to hear that," Abby said, scratching off a blotch of paint from her pinky that she'd missed with the solvent. She hesitated. "Is therapy helping?"

Jenny shrugged. "Probably best to leave it at that for now."

Abby got the message. "How about we head downstairs then and I show you my new painting?"

Five minutes later, they stood in front of the covered easel, turned toward the wall, mugs of freshly brewed coffee in hand.

"You have to promise to be brutally honest," Abby said.

"Am I ever anything else?"

"Good point."

"Turn it around already," Jenny said impatiently.

"Close your eyes," Abby said and uncovered the painting, placing it in front of Jenny. "Okay."

The first thing that hit Jenny was the composition—a tranquil central image with satellite scenes that created exquisite narrative tension. Her eyes were drawn from composition to composition, trying to make sense of the whole. Abby's lines were assured, unraveling with intention, guiding the viewer across the canvas.

"It's stunning," Jenny whispered, watching hidden scenes surface—so many stories, so much movement. "Absolutely stunning. I think"—dare she say it?—"this is a masterpiece."

Abby sank onto the sofa, visibly relieved, as Jenny continued to study the work. Each time she blinked, lines would recede and advance, creating images that would mutate like shapes in clouds: a tiny being blossoming in a torso; an iris-like aperture overlaying the whole; two children tangled in a curious knot.

Ken

By the time Ken arrived home, it was close to midnight. Jenny was curled on her side, facing away from the door, snoring delicately. He slid in beside her, spooning his body around hers. He'd had a productive few days in Boston. In between meetings with lawyers and bankers, he'd even found time to procure all the materials he'd need—balsa wood sheets, dowels, an X-Acto knife kit—to build a perfect model replica of the retirement home he planned to give his father for his seventieth birthday. And, as if that wasn't enough, his trip was capped off by the best session he'd ever had with George. Turned out, his algae-muncher therapist *had* been listening, after all. At long last, George was speaking a language Ken understood, a language that included terms like *objectives*, *timelines*, *goals*, and *accountability*. Finally, Ken left with action items he looked forward to ticking off over the next week.

1. No working on the weekend—that included emails, texts, and calls.
2. Be present with Jenny—attend to her feelings.
3. Create meaningful family time.
4. No chat room visits, no matter how stressed.
5. Make space for self-reflection.

Okay, number five was a little much, but that was to be expected. It was therapy, after all. With his arm already wrapped around his wife, Ken figured he'd start with number two. Did it count as being present if she was asleep? *Yes, it did,* he thought, giving himself permission, tucking himself more snugly around Jenny. He closed his eyes and inhaled the molecules of perspiration and salt at the base of her neck. George had suggested he try to recall the euphoric feelings of falling in love, and Ken pictured the first time he'd ever laid eyes on Jenny. She'd been climbing out of Abby's red convertible VW Bug in cut-off shorts and a bikini top, a beach towel slung over her shoulders, her hair a windblown mess, when Abby, still in the driver's seat, said something that caused Jenny to erupt in laughter and fall back into the passenger seat, and then into Abby's arms. They were so joyful.

Jenny moaned and shifted slightly, which caused her backside to press against him. It took all of two seconds for him to become wolfishly aroused. It had been months since they'd had sex. She hadn't let him anywhere near her since she'd walked in on him in the chat room that day, and he still had no idea how much she'd seen or heard. He pushed the thought out of his head, and lightly brushed his finger across her nipple, which hardened under her camisole. His wife's breast was just inches from his mouth, and he decided he would kiss his way toward it. But no sooner did he press his lips to her shoulder then Jenny rolled away onto her stomach, pulling the sheet around her in the process. Ken felt the familiar sting of rejection, followed by a dull throb of anger.

He jerked off sulkily, missing the sex life he'd had with Jenny before they'd become parents, unaware at the time that her libido had already peaked and was sloping toward its extinction. Then George popped uninvited into his head, reminding him that he was doing it again, blaming Jenny. But it *had* been Jenny who'd pulled back. Even a dozen years later, Ken could recall how instantaneously his wife had redirected all her resources, all her concern and tender embraces, to the twins.

"Chop, chop, family," Ken called upstairs, eager to get the day underway. Outside, it was sunny and bright with clouds skidding across the sky on gusts of wind. A perfect day for the first sail of the summer. Frannie was already at the breakfast table, but Tessa hadn't yet emerged from her room, and Jenny seemed to be moving in a fog. His wife was not a morning person. "The *Francesca* sets sail at ten thirty," he bellowed.

"It's Saturday—" Tessa's voice from upstairs. "Give us a break."

"Not joking, Tessa. Ten thirty," Ken called back. Lately, Tessa seemed to take pleasure in making even simple tasks challenging. Something as benign as asking her to clear her plate could lead to an epic fight. "Jenny, would you please let your daughter know I'm serious."

"Funny how she's *my* daughter when she's being difficult," Jenny said, cinching the bathrobe around her waist as she descended the stairs. "I didn't even hear you come in last night." At the bottom, she gave him a peck on the cheek. "How was Boston?"

"Great. I saw Stefan and Brian about the deal. Schmoozed donors for the campaign. Got more done in forty-eight hours than most men—"

"—get done in a month," said Jenny and Frannie, finishing his sentence for him.

He smiled and surprised them both by scooping Jenny up and spinning her around before putting her back down on her feet.

"What on earth is going on with you, Ken Gardner?" Jenny said, slapping his shoulder playfully.

He didn't know. He just wanted the day to be perfect. "What? A guy can't twirl his wife without getting the third degree?" Ken clapped his hands. "Let's get going, ladies. The sandwiches aren't going to make themselves."

"OMG, Dad, chill. Don't you know that breakfast is the most important meal of the day?" Frannie said, smirking as she shook the box of Special K. "Would you grab the milk?"

At least this one was still talking to him, Ken thought. He flashed back to how he used to make waffles with the girls on Sunday mornings when they were little. He'd man the iron, and they'd oversee the decorating, a free-for-all of whipped cream, chocolate chips, sprinkles, and syrup. He loved the way they hung on to him, arms wrapped around his leg or neck, sticky hands on his face. He wanted to ask Frannie if she remembered those mornings. Instead, he said, "Can you imagine what your gramps would have said to me if I asked him for the milk when I was closer to the fridge?"

"In fact, I can," said Frannie, waggling her brows theatrically. "As a boomer, Gramps would have given you a sob story about walking a mile in the rain to milk a cow. But you know what?" The kid was on a roll.

"You'd have never asked because you were a self-sufficient, latchkey Gen X-er."

"Damn straight," Ken said, enjoying his daughter's schtick.

"As for me," Frannie continued, "I'm just a sorry, spoiled little Z, addicted to my phone and used to getting trophies for last place."

Jenny pulled Frannie in for a hug. "Losing is the new winning, sweetie!" she said, and winked.

"So long as we're all in agreement," Ken said.

"Come on, Daddy-O." Frannie pouted. "Milk, please."

Ken smiled and opened the fridge. He'd pick his battles today.

An hour later, Ken and the girls were prepping the boat while Jenny packed lunch. He checked the weather report on his phone again—the wind was steady, and the tide would be cooperating in both directions. He slipped the device back into its waterproof pouch without even sneaking a peek at his emails.

No Working on the Weekend? Check.

Create Meaningful Family Time? Check.

No Online Encounters? Check.

Ken was crushing therapy.

As Frannie and Tessa opened the hatches and drop boards, Ken swelled with pride. He might not have a son to carry on the Gardner name, but his girls knew their way around the *Francesca*. They scampered down into the cabin, retrieving cushions, winch handles, binoculars, and sunscreen. They made sure the lines were clear and scrubbed the seagull droppings from the bow, high-fiving each other with each task completed. Gen-Z jokes aside, his daughters were stellar first mates. Plus, they made a great team and always had each other's back. Given his childhood, the fact that he'd somehow created happy and well-adjusted children was remarkable to him. Above all, he loved their friendship. Abby had been his closest ally once, but at some point along the way, she discarded him without looking back.

Ken turned the power on and did an engine check—coolant, oil, fuel.

Everything was good to go. The girls were taking turns cannonballing off the bow as he rowed the dinghy back to the dock to pick up Jenny and the cooler. He felt an unexpected rush of love and appreciation for all he had. Yes, this was going to be a perfect day.

Once everyone was aboard, he motored the *Francesca* out of Stage Harbor and into Nantucket Sound where there was plenty of space to maneuver. He steered the boat into the wind.

"Free the ties!" he ordered. "Rig the halyards! Loosen the sheets!"

The girls were on it—*Aye-aye, Captain*-ing him at every command. He told them to winch up the sails and they obeyed. Here on the water, everyone understood that he was king.

"Ready?" he asked.

"Ready," they answered in unison.

Ken switched off the motor and turned the vessel off the wind. This was the moment when the world fell away. He watched the pattern on the water, dark smudges rippling across the surface toward them. Wind. Then—*swoosh!*—the sails filled and off they went, magically carried by an invisible force. Ken listened to the gurgle of water moving beneath the boat, watched seaweed and shadows pass beneath them, and felt the hull cut through the ocean, the tension in the sheets, and the gentle tug of the wheel as it tried to recenter. But more than anything, Ken felt his mother's presence on the water, along with a sense of well-being and a connection to something larger than himself.

An hour in, the wind was gentle and steady, the water mostly smooth, and the girls lay on their stomachs, peering over the side as they stared into the depths, the rising and falling of pale green below. Nantucket Sound, an ecologically rich and shallow basin of constantly shifting sand and shoals, was protected from the open ocean by Martha's Vineyard, Nantucket, and other islands south of Chatham, and offered wonderful opportunities for discovery, both natural and man-made. Over the years, they'd spied all manner of fish, sharks, marine mammals, sea turtles, jellies, and more. Plus, thanks to reliably treacherous conditions, the sound was also home to dozens of shipwrecks: schooners, sloops, brigs, and barges, although they'd yet to come upon one of those. The rule was, when Tessa or Frannie saw something worthy of further investigation, they'd shriek "Halt!" and he'd point the *Francesca* into the wind and drop anchor so that they could explore.

"Halt," the girls screamed. "Halt, halt!"

Likely, it was a false alarm, but why not stop? It was lunchtime and this was as beautiful a spot as any to swim. Ken turned the boat toward the direction of the wind until the sails luffed.

"What did you see?" he called from the bow where he released the anchor.

Frannie and Tessa were already at the stern, waiting for the *Francesca* to slide back over the mysterious treasure.

"Unsure," Frannie said, a hand on her brow to shield her eyes. "It looked man-made. It was sticking up funny."

"I saw a flash of color, maybe gold," Tessa said and hurried below to grab their masks and fins.

Seconds later—*splash!*—the girls had hurled themselves off the back of the boat.

"Good luck," Jenny called down to Frannie and Tessa as they treaded water and adjusted their masks. Then she donned a preposterously large sun hat.

"And the adventure begins," Ken said, taking a seat beside Jenny and putting a hand around her slender ankle.

"Nice work, mister. They're having a great day." Jenny tilted her head back, closed her eyes, and smiled at the sun.

"And what about you?" Ken asked. "Are *you* having a great day?"

"Well, let's see. Children deliriously happy. Husband not working. Day on the water." Jenny pretended to consider it carefully. "I'd have to say yes. So far, so good."

Ken understood that the day was still his to lose. "Excellent. All part of the master plan. Stay exactly where you are. I'll get lunch ready." He lifted the side brim of her hat and placed a kiss where her hairline met her neck.

Jenny's eyes popped open, her carefree look suddenly gone.

"Hey, sorry. Didn't mean to get ahead of myself. Go back to your Zen state, please," Ken said, getting up.

"It's okay," Jenny said, touching where he'd kissed her. "I just wasn't expecting it."

"I hope we can get back to a point where you are expecting it and maybe even welcoming it," Ken said, smiling. "I'm trying. I really need you to know that. I'm working on all of it."

"Good. That's good to hear," Jenny said, applying sunscreen.

Ken could tell his wife had something on her mind. He knew how to read people and in Jenny's case, he knew he wouldn't have to wait long to find out what was up.

"I need to talk to you about something," she said. "Not necessarily right this moment, but soon."

Ken sat back down, knowing if he remained silent, she would fill the void.

"Look, I know I'm not supposed to get involved. And I will never fully understand what's up with you and Abby"—Jenny lifted the brim of her hat to look Ken in the eyes—"but something has got to give. The Arcadia situation must change. I've stayed out of it, but that doesn't mean I don't have an opinion."

Ken stiffened but nodded agreeably.

"It's just, well, you need to make things right there, Ken. Everyone knows that Abby deserves to own that place outright. It's what your mother would have wanted."

At the mention of his mother, Ken felt his muscles clench and his chest tighten. Who exactly was "everyone"? He stared at his hands, which were balled in his lap. He relaxed his grip, took a breath, and concentrated on smiling. "As I mentioned, I'm working on all of it in therapy, just as I promised you I would."

Jenny's face softened, but the moment was interrupted by hysterical shouts from the water.

"Mom! Dad!" Tessa shrieked. "You have to see this."

"What?" Jenny asked, leaning over the stern pulpit.

"Part of a ship's wheel," Tessa said. "I couldn't get as close as I wanted to."

Frannie was already halfway up the ladder, looking as if she'd seen a ghost. "What if there are bodies down there?"

Through the wobbling current, Ken saw the thing: an uneven circular shape. Spokes and handgrips possibly? Whatever it was was misshapen by barnacles, seaweed, and moving water. He dove in without a mask or fins, propelling himself porpoise style down to the ocean floor, equalizing his ears as he went. He grabbed the object and tugged hard, but it wasn't going anywhere. By God, the girls were right. It *was* a ship's wheel, half-buried in sand and marine life, still firmly attached to whatever held it from below.

Ken spent the next two hours trying to raise it with the girls—diving, gripping, tugging—but to no avail. Still, what a day, a true adventure! And Ken enjoyed every minute of it, basking in his daughters' adoration.

Six glorious hours later, they motored back into Stage Harbor, pleasantly exhausted. There had been no squabbles, no insubordination, no mutiny, Ken thought happily, as he rowed his family to shore, already imagining how he would report it all back to George.

"Let's get lobster rolls for dinner," Frannie suggested, strolling down the dock.

"Better yet, sushi!" Tessa suggested. "This is the kind of day that deserves Sushi Den."

Frannie nodded. "Credit card, Daddy-O."

"How about: 'Thanks for the amazing day, Dad'?" Ken said. He was going for funny but ended up sounding needy. No wonder Tessa thought he was an idiot. Ken was incapable of being cool—just as Danny McCormick had pointed out decades ago. A wave of loneliness tugged at him. What was it that George had said about loneliness? That children experienced it like shame.

The smell of hot dogs grilling hit Ken as soon as he stepped off the dock. Then he heard the voices. A family was settled in just beyond the path to his house. A semicircle of beach chairs, two big ones and three smaller ones, set around a folding table covered with picnic stuff. The kids were digging a huge hole—pulling up the native grasses he'd planted to combat the erosion. Parents tipped back in their chairs, guzzling beers and shelling peanuts. An open fire. Charcoal briquettes. The stink of lighter fluid.

"Hey," Jenny said, taking his wrist as if reading his mind. "Ken, how about you just ignore them? It's been a perfect day. Let's go inside, shower, and top it off with a decadent dinner."

Jenny was right. Ken should listen. He knew he should. George had told him to count to ten before he reacted to things, explaining that in that short time was the power to choose a response. 1, 2, 3, 4 . . . Nope! He couldn't do it. There was something about the way the dude was discarding his peanut shells, tossing them over his shoulder onto the sand, his sand, that made it impossible for him to keep counting. Ken shook his wrist free from Jenny's hold and marched toward the family.

The guy looked up and raised his beer as Ken approached. "Doesn't get any better than this, does it?"

"It sure doesn't," Ken said, taking in the man's "Life is great, so is beer" koozie and moving on to the ugly plastic beach toys, no doubt purchased for a dollar at the Christmas Tree Shops and destined for the landfill in a matter of days. The oldest child, a girl, was braiding his beach grass into a necklace—American dune grass that he'd planted himself to protect his precious coastline. The wife's white thighs spread like cake batter on her chair.

"I'm sorry to ruin your picnic, but this is delicate coastal habitat and private property," he said. "There are no fires allowed."

The couple stared at him blankly—dumbfounded or dimwitted, Ken couldn't tell which.

"Whoa. Sorry, man," the guy said, getting up. "I'm Fred. This is my wife, Nancy. We're renting a place down the road." He pointed vaguely across the bay. "We just arrived. Long drive. It's our first day of vacation and the kids wanted to see the wildlife." He reached out a meaty hand.

Ken gave it a perfunctory shake and watched the oldest boy evict a hermit crab from its shell. *See it or kill it?* he wondered. He gave the parents directions to the Monomoy National Wildlife Refuge less than a mile from where they sat.

"Dad!" Tessa shrieked from the dock. "I need to talk with you right now."

Ken turned to see his daughter scooping up armfuls of air, beckoning frantically for him to come back.

"Cute kid," Fred said.

An empty plastic hot dog bag blew off the table and into the water. That was it. Ken had had it with tourists—the litter, the erosion, the carelessness.

"I'm sorry, Fred, but you're going to have to move your picnic."

"Look, we just put the franks on," the man whispered tightly. "Long drive, hungry kids. We'll keep it quiet."

Not his problem, Ken thought. But for Tessa's sake, he'd compromise. "Eat the dogs, clean up, and leave quickly."

"Doesn't the beach belong to everyone?" the wife huffed.

"Not this one," Ken said matter-of-factly. "You have twenty minutes to wrap things up. And please, use plenty of water on those coals." He turned and walked back in the direction of the dock, where his daughters stood. Jenny had already retreated to the house.

"What an asshole," Fred muttered under his breath.

"Really, Dad? Really?" Tessa said. "You had to be *that* much of a jerk?"

"Drop it, Tessa," Frannie warned. "Dad's protecting the environment."

This was a teachable moment, Ken thought. He would not lose his temper. "Tessa, mutual respect is the key to coastal access."

Eye roll. The apex of dismissiveness.

"I thought you were an environmentalist," he said, trying a new tack. "They caused more erosion in ten minutes than we have all year. They had an open fire. The kids were murdering sea critters."

Eye roll. Eye roll. Ken hated when his sister's face made a guest appearance on one of his daughters. But there was Abby, written right into Tessa's expression.

"Did you not see them littering?"

"It's just not fair," Tessa said.

"What's not fair?" Ken said, starting to lose his patience.

Tessa crossed her arms in front of her chest. "Dad, have you ever considered that over sixty percent of the *Titanic*'s first-class passengers survived and less than twenty-five percent from steerage did?"

What did that have to do with anything?

"Honey . . ." he started to explain, but Tessa continued, indignant.

"This land belongs to the Wampanoag tribe," she said. "All of Chatham, really, all of the Cape, was stolen. We don't *own* any of this."

Ken knew that to respond was to risk lighting up a network of adolescent outrage that lay like a power grid just beneath the surface. He reminded himself that Tessa was not yet thirteen. It was her job to question everything. But what the fuck! *Stolen land? The Wampanoags? Was this the education his tax dollars paid for?*

Tessa uncrossed her arms and placed them on her hips. "I'm just saying, it's not fair. The system's rigged. We live in a McMansion while people around the world starve."

Yes, life was unfair. But since when did providing well for your family make you the bad guy? Ken knew what he *should* do—he *should* tell his daughter that he loved her, that he was proud of her convictions—but the smug expression on Tessa's face was too much. How dare she refer to their beautiful home as a McMansion, as if it was some tacky display of wealth? He looked up at his grand house. It was tasteful, wasn't it? Or was it pretentious? *Jesus, pull it together, Gardner.*

"You know what, Tessa?" Ken said, stepping closer so that he towered over her. Then he put his face at her level and lowered his voice into an angry hiss. "The rigged system didn't seem to bother you ten minutes ago when you were deciding between lobster rolls and sushi."

As his words hit their mark, Ken watched his daughter's face transform with humiliation. And like that, his near-perfect day circled the drain. God, he hated himself. He would hate himself even more later; the aftermath of his rage always felt worse than the rage itself. Why couldn't he be the father he wanted to be? He'd been so careful to sidestep the ancestral muddle, determined to be different than his own father, that he stepped into a fresh cycle of mistakes, all his own. "Honey, I'm sorry. I didn't mean that to come out so harshly." He wanted a do-over. "How about this: when you and Frannie inherit the property, you two can do what you want with it. Turn it into a commune, for all I care."

Too late. Tessa wouldn't meet his eyes. "Already in the works," she said coolly.

Ken looked to Frannie for an explanation.

"It's kind of true," Frannie said, giggling. "It's what Aunt Abby says she's going to do with the Arcadia. Turn it into an artists' cooperative."

"Is that so?" said Ken. So, once again, it was Abby. It should come as no surprise that his sister was behind this insurrection. But Abby didn't even own the Arcadia, now, did she? An artists' cooperative over his dead body. And not even then, according to his will.

Adam

In the parking lot of Tzuco's, Adam swallowed a couple of clonazepam dry and watched the setting sun pink the sky over Provincetown's harbor. His mind had been revving and idling all day. "Rapid cycling" was the clinical term, and the highs and lows he'd been experiencing gave him a new appreciation of the saying, *What goes up must come down*. His heart felt like a jack-in-the-box with a faulty lid—every time he pushed it down, it sprang right back up again.

Adam gazed at the shoreline, where gulls crouched on shaggy-weeded rocks and wind gusts rippled the water, willing the drugs to kick in. Through the car's open window, Adam heard the faint pebble clatter of retreating waves. He looked through the water and conjured the strange and beautiful happenings beneath the choppy surface: blue lobsters exploring meadows of eelgrass with sensitive antennae, starfish regenerating limbs, anglerfish dangling bioluminescent lures. As these images lapped the edges of his mind, a poem swam to shore.

How is it that the anglerfish glows?
Or the flying fish flies?
Ask the whale. Ask the whale. He knows.

Welcome, Adam thought, delighted at the prospect of a poet chiming into his aural hallucinations. If only the jabberwocky of other voices would pipe down, he'd like to hear what this one had to say. One of his granddaughters wanted to be a poet. Which one was it? Tessa, of course. Now he knew where she got her talent from. She was tricky, that one. A tomboy, only you weren't allowed to call a girl that anymore. Even when she dressed like a boy, which Tessa did from time to time, you were just supposed to act like everything was normal. He closed his eyes and tried to listen, but was distracted by swirls of color blossoming behind his lids, delineated by ferns of veins—like frost on a window, only red. Then a rapid sequence of unpleasant scenes flashed before him: Emily collapsing on the hospital floor; Ken returning from school with a black eye; Abby pushing food around her plate, refusing to eat; Gretchen hurling a mug at him. Sweat prickled like ant bites over the surface of his skin. Adam opened his eyes. He needed a drink.

"Well, if it isn't the Socrates of Wellfleet," said his favorite bartender, Joe, greeting Adam while garnishing a couple of cocktails, which he placed on a tray.

"For God's sake, Joe, get your philosophers straight," Adam said, secretly pleased with the moniker. "Do I strike you as the kind of man who would brag about knowing nothing?"

"My bad," Joe said, slapping a bell to alert the waitress. "What can I get you tonight?"

"Bourbon on the rocks."

Tzuco's bar was a classic L-shape with a mirrored wall running the length of it, creating drinker camaraderie and optimal visual access. Secured on his favorite stool at the L's hinge, Adam had the best view in the house. Joe placed the drink on a coaster in front of him. "How are all things aquatic?"

Adam exhaled with relief. Joe's chatter was drawing him out of his head. "You want the good news or the bad news?"

"The good news, of course," Joe replied.

"Spoken like a true knucklehead," Adam said affectionately. "I'll win the Nobel for keeping you in the dark." He took a sip. "Here are some facts that I'll *forgo* mentioning: The earth's carbon dioxide levels recently surpassed four hundred parts per million. This year has been the hottest on record. The ice is melting. The reefs are bleaching." Adam gazed upward as if searching the ceiling for more catastrophic data. "I'll say no more. Ignorance is bliss, after all."

"Thanks," Joe said.

Adam looked at the kid: sweet dope. He pointed at his empty glass, already feeling so much better, elbows on the bar, feet on the rail. "Another three fingers, please."

Joe gave him a generous pour.

"All right, here's the good news," Adam said. "The endangered right whales are back on the Cape in good numbers this spring. There are only about five hundred remaining in the world total, and they're here"—Adam pointed to the bay—"to dine on our copepods."

"Cool," Joe said. "They're the whales you study, right?"

"Your tip just fell to ten percent," Adam said, grinning. He loved this kid. "Humpbacks. I study humpbacks, you moron. Clean the wax out of your ears."

Joe shrugged. "Menu?"

Adam took the slim leather-bound booklet and placed it unopened on the counter beside him. It was a formality. He always ordered the calamari.

The place was filling up, and Joe got busy with other customers, shaking elaborate concoctions filled with elixirs, syrups, and infusions, girly cocktails that cost eighteen bucks a pop. Highway robbery. With summer just around the corner, Adam knew that soon he'd be fighting for his coveted corner barstool. Secretly, he enjoyed the tourists. People-watching was his favorite pastime, especially in P-town where the ecosystem attracted such variety. Adam played a game with himself at the bar. He'd pick someone to study and observe and eavesdrop on until he could guess three things about them: what they did, where they were from, and their greatest fear. Then he'd solicit a conversation to confirm his guesses. He was an expert at reading people.

Standing beside him was a hairy-legged young man wearing a tartan skirt, combat boots, and a black leather jacket. *Speech pathologist. Upstate New York. Getting fat.* Adam was uninterested. Occupying the two stools on the far side of the kilted punk was a middle-aged couple, sightseers from a midsize town in Ohio. From the cheery cardigan, Adam pegged the woman for a retired teacher. The husband, who had a spray of fuzz sprouting from the last productive follicles at the base of his head, was likely in insurance. They'd probably spent the day on a whale watch. *Yawn. Yawn.* Moving on. Three biotech bozos—Silicon Valley or Cambridge, hard to tell—celebrating a deal with rounds of Manhattans at the far end. The dullest sort.

With no one to capture his imagination, Adam found himself twisting down a whirlpool of thought: How was it possible that all these people—"extras," as it were, on the set of his life—believed they had experiences and emotions as rich and complex as his own? From there, he began to question his impressions about reality: Was it just a universal hallucination? At its core, might his mania be a refusal to go along with the status quo? He liked that idea, even as it drifted from him, and once again, he found himself splashing around for something to cling to. Why the hell wasn't he feeling the clonazepam more?

Adam took a long sip of bourbon and felt a prickle at the base of his neck, alerting him that he was being watched. He looked into the mirror and perused the line of reflected faces: the lonely one, the inebriated one, the anxious one. Then he found the source of the feeling: a dark-haired young woman observing him from the far end of the bar, a tall glass of something-and-soda in front of her. She wore a tan leather jacket over a pale-green shirt and had sleek, dark hair, a beguiling cleft on her chin, and a thick fringe of eyelashes visible from where he sat. She was a compact and tough-looking girl, but the toughness was countered by stunning beauty. More importantly, she looked intelligent and inquisitive. A splash of color in a sea of beige, and that was saying something in P-town, where everyone tried to stand out. Adam locked eyes on her reflection, lifted his glass, and smiled as if she was an old friend he'd spied from a distance on a train platform. *Greetings*, he thought, expecting a smile in return. Instead, the woman's eyes hardened like a flexed muscle.

At that same moment, Joe placed a plate of fried calamari in front of him, each ring lightly seasoned with spices, drizzled with a creamy chipotle sauce, and topped with a few freshly chopped cilantro leaves. The citrusy aroma shot through his limbic system. Adam decided to switch over to wine, choosing a crisp chenin blanc, and dove into his meal. The calamari at Tzuco's was the best on Cape Cod—slightly sweet, vaguely nutty, never greasy. His favorite bites were the arms and tentacles, which looked like delicate dried flowers on the plate but were the most powerful parts of the animal when alive, propelling it through the water and enabling it to grab and hold its prey.

Seeking conversation to accompany his calamari, Adam decided to give the bland couple from Ohio a shot. "How are the mussels?" he asked. They were sharing the dish as an appetizer, placing the empty purple shells in a neat row in a bowl between them, and possibly had been waiting their whole lives for such a riveting question. The mussels were delicious. The sauce, to die for. And wasn't the Cape beautiful this time of year? They'd been coming to P-town for thirty years, renting the same cottage. Their grandchildren, three and seven, a boy and a girl, were arriving on Saturday . . . Adam had the dreadful feeling he'd soon be hearing about their sandcastle-building plans. His rescue came in the form of a slender hostess who announced their table was ready. Sayonara, nitwits.

"Is everything okay?" Joe asked Adam as he cleared the couple's plate from the bar.

Adam was ready for some more witty banter, but Joe had already turned away and was bullying a rag down the length of the bar. *Subpar service*, Adam thought. And what a stupid question: *Is everything okay?* How could everything *ever* be okay? No, *everything* was not okay. Adam needed to correct Joe's false impression that his calamari had created equanimity. It had not.

Adam raised his hand to call Joe back, a lecture forming itself in his head when he noticed the woman looking at him again. Only this time, she held his gaze with a look so concentrated that it shimmered the air around her like heat coming off asphalt. She was decidedly not your average tourist taking in the gay scene or the bay views. She looked purposeful—as if she was here for a reason. Adam scrolled through his matrixes: A restaurant critic? A community activist? A fellow scientist? He was stumped. One thing was for sure, he'd found the most interesting person in the room.

Adam looked down at his empty plate and pushed it away from him.

When he looked up again, to his great surprise, the woman had drained her drink and was marching toward him.

"Do you mind if I sit here?" she asked.

Speechless, Adam gestured to the empty stool beside him.

She slipped onto it and grinned. "Just so you don't get the wrong idea, I'm not hitting on you. I just feel self-conscious sitting at bars by myself, and you looked like you could use some company. Steph Murphy," she said, extending her hand.

She had a lovely smile, one tooth slightly forward. "Delighted to make your acquaintance. May I call you Stephanie, which I assume is your given name?" he said, taking her hand. That crooked tooth sure was charming. Braces—that's what was wrong with the world. All those generic smiles.

"O-kay," she said uncertainly.

"I'm Adam Gardner, marine biologist and"—he paused for a thoughtful moment—"poet. May I buy you another—?"

"Cranberry and soda," she said. "Thanks."

Adam signaled to Joe for another round. "So, where are you from and what brings you to the fair shores of Provincetown?"

"I live in Jamaica Plain, but I've been coming to P-town since college," she said, looking beyond him to where the setting sun was as orange as a cigarette end.

"I've spent a lot of time in Boston," Adam said. "What do you do there?"

"I'm on the force," Stephanie said.

Adam was sure he'd never met a female police officer before. "What drew you to that line of work?"

"My father and his four brothers are all with the Boston PD. So was my grandfather. I guess you could say I was born into it, although I am the first woman in the family to wear a badge."

"Fascinating," Adam said.

"Trust me, it's not quite as glamorous as it seems on *Law & Order*. There's a lot of paperwork." Then Stephanie gave him a curious smile. "I'm here to look into a cold case."

Adam knew she'd be interesting, but this was more than he'd hoped for. "Murder?"

"More like a missing person."

"Intriguing," Adam said. "And in a million years, I would have never pegged you for a cop."

"I get that a lot," she said. "For what it's worth, you're my first poet-slash-marine biologist. I didn't know those things went together."

Adam loved a woman who could banter. This one reminded him of one of those fast-talking women right out of an old black-and-white movie. "Poetry and science? Same skill set: pay attention, be surprised, talk about it," he said, butchering Mary Oliver's lines. *What was the saying? Good writers borrow, great writers steal.*

Joe set down their drinks.

"What unit are you in?" Adam asked, priding himself on knowing a little bit about almost everything. He read the *New York Times*, *Boston Globe*, and *Cape Cod Times* cover-to-cover daily and had done so for decades. There was no subject he could not speak knowledgeably about.

"S.T.O.P.," she said.

Adam tried to figure out the acronym.

"Special Tactics and Operations team. You know, the good stuff: armed suspects, hostage situations, that kind of thing."

"Impressive. So, tell me about your missing person," Adam said. "Maybe I can help. Is he on the lam? Aware you're tracking him? I assume your target is a man."

"Yes, a man. And no, he doesn't have the first clue."

Adam was enjoying their little game. "What do you know about him?"

"Just the basics: his name and address," said Stephanie. "I'm in the early stages, gathering info, doing recon, that kind of thing." She smiled at him, which had the effect of deepening the cleft in her chin. What was it about that cleft? "I have the whole summer to find him."

Adam was pleased to know that Stephanie would be in town for a while. Maybe he'd invite her out on the boat for a private whale watch. "May I inquire as to the nature of his crime?"

"Did I say he was a criminal?" she asked, giving him a closed-lipped smile.

Oh, she was good, this one! "You did not," Adam conceded.

"He could be a criminal, I suppose," she said, her eyes following a swollen drop of water that rolled down the side of her glass. "But I doubt it. I think he's just a typical man. You know, someone who takes what he wants without thinking twice."

Ah. A feminist. And a feisty one! Adam thought about his daughter, Abby, whose buttons he loved to push. He considered making a smart-ass retort about women and their ever-changing minds but decided against it. He was enjoying Stephanie and didn't want to offend her. At least, not yet. Who knew if she had a sense of humor about all of this? A lot of women didn't, at least not these days. He'd figure out a way to let her know he was one of the good guys. Hell, he planned to vote for "Shillary" in the fall; he should at least get some points for that. "Don't be too hard on us poor men. The rules have been changing fast. We're doing our best to keep up."

Stephanie's phone lit up. "Shoot," she said with alarm, popping off her stool. "Sorry, Adam. I need to get going. I told my wife I'd be back twenty minutes ago and my baby, Jonah, needs to be fed. You're looking at the milk supply."

Wife? Baby? Adam hadn't picked up on either. He tried to play it cool, but he didn't want her to leave. "Let's stay in touch. I've lived on this sandbar for a long time," he said, handing her his business card. "If you need any help finding your guy, give me a shout. If I don't know him myself, I'm sure I know people who know him."

"I'm sure you do," she said, running a finger across the embossed lettering on the heavy card stock. She held it by the corner and waved it at him. "Sweet. Old school."

Adam felt ancient and foolish. "It helps to know where to send the telegrams," he said.

To his delight, the joke landed, and Stephanie's face broke into a smile. Perhaps he should invite her to his birthday party? That was an idea. Young and beautiful guests might show his colleagues he wasn't a relic.

Stephanie picked up his phone and typed in her contact information. "How the kids do it, today. Text me," she said and exited the bar without looking back.

A few hours later, Adam smoked a joint—whoa, the stuff was stronger than it used to be—and felt his body relax into a pleasant lethargy, pinned to his deck chair beneath a velvet blanket of sky. With his birthday less than two months away, he felt less sure than ever about his discovery. He reminded himself that doubt was a critical part of scientific inquiry. He was in the belly of the beast. Yes, that was it—the belly of the beast was the right metaphor. He was going to have to find a way to stay comfortable with feeling a bit lost. Or maybe he was just stoned. Adam looked into the night sky for a sign. There were some twinkles, but nothing obvious. He thought of the young woman he'd met—a terrific girl—and pictured her racing out of the bar to nurse her son. Jonah, she'd called him. Jonah, the recalcitrant prophet. Jonah and the whale. That was his sign! *Three days*, he thought. He would only be in the belly of the beast for three days, or so the legend went. Then, he'd be vomited back on terra firma.

Steph

Steph awoke to floorboards creaking, coffee beans being ground, and a toilet flushing—familiar sounds that heralded a new day. She blinked open her eyes. Jonah lay in his bassinet beside the bed, quietly gurgling, eyes open, seemingly mesmerized by the dust-fringed blades of the overhead fan.

"Good morning, sweet boy," she said, stacking pillows against the headboard behind her and drinking from the glass of water she'd left by the bedside the night before. "Are you ready for breakfast?" Jonah's legs peddled the air, and Steph collected him, inhaling the fragrance of his downy head where a web of tiny veins moved blood beneath the surface. One sniff was all it took for the sweet pins-and-needles sensation of her milk letting down to begin and oxytocin to flood her with a sense of well-being.

Toni appeared in the doorway, two mugs of coffee in hand, which she set down on the bedside tables. Then she slipped back under the sheets beside Steph. "Tell me everything," she said.

Steph didn't know where to begin. After leaving Adam at Tzuco's, she'd phoned to let Toni know that she wouldn't be home in time to feed Jonah. Toni didn't ask questions, and Steph didn't offer any explanation. Her head was full of noise. She'd just conversed with a man with whom she shared twenty-three chromosomes. A whale scientist. A man so unlike her dad (or any dad she'd ever known) that she felt dizzy trying to retrofit her life around the new information.

She'd left Tzuco's and meandered in the general direction of their house. She passed tourists off cruise ships anchored in the bay, tattooed bikers, drag queens, and fishermen; galleries, shops, and bungalows with pocket gardens full of gargantuan blooms—all of it illuminated by the evening light for which Provincetown was famous. She turned onto the bay beach as the first stars were becoming visible in the darkening sky. As soon as her feet hit the sand, she stopped, shed her jacket, and lay down.

Salt air filled her nostrils and sand shifted beneath the weight of her body. Steph felt comforted by the murmur of the bay, a sound that made her think the world itself was breathing. Or it could be that she was hearing whale exhalations, which Adam had told her was possible. Adam! Her biological father. Charming, eccentric, magnetic.

Steph stopped herself. Why was she glorifying him? She'd met her sperm donor, that was all. The salt air settled over her like a blanket and she lay still, fixed to the sand, tracking cruising satellites and identifying what few star clusters she could: the Big Dipper, Orion's Belt, the murky dusk of the Milky Way. Why was she here? Then, Steph experienced a sensation of lightness that made her feel like she'd been levitated off the sand. For several minutes, she floated on this tranquil wave of consciousness, feeling as if the universe was endless. Then the mosquitoes found her. So much for transcendence.

"Maybe start with how you broke the ice?" Toni suggested.

"It wasn't like that," Steph said. "I saw him . . . and I just marched over and introduced myself."

Toni nodded as if she'd expected this. And the truth was, Toni had pretty much predicted all of it—not only had she been sure that Adam Gardner would be at the bar, but she'd also insisted he was searching for Steph, too, if only subconsciously. Normally, Steph felt put off by Toni's everything-happens-for-a-reason mindset, but her fleeting experience with transcendence the night before had been revelatory.

"What was he like?" Toni asked.

The coffee, strong and sweetened only with warm milk, anchored Steph. The man was not easy to sum up. The weirdest part had been seeing herself in him. Not the obvious physical stuff, but what she thought of as tiny DNA flashes—versions of his gestures that she knew she shared. Like the way he rubbed his thumb and forefinger together when he tried to articulate a feeling.

"Charismatic," she said, the first word that came to mind. "Intense. He's completely obsessed with whales." *Adam was a showboater, too,* she thought. She'd been rapt. Her teenage mother would have been defenseless against his charms.

"What else?" Toni asked.

"Possibly slightly unhinged," she added, recalling Adam's gesticulations and rapid-fire speech. "I don't know. I liked him. He was funny."

"Huh. So, how long did you guys talk?" Toni asked.

"Not sure, maybe forty-five minutes?"

"Any surprises?"

The only real surprise was that Steph had gone in intending to interrogate Adam, and he'd asked lots of questions, too. "Not really," she said.

"No red flags?"

Steph knew what Toni was really asking. The man had taken advantage of her mother as a teenager. It wasn't much of a leap to assume he was a lech when it came to attractive younger women.

"Not really," Steph said. "In fact, we exchanged contact info." His business card sat on the bedside table. "I'm pretty sure he'll reach out. He offered to take me to the whale sanctuary where he does his research."

"Hmm." Toni sipped her coffee. If she had any reservations about Steph spending time alone on a boat with a stranger, she didn't say. "So, how do you *feel* about all of it?"

Toni never tired of talking about feelings.

"Bewildered," Steph admitted. She was the bewildered daughter of a new father, the bewildered half sister of two strangers, and the bewildered mother of the little guy in her arms. Steph looked into Toni's wise, blue-gray eyes and tucked a stray strand of her wife's blonde hair behind her ear.

"I love you," Steph said and leaned over to kiss Toni. "I guess I thought meeting Adam Gardner would bring some kind of closure, but I feel cracked open."

"In a good way?" Toni asked.

"In a guts-spilling-out way," Steph said. Jonah's eyes were half shut; his fists squeezed rhythmically alongside her breast as he suckled. "Want to know something cool about humpbacks?"

"Who doesn't?" Toni replied.

"They make pink milk!" said Steph, having no idea why, out of all the fascinating humpback whale facts Adam had imparted—the behemoths migrated five thousand miles between breeding and feeding, had hearts that weighed four hundred pounds, and sang songs that could be heard twenty miles away—pink milk felt the most extraordinary. Maybe it was because, as a lactating mammal herself, she felt a kinship to all mothers, cetacean (she'd learned the word from Adam) and otherwise. Steph wasn't used to these thoughts or feelings.

"That *is* cool," Toni said. "By the way, your parents called again."

Steph groaned.

"They'll be here for the fourth, like always. They're staying at a bed and breakfast in Wellfleet."

Steph didn't feel ready to deal with them. "I have no idea how to talk to them about any of this."

"Well, they don't, either. But it's time. Your father knows the truth now, and everyone has had a chance to process it. You three are going to have to talk it out sooner or later," Toni said. "Plus, they're dying to see their grandson."

Jonah had unlatched, and Steph adjusted him so he was sitting with his back against her knees, facing them. She held a tiny wrist in each hand. "And what did you and Mommy do last night, mister?" she said in the universal singsong of mothers.

"While he slept," Toni said, "I consulted the Tarot."

Steph sighed.

Toni handed her a card, the Ten of Swords—a man on the ground, ten swords sticking out of his back.

"That's pleasant."

"Your half-siblings are working through some trauma," Toni said.

Who the hell wasn't? Steph returned the card.

"And it's not your run-of-the-mill trauma," Toni continued. She placed the card in the middle of the deck and shuffled. "It's big-time stuff. In fact, the whole spread told the story of wounded people."

"Come on, Toni," Steph said.

"All I'm saying is, pay attention," Toni said. "Wounded people wound."

Abby

What had started as a mercy mission twelve years ago—giving Ken and Jenny a twenty-four-hour break from their six-month-old twins—had become Abby's favorite day of the summer and sealed her standing as Best Aunt Ever. Not that she had much competition—despite Rebecca's ridiculous insistence that she be called "Aunt Becky"—Abby was their only real aunt. And every year on June 30, she did her best to make Frannie and Tessa's half-birthday outshine the real one, which could get lost in the holiday shuffle, landing between Christmas and New Year's. The "half-a-palooza," as they called it, included gifts, adventures, and a hard-and-fast ice cream-for-lunch policy. But the best part of the extravaganza, added to the tradition when the girls were seven and a half, was an overnight stay at one of the coveted dune shacks in Provincetown. How exactly Abby secured a cottage each year, she told no one. But there in the dunes, without electricity or plumbing, the three of them roasted marshmallows, watched shooting stars torch the clear black sky, and shared secrets.

By the time Abby pulled into her brother's driveway around 10:00 a.m., it was already 80 degrees and Stage Harbor was bustling—paddleboarders and kayakers skimming along the marshes; beachgoers loading up whalers with folding chairs, towel bags, and coolers; and dogs springing through the shallow water to retrieve sticks and tennis balls. The brief and frantic spring had come and gone, replaced by languid summer days. Strawberries raced their runners across the ground in the patch near the driveway, small red berries weighing down the stems.

Ken was at the far end of his vegetable garden, hunched over and so focused that he hadn't noticed her pull in. Abby couldn't make out what he was doing. He seemed to be holding something in one hand while untangling something else with the other, his concerned expression reminding Abby of childhood summers spent rescuing woodland creatures, shorebirds, and tadpoles in the Wellfleet Woods. Ken had always had a soft spot for wild animals.

Abby watched Ken straighten up, cupping something in his palms. He brought the handful to his face and Abby had the irrational fear that her brother might stuff it into his mouth or smash it between his palms. But no, his lips were moving. He was saying something to the creature. Then Ken smiled and threw his arms over his head, opening his hands. Out burst a goldfinch, a blur of yellow undulating over the lawn and into the nearest tree. Tears pricked Abby's eyes. Earlier in the week, she'd felt the baby move for the first time—a sensation followed by a wave of love so forceful that it knocked over everything that had been there before. Since then, pretty much anything could bring her to tears from the sound of a foghorn to the loyal thump of Frida's tail. Abby placed a palm on her belly where a creature swam in the dark ocean of her.

She got out of the car and called hello to her brother, raising two white bakery bags, which they both knew contained his favorite treat: dirt bombs, cinnamon donuts masquerading as muffins. Ken acknowledged her with a perfunctory wave and turned his attention back to his vegetable garden, where he struggled to reposition the mesh on the pole. Abby lowered the bags, deciding not to let her brother's dismissiveness affect her good mood. She closed the car door with her hip, which gave a satisfying slam, alerting Frannie and Tessa to her arrival.

"Aunt Abby's here! Aunt Abby's here!" came the delighted shrieks from the house.

The screen door banged shut and the two girls dashed down the stone steps and across the lawn, barreling into Abby as they'd done since they were toddlers. Every year, Abby wondered if this might be their last half-birthday palooza. Frannie and Tessa would be teenagers in six months. How much longer would they want to hang out with their aunt? And next year, she would have a baby at home. They each grabbed a bag of muffins and hooked arms with Abby, steering her toward the door.

"Dad," Frannie shouted in the direction of the garden. "Time for dirt bombs."

"Hurry!" Tessa ordered.

"Hold up," Ken called back, waving them over. "I need some help here first."

Killjoy, Abby thought.

The girls looked to her for rescue. Abby would take the high road. The dirt bombs would have to wait. "Go help your dad," she said, taking the bags from them. "I'll set the table and we'll start the party in just a few minutes."

Frannie and Tessa trudged toward their father.

From the wraparound deck, Abby entered through the kitchen: white walls, terra-cotta-tiled floors, large picture windows, and a long peninsula counter separating the kitchen from an oak dining table. Inside, Jenny raced around with a hamper balanced on her hip, picking up a mess of bikini bottoms, flip-flops, and hair bands. A familiar sight. Despite Jenny's best efforts to be tidy, it didn't come naturally. If she took off a cardigan in the living room, chances were it would stay slung over the arm of the sofa until her cleaners came.

When Jenny noticed Abby, she dropped the basket. "I know what you're thinking," Jenny said, giving Abby a peck on the cheek. "How is it possible that this place always looks like a bomb's gone off?"

"Do you know who you're talking to?"

"Well, you're an artist," Jenny said. "No one expects you to be neat."

Abby tried to decide if she should be offended. "Slob to slob, you must know that the only thing anyone notices when they walk into this house is this," she said, gesturing to the view of Stage Harbor. She started to help, tossing scrunchies and a lip gloss into the basket. "You could be ankle-deep in underwear in this room and not care."

"And that's what makes you you!" said Jenny. "Trust me, yours is not the common opinion."

"I'm just saying, you have better things to do with your time." As the words left her mouth, Abby hoped she hadn't sounded judgmental.

But Jenny laughed in agreement. "True. Lots of better things. But my garden tour starts in an hour, and there's always at least one snoop who looks through the window."

"So what?" Abby said. "They see that you have a life."

Jenny exhaled. "People want the fairy tale, Abby. *Voters* want the fairy tale. They want to see what their vote will get them. Perfect garden, perfect house, perfect wife, perfect life." Jenny opened the jam-packed closet in the hall and a tennis racket tumbled out. She shoved it back in with her foot. She placed the basket onto the heap and leaned her weight against the door until it clicked closed behind her. "Voters do not go easy on women with sloppy homes."

Neither does my brother, thought Abby.

The two got to work making coffee and setting up the screened-in porch for breakfast: mugs, plates, napkins, juice. Abby placed the pastry bags in the center of the table.

"So, what are the big plans for half-a-palooza?" Jenny asked.

"You know, the usual: lots of sugar, the beach, a project or two," Abby said. "I was thinking if you didn't already have something in mind, I'd help get them started on a gift for Gramps's birthday."

"That would be awesome," Jenny said, filling a small pitcher with half-and-half. "Thanks again. You have no idea how much they look forward to this day each summer."

"Me, too," Abby said.

"How are you feeling?" Jenny asked.

"My back aches, I'm starving, and I have to pee, like, all the time."

"Ah, the trifecta of pregnancy," Jenny said, smiling, and then lowered her voice. "Have you told David yet?"

"Any romantic plans for your night alone?" Abby volleyed back.

Then the girls flew through the door, making a beeline for the dirt bombs.

"Stop," Jenny said, pointing to the sink. "Hands first!"

"Aunt Abby, did you know Dad just saved a goldfinch?" Frannie asked, lathering soap beyond her wrists as the surgeons on her beloved *Grey's Anatomy* did.

"Yes, I saw it fly free." Abby smiled at Ken, who came in behind them. Their father had taught them to love birds, how to identify songbirds by their calls—a skill he'd learned from Adam. All those flitting shapes like darting apparitions or figments of spirits. "Ken, do you remember the time we dropper-fed that nest of baby wrens after a cat killed the mom?" She did this from time to time: brought up happy memories from their childhood, as if reminding him of their past closeness might awaken some affection.

They moved to the table on the screened-in porch.

"I remember you wanting to bake for them," Ken said, smirking. His mouth settled into its downward grooves. "Your aunt Abby wasn't too thrilled when she learned their diet consisted of worms and insects."

"Pretty gnarly cookie," Frannie agreed.

"If you really cared about the birds, Dad," Tessa said, "you'd ditch the mesh."

The comment was greeted by silence.

When had Tessa become so hard on her dad? "How about we get this party started?" Abby suggested, hoping for a reset. "Happy half-birthday to the two best nieces in the world!"

The girls each took a bag and unfolded the tops, releasing a wave of buttery cinnamon fumes. They dug in. Ken devoured his first bomb in five bites and immediately reached for a second. Jenny quartered hers, then halved the quarters, popping the perfectly sized chunks into her mouth between sips of coffee. Tessa ate hers from the bottom up, saving the crispy edges for last, and Frannie ate only the outside, leaving the interior ball of bland muffin on her plate. There was no wrong way to eat a dirt bomb—although as a family, they frowned on dunking. When Abby brought hers to her mouth, she felt nauseated. She hadn't experienced much morning sickness, but when she did, it came on forcefully. As it did now. The sight of her family licking their sugar-coated fingers revolted her. Saliva pooled in her mouth. Abby dropped the muffin onto her plate and leaned back in her chair, creating distance. What she craved was a bacon, egg, and cheddar sandwich on a toasted roll with hot sauce. This day might be harder than she thought.

"Where do you stand on the garden netting, Aunt Abby?" Tessa asked. "As a bird lover, don't you agree that we should take it down? Who cares if they nibble on our veggies?"

Abby looked at her brother and hesitated. His jaw shifted back and forth the way it did when he was agitated. Time to de-escalate things. "It's complicated, sweetie, but I think your dad's just trying to protect his—"

Ken pushed back his chair. "Your aunt Abby doesn't get to have an opinion on my garden," he interrupted.

Abby blinked. Why had she even tried to defend him? Why were they all so hell-bent on placating him? Well, at least not Tessa anymore. *Good for her*, Abby thought. She hadn't had that kind of fortitude or confidence at twelve and a half. Hell, she didn't have it now, at thirty-eight. She still tiptoed around her brother's moods. Her father's, too, for that matter.

"Have a great half-birthday, girls," Ken said, exiting without a word of thanks to Abby.

"Oh, Kenny-loo." Abby muttered the words softly enough to pretend she hadn't intended Ken to hear them. "Kenny-loo" was what Danny McCormick used to call her brother in grade school, code for "He was fat enough to break the loo." It was mean, and she regretted it instantly. What was it about siblings that made you shrink back to your worst childhood self?

Ken flinched at the words, freezing mid-step like a basketball player suspended at the hoop. Then his foot hit the ground and he was gone.

At the slam of the screen door, Abby smiled apologetically at Jenny. "I don't seem to bring out the best in him, do I?"

"Ignore him. He's probably just mad he ate two dirt bombs," Jenny said. "He'll be on the treadmill repenting for hours."

"It's the garden tour," said Frannie. "Flower ladies give him the creeps."

Tessa shook her head. "Stop making excuses for him. Dad's just being a jerk . . . as usual."

"Oh shit! The flower ladies," Jenny said, jumping to her feet and straightening her dress. "The tour starts in ten."

"That's a dollar, Mom," Frannie said.

Jenny ignored her, stacking plates, and brushing crumbs onto them. "Help me throw these in the dishwasher. And then get out of here, ladies!"

By the time Abby and the girls got in the Jeep, there was already a haphazard line of people, mostly women, filing down her brother's driveway. She released the brake and the vehicle crept forward, inching past tourgoers already impressed by a stretch of landscape that Jenny had transitioned to native grasses, flowering shrubs, and ornamentals, each selected to support an ecosystem of local pollinators: hummingbirds, bees, and butterflies, every blossom surrounded by vibrating wings.

Then Abby saw them, the couple who'd visited her at the studio a few weeks back. Yes, it was them—the dark-haired one was carrying the baby, the blonde followed. They were wandering up the driveway, plucking honeysuckle from a bush and pulling stems through to extract drops of honey. The sight made Abby flash back to an early memory: Kenny placing drops of honeysuckle on her tongue. How old had she been? Four? Five? They used to pretend that the nectar gave them superpowers: hers was invisibility, his was strength. She remembered the feeling of wanting more, but the second she could taste the honey, it was gone.

Abby stopped the Jeep alongside the couple, who were too captivated by the blossoms to look up. She remembered that the baby's name was Jonah, but the moms' names eluded her. She rolled down the windows.

"Hey there," Abby called out.

The dark-haired one looked up.

"Whoa, they're pretty," Frannie whispered from the back seat. "The one by the bush looks like a blonde Natalie Portman."

"And look at the other one," Tessa said, narrowing her eyes. "I know her from somewhere."

Strange, that was exactly how Abby had felt when she'd first met Steph.

"Toni," said the dark-haired one, tapping the blonde's shoulder, "look who's here. It's Abby from the Arcadia."

"Nice to see you again, Abby," said Toni, standing up, butterflies waltzing behind her.

"What are you two doing here?" Abby asked. To her relief, their names came to her.

"We're here for the garden tour," Steph said. "You?"

"If you can believe it, this is my brother's place. And these two," Abby said, twisting toward the back seat, "are my nieces, Frannie and Tessa. Frannie, Tessa, this is Steph and Toni. They came to see my work at the studio a while back."

The girls waved.

Steph bent down in front of the open back window, the baby strapped spread-eagle to her front, and took a long look at Frannie and Tessa. "It is so, so, so nice to meet you, girls," she said. "This is Jonah."

"Hi, Jonah," Frannie said.

"He's super cute," said Tessa, reaching out to touch one of Jonah's knitted fists, wriggling her pinkie into its center. "Look, he's holding my finger!"

"He likes you," Steph said. Finally, she broke eye contact with the girls and turned back to Abby. "Did you finish that painting? I haven't been able to get it out of my head."

"I did," Abby said. She was about to thank her for asking when panic swept over her as she remembered confiding in them about her pregnancy. It hadn't occurred to her she might see them again, let alone with her family. Steph and Toni had no way of knowing it was a secret. "I'm so sorry, but we're in a bit of a rush. Catch up with you later." She attempted to convey both explanation and apology with a grimace, rolling her eyes in the direction of the twins behind her.

Steph straightened up, looking confused.

Abby lifted her foot off the brake. "Great to see you again." The car lurched forward, crunching shells beneath its wheels.

They sat at a picnic table on the side of Route 6 where yellowjackets swarmed around trash cans and cars sped by, funneling tourists to their destinations. The twins were aghast that Abby ordered a well-done cheeseburger, a breach of half-a-palooza protocol. They'd both ordered their usuals, a vanilla soft serve for Frannie and a banana split for Tessa, but it was so hot—almost 90 degrees in the shade—that the ice cream was turning into soup faster than they could eat it.

"How's it possible that no one's come up with non-melting ice cream?" Tessa asked.

Frannie perked up. "Sounds lucrative."

"You sound like Dad," Tessa said.

"Want to know what my first business idea was?" Abby asked.

"*You* had a business idea?" Frannie said. The girls erupted in laughter.

Abby mimed removing a dagger from her heart.

"You have to admit—" Tessa said.

"Honeysuckle honey," Abby interrupted. "Yes, I planned to make my fortune bottling and selling honeysuckle honey." More laughter. "What's so funny about that?" she asked, smiling.

"Talk about a 'mouse-milking' operation," Tessa said, stealing one of her gramps's favorite lines.

"It's always easy to be a critic." Abby dragged her burger through a blob of ketchup. "The idea was genius!"

"How old were you?" Frannie asked.

Abby thought for a moment. "Eight? Maybe nine?"

Tessa pushed her banana split aside and wrote "honeysuckle honey" in her notebook, the one Abby had given her when she announced her intention to become a poet.

"You have to admit, Aunt Abby, it does sound a bit labor-intensive," Frannie said with a smirk.

"Well, so's harvesting caviar, and yet, people pay hundreds per ounce for that," said Abby.

"And with honeysuckle honey, no animal dies in the process. I'm in," Tessa said, offering Abby her palm for a high-five.

"Reality check, you two. How many droplets to fill a jar?" Frannie asked. "A hundred thousand? A million?"

They made a quick pit stop at the Arcadia to use the bathroom and pick up Frida and supplies—dinner, s'mores makings, a ukulele—and then drove toward Provincetown, parking at an unmarked trailhead. From there, they donned backpacks, kicked off their flip-flops, and followed Frida up a giant hill of sand. At the top was an alien, wind-swept landscape, which looked like the earth was trying to imitate the sea, with miles of dunes cresting and falling like waves. There were oases of vegetation in the troughs—patches of scrub oak, bayberry bushes, even a few cranberry bogs—and tall ridges of sand covered in dune grasses. They'd entered the Peaked Hill Bars Historic District, 1,960 acres of preserved shoreline where, for as far as the eye could see, there was a corrugated pattern of green, khaki, and blue.

The girls ran down the steep slope, arms wheeling, and waited for Abby at the bottom. From there, they heel-toed through the soft sand, following a path bordered by wild roses, poison ivy, and wormwood, with Frida in the lead, pink tongue lolling. The sun felt hot on her shoulders and Abby silently acknowledged the Wampanoag tribe who'd roamed Cape Cod for thousands of years before the Europeans arrived, back when this barren landscape was a thriving, deep-rooted forest before settlers cleared the trees for firewood and to farm, creating the first of many ecological disasters. Lost in the surround sound of the ocean, Abby watched gulls pass lazily overhead and swallows turn and shift in concert.

Soon the dune shacks started appearing, nineteen in total, some nestled against the sides of bluffs, others standing atop hills of sand, others half-buried in drifts, all with a rich history, collective and individual. The original huts, lifesaving sheds designed to provide emergency shelter to survivors of shipwrecks, were long gone, having tumbled off dune cliffs and been dragged into the ocean, destroyed by storms, or long buried beneath shifting sands. The "new" shacks, built in the 1920s and '30s, were designed to surf the dunes and constructed on pilings to float like wharves over the sand. Some were made from driftwood, others recycled from flotsam left by the abundant shipwrecks.

Each shack had a distinctive character, but all were ramshackle, weathered, and without electricity or indoor plumbing. In the five years that Abby had been taking Frannie and Tessa to the dunes for their half-birthday, they'd never stayed in the same hut twice. This year, their cabin was a shingled, one-room box with a slanted roof, built behind a barrier dune. The cottage had a driftwood fence, a solar shower, an outdoor privy, and a hand-painted sign that read: STANDING SINCE 1931. Tessa dropped her backpack, opened her arms, and spun around, taking in 360 degrees of pristine dunes and ocean. Frannie hoisted aside a weathered log propped against the door to hold it shut, and Abby lifted the cloth covering that protected the lock from sand and turned the key. They pulled the door open and peered in: bunk beds, a wood stove, a compact kitchen with a propane two-burner cooktop and fridge, and a small table with mismatched wood chairs. Heaven.

After unloading their gear, setting up camp, and taking a dip in the ocean, they gorged on shrimp kabobs cooked over a small fire. It had been a near-perfect day and Abby was exhausted from all the exertion.

"Mom told us you're making a special painting for Gramps for his birthday," Tessa said.

Abby wondered what exactly Jenny had told them. "Yes, I am," she said. "You know, seventy is a big deal. Have you guys got a gift in mind?"

"It's over a month away!" Frannie said.

"That's not a lot of time. Let's brainstorm," Abby said. "You want to make something for him at the studio?"

"And compete with our famous aunt?" Frannie said.

"No way," Tessa agreed.

"Then what?" Abby asked.

"How about we write a song?" Tessa suggested.

"I love that idea," said Abby. "Frannie?"

Frannie mulled over the idea. "How about to the tune of something we know, like 'Shake It Off'? That's catchy."

"Not Taylor Swift," Tessa said. "Lame."

Abby said, "It might be better to pick a tune that your gramps and his friends would know."

"What would that be?" asked Frannie. "Bing Crosby? Frank Sinatra?"

Abby laughed. "The Stones or the Beatles would probably do the trick. Just something familiar to everyone."

"What about 'Hey Jude'?" Tessa suggested.

"That works," Frannie said, nodding. "But what rhymes with 'cetologist'?"

Abby reached for Tessa's notebook. "Do you mind?" she asked, taking the pad. "You two free-associate. I'll write down your ideas. Don't overthink. Just close your eyes and be Gramps."

"Don't tell me what to do," said Tessa, imitating her grandfather's gruff voice.

"It was a joke! Can't you take a joke?" said Frannie.

"Have I ever told you about the time . . ." said Tessa.

Frannie laughed. "We just found our refrain!"

The fire crackled, smoke curling upward.

"Keep going," Abby encouraged. "Just say whatever pops into your head . . . We'll make it pretty later."

"Return addresses are for fools," Frannie said with bluster. "Who but an idiot wants something they send to come back?"

Abby smiled, scribbling down the words as soon as they left Frannie's and Tessa's mouths.

The twins had found their groove.

"I only swim in no-swim zones."

"Drive against traffic."

"How about a smile, pretty lady?"

"Enough about you . . ."

"I gave that idiot a piece of my mind."

"No-neck monster."

"Cro-Magnon."

"Kids today."

Then they looked at each other, having one of those twin moments where their minds melded. Together they shouted, "Women!"

"Whoa, girls," Abby interrupted. "This is great. But maybe we need to sprinkle in some of Gramps's good points."

They sat listening to the hissing of the wood, mesmerized by hot ribbons of light.

"How about this," Frannie offered, "Gramps is never boring. That's a compliment!"

"Really?" Tessa said, incredulous. "Do you think Gramps would want us to go easy on him? He never goes soft on us, and we're children."

Tessa was right, Abby thought, considering her father's vague contempt for women. Yes, it was a generational thing, but that didn't make it less annoying. The guy was still towing the Bernie Sanders line, even as Hillary was the presumptive nominee. She knew he'd vote for her in the end, but the idea that he could only get behind a woman reluctantly irritated her. "I hear you," Abby said. "But maybe we should take the high road anyway. It's a special occasion. Let's roast him, then toast him. Bring him down, then lift him up."

"Gramps can dish it out, but he can't take it," Tessa said. "Kind of like Dad."

Abby lay back onto the sand, cupping her head in her hands, trying to figure out a response when Frannie said, "It's why you don't have a boyfriend, right, Aunt Abby? So you don't have to put up with that stuff?"

"Well, there's more to it than just that," Abby said, thinking of David. "But living without having to cater to men's BS is not to be underestimated." She smiled, enjoying being able to take them into her confidence and treat them a bit more like grown-ups.

Tessa skewered a marshmallow and dipped it in and out of the flame, and Abby saw that her niece wasn't going to give her a pass. Tessa leveled her gaze at Abby. "What is the deal with you and Dad, Aunt Abby? Like, really, what's the actual deal?"

July

Ken

"Hi, George," Ken said, taking his place on the sofa.

Ken had canceled three sessions in a row in June, his way of putting George on notice that he, Ken, was calling the shots. He was a busy man, after all, and George needed to understand that. But something had changed in the office since he'd last been here and it bothered Ken that he couldn't figure out what. Everything seemed to be in its usual place, same old throw pillows, Kleenex boxes, lamps. He studied George's bookshelves. Interspersed with the classics were *Mating in Captivity, The Power of Habit, I Don't Want to Talk About It*, and other pop-psychology books. George looked unkempt as usual, dark green flecks of nori on the shelf of his belly. Possibly, he'd even put on a few pounds this last month, the buttons on his shirt straining more than usual. *Schlub* was the word that came to mind. The guy had no self-restraint.

Then Ken figured out what had changed. There was a new mask on the wall directly over George's head—primitive, stylized, ugly. Dr. Kunar's taste was reliably bad. The new mask was every bit as hideous as the others, possibly Native American, with a human-ish face flanked on either side by snakes. Strands of sinew hung down and Ken deduced it had moveable parts and that the snake panels could be pulled together.

"It's good to see you, Ken," George said. "I've missed you."

Missed me? What an awkward thing for a guy to say. Ken cleared his throat. *More like you've missed my checks*, he thought. "Sure thing. It's good to see you, too."

"Obviously, it would be ideal if we could stick to our weekly schedule"—and here, George paused to give Ken a chance to respond, which he chose not to do—"but if this is the way we're going to proceed, let's get straight down to business."

"Music to my ears," Ken said, smiling.

George didn't smile back. "As you know, in my practice, I focus exclusively on men," he said.

Had Ken known this? He didn't think so. When he and Jenny agreed to go the therapy route, Jenny's analyst had recommended Dr. Kunar, and when Ken Googled the guy and saw that Kunar checked out as one of Boston's best psychoanalysts, he set up an appointment without further research. Box checked.

"Here's what I know from twenty-five years of practice. For men, shame is the invisible twin to childhood trauma. It's deeply rooted in the male psyche, part of the legacy of the patriarchy, and, from everything you've told me, embedded in your family's pathology. A pathology, I might add, that has likely rolled from generation to generation," George said. "So, let's start there. Are you going to be the guy with the courage to stop the pattern and spare your children? Or the guy who sleepwalks through life and repeats his ancestors' mistakes?"

Where did beta George go? Ken bristled at the summary. He was sick and tired of all social ills being blamed on what had been the ruling order for centuries. Ken hadn't invented the patriarchy. It wasn't his fault that the world's leading scientists, CEOs, and politicians were—and had always been—white men. Moreover, it didn't make them monsters. He heard enough of this cavalier patriarchy crap from the women in his life; he didn't need it from his shrink, too.

"George, you're making sweeping generalizations that I don't agree with. There's no way I'm going to assume responsibility for all of history, so how about you rephrase your question."

"Okay," George said, tenting his fingers. "How about this—would you agree that there's a direct connection between childhood trauma and shame?"

"Define *shame*."

"Contempt turned inward," George said, "and the hallmark of a certain toxic masculinity."

Ken considered how his father plunged into shame after each manic episode.

"The flip side of which is grandiosity," George continued. "Contempt turned outward."

Okay, maybe George had a point. Ken's father was nothing if not grandiose, the hero of every story—always saving the day, righting wrongs, speaking truth to power. Ken wasn't used to agreeing with George, but today, his therapist seemed to be nailing it when it came to his self-righteous father.

"What I'm getting at is it's a tough time to be a man," George said sympathetically. "The rules are changing on us fast, right? Women are speaking up, making demands, wanting to be heard."

Even as Ken sensed a trap being set, he found himself nodding. Amen. It was an undeniably terrible time to be a man. George was making perfect sense for a change.

"And we men are being forced to reckon with how we've subjugated women to maintain our power."

What the hell. How had the conversation veered back into this territory?

"It's like a cozy blanket of denial has been ripped off of us, exposing our nakedness and shame," George continued, nodding as if they were still in agreement. "And I imagine, Ken, that the part of you who is a father, husband, and brother welcomes this. But it doesn't make it easy, does it?" The therapist's voice was silky. "It's never easy to let go of power and control."

It *was* hard. But had George been suggesting that it was Ken, not his father, who suffered from shame and grandiosity?

"As I see it, there are two competing versions of masculinity: the traditional one, which values power; the more powerful you are, the more manly you are," George continued. "And a more progressive version, which is collaborative and values vulnerability."

"Dare I hazard a guess as to which one you think is best?" Ken said.

George chuckled. "Guilty as charged. I throw any convention of therapist neutrality out the window on this subject matter." He leaned toward Ken, and Ken worried that he might reach for his hand. "The new version of masculinity is healthier in every way. Ken, you might not consider what you do online as infidelity, but Jenny does. You do it with impunity simply because you can. Grandiosity has always been the master narrative of your relationship."

George *was* talking about him.

"You wanted me to get to the point quicker," George continued. "Well, here goes. If you want your marriage to work, you've got to stop acting out and shutting down. You must investigate the unresolved pain behind your actions, which is causing you to look for comfort outside of your marriage."

Ken felt suddenly hot.

"Ken, this is a safe place. Think about what caused you the most shame as a kid."

Being fat. Feeling lonely. Missing his mom. Needing Abby more than she needed him. Being rejected by her. His stepmother Gretchen's accusations and judgment. Never being able to get his father's full attention. Ken pulled at his collar.

"Ken, you have the power to choose to use your adult brain. As a child, things were out of your control. But as an adult, you can connect with Jenny and everyone else in your life—business partners to friends to your children—with patience and love."

Time to take the reins. "Patience and love are not how successful people accomplish things in business." Ken thought of Steve Jobs, Mark Zuckerberg, Jeff Bezos, Bill Gates. "I defy you to name a patient and loving billionaire." The masks on the wall seemed to be frowning at Ken for his evasions. Screw them.

To his surprise, George threw up his hands. "Ken, would you agree that from an early age most boys are discouraged from being emotional and empathic?"

So, George had a little fight left in him. Ken nodded with a small smile. He'd give him that.

"We celebrate the alpha male, right?" George said.

Nothing wrong with alpha males, Ken thought and nodded again.

"What are you so scared of?" George asked, leveling his gaze at Ken. "You have nothing to lose. Nothing you say in this room will ever leave.

So why not take a chance and tell me about your pain? What do you get in that chat room that your wife can't give you?"

Was George actually growing a pair? Maybe his shrink should be paying him.

"Since we've missed three weeks, I'm going to synopsize here," George said. "You lost your mother tragically when you were three and a half years old, which I imagine felt like profound abandonment. On his best day, your father was not emotionally available. On his worst, he was out of his mind. He got married twice while you were young, and both those marriages failed. More abandonment. So, you turned to your sister." Here George paused, an idea forming. "Is it possible you relied on her too much?"

Ken felt a prickle behind his eyes.

"Maybe you turned Abby into a mother figure. Or . . . maybe something else?" George was fishing. "For sure, you needed love. And none of this was your fault; you were a kid. Childhood is all about survival, and you did what it took to survive."

George stated these hunches as facts, as if he were reciting the periodic table. Where was all of this coming from?

"At some point, your needs and expectations became too much for your sister." George sat up tall, a meaty hand on each thigh. "And that's when she disappointed you, too? By withdrawing her love and taking up with your best friend, David?"

Silence.

"Am I getting close?"

More silence.

"Female abandonment is a dominant pattern in your life." George sat back. "Do I have this mostly right?"

Ken sat frozen, the hairs on the back of his neck individuating and standing up. He concentrated on the equation for mortgage payments, an old trick he used when he didn't want to come too soon during sex.

George seemed to accept that Ken wasn't ready to speak. "Ken, you've read Steinbeck, right?" he asked. "*East of Eden*, *The Grapes of Wrath* . . ."

"Of course I have," Ken said, but in truth, he hadn't read much fiction since college, and those guys—Steinbeck, Hemingway, Faulkner—all kind of blurred together. He preferred nonfiction like Malcolm Gladwell and Michael Lewis.

"Steinbeck called rejection the hell of fears." George closed his eyes and recited: "'And with rejection comes anger, and with anger some kind of crime in revenge for the rejection, and with the crime guilt—and there is the story of mankind.' If you haven't read *East of Eden* recently, I think it might resonate."

Ken dimly recalled the book from tenth grade. What did this have to do with anything? He was not in therapy for a damn literature class.

"I'll bring it up with my book club," Ken said. "Personally, I'm more the Hemingway type. Give me a bullfight any day." He felt proud to have pulled this literary tidbit from the recesses of his mind, but George did not look impressed. Ken reminded himself he could cancel his next session. Hell, he didn't need to return ever if he didn't want to. "How about you finally answer my questions about the masks," Ken said. "I've been waiting with an abundance of—how did you put it?—'love and patience' for an explanation."

George exhaled in audible frustration and reached into the drawer of the side table to his left, withdrawing what looked like one of Frannie's lip glosses, the kind with a rollerball on top. He glided it over the inside of one wrist and rubbed the other wrist against it. He brought his palms to his face and inhaled.

Ken smelled the lavender essential oil from three feet away. Good grief.

"You want to know about the masks? I'll tell you about the masks," George said, rising, seaweed crumbs drifting to the floor. He lifted the new one from its hook on the wall. "My collection is composed of what are known as transformation masks because, to state the obvious, they turn into something else." George demonstrated, folding the moving parts together into the closed position, which turned the mask into a fierce eagle that looked like the Seattle Seahawks logo. Then George placed the contraption over his head.

Jesus. Were there no rules in therapists' offices? No best practices? This guy's license should be revoked. Ken shifted on the sofa.

"We all put on masks from time to time, Ken. It's called self-preservation," George said. "You had to wear one after your mother's death. Brave boy. You were dealing with stuff no kid should ever have to deal with." His voice fairly dripped with compassion. "You had to project an image of strength while everything that made you feel safe and secure vanished."

A lump formed in Ken's throat, making it impossible to swallow or speak.

"But the question you must ask yourself is: How well is your mask working for you now? Protection can exact a steep price."

Ken's armor had served him well. His hyper-vigilance—a strict diet and exercise regimen, attending Sunday services, and never having more than three drinks—was what made him who he was. He'd been able to show the Danny McCormicks of the world just how wrong they'd been about him.

George continued, "Hiding your feelings doesn't signify a mastery of them."

"Presenting a strong exterior hasn't failed me yet," Ken countered.

"Are you sure?" asked George, his voice muffled beneath the mask. "I think you're wrong, Ken. I think if you don't remove your mask soon, it will fuse to your face, and you'll never be able to feel deeply. Not only pain but also joy."

Ken's smile deserted him. What was so great about feeling pain? Not feeling it had been working just fine for him.

Then George pulled the cord and the eagle's face and beak split down the middle, revealing the interior. "It's what we're meant to do, Ken," he said. "Transform."

The primitive features reminded Ken of the monsters in *Where the Wild Things Are*. Then he heard his mother, clear as a bell, speaking into his ear. "Kenny, you're just a boy, pretending to be a wolf, pretending to be a king."

Ken glanced at the digital clock. Thank God, their session was just about over.

George took the mask off and placed it gently on the floor beside him. "Ken," he said, and waited to continue until he had Ken's full attention.

"You're making progress, even if it doesn't seem that way. You can count on me. That's what I'm here for."

Ken wasn't buying it; therapy was paid friendship.

But George held his gaze. "I want to remind you that you can call me in between appointments if you ever need to talk."

Had Ken been paying for some special concierge treatment he didn't know about?

"I'm dead serious, Ken—you call me *anytime*, day or night."

As if, thought Ken. "Sure thing, George," he said.

Steph

The lobsters, dozens and dozens of them, were three deep in shallow basins that ran half the length of the Provincetown fish store. Steph peered into the tanks and watched them crawl over one another on jointed legs, brandishing banded claws and staring up on stalked, black eyes, like giant sea insects.

"Four one-and-a-half-pounders, please. Females with hard shells," Steph said. She knew what to look for. "I'll also need two pounds each of mussels, littlenecks, steamers, and oysters."

Serving her was the quintessential Cape Cod teenager, a spray of freckles across his nose and cheeks, and a flop of salt-separated hair in his eye. "Beach or pot clambake?" he asked, reaching into the water and pulling out a glistening lobster, claws hanging down. Before Steph had the chance to veto the selection—its stubby antenna indicated it had been in the tank too long—he released it back into the basin and searched for another.

"It's not a real clambake if it's cooked in a pot," she answered.

The kid lined up four good-looking females on the counter, their swimmeret legs clicking against the tiles. Steph squeezed their sides and checked the color of their underbodies. Satisfied, she handed over her credit card and watched him bag the beasts.

For as long as she and Toni had been vacationing in Provincetown, Steph put on this annual clambake to celebrate her parents' arrival. And every summer, she swore it would be her last. Clambakes required more strength than talent. They were physically demanding events in the best of circumstances, and July—with its heat and humidity—was far from ideal. Steph preferred preparing fiddly dishes that could curdle or fall and showed off her skills. Any brute with a shovel could dig a hole. Still, it was a crowd-pleaser.

Their rental cottage was just yards from the bay beach where, earlier in the day, Steph had dug the pit, using the backside of the shovel to pack the sand and create solid walls. She lined the hole with a layer of softball-size rocks and arranged logs in the shape of a teepee over the stones. She set two bags of charcoal—frowned upon by true bake masters—off to the side as a precautionary measure in case the logs were damp.

In the afternoon, she lit the fire. It would take several hours for the rocks to get red hot. In the meantime, she made herb butter with garlic, fresh basil, and thyme; washed and scrubbed the clams and potatoes; partially shucked the corn to remove the interior silk, repackaging each ear in its husk; gathered an enormous pile of wet seaweed, the green-brown stuff called bladder wrack, and lugged up two large bucketfuls of saltwater, which she left next to the fire. When the wood had turned to coal, Steph raked the red-hot chunks evenly over the rocks, set cinderblocks in each corner, and balanced a grate over them. Now came the fun part, layering the ingredients: seaweed, potatoes; seaweed, corn; seaweed, linguiça; seaweed, lobsters; seaweed, clams; followed by a final layer of wet seaweed. She nestled an egg discreetly in a corner, a foolproof way to time the meal. Then she spread a canvas tarp over the bake.

Soon enough, the seaweed was hissing and popping, and Steph found herself wondering, of all inane things, if lobsters felt pain. What the fuck? She'd never been squeamish, especially not when it came to food. Her favorite meals involved innocent ducklings and lambs. She'd never felt even an iota of guilt at the thought of force-feeding geese—foie gras seemed worth it. Motherhood must be making her soft.

She distracted herself by arranging the picnic: unfolding chairs, spreading out the blanket, and weighting down napkins and disposable lobster plates with smooth stones. She brought out the necessary tools—nutcrackers, kitchen shears, cocktail forks, a cleaver, and a shucking knife for the oysters—and stood them upright in a bucket. She'd already made cocktail sauce, spicy with freshly grated horseradish, and coleslaw with her signature vinaigrette dressing; the lemons were sliced; the Portuguese rolls were in a basket draped with a kitchen towel; and six citronella candles were at the ready. Everything was set, and yet, Steph couldn't shake the feeling that something wasn't right.

If the lobsters weren't dead by now, they would be soon, she thought, staring into the blurry heat. She doused the bake with a few ladles of seawater, creating a briny burst. She peeked under the canvas and leaped back at the sight of a red claw poking out from the seaweed, a lobster's attempt at escape. A baby cried. Was it Jonah? No. A bottle rocket went off. Jesus. Steph didn't know why her nerves were frayed.

When Michael and Mary Beth arrived at the cottage, they went straight to their grandson, whom they hadn't seen for five weeks. Steph watched from the kitchen.

"Just look at how big you are, Jo-Jo," her mother said to Jonah, who sat in a portable baby seat on the table, the backside of his fist stuffed improbably into his mouth. "Such a big boy. And you've discovered your hands, haven't you? Are they yummy?"

Her dad nudged his pointer finger at his grandson, who reached for it with a saliva-coated hand. "Hey, little man," he said. "How do you like the Cape?"

"Hi, Dad," Steph said, entering quietly.

"Hi, hon," he answered.

There was new pink skin behind her father's ear, a sign of a recent haircut, and for some reason, that small detail on this kind and decent man made Steph yearn for her previous life—when she believed her parents' marriage was perfect, and didn't consider a lobster's pain.

"How about a drink?" Toni said, already getting their usuals, a can of beer for Michael and a glass of chardonnay for Mary Beth.

With refreshments in hand, they moved out to the beach, Jonah in a sling across Toni's chest. They sat on beach chairs arranged in a straight line, looking out at the water, coppered now by the late-afternoon sun. The bay was full of ambient sounds—waves roiling pebbles, gulls wailing, families packing up to go home. As often happened at dusk, a fracas erupted offshore—bluefish, crazed with hunger, thrashed and arced open-mouthed, having corralled a school of bunkers to the surface. Overhead, terns screamed, diving into the fray to collect the spoils. The chaotic pattern slid across the bay and then stopped as abruptly as it had started.

In the distance, Steph saw a plume, a small puff on the horizon. She stood, shaded her face, and squinted into the sun, scanning the horizon. Could it have been a humpback? She recalled Adam Gardner's description of these intelligent and empathetic mammals and longed to see one. In his enthusiasm to impart their majesty to her, he'd drawn something called a "bubble net" on his cocktail napkin, a spiral of circles rising to the surface of the water. Later, she found a video of the phenomenon on the Internet where a pod of whales, working in concert, exhaled giant bubbles that created an aerated cylindrical wall, encircling enormous schools of fish and krill. The whales emitted high-pitched cries that reminded Steph of piglets squealing, disorienting their soon-to-be supper. Then they shot up through the bubble tunnel, enormous mouths open and throats expanding like accordion bellows, swallowing everything in their path. Steph had never seen anything like it. Adam told her that humpbacks consumed up to three thousand pounds of food a day.

"What are you staring at?" her mother asked. "Steph?"

Steph continued to scan the horizon. "I think I just saw a blow."

"A what?"

"A blow. A spout," Steph said, glancing at her mother. "You know, whale spray."

Mary Beth's expression changed instantaneously.

"Hey," her dad interrupted. "What's a guy got to do to get another beer around here?"

"Follow me," Steph said, leaving her mother to stew. Steph refused to feel guilty for wanting to know her biological father. On the way to the cooler, she downed her glass of wine. That helped. Toni would be mad that she'd destroyed yet another eight ounces of breast milk, but Steph would do whatever was necessary to get through this night. She retrieved a frigid bottle of Sam Adams for her dad and refilled her wineglass.

"Think the lobbies are ready?" her father asked.

"Let's check," Steph said, grabbing tongs and a pair of fireproof gloves.

With a protected hand, she reached into the seaweed, found the egg, and cracked it open. The yolk was cooked through—the clambake was ready. They rolled the tarp off the pile and were smacked by a pungent wall of briny steam. Steph excavated the lobsters one at a time with the tongs, depositing them on the platter her father held.

"How about a walk after dinner?" he suggested. "Seems like you and I are overdue for a talk."

So, he was opening a door. Steph nodded and looked down.

Her father slung an arm over her shoulder. "Kiddo, you must know that nothing could ever change how I feel about you."

Steph felt a sad sort of relief as she relaxed into the familiarity of him, nuzzling her head against his chest.

"Thanks, Dad. I love you, too."

Later, Steph wouldn't be able to remember much about the meal itself. Not the faintly metallic taste of the oysters or the tearing apart of the lobster before sucking out meat from the claws, or the alternating flavors of salty linguiça followed by sweet corn. The night was a blur, not because of the wine, although she'd had several glasses, but because she wanted it to be over so that she and her father could talk. When at last Toni and her mother left the beach to put Jonah to bed, she and her dad poured seawater over the coals and left on their walk.

She led them in the general direction of the Race Point Lighthouse, named after the deadly crosscurrent that shot along the shore, causing hundreds of shipwrecks over the years. The light on the original tower, built two hundred years earlier, had been fueled by whale oil and could be seen up to nineteen miles away. The new lighthouse, rebuilt and solar-powered, was functional but dimmer.

"The past is the past, kiddo," Michael began. "Your mom regrets what she did and the pain she caused." He went on to tell her that her mother had confessed to Father Mulligan, with whom she was in counseling. He sounded like he was on autopilot. Overhead, fireworks arced and burst into glittery showers, a preview of the next night's show.

The past didn't feel like the past, at least not to Steph. "This is my present, Dad," she said.

"I know it's a lot to process, hon," Michael said. "But the only direction is forward. The future is what's important; that and staying together as a family."

Steph's thoughts were as scattered as the pyrotechnics overhead. "I'm afraid I can't sidestep the present. I'm hurt."

A tidal flat forced them to head inland and walk up and over the dunes. The sky was darkening, and a stripe of silver moonlight shimmered on the bay.

"What good will focusing on the hurt do?" Her father's voice was unbearably gentle. "We need to forgive your mother and move on."

Steph faced her father. "You can't get past pain without going through it," she said, a mantra of Toni's. "It's called denial."

Michael shut his eyes and whispered the Serenity Prayer. "God, grant me the serenity to accept the things I cannot change."

At that, anger hit suddenly, the way the ground came toward you in a falling dream. Couldn't her father ever just take her side? He'd been wronged, too. Yet still, he was going to present a united front with her mother. "Just stop, Dad," Steph said. "I know you've been hurt in all this, too. But I've been cheated out of knowing who I am. It's not fair to ask me to put all this behind me."

Her father's knees gave.

In thirty-eight years, Steph had never seen the man cry. The shiny spot on his skull was bigger than she remembered, and she placed her arm across his back. "Oh, Dad, I'm sorry," she said. "I'm so sorry, but I have to find out who and where I come from."

"I don't want to lose you over this," Michael said, trying to compose himself.

"You're not going to."

"That man . . . he's not your father. I am. I raised you. You're the only daughter I have," he said.

"And nothing will change that. Ever. I promise. I swear." Steph would do almost anything not to hurt him. "But I have a medical history, half-siblings, a whole other family history that I have a right to know about. And Jonah has cousins. You must understand why I want to know him, right?"

"Your 'father'"—he held up air quotes—"is a man who got a teenage girl drunk and took advantage of her while his wife was pregnant," her father said, eyes narrowing. "So, no, Steph. I really don't know why you want to know that man."

Abby

Abby held the rigger brush in her right hand. To most people, an artist's signature was a simple validation of authenticity. But to Abby, it was essential to the whole. Color, placement, size, all of it vital. She liked to surreptitiously incorporate her signature into the work itself, the way that *New Yorker* cartoonist embedded his daughter's name into the fringe of rugs or characters' hair. Her signature needed to complement the painting without drawing undue attention to itself. She had a hard-and-fast rule that once she'd signed and dated a work, she couldn't touch it again. No adding paint. No scraping. No nothing. Abby believed that paintings captured their artist as well as their subjects. To tweak a brushstroke a month or a year later felt dishonest. In this way, her signature was her word.

Now she was just stalling. She'd been worrying over the same corner of canvas all day, studying the lines, the light, the colors, the story. Jenny had deemed it a masterpiece. Her stepmother Gretchen always said that art was a vehicle for truth. "Stop letting yourself be silenced," she'd said on their last phone call, the words ringing a bell inside Abby that had not stopped since. What was she waiting for? Written permission?

"Just sign it already," Abby said aloud, ignoring her phone, which buzzed and buzzed. One of the best things about pregnancy was that you felt less deranged talking to yourself—there was always someone else in the room.

Abby looked at the scene in the lower-right corner, two entangled children, naked, cuddling. She was still holding back, following a path carved by her desire to please others. This painting did not have to be beautiful, but it had to tell the truth and one line was missing, one that few people would understand. Still, the repercussions scared her. Abby had always been an anxious person. As a child, she'd feared the way horseshoe crabs skulked along the shoreline, the character of Aunt Sponge in *James and the Giant Peach*, getting called on in math, and her father's rapid-fire speech and racing thoughts, preludes to his episodes. She reminded herself that she was no longer a frightened little girl. She was stronger now. More settled in her skin. Capable of growing a new life inside of her. But then she pictured Ken's blame-thirsty finger pointing at her—*How dare you, Abby. You promised not to tell*—and her heart raced.

Had what happened between them all those years ago been more his doing than hers? Gretchen certainly thought so. Abby had overheard her stepmother telling her father that he needed to do something about Ken's "inappropriate" behavior, and her father telling Gretchen to mind her own business, that they were just kids. Abby hoped that might be the end of it, but once Gretchen had put the notion out into the world, there was no bringing it back. Ken had heard the hushed arguments, too. Within a few months, Gretchen left their house once and for all. Neither Adam nor Ken had ever mentioned her by name since. Their family was a conspiracy of silence, and anyone who broke the silence should not expect to be forgiven. *Had* Ken been old enough to know better? Had it been his fault? Abby didn't know. He'd been a child at the time, too. Still, why did he get to be both—perpetrator and victim? Why did he get to be the angry one?

Abby turned on the electric kettle and made a deal with herself. Twenty minutes. The time it took for water to boil, tea to steep and become cool enough to enjoy, and not one minute longer. Then she'd paint the line and be done. Soon enough, bubbles jostled furiously against the glass, and Abby took down her favorite mug, pouring water over a tea bag and watching the amber swirl. The mug, pale blue with irregular channels of gold running through it, had been made by Jenny during her *kintsugi* phase, back at RISD. Abby still remembered how furious she'd been when she'd found Jenny hunched over it, having broken it into a half dozen pieces.

"Jenny, what the hell—?" Abby said. The rule was Jenny could destroy her own stuff in the name of art, but Abby's stuff was off-limits.

"Close your eyes! It's supposed to be a surprise!" Jenny shouted, throwing a towel over the pieces. "Trust me, you're going to love it."

"I doubt it," Abby said, slamming the door on her way out.

But when she returned several hours later, her ordinary mug had been transformed into a work of art. Beneath it, a note: *Our scars are what make us unique. Nothing broken is ever lost. Jenny.*

Where was that Jenny now? Abby sighed and went back to confront her painting. Would Ken recognize himself in her art? Probably not. For all she knew, he'd blocked this part of their past from his consciousness altogether. But who else might make the connection? Jenny? Possible, but unlikely—she was too invested in the sunny image of the Gardner family she was propagating to get Ken elected. David? Also possible. He'd witnessed Ken's possessiveness of her when they were children. But David had been a kid, too, so maybe he didn't think anything of it. In all their years as a couple, he'd never mentioned it. Her father? Well, that was the real question, wasn't it? Deep down, Abby wanted her father to know what she'd gone through. But Adam Gardner was the king of denial, and Abby knew that he'd look no further than the central image—Abby pregnant with his grandson—and puff up at the thought of his name and lineage continuing. Likely, this mess of lines would be a head-scratcher for all of them. She just needed to say her piece and get on with it.

She took a deep breath. Her signature, she decided, would be periwinkle, her mother's favorite color and the elusive shade of the sky at dusk. Abby blended blue, white, and red but couldn't achieve the hue she was after. Periwinkle was more a quality of light than a color—bolder than lavender and fainter than purple. Frustrated, she chucked a tube of paint across the studio, where it knocked over a jar of mussel shells, which tinkled and scattered on the floor. A solution came to her. She'd make her own pigment. She used to do it all the time, creating colors from berries, roots, bugs, and whatever else she could find.

Abby grabbed a mallet and towel and a mason jar full of mussels and sank to the floor, where she dumped out the shells. She used a razor to scrape off the outer black membrane and put what remained into the center of the towel, folding it over itself. As she started to smash the mussel shells, Frida cocked her head, her front paws sliding forward until she lay prone.

"It's okay, girl," Abby said. "This is fun."

And it was. Why on earth had she ever stopped making paint this way? The muffled thunk, the satisfying work of pulverization. With each wallop, some bit of anger came loose. Her not owning the Arcadia. *Whack.* All the times she'd felt silenced or smothered. *Whack.* When men told her to smile. *Whack.* The misogynist comments of a certain presidential candidate. *Whack.* "Jailbait," her brother's word. *Whack.* Her father's mood swings and absences. *Whack.* David's marriage. *Whack. Whack. Whack.*

Glistening with sweat, Abby ground the shards with a mortar and pestle until she had a bowl full of opalescent grit, which she sifted twice through a fine screen until it had a powder-like consistency. Then drop by drop, she added linseed oil, blending the mixture into a luminous shade of violet. Now she was ready. She'd been trapped inside this canvas long enough. She kissed one of her mother's serpentine ceramic fragments for courage, then dipped the rigger brush into the pigment and in tight, cursive letters formed her signature, using the base of her middle initial, E—for Emily, after her mother—to create a bean-shaped splotch across the upper-left buttock of the boy in the scene. Then, all at once, the title came to her: *Little Monster*.

"Hey, Sleeping Beauty." A gentle voice followed by rapping.

Abby started.

"Sorry," David said, "but I texted you a dozen times this morning, letting you know that I was free."

She blinked David into focus on the other side of the screen door, squatting and pressing his hand to Frida's nose, mumbling sweet nothings to her dog, whose tail wagged ecstatically. Behind him, monarch butterflies danced around the milkweed. A bright column of particle-filled light. The throb of Lou Reed. A piece of ceramic squeezed in her fist. What time was it? Abby rubbed her eyes, swung her legs off the sofa, and got to her feet.

"Since when do you knock?" she asked as she crossed the room, tossing a cloth over the painting.

"Since when do you nap?" David said.

They embraced in the unhurried manner of people who'd loved each other their whole lives. Abby leaned into the warm bulk of him, waiting for their breath to synchronize. The baby fluttered inside her, and she lost her bearings in the entwinement, worried that her news might change everything.

David pulled back to take her in. "Rebecca and Peony went to Martha's Vineyard for the day," he said, tucking a strand of strawberry hair behind her ear. "So, we can have the whole afternoon to ourselves." He started kissing her neck.

She felt her body start to respond and placed her palms on David's chest. "Hey, slow down, sailor." He was going to find out about it, sooner or later, but later might be better. *If* Abby did decide to tell him that he was the father, she'd let him know that she expected nothing. Nothing. She'd raise the baby alone and never breathe a word. Oh shit. Of course she needed to tell him.

"I need to talk to you about something, David."

"Me first," he interrupted.

"But—"

"Please, Abby," David said. "I don't want to lose my nerve."

Abby's heart started to sink; it sounded ominous. She led them to the sofa, reminding herself that David was married, and she could do this alone. She sat and placed her hands in her lap, preparing herself for what was to come.

"I'm leaving Rebecca," he said.

Not what she was expecting.

"I know I've said it before, but this time is different." David touched her cheek and allowed his finger to trace down her neck. "And before you start blaming yourself, I need for you to know that you are not the reason . . . Or not the *only* reason . . . Or not the—" Whatever script David was trying to follow was eluding him.

David was going to leave Rebecca. Did she even want that?

He began again. "Abby, I love you. I've always loved you. Please keep waiting for me, just a little while longer."

Is that what he thought she was doing, *waiting for him*? "What's changed?" she asked.

"A lot of things and nothing. We fight constantly. Rebecca deserves better than what I'm giving her."

Rebecca did deserve better, Abby thought. *And so did David.*

David took both of Abby's hands in his. "I've stayed in this marriage as long as I have because of Peony, and Peony's going to be fine."

When Abby tried to speak, David put a finger to her lips. And then kissed where his finger had been. "The marriage is over," he said with finality.

Abby considered this. "Does Rebecca know it's over?"

"Deep down, yes, I think so," David said.

Deep down. Rebecca probably didn't have the first clue.

"What?" David asked.

Abby's thoughts wouldn't organize. It felt as if a dam had burst and was causing everything, the good and the bad, to pile up like wreckage along the shore.

He reached for Abby's hand. "Tell me what you're thinking."

Abby hesitated. She didn't want to place a thumb on the scale or muddy his convictions. David needed to do whatever he was going to do with Rebecca on his terms, not because of this pregnancy. The baby, who'd been fluttering since David knocked on the door—insisting his presence be felt—stilled. "Nothing, David. It can wait."

"Well, I'm not sure I can," he said, and resumed kissing her, but Abby pushed him away gently. "Your timing is off, as usual. Jenny will be over any minute," she lied.

David sank back, disappointed.

"Soon," Abby promised, noticing for the first time that his dark hair was flecked with gray at the temples.

Adam

When it came right down to it, what did Adam Gardner really need an office for? The answer: *Not a thing, not a goddamn thing.* If the CCIO wanted to free up space for some ass-kissing, grant-grubbing, up-and-coming scientist, well, good fucking riddance. They could have his corner office. Adam's work took place in the vast ocean of his mind, not in some rectangle of glass and concrete. He was not a paper shuffler. He was a genius whose job it was to contemplate the boundless wonders of the deep, soar along the silent floor of the sea, and listen to what the whales were telling him. He didn't need this meager workstation and he certainly didn't need the bullshit that went with it.

With that, Adam got busy dismantling forty-five years of professional life, tossing old files and press clippings into an industrial-size waste receptacle placed in his office for just this purpose. He took care with the items he deemed valuable, acknowledging those books, trophies, photographs, and other memorabilia that "sparked joy" before boxing them up. Once again, Adam marveled at his liberated mind's access to facts. He couldn't recall ever having read Marie Kondo, and yet . . .

Adam started with the shelf that held his collection of shore and seafloor treasures, moving methodically from left to right. First, his queen conch—a marine gastropod mollusk from the family of *Strombus gigas*—with its lustrous orange-pink cleft. This shell had set Adam on his pelagic path. He'd been eight, on a family vacation in the Florida Keys, when he found it in less than a foot of azure water. His father had put the shell to Adam's ear, where Adam heard the circular sounds of waves breaking, somehow embedded in its spiral. "Who is the shell calling?" he'd asked his father, convinced that the conch was a telephone of sorts. The innocent question became family lore. His father set him straight right away, explaining that what sounded like the ocean was the murmuration of his pulse in his ear. Intellectually, Adam understood this, then and now, but part of him had never stopped wondering who the shell was calling. Adam placed the conch in a box.

Next, his most valuable treasure, a football-sized chunk of ambergris—taken from the old French *ambre gris*, meaning "gray amber." Ambergris sold for north of $10,000 a pound and this nugget weighed just shy of three pounds. He and Emily had found the egg-shaped lump on their honeymoon, along the rugged coast of Cornwall, and joked that it would be their retirement plan. Most people thought ambergris was whale vomit, but it usually came out the other end, fecal debris. Sperm whales, whose diet consisted largely of squid, were the producers of the unlikely substance, which was composed mostly of squid beaks and other indigestible bits. He and Emily deemed the find a harbinger of good things to come. Adam put his nose to the ambergris and inhaled deeply. The scent had diminished over the decades but was still there with hints of cigars, horse stables, and damp seaweed—sweet, musky smells that reminded him of sex. *Focus*, Adam reminded himself. He didn't need a boner right now. He swaddled the ambergris in bubble wrap and lay it in the box alongside the conch.

The next keepsake on the shelf was a dried seahorse, what the ancient Greeks called hippocampus, "half-horse, half-fish," and the only one of Adam's specimens not found by him personally. This seahorse, about four inches long, had been part of a goodie bag from a benefit for the New England Aquarium eons ago. *Imagine the public outcry if the New England Aquarium tried to pull a stunt like that today*, Adam thought. He flipped the translucent, bony-plated body over in his hands, admiring its trumpet snout, pouched torso, and coiled tail in the shape of a question mark—yet another example of a mysterious spiral. No surprise that these creatures were considered mythological, pulling Poseidon's golden chariot, etc. They were unlike any other fish. But should Adam hang on to this memento? He'd kept it as a reminder of his greatest regret, a drunken night almost four decades ago, the only time he'd cheated on Emily. And even though he knew the infidelity and his wife's death were unrelated, his brain had fused the two events. The real kicker, symbolically speaking, was that seahorses—unlike most other fish—are monogamous and mate for life and are among the only species on earth in which the male bears the unborn young. For thirty-eight years, this little fucker had been reminding him of his betrayal. *No more!* He crushed the equine body in his palm and poured the chunks into the garbage.

Adam needed to speed up this packing operation. He considered confronting his desk, a mess of paperwork. That was something he'd miss, administrative support. Though it hadn't been the same since Debbie left fifteen years ago. Instead, he lifted a black-framed photo off the wall, a picture of him free-diving in a wetsuit, arcing away from a humpback and her calf. What a privilege it had been to witness their sentience up close. Next, a triptych of shots taken a year apart, the stages of a whale fall on the seafloor—leviathan transformed into garden. The flesh was the first thing to go, followed by the fat-filled bones, which could support a bonanza of marine organisms for decades after the death. Oh, to witness those extreme abyssopelagic ecosystems that existed in permanent darkness, in depths beyond diurnal time, where life took hold despite conditions that scientists used to insist made life impossible. Adam knew that the biological communities that arose from this one whale corpse would outlast him. Hell, all sorts of unknown life might emanate from it. The deep seafloor could be a source of new species, he felt sure of it. This was not an ending; it was a beginning! He looked forward to the day that the CCIO regretted foisting retirement upon him. Adam wrapped the photographs in a protective armor of bubble wrap, standing them on their sides in a tidy row.

What else would he miss? Not a thing. Not a goddam thing. But just then, a pod of young biologists slowed as they walked past his office, speaking in hushed tones. Okay, Adam could admit it . . . he'd miss the stealthy glances of fledgling scientists at the precise moment of recognition, their faces upturned in awe: *Was that* the *Adam Gardner?* Adam turned a turtle-shaped pinch pot over in his hand, paper clips falling out of it in the process, tinkling as they scattered onto the floor. Carved into the back was an inscription: *Ken, 1984.* His son's rendering of Charon.

Oh, how Kenny had loved that old snapper. A keeper. He dropped the vessel into a box loaded with knickknacks and small mementos.

A rap on the glass and a wave. It was Stanley, one of the few colleagues who'd been around for as long as he had. Adam guessed he'd also miss this kind of impromptu encounter, an opportunity to reminisce about the good old days. He waved Stanley in and handed him a Xerox of the invitation to his birthday bash, which Jenny had illustrated and designed herself. He'd handed out quite a few of these today and worried momentarily that he was supposed to be keeping track. Too late now . . .

"Hope you and Maggie can make it," Adam said.

His friend gave a low whistle. "Seventy," Stanley said, admiring the line drawing, Adam riding a whale into the sunset on the open ocean. "How'd we get this old?"

"Seventy is *not* old," Adam said, bristling. He thought of the way Ken had suggested he move out of his beautiful home in the Wellfleet Woods and into something more sensible. "Time to downsize, Dad. You want to stay ahead of the curve," his son said, pointing out the challenges that would arise once he could no longer drive. As if *that* was inevitable. Adam knew the stories about kids making deals with local police departments to have car keys removed from their elderly parents. *Cowards!* "You know you can't stay in this house forever," his son had informed him. "Uneven floorboards. Narrow steps to every room. It's not sensible." Adam knew enough to play it cool, nodding as if considering solid advice. *Well, guess what, Ken?* He did have a plan. The plan was to leave his home in a pine box.

"'Old' is relative, I guess. Maggie and I'll be there," Stanley said, giving him an awkward back pat before retreating from the office.

Adam was almost finished. He swept his arm across the desk, shoving all the paperwork into a box. All that was left was the eight-by-ten framed family picture that had graced his desk for close to four decades—Emily, Kenny, and him on the beach, Abby inside her mother's belly. If Adam had only known how little time they had left together. It bothered him that he couldn't remember who'd snapped this picture, catching such an intimate family moment. He felt choked up at the sight of it—him, looking adoringly at Emily; Emily, looking adoringly at their son; Kenny, looking adoringly at his mother's belly, all of which made Adam draw the obvious conclusion that his unborn child was looking adoringly at him through the walls of her mother's womb. In Hebrew, the name Abigail meant "father's joy" or "cause of joy." Was that true? Adam Googled it. *Correct, again!* When his children were young, he'd made copies of this photo for them, and felt gratified that they both still displayed the picture prominently in their homes. If there was one thing Adam had done right, he'd kept Emily's memory alive, telling his children stories about their perfect marriage, their extraordinary love. Then the image of that young woman at the New England Aquarium gala intruded into his thoughts, her dress pulled up, hair across her face. That memory had become as persistent as a terrier lately, which didn't seem fair. He'd had one indiscretion. One! He shoved the family portrait in between some books and sealed the box.

When it was all done, Adam sank into his formidable office chair. It was the kind of chair that conveyed a certain privilege, like a king's throne or the seat at the head of a long table. Yes, he would enjoy it one last time, occupying his rightful place on his impressive chair in his impressive office. But his mind bounced again, this time landing on van Gogh's infinitely sad and iconic painting of an empty yellow chair. Van Gogh was absent, just as Adam would soon be absent. Had Vincent chopped off his ear by the time of this painting? Adam didn't think so. *Goodbye, chair,* he thought. *Thank you for your service.* What was up with all this nostalgic crap? It was a chair.

Do you know what he wouldn't miss? The relentless meetings, the petty politics, the race for professional advancement, and the emphasis on grant getting. Sometime over the last decade, there'd been a shift in priorities. No one cared about the past or wanted to hear Adam's stories. Gone were the days of discussing the wonders of the deep. What mattered now was productivity, the efficient use of time, and how to quantify those things, which as far as Adam could tell came down to citation tracking, the scientific equivalent of being popular. *Good riddance, lemmings!* What had happened to scientific observation, serious contemplation, and the meticulous construction of theories? That was where discovery took place, in the fertile froth of churning ideas. Sadly, this notion was beyond the grasp of the CCIO's head honchos. Contemplation didn't pay the bills and that's what it came down to. Adam had been given an ultimatum a few years back. If he wanted to keep his corner office, research assistants, coveted parking spot, and other privileges . . . well, he needed to contribute just like the rest of them.

Adam had given it the old college try. But once scientists were tasked with making money, it was a slippery slope; lines blurred. Churning out papers and applying for grants were activities that fed on themselves, a serpent eating its own tail. Above all, Adam prided himself on his integrity and scientific rigor. Flattering wealthy donors, writing recommendations for their lackluster relatives, producing report after report for family foundations—all of it, a waste of his time. Had Adam wanted to be a nonprofit executive, he'd have studied accounting, not biology.

And don't even get him started on all the crap around white male privilege in science. Ridiculous. How many marine biologists could boast the kind of professional success he'd had? Zero, that's how many. And now Adam was supposed to accept that his successes were somehow based on the oppression of others. Bah!

Finally, Adam's office was bare, no books on the shelves, no photos or plaques on the walls, nothing remaining in his desk drawers. It took only two trips with the dolly to get his entire professional life into his car, and this thought made him want to cry. No, he would not cry, absolutely not. Adam turned the key, slung an arm over the passenger seat headrest, and backed out of his reserved parking spot for the last time.

He would show them.

Jenny

Perched on a tall stool at the kitchen counter, Jenny squinted at her open laptop, finding her emails impossible to read, the computer screen bathed in so much morning light. A first-world problem if ever there was one. She inhaled the aroma of freshly brewed coffee, the smell that separated night from morning, and enjoyed a tranquil moment: the girls still asleep, Ken in Command Central, and Jenny headache free for the first time in weeks thanks to a rare night of avoiding the bottle.

An elusive but familiar dream was taunting her from the edges of her consciousness. She'd awakened thinking about it, but the images and words blinked in and out like a faulty connection. It had been about her mother, that much she was certain of, a replaying of their final moments together. She'd had a version of this dream before, but it was different this time. Normally, it hewed closely to the actual events: her mother on an adjustable hospital bed in their living room; Jenny promising to do right by the family name; her mother replying, "Just be a Lowell," and then, fade out to black.

Jenny shut her eyes and reached for the dream, concentrating on pulling what images she could remember to the surface. Trees and animals streaked beneath them. They'd been flying—that was it—soaring over the earth with their arms outstretched. But then her mother steered her toward the stars, higher and higher and higher until they could see the whole planet at once.

"Just be *Jennifer* Lowell," her mother said, a single word that changed everything.

Be *Jennifer* Lowell, not just *a* Lowell. Had that always been her mother's message? She'd bring it up in therapy. For now, she needed to get to work.

"Alexa, lower the shades, please."

The room dimmed, illuminating her screen. Jenny clicked on her Gmail icon and the pinging started as her inbox filled. Whoa. What the hell was going on? People who weren't on the guest list, people she'd never even heard of, were RSVPing to Adam's party in droves: bettythebarista@gmail.com, Stephanie.Murphy@Boston.gov, JoeFlynn@hotmail.com, and at least a dozen addresses ending in CCIO.org. Had she even had this many invitations printed?

When Adam had insisted on a formal, sit-down dinner rather than the cocktail party Jenny had proposed, they'd compromised, agreeing to cap the invite list at fifty people. According to the mathematical laws of dinner parties, fifty invites should result in approximately thirty guests, a manageable number that could be handled with four rented round tables in the great room. But this? *This* was not manageable. In the past twenty-four hours, twenty-seven people who were not on the guest list had RSVP'd yes. That brought the total yeses to fifty-two. Jenny mentally rearranged the room to see what would happen if she squeezed in another table and added a couple of chairs to each. Even in her mind's eye, the space felt claustrophobic, all those knees touching. And she was still waiting to hear from close to twenty people from the original guest list. Damn Adam! His self-centeredness astounded her.

Jenny took a slug of hot coffee, scorching her throat in the process. This was what this day was going to be like. She felt furious. Why was this all *her* problem? Her therapist had been trying to help her prioritize her time. If something didn't have a direct impact on Ken's career, her children, or her gardens, it was supposed to take a back burner. Well, Adam's party didn't directly serve any of these goals and yet it occupied a lot of mental real estate. And was Ken doing his part and sharing the worry? No, he was not. Adam was *his* father. But Jenny suspected her husband hadn't given his father's party a second thought.

Well, she'd be damned if she was going to handle this mess alone. Jenny strode across the lawn, mentally berating Ken for shirking his responsibilities, hiding out in his office, and working twelve-hour days in the summer. She considered pounding on the door—that might be satisfying—but instead threw it open without warning.

"Your father is out of control, Ken," she said as the door hit the jamb with a bang. "And there's no way this is going to be my problem alone."

Ken jerked back, startled, dropping something on the floor. "Ouch. Jesus! What the—?" he cried, putting his thumb to his mouth, regarding Jenny as if she was crazy.

Jenny picked up the X-Acto knife that had clattered to the ground and took in the mayhem of his normally immaculate office. On the floor: wood shavings, scraps of cardboard and Styrofoam, slivers of discarded balsa wood and cork; on his desk: large sheets of grid paper, strips of material organized by size into neat piles, tiny homemade trees stuck into clay bases, dowels, blades, brushes, and an antique tool kit containing small vises and clamps, picks, probes, and various tweezers and mini pliers.

"What is all this?" But as the words left her mouth, Jenny was already making sense of the scene. She picked up a miniature sign and brought it to her face: GARDNER SENIOR LIVING. Handwritten but so neat it looked professionally typeset. She circled the desk, taking in the model from every angle: the layered cardboard topography, the miniature landscaping, the perfectly to-scale building, and the mid-century modern furniture within.

"What do you think?" Ken asked shyly. He seemed genuinely nervous. "Do you like it?" And then, "Do you think my dad will?"

And suddenly, there he was, the young man she'd met and fallen in love with all those years ago. The one who made her mixtapes and left Post-it love notes affixed to her coffee cup. The old Ken, the sweet Ken, the vulnerable Ken. Jenny pulled a tissue from a Kleenex box and wrapped Ken's thumb in it. "Apply pressure," she said. "Sorry to have startled you."

Jenny brought her face close to the model to examine the details. Ken had made shingles and floorboards. He'd glued down stones—slivers of rocks he must have found on the beach—to create a pathway to the dwelling. The handmade furniture even had hardware. How had he found time for this?

"Do you think he'll like it?" Ken asked again, picking up a tiny tree and spinning it between his thumb and forefinger.

Jenny placed a hand on the side of his face, turning his head so that their eyes met, a fine network of lines branching from the corners of his. "It's beautiful," she said. How could Adam not be touched by all the time that Ken had put into this? "Your father will love this, Ken." Though she felt far less sure he'd love the condo itself.

"I was going to give him one of the prototypes the architects made," Ken said. "But then I decided to build one myself. Between the girls writing their own song and hearing you go on and on about Abby's painting, I thought I better step up my game." He took her hand from his face and kissed it. "I've been at it for weeks. And check this out"—he pointed at the toolbox—"I found it in the basement. It was my mom's."

The box, an antique, was made of wood and designed specifically to hold the tiny implements of model building. There were things that Ken rarely discussed, and his mother was one of them. Jenny perked up.

"It'll sound crazy, but I swear, she helped me with this project," Ken said.

"Your mother *helped* you?" she repeated. "Helped you how?"

Ken's eyebrows rode high on his forehead. "Never mind, I told you it was crazy."

"No, it isn't. Say more."

But Ken had already moved on. "And to think, this isn't even the *real* gift," he said, fitting the Gardner Senior Living sign back into snug grooves carved into the baseboard. "Just picture my father's face when he crosses the threshold of his state-of-the-art new home." Ken smiled at the thought. "Viking stove, Eames chair, Bose stereo system . . ."

Her father-in-law wouldn't know what to do with any of those things, and he loved his home in the Wellfleet Woods. Jenny couldn't picture him leaving it *ever*. But she kept those thoughts to herself.

"Now, by 'out of control,' what exactly are we talking about?" he asked, bringing the conversation back to where it started when Jenny had stormed in.

Jenny was about to tell him everything about the ballooning RSVP list but suddenly felt embarrassed. Her mother would never have bothered her father with this type of stuff.

"You know what?" she said. "Never mind." She'd make the problem go away by throwing money at it. One hundred guests? Easy. They'd just move the dinner outside, rent a large tent, hire more staff, increase the catering budget, and embrace the madness.

"That's my girl," Ken said, pulling Jenny in for a hug. "Now, I have an idea for how you can help me with this," he said, pointing to his model. "How about you shred the ugly Neiman Marcus tie your father gave me for Christmas and make a rag rug and some curtains for Dad's new home?"

Abby

"Hey, Abby," Jenny said.

Even with bad cell reception, Abby could tell that something was amiss. "One sec, Jenny," she said and moved to the corner of the Arcadia with the best reception. She covered her non-phone ear. "Okay, go ahead."

"Did I catch you at a bad time?" Jenny asked.

"No. Um, well, kind of," Abby admitted, looking over her shoulder to where Richard Luong—*the* Richard Luong—was setting up his equipment for their shoot: tripod, backdrop, lights.

"Everything okay?" Jenny asked, sounding alarmed.

Since finding out about Abby's pregnancy, Jenny had made up excuses to call and check in daily. Abby would have found it irritating if she weren't so relieved that their friendship was back on track.

"Yes, fine," Abby said, lowering her voice. "I'm just busy."

"Doing what?" Jenny asked.

"Jenny, please. You called me. Out with it. What's up?"

"Your dad's what's up," Jenny said. "As in *really*, *really*, *really* up."

"Oh, shit," Abby said. Her father's timing, as usual, was terrible. "Hold on, Jenny," she said, pressing the mute button and excusing herself from the photographer. She stepped outside where she unmuted herself. "Jenny?"

"Still here."

"Okay, the *Reader's Digest* version, please," Abby said, watching Frida walk a wobbly line, steered by a nose that followed invisible whorls of aroma.

"Well, your dad's been passing out invitations to his party like candy," Jenny said. "RSVPs are rolling in from people I've never heard of."

Abby closed her eyes and lowered herself to the stoop. Had Richard

Luong not been directly on the other side of the wall, she'd be knocking her head against it now. What a fool she'd been. Of course, her father was cycling. She'd known it all along and kept talking herself out of knowing it because . . . well, if she were honest about all of it, she hadn't wanted to deal.

"Abby?"

"Still here," Abby said.

"Look, I'm sorry to add to your stress," Jenny said. "I just thought you'd want to know."

"Of course I do. Thanks for telling me," Abby said. She snapped her fingers together softly, all it took to get Frida back to her side. "How about you send me the RSVP list and when I'm done here, I'll have a look. We'll figure it out."

"What *exactly* are you doing there, Abby?" Jenny asked.

Abby thought about how to answer. "Does our agreement hold? What is said in the Arcadia, stays in the Arcadia, even if you're not here?"

"I promise."

"I'm getting photographed by Richard Luong for *Art Observer*. Like, right now!"

"How could you *not* have told me?" Jenny was clearly thrilled.

"I'm already nervous enough without you hovering."

"You better be wearing blue, Abby. Tell me you're wearing blue," Jenny said.

Abby *was* wearing blue, the robin's-egg shade Jenny insisted was her color. The blouse skimmed the edges of her shoulders. She'd even put on makeup.

The shoot was stark and simple. Richard had arranged a stool beside *Little Monster* in a sun-drenched corner of the Arcadia and invited Abby to take it. With her permission, he freed a single lock of hair from her messy bun and curved it around her cheekbone.

Richard smelled like cigarettes and peppermint. "Are you ready?" he asked, returning to his camera, hovering over it, alternately looking at her directly and through the lens.

"I guess," Abby said, staring at her hands placidly folded on her lap. "Are you going to tell me what you want me to do with my hands?" She lifted them. "Or where you want me to look?"

"No," Richard said. He moved away from the tripod, holding a shudder remote control in his hands. "This is your story. You tell it to me."

Hours later, long after Richard packed up his equipment and left, after her nightly walk to the beach with Frida, Abby allowed herself to consider her father's situation. She recalled the way he'd shaken his fist at the edge of the pond, hollering at Charon. When had that been? May? Surely, he'd have gone to see Dr. Peabody right away. That was their agreement. That was what he always did, his way of honoring the mistakes he'd made when she and Ken were young. And yet, it didn't seem possible that her father could be ten weeks into a manic episode that was still going strong if he were being properly medicated.

Abby shed her shirt, letting it fall to the floor. She hooked her thumbs into the belt loops of her shorts and tugged them down, stepping out of her flip-flops at the same time, leaving a circular pile of clothing on the floor, underwear nestled in the center. She flopped onto the bed. She'd been self-absorbed of late: with her painting, her pregnancy, the possibility (or not) of a future with David, and—as uncomfortable as it was to admit—the heady prospect of fame. She'd been consumed by all of it and had stopped making regular visits to see her father. And now, she had no idea what level of mania they were dealing with. Hopefully, it was standard-issue grandiosity, irritating but manageable. But if Dr. Peabody had chosen not to treat it aggressively or if her father had for some reason not followed instructions . . . Well, she knew how bad it could get. When had she last talked to her dad? It had been over a week. Abby's mind flitted to a terrifying moment from childhood when their father, convinced that he was being followed, took them on a survival adventure where they'd had to endure three cold days and nights without supplies in the woods. Abby closed her eyes as a laundry list of worst-case scenarios presented themselves: her father diving overboard to swim with whales, lying broken at the bottom of a cliff, driving the wrong way down Route 6.

The ping of an incoming email snapped Abby back to the here and now. It was from Jenny. Abby scrolled down the long list of RSVPs. Who were all these people? There were at least a dozen colleagues from the CCIO she'd never heard of; her dad's favorite Tzuco bartender; Betty from Plover; his plumber; several fishing buddies; and someone named Stephanie Murphy who, judging from her email address, worked for the city of Boston. Abby paused at that name. It was familiar, but she couldn't place it. She Googled "Stephanie Murphy, city of Boston" and a photo appeared, a woman in uniform, a cop. Abby magnified the image. It was *her*. The woman who'd visited her in the studio a few months back with her wife and baby boy. She'd seen them again in Ken's driveway—they were purportedly headed to Jenny's garden tour—as she was whisking her nieces away to the dune shack. At the time, Abby assumed it had been a coincidence. An irrational thought made its way to the surface. The woman was a police officer . . . maybe their family was being investigated. But for what? Could this have to do with Ken's campaign? Abby closed her laptop. She needed to focus on the problem at hand: her father.

She pushed herself off the bed, picked up her dirty clothes, and tossed them into the hamper. She walked naked into the bathroom to brush her teeth. She'd always felt safe in the Arcadia, deep in the woods, no prying eyes. Standing in front of the sink, she took in the scum around the faucet; two dead, raisin-size flies on the sill; a dingy, gray-yellow circle in the john—ugh. She didn't care, these things could wait. She caught her reflection in the long mirror that hung from the back of the door and saw that she was looking pregnant in earnest. Not big-bellied, but with an undeniable bump. She ran a finger along the dark line that stretched from her belly button to her pubis. Her father's party was just weeks away now. Oblivious as the men in her life were, her secret would not keep much longer. And certainly not in the dress she'd bought for the occasion, ruched to highlight the pregnancy. That said, for all she knew, David wouldn't even be there. He'd been off the Cape more than on it this summer, zigzagging across the country alongside the Clinton campaign.

First things first. She needed to confront her father. Maybe there was still time to straighten all this out before his party. She'd go with him to see Dr. Peabody right away. No, that wasn't possible; it was Friday. She'd have to take him in next week, which put them into August. Luckily for her, her father was a creature of habit, a man of routine, and she could find him easily. Daily, he picked up a cappuccino at Plover. Weekly—during the summer, that was, and weather depending, of course—he piloted his boat to the Stellwagen Bank National Marine Sanctuary to record his beloved humpbacks. After that, he always went to Tzuco's to shoot the breeze with Joe and enjoy a plate of calamari. Decision made. She'd meet him after a day on his boat and stage her intervention there. He invariably returned from those research adventures refreshed and inspired.

With that, Abby went back into the bedroom, crawled onto her bed, and lay on her side, no longer comfortable on her back or stomach. She pulled the soft sheet over her and succumbed to the tug of sleep, welcoming random images that slipped past—a periwinkle sky, Charon in his aquarium, a pattern of stucco memorized from the crib.

Steph

Steph awoke to the muffled sound of Toni's voice from another room and the fleeting sensation of not knowing where she was. Then a gull called, luring her consciousness back to Provincetown. She flexed her feet and stretched her arms overhead until her whole body tingled. It was past 6:00 a.m., which these days counted as sleeping in. It didn't seem possible that July was almost over. Like every other first-time parent, Steph had underestimated how all-consuming caring for a newborn was. It felt like they'd just arrived on Cape Cod, but they were already two months into their three-month leave, and she hadn't made nearly the progress getting to know her biological family that she'd expected by now.

Thus far, she'd had only two interactions with her half sister—one intentional and the other a surprise encounter in Ken Gardner's driveway. She hadn't even managed to get back to Abby's studio for some one-on-one time. Things were better with Adam, who'd been texting her regularly since they met at Tzuco's. He was so old school that he signed his texts, a fact that charmed her. And just last night, he'd finally made good on his promise to ask her to go out on his research vessel.

But Toni didn't think this was a good idea. "You can't keep inserting yourself into their lives without telling them who you are," she said. "It's creepy."

"Does going on a boat ride really count as inserting myself into his life?" asked Steph.

Toni looked exasperated. "How about accepting an invitation to his seventieth birthday party? You barely know the man."

It wasn't as if Steph had tricked him; Adam had suggested it.

"Look, it's obvious you want a relationship with them," said Toni.

Did she? Steph thought of her dad begging her not to pursue this.

As usual, Toni read her thoughts. "Your parents will be okay with this. They're just adjusting to the shock. But if you keep being sneaky with the Gardners, you're going to blow their trust before you've had the chance to earn it. Do you think they'll want a relationship with you if they feel like you spied on them? You're giving them reason to question your motives."

Toni was right. Steph needed to figure out how to tell Adam the truth, and five hours on a boat would provide ample opportunity.

She reached for her phone and saw that she had a new message.

I assure you; this will not be your typical tourist whale watch. You will be witness to scientific research in action and a major discovery unfolding. It should be quite special. Yours, Adam Gardner Ph.D.

A semicolon in a text message! It had come in at 1:42 a.m.

She wrote back: **sounds great. when? where?**

To her surprise, Adam responded immediately. Did he not sleep? **Tuesday. Meet me at the Provincetown Marina at 10 AM. Yours, Adam Gardner Ph.D.**

She inserted a thumbs-up emoji. **what to bring? how long?**

The ellipses bubble reappeared immediately.

You will need sunscreen, a hat, and sensible shoes. We will be out the whole day.

Steph wrote back, offering to bring lunch. Adam might wow her with whales, but Steph would wow him with her cooking.

Adam accepted and signed off with: **I'm looking forward to introducing you to some of my favorite mysticete, who will serenade you. Yours, Adam Gardner Ph.D.**

Mysticete, another word to look up. According to Wikipedia, they were baleen whales, the kind that had plates in their mouths to sieve planktonic creatures from the water. Steph read on. Baleen whales had split from toothed whales around thirty-four million years ago. Who knew?

looking forward! she pecked.

It will be my pleasure. Yours, Adam Gardner Ph.D.

Now, all she had to figure out was how to get to Ken. To date, the closest she'd gotten to him was a fleeting glance through the window of his fancy man cave while pretending to admire a flowering vine crawling up a trellis affixed to its wall. She thought she'd been stealthy, maneuvering away from the rest of the garden tour, but as soon as she got close to the outbuilding, an automatic shade lowered and prevented any real snooping.

Steph returned to her most reliable source, Jenny's Facebook feed. Ken sailing, Ken golfing, Ken shaking hands at $1,000/plate fundraisers—nothing that provided a way for Steph to casually bump into her half brother. But then—eureka!—a new post from Jenny, featuring one of her stunning floral arrangements above a caption that read: "Fundraiser to benefit the Chatham Episcopal Church, today." God, these Gardners were early risers. The details followed: the event would be held outside the church immediately following the 10:00 a.m. services. They'd be there.

Steph scooted up on the pillows. "Guess where we're going today?"

Ken

It wasn't until they parked and got out of the car that Ken got a good look at his daughters, their heads bowed over their phones, as usual. They wore the same outfit—a nod to their twinhood reserved only for church these days—but the dress fit Frannie differently, riding higher on her thighs and tighter across her chest. Tessa still looked twelve, coltish and compact, but Frannie had changed. Her body looked liquid.

Frannie looked up at him. "What?"

"Phone," he said sternly, and she handed it over. He put his open palm in front of Tessa, who took longer to relinquish hers. He tucked the devices into the glove compartment and went around to open the trunk where Jenny's floral arrangements were carefully packed.

Four boys approached to collect the auction items.

"Hi, Mrs. Gardner," one said. "Can we help?"

"That would be great, boys," Jenny said.

"Hi, Frannie," the same kid said, rearranging his flop of bangs with a flick of his head. "You look awesome."

"Hi, Luke," Frannie replied, giving him a little wave.

Luke peered into the trunk. "Wow, Mrs. Gardner. I've never seen hydrangeas in so many colors."

"Thank you, Luke," Jenny said. "I'm impressed you even know what a hydrangea is. Let's hope people bid generously."

"They'd be crazy not to," Luke said.

Flattery will get you everywhere, kid, Ken thought.

"Mr. Gardner," Luke said.

So, it was his turn now.

Luke whistled. "You just killed it on the eighth hole last week."

Ken had forgotten that Luke caddied at the club. The kid was right, it had been a near-perfect hit; he recalled the feel of his club face nailing the ball, watching it speed bullet-like down the fairway.

Luke gave a self-satisfied smile.

"How about getting a move on," Ken said, doling out the vases to the boys, who took off in the direction of where the tables were being set up on the lawn beside the church.

Frannie and Tessa started after them.

"Whoa," Ken said. "Hold up!"

The girls froze.

"Ken"—Jenny's voice was low—"Let them go with their friends."

The twins didn't wait to see how the discussion unfolded but instead ran to catch up with the boys, who were congregating with a bunch of other young people.

"What's up with you, Ken?" Jenny asked, folding her arms across her chest.

"The kid was checking out Frannie," he said. "She's twelve."

"Luke's a kid, too, Ken. Maybe fourteen," Jenny said calmly. "Besides, Frannie's had a crush on him forever."

Clearly, he needed to start paying more attention. Even if Luke was only fourteen—and he looked older—two years was a big difference at their age. Besides, Ken knew what went through the mind of a fourteen-year-old boy. "Frannie's dress is a little short, don't you think?"

Jenny cocked her head. "*That's* what this is about? Mid-thigh is the style."

Ken karate-chopped his upper thigh. "Nothing 'mid' about it."

"Oh, Ken," Jenny said, pleasure brightening her eyes. She moved directly in front of him and patted his lapel, a condescending smile on her face. "You'd best prepare yourself. Boys will be checking out your daughters from here on out. And that will be the *least* of your concerns."

There was glee in his wife's voice.

Then she gave the knot of his tie a sharp tug, tightening it around his neck. "Men will also stare and have their disgusting man thoughts."

There was no missing the accusation in Jenny's words. Ken flashed to Peony and her friend on the dock. As Abby predicted, the term "jailbait" had taken on new meaning vis-à-vis his daughters. He hated when his sister was right.

"Discussion over," Ken said, sticking a finger into his half-Windsor and loosening the noose. He took Jenny by the elbow and guided her toward the entrance of the church, waving the girls over. The family gathered on the steps and arranged themselves: Jenny in the front, followed by Frannie and then Tessa, with Ken at the rear. An instrumental prelude ushered them down the aisle and into the nave, where they took their usual place in the front pew. Ken found comfort in the smell of incense, the feel of the solid wooden bench beneath him, and the squeak of the cushioned kneeler as he went down for a quick prayer.

The sermon was about the seven deadly sins, a bit heavy for a summer weekend, but whatever. The reverend asked the congregation to reflect on which sin they were most guilty of. Ken ruled out sloth, gluttony, and greed quickly, but considered lust. No doubt Jenny would peg that as his issue, but lust wasn't what drove him. Sure, he liked to get what he wanted when he wanted it—who didn't?—but that was about power. And power, he noted, hadn't even made the list of sins. Probably because God respected people who thought they should be running the world. Ken straightened in his chair. Envy was also out—he had what everyone else wanted. That left pride and anger. Analysis over.

In the end, the highest bid for Jenny's prize arrangement hadn't come from a congregant or even a local but rather from a tourist couple from Boston who were in Provincetown for the summer. Lesbians, no less, two attractive ladies—one blonde, one brunette—with a baby boy. Ken wondered if "lesbian" was still the correct term. He'd have to ask Tessa, the family expert on all things PC. There was no question, despite his relative social progressiveness, he was in for an uphill battle when it came to the gay vote. Which didn't mean he shouldn't give it his all. Provincetown was part of the ninth district, and here was a perfect opportunity to show he was gay-friendly.

"Congratulations," Ken said, introducing himself. "What brings you to Chatham?"

"Actually, we came specifically to bid on your wife's amazing flowers," said Steph, letting him know they'd been on a garden tour that included his home. "We were hoping to meet you, too. You have a spectacular home."

"Thank you. That's very kind of you to say," Ken said and slid an arm around Jenny's waist, giving her a small squeeze of thanks. He'd like to get a photo of this couple up on his website. Social media gold, as it were. "And who's this little guy?" he asked, leaning in. Jenny had impressed upon him the importance of acknowledging babies.

"Jonah," Steph answered, clearly charmed by the attention Ken was giving her son.

"Great name," Ken said.

"Are you a gardener, too?" asked Toni. "Or are flowers your wife's domain?"

Ken detected an edge to the inquiry. No matter, he'd win her over. He gave a toothy grin. "Jenny gets full credit when it comes to making our home beautiful," he said. "I'm just the man who's lucky enough to live with her." If the line was good enough for Jack Kennedy, it was good enough for him.

Jenny smiled.

"I'm a conservationist, especially when it comes to wetlands and waterfront," Ken continued, launching into his campaign talking points. "The environment is always front of mind and that includes when it comes to our landscaping decisions. I'm sure Jenny spoke about our commitment to indigenous plants." In truth, the conservation commission hadn't given them much choice in the matter. If Ken wanted to build an external office and shore up his revetment, that was the price. "Environmental conservation is a critical part of my platform," he said, snapping a red-and-blue *Gardner for Congress 2018* business card on the table beside their bouquet.

The gesture was met with an awkward silence.

"How about a picture of you two and Jonah with the hydrangeas?" Jenny suggested, coming to the rescue.

"Sure," Steph said and positioned herself beside Toni behind the colorful bouquet. She adjusted Jonah's sun hat to shade his fair skin.

Ken click-clicked as Jenny made faces to get the baby to smile.

"How about you two get in the shot?" Steph suggested. "That way, when you're a congressman, I can impress my friends."

To think, Ken hadn't even had to propose it. He called to Tessa, who came running. There was no need to give her instructions; the whole family knew the photo-op drill. He palmed the phone to his daughter, and arranged himself with Jenny, sandwiching the couple.

No sooner had Tessa started snapping photos than she lifted her face. "Hey, I know you," she said, looking at Steph.

"It's good to see you again," Steph said.

"Wait. You two have met?" Ken asked.

"At the garden tour. Your daughters were leaving as we were walking in," Steph said. "We met your sister, too."

"What a talented artist," Toni added. "We checked out one of her open studios."

Ken twisted his wedding ring but maintained his camera smile.

As Tessa handed him back his phone, she whispered, "Dark-haired one look familiar or what?"

Tessa was gone before Ken could ask what she meant. He took a long look at Steph. Pretty face, great body, shiny hair . . . Sandra Bullock? When she caught him staring, Ken pointed toward Tessa, now back with her friends. "She's an ally."

The statement was met with another awkward silence.

That was the expression, wasn't it? Ken hitched up his pants. This PC stuff would be the death of him.

Thankfully, their baby started to fuss, drawing attention away from Ken's clumsiness, and Steph and Toni started gathering their things in that harried, new-parent way. So much for impressing them. At least he'd gotten a photo with lesbians. Ken offered to carry the bouquet to their car. "It's heavy," he said.

"We'll manage," the blonde replied curtly, hefting the vase onto her hip. She wasn't exactly friendly.

At least the Sandra Bullock one was pleasant. She provided her contact information, and it turned out she was a cop. Talk about striking gold, a gay police officer.

"Please send me copies of the pics," she said.

"Will do," Ken promised.

On the car ride back to Stage Island, everyone was in high spirits, a rare phenomenon these days.

"What did you think about the sermon?" Ken asked.

"Not bad," Tessa said. "I'd never given any real *thought*-thought to the seven deadly sins before."

"Did you figure out what your sin was?" he asked.

"Did you?"

Everything was a challenge with Tessa.

The next thing he knew, she'd proposed a game: each person would say what they *thought* their sin was, and then the rest of them would tell them what their actual sin was.

"Sounds fun," said Frannie.

Ken wasn't so sure.

"I'm in," said Jenny. "You can even start with me. Bring it on, sweet family."

The response was instantaneous. "Sloth!" the three said in a rare moment of family accord.

Jenny's mouth dropped open in mock hurt.

"Sorry, Mom," said Tessa. "But you are seriously slothy."

"Me?" Jenny said, fanning her perfectly manicured nails around her perfectly made-up face and perfectly coiffed hair as if to say, *No sloth could accomplish all this*. "Well, in my defense, slothfulness is a pretty benign sin," Jenny said. "No one gets hurt."

"I'm not sure Dad would agree," Tessa said under her breath.

"Well, with any luck," Jenny continued, "my slothfulness will cancel out your dad's OCD, and you two will lead normal, productive, and balanced lives."

Ken coughed to register his dissent.

"So, Daddy-O," said Frannie, "any thoughts as to the sins of your sweet, innocent daughters?"

Ken glanced in the rearview mirror. All smiles. What the hell? He was enjoying the banter. "Despite what your mother said, you're both sloth contenders." He checked for their reactions. So far, so good. "But if I had to pick fresh sins for you, I'd say pride for Tessa and greed for Frannie."

"Greed? Ouch," Frannie said. "How so?"

Ken felt emboldened by her smile. "Have you ever watched any Gardner Christmas videos?"

Frannie pouted. "The whole point of Christmas is getting presents."

"News flash," Tessa said, laughing. "The whole point is *giving*."

"Whatever," Frannie said.

"And stealing runs counter to the spirit of the holiday," her mother added.

"Six! I was six when that happened. You people are the worst," Frannie said, but the grin hadn't left her face. "I'll have you know that my cardinal sin happens to be far more interesting than greed." She arched an eyebrow provocatively at her father's reflection in the mirror.

Whispers and giggles came from the back seat.

Had Ken heard the word "lust"? *Do not take the bait*, he told himself.

"On to you, Tessa," Jenny prompted.

"*Moi?*" Tessa rapped the window with the back of her knuckles. "Truth is, Dad got mine right, too," she said. "But I'm proud of my pride. Humility hasn't gotten women very far, now has it?"

This was where a son would come in handy. Another Y chromosome to balance things out.

"It's Dad's turn," Tessa said.

Jenny reached across and squeezed his thigh. "Ready?"

Sure, he was ready. Ken thought of George in that nutty mask. He'd do vulnerable like a champ. "It may surprise you to know that I can admit to more than one sin."

"No!" said Tessa.

Ken would rise above her sass. "I can own a dash of pride, a pinch of wrath, and a smidge of gluttony," he said, thinking of his childhood chubbiness. He was going for laughs and felt pleased when he got them. Only the laughter didn't stop. "All right, all right. Perhaps ample amounts of each," he said, still playing along.

"Oh, Ken," Jenny said, patting his leg condescendingly.

"What?" he asked.

Jenny looked back at the girls. "It's possible your father doesn't know?"

There was no way his wife would suggest lust in front of his daughters. Would she?

"Shall we?" Jenny said.

The girls nodded.

"On the count of three, then," Jenny said. "One, two, three . . ."

They shouted "Envy" in unison.

Ken felt as if he'd been stabbed. That was absurd. People were envious of him, not the other way around. "Don't be ridiculous."

"What about Aunt Abby, Dad?" Tessa said.

August

Adam

Adam wasn't much of a baby guy—what self-respecting man was?—but this Jonah was an interesting specimen, what some might call an "old soul," which sounded like malarkey, even in his thoughts. But no doubt about it, he and the kid were having some seriously sustained eye contact. The baby was reaching for him, pulling hard away from the woman he was strapped to, mom number two, who introduced herself as Toni.

"Short for Antonia, I presume?" he asked. "A lovely name. May I use it?"

"Go for it," Toni said.

Adam offered the baby a finger, which Jonah took.

"He likes you," Toni said.

"Well, I did raise two all on my own," Adam said, his go-to line. "Thanks for letting me steal your mom for the day, Jonah," he said as he removed his finger and forfeited their staring contest.

Adam was pleased to see that Steph had dressed properly for the day: a lightweight, long-sleeved shirt, sneakers, a baseball cap, and sunglasses. Lots of coverage.

"Which vessel is yours, Captain?" Steph asked.

"Follow me," he said, picking up Steph's bags, a large canvas tote and a surprisingly heavy cooler. He led them down the dock past boat after boat to where his scuffed Grady-White was tied to a piling, dwarfed by fishing boats and cabin cruisers that bobbed in slips. "Your chariot, milady."

Steph climbed aboard cautiously, sitting on the gunnel and swinging her legs over. She was muscular and had good balance, but it was clear that she hadn't spent much time on boats. She'd find her sea legs soon enough. Adam lowered the bags with a grunt—how much lunch had she brought?

"Don't judge," she said. "You'll thank me later."

Ha! She was a pistol, this one, and Adam delighted in the prospect of spending five hours on the open ocean with her. "Landlubber," he said, hopping in and untying the boat from the dock.

"No. Really. You *will* thank her later," Toni said from above. "Her scones have won prizes."

Come to think of it, Adam was a bit hungry. Another sign he was coming down. He pushed the thought away and bid Antonia and Jonah farewell, promising to have Steph back before 5:00 p.m. Then he shoved off from the dock, turned the ignition, and the outboard engine sputtered to life. He motored out of Provincetown Harbor slowly to allow his passenger time to adjust to the water. As he circumnavigated Long Point, Adam pointed out the extreme tip of the Cape, once home to a coastal artillery post during the Civil War. "'Fort Useless' was what the locals called it." He cruised past Herring Cove Beach, where sunbathers transformed into speckled dots on the shoreline, and continued northward, Race Point Lighthouse shrinking in the distance. Ahead of them, nothing but sea. The conditions were near perfect: a crystal clear day, practically no wind, and a calm ocean rising and falling beneath them like a sleeping giant's chest. *Please let today be the day.*

With Provincetown receding, Adam pushed down on the throttle, accelerating until the boat was going full tilt, flying over the water. He took a wide stance, hands at ten and two, knees absorbing the gentle swells. At this rate, they'd reach the base of the invisible trapezoidal shape of Stellwagen in about seventy-five minutes. Over the salt-freckled windscreen of the front console, Adam studied the top of Steph's head, admiring her shiny black ponytail poking through the closure of a navy-blue Red Sox cap. Her chin was up, and her head moved back and forth. He could tell she was taking it all in—the salt air, the seabirds, the unknown below. Adam couldn't wait for her to see her first whale up close. He reminded himself to slow down and let the experience unfold organically but there was so much he wanted to say . . . about whales . . . about language . . . about the meaning of the universe.

Why was it that his mind could never stick to the speed limit? It either wreaked metaphorical havoc on the highway at 10 mph or careened down a country road at 120. Despite how attentive Adam had been to his mania, coaxing it along with pharmacological treats, he could tell that this cycle would be ending soon. He'd slept a full eight hours the night before. The thought of crashing without being able to show the world what he knew but could not yet prove was devastating. It didn't make sense. Nothing made much sense anymore. There was nothing Adam felt sure of, except that he would die someday, and that day kept getting closer.

Focus. He had a feisty young woman on his boat who wanted to see whales. That would be his goal for the day: to show Steph Murphy the first whale of her life.

Adam slowed the boat as they neared the border of Stellwagen. He had three pills in his pocket, two fast-acting Ritalin and one clonazepam. *What's it going to be, Hamlet? Up or down?* The smart thing to do would be to stay cool, of course. Adam knew that. But revving up always felt better than slowing down. Might as well go out with a bang, he reasoned. He tossed back the Ritalin and swallowed them dry.

"You've just entered one of the most important ocean sanctuaries in the world, where the whale watching rivals California and Hawaii," he said, following the well-worn grooves of a monologue he'd delivered countless times about the sanctuary's mission to conserve, protect, and enhance the biological diversity, ecological integrity, blah, blah, blah. About ten minutes into his spiel, Adam felt a familiar kick in his chest—a heavenly jolt followed by a fluttering sensation that traveled to his neck. His heart hard at work, pumping blood to his brain, where delightful jitters seemed to shake loose thoughts. This big-picture sermon he was preaching was for the birds. Far more interesting words and thoughts were piling up in his throat. Stellwagen needed to be explained from the bottom up, not the top down. All at once, the dam burst, and words rushed out—"nitrates," "phosphates," "phytoplankton," "zooplankton," "photosynthesis," "chemosynthesis," "rotifers," "copepods"—and Adam explained the aquatic food chain from the base of the pyramid.

Steph seemed unfazed by the diatribe. "What makes the Stellwagen's buffet different from any other part of the ocean?" she asked.

Impressive! She was keeping up! This was just what his wavering confidence needed, a rapt audience. Yes, his mania might be receding and his connection to his idea might be fraying, but all was not lost. Not yet anyway. This charming young woman might hold the answer. Aware as he was that this line of thinking was not exactly logical, it took hold. Adam's pulse continued to soar. Stephanie Murphy might just be his ticket to Stockholm. Perhaps, just perhaps, if he could bedazzle her with his Nobel-level genius . . . if he could make her see what he was onto . . . if he could convince her what he was capable of . . . All he had to do was introduce her to his jazz-singing giants and allow her to become mesmerized. Then, just when she thought it couldn't get any better, he'd pull out the ultimate party trick.

"Adam?"

He snapped back to attention and put the boat in neutral.

"Everything okay?"

How long had he been gone? Adam bought himself some time by pretending to adjust a long-broken dial on his console. He patted the instrument as if he'd fixed the problem. "Sorry. Can you repeat the question?"

"What makes Stellwagen special?" she asked. "Aren't all oceans more or less the same?"

Did she also think the world was flat? But her expression was so earnest that Adam softened, remembering a time when his own children were curious. "My dear girl, oceans are as different as gardens." He chuckled softly. "What makes Stellwagen special is an array of unique marine and topographic features—near-shore geology, contours of the ocean floor, marine currents, density, and chemistry of the water—working in concert. It's the combination that creates an ideal habitat for the phytoplankton and algae, the bases of the aquatic food chain."

Steph nodded, and on her face, Adam saw genuine awe.

"How about a little breakfast?" she suggested, moving to the bow so she could face him. From her canvas bag, she excavated a thermos, two shiny steel mugs, and a neatly wrapped tinfoil package.

His hunger was gone but he'd make himself eat. He turned off the ignition and took a seat across from her.

"Thanks so much for having me, Adam. I can't tell you what it means to be here," she said, pouring dark coffee into travel mugs. "Cream? Sugar?"

Was she for real? "Cream," he answered, watching her thumb stroke the top of the mug handle absently. Back and forth, back and forth. Funny how a small gesture could elicit a big memory. His mother had had the same nervous tic. She'd worn down the glaze on her favorite coffee cup with all her rubbing.

Adam fingered the remaining pill in his pocket, a clonazepam, but decided against it. There was still a chance that today would be the day when everything fell into place. He had to be on high alert. He'd try to bring down his racing heart by concentrating on the ocean and allowing its sounds and rhythms to go to work on his parasympathetic nervous system. It worked a bit, helped by the fact that Steph was transfixed by a large northern gannet that plunged into the ocean like a torpedo.

"That happens to be one of the most impressive avian hunters out there," Adam said, putting on his nature narrator voice.

Steph stared at the spot on the ocean where it had dived, thumb still working the mug. "He's been under for a long time."

"Not to worry. Gannets can stay under for a while," he said. "You like birds?"

She nodded. "I love them. We have a feeder in our backyard."

Adam could picture it: a dingy, forest-green tube hanging from a branch and attracting all the usual ornithological riffraff, English sparrows and house finches.

The gannet popped to the surface.

"My dear, you're in for a treat today," Adam said. "Seabirds are like the all-terrain vehicle of the avian world—they can dive, float, swim, and fly." He listed some of the species they'd likely encounter—gulls, terns, various sea ducks, shearwaters, and jaegers—elaborating on the anatomical oddities that made each species unique: long wings for gliding, reverse coloration for hunting, airbags to cushion their bodies for high-octane plunges. "Some of these birds go years without ever touching land."

Steph whistled.

Adam bit into one of Steph's chive-and-rosemary-flecked cheddar scones, crunchy on the outside, buttery soft on the inside. In a word: sublime. "Worth the additional cargo tonnage," he said.

Steph beamed. "Just wait until lunch."

In the distance, a tall columnar blow. It was showtime.

"You ready to meet my friends?"

Adam's beloved humpbacks did not disappoint, performing pretty much every display he'd hoped to show Steph—breaching, flipper and tail slapping, and his personal favorite, spy-hopping, when the animal poked its head above water to say hello. Steph was rapt, oohing and aahing at every sight and sound, and Adam experienced the paradoxical sensations of soaring and calm. Nothing beat giving this gift—the majesty of these creatures—to someone uninitiated. It was life-altering, and he knew it. Adam couldn't decide whether to bombard his guest with facts about their coloration or how the irregular bumps on their pectoral fins made them counterintuitively *more* hydrodynamic or simply stay quiet so he could bask in her awe. He decided upon the latter.

"Adam," she said, finally looking away from the water. "There's something important I want to tell you." She patted the space beside her on the bow.

"I'm all ears," Adam said, taking a seat beside her. It had been a long time since anyone had taken him into their confidence. He felt honored. But just then Rattan showed up, starboard side, exhaling wetly and loudly, a small rainbow shimmering in his blow. *Could this day possibly get any better?* Adam leaped to his feet. The whale wasn't twenty feet from the boat.

He pulled Steph to her feet. "Watch for it! Watch for it when he dives."

The whale moved gracefully, his low-slung dorsal fin arcing out of the water and his back rolling by as if it had no end.

"Don't take your eyes off him," Adam said. "Don't even blink. I am going to show you how to identify a whale. Note the pattern on the underside of his right fluke. Rattan is a show-off."

And like that, the bull dove, graciously holding his tail aloft, as if just for Steph's examination. A second later, he was gone.

"Did you see it?"

"Uh. Not sure. See what?"

How could she have missed it? Rattan got his name from the plait pattern on his right fluke. Adam explained that every whale tail had unique markers—barnacles, scars, patterns of color.

"The weave pattern?"

"I'm afraid not," she said.

"And you call yourself a cop," Adam said. "Some people can't see what's right in front of them."

"I'll remind you that you said that later," she said. "Now, please, let's sit. I want to tell you—"

"Not yet. There's more," Adam said, pointing to a slick round patch of still water on the ocean surface. "That's what we call a 'fluke print.'"

Adam took a breath for courage. It was time to put the touristy part of their whale-watching adventure behind them and bring Steph into the fold. "I have something I want to tell you. How are you with secrets?"

"A vault," she said. "How about you? I have one for you, too."

"Well, mine is more of an experience," he said, focused on his own. "Close your eyes and prepare to have your mind blown."

Steph held the rail and shut her eyes.

"What do you hear?"

Her brow furrowed. "Oceany stuff? Gulls, waves . . ."

"Listen deeper."

Silence.

Clearly, she wasn't getting it. Adam would lead by example, so he shut his eyes and allowed the topography of the seascape to enter through his ears. "Concentrate on the ocean floor," he instructed. "Listen for it."

"Come again?"

This was not going to be as easy as he thought. He'd have to coach her step by step. "You must tap into your deeper sense of hearing. Pretend you're an acoustic ecologist and feel the world through your ears." He gave her a moment and then said, "Are you with me?"

"That would be a definite no," she said. "You okay?"

Adam chose to ignore this, so intent was he that she experience the multidimensionality of sound. "You can do this. You just need to concentrate." Adam was now hearing in color, traveling through deep blues until he got to the ocean floor. He was inside the sound. "Remember, hearing is your most important sense."

"How so?" Steph asked.

"Well, there are no such things as earlids, are there? If we could afford not to hear, we'd be able to turn off our ears just like our eyes." Adam felt layers of echoes start to reverberate in his mind. "Plenty of animals are born blind, but virtually every species hears." All at once, Adam could tell that whales were approaching. He could feel them. "Do you hear the whales? Listen, Stephanie. Listen!" he whisper-shouted.

Steph cleared her throat loudly.

Adam blinked open his eyes to find her regarding him with concern, possibly alarm. *Uh-oh.* He'd gotten ahead of himself and scared her. He lifted his hands in surrender. "Sorry. Sorry. I should know better than to try that with a layperson. Let's start with something more basic." From a storage box in the stern, Adam retrieved two headsets and a long rod with a microphone affixed. "This will knock your socks off."

Adam lowered the device into the water and attached the handle to a clip on the gunwale. *Let there be sound*, he thought, fidgeting with the volume on a small black box. A few seconds of static and then—behold!—a dulcet composition of moans, chirps, howls, and snores, all below 4 kHz in frequency.

Steph's face lit up and the apprehension on it disappeared. She sank onto the padded bow cushion, closed her eyes, and bent her head down, giving the whale song the attention a miracle deserves. She pressed the speaker cushions against her ears. "Oh my God. Oh my God, Adam. Is this . . . is this what I think it is?"

There was so much to tell his new friend, his student, his maritime Helen Keller. Adam wanted to explain how sound worked differently in the ocean, where waves could bend around the horizon and travel great distances, allowing the past and present to be experienced at once. But that would be too much too soon. Perhaps it would be okay to mention that humpbacks employed repeating patterns structurally resembling human rhythm? For all they knew, they were listening to a cetacean Homer, composing songs in the whale equivalent of dactylic hexameter. Damn, he was good. It had been at least fifty years since he picked up an epic poem, but some venerable facts were still banging against the bars of his steel trap. Adam admonished himself to keep quiet. He didn't want to overwhelm her again. For now, he needed to let the magic unfold and find contentment in witnessing Steph experience whale song.

But this particular canto was a favorite of his, one he knew by heart. He hummed softly and swayed to its discordant rhythm. The acoustic waves reverberated through his chest, lifting his spirits until he was overcome with emotion. A love song. Language was a tool of consciousness, and his friends were inviting him to sing along with them. Adam moved past where Steph sat in concentration and went to the tip of the bow where he stood bracing himself, shins against the railing. Then he opened his arms, tilted his head skyward, and bayed in concert with his comrades.

Abby

Abby sat on the beach on an upside-down kayak watching three sailboats skim alongside one another, waiting for her father to return from Stellwagen. She felt twitchy and unsettled in her body. David hadn't called or even texted since he'd visited her at the Arcadia; not unusual, but given the declaration of his intention to leave Rebecca, Abby thought she'd have heard something by now. She tilted her face into the afternoon sun and touched the soles of her feet together to form a diamond. Holding her ankles, she bent forward toward her toes, only to be met by resistance, something solid, her uterus. She no longer had any nausea and had started to put on weight. And even though she'd only gained seven pounds—not noticeable in her oversized Oxford shirts—her internal corsetry had changed. Her skin felt tight and itchy around her belly and breasts. Abby longed for her mother differently than she had in the past, in a way that couldn't be satisfied by shards of ceramics or a vague ethereal presence.

In the distance, the familiar shape of her father's powerboat skirted Long Point, where a lambent glow suffused the spit of dunes at the Cape's outermost tip. The sun reflected against the hull, sending a clear, prismatic flash of marine light into her eyes. She got up and followed a set of footprints to the water's edge where well-rounded pebbles massaged the bottoms of her feet. The tide was low and revealed an abundance of moon snail collars, which looked like rippled toilet plungers but were actually mucus sand nests made by industrious mothers, who curled these gelatin casings around themselves and embedded their eggs. Motherhood as sculpture. Alongside a jetty, mussels gripped rocks with long beards, and strands of mossy seaweed swayed hypnotically in the water. She considered her father and the interaction that lay ahead—the fortress of his personality and what she knew would be his vehement denial. He'd always been able to make her doubt what she knew to be true. Bullying and control and egotism all mixed up with incredible love. Their cycle.

This time, she would not let herself be intimidated by him. Abby knew the conversation had to be had today. She headed toward the dock in ankle-deep water. The beach was crowded with summer tourists—bearded lugs in cargo shorts and tank tops, gay men in bikinis, and families of every sort chasing children. Two towheads caught her eye, an older brother and a younger sister. They were playing king of the hill on a mound of sand, and the girl, about four, didn't stand a chance.

Adam's boat slowed in the no-wake zone and proceeded toward the dock carefully. Abby had already decided it would be best to broach her father's mental state when they were sitting at Tzuco's bar, where hopefully being in public would prevent things from getting out of hand. She mentally rehearsed the conversation. She'd start with the RSVP list—what to make of all those invitations he'd been handing out willy-nilly. If Adam was in full-blown mania, he'd go on the attack, prosecuting her to defend himself—gaslighting, his go-to response. If he was coming down, he might slide into despair, anguishing over his failures. But no matter where her father was on the continuum, Abby wasn't going to be cowed. She planned to confront him.

For as long as she could remember, Abby had been a minor character in their family drama, a backup to her father's and brother's starring roles. Her main job was to let them shine. When things didn't go their way, they had tantrums and changed the narrative, and Abby—peacemaker that she was—tended to follow their lead. Abby picked up a smooth flat stone and skipped it on the water. Nine flips! Huzzah!

The baby kicked her side, a reminder of the future ahead. A whole new world spun inside her, and 2016 was going to be a game changer. Earlier that week, Rachel Draper had called with the news that Abby had been hoping for: *Little Monster* was going to grace the cover of the fall issue of *Art Observer*. The cover! Big buzz was already underway, and this time, Abby planned to capitalize on the exposure. Not only would her work be admired by over two hundred thousand subscribers—art enthusiasts and buyers—it would also be seen by countless people who passed it on newsstand racks. She pictured Ken doing a double take as he walked by Barnes & Noble. There was her upcoming group exhibit to look forward to, too, already generating publicity. The gallery had provided a studio assistant to overhaul her website and amplify her social media presence. Abby had already informed Nauset High that she wouldn't be returning in the fall. She'd miss her students, of course, but she only had until November 22—her due date—to give this her all. She planned to paint right up until that first contraction.

As her father's boat reached the dock, Abby considered how he might react to the *Little Monster* unveiling. He likely wouldn't get it, at least not at first glance. Her paintings revealed themselves like novels, unfolding over time. Her father would see what he could see when he was ready to see it. He'd once told her that art was the soul's need to speak. Well, Abby had finally initiated a long-overdue conversation. Response . . . no response . . . that was beyond her control.

She considered how good it felt to be a creator of life and a maker of art. Thanks to her upcoming profile and exhibit, soon she'd also have an audience and reach. "Platform" was the new buzzword. And platform trumped wealth. Ken might have the money to secure the corner table and impress his friends, but he didn't have a platform. Not yet anyway. Abby felt giddy. So, this was what power felt like. Being consequential, having a voice, feeling *relevant* . . . It was undeniably thrilling. The trick would be to leverage it well. Abby wanted—no, she *needed*—to own her home, if for no other reason than to leave it to her son.

Abby felt roused by her own power-happy internal monologue. God bless pregnancy hormones! The old Abby would have been terrified by all the unknowns that lay ahead, but this woman, jacked up on estrogen and progesterone, felt ready to leap into the future.

When she was a short distance from the wharf, Abby noticed something unexpected: a second figure on the boat, a woman, her black ponytail swishing from beneath a baseball cap. Abby squinted harder and stared. The woman clambered onto the dock and her father passed her a canvas bag and cooler. There was a short exchange. A wave. Nothing too intimate. Then the woman hurried down the pier. If Abby wanted to get a good look at her father's mystery guest, she needed to hustle. But that wasn't necessary. The woman, possibly sensing she was being watched, turned and looked right at Abby. It was that police officer again. Steph Murphy. Only she looked shaken.

"Hey," Abby called out, moving to intercept her. "Stop. Wait. What's going on here?" This was no coincidence. The visit to the studio, the garden tour, the RSVP list, and now this. Their family *must* be under investigation. Was it her father? Could he be in trouble? Or had Ken broken a campaign law? Taken money from a shady PAC? Behind Steph, Abby saw her father push off from the dock. It would take him at least five minutes to moor the boat and paddle the dinghy to shore.

"Seriously, what the hell?" Abby said, her heart racing.

An expression crossed Steph's face that was inscrutable to Abby.

"What's going on? Are we in trouble? I mean. You're a cop. Are you investigating us?"

"Oh, God no," Steph said. "It's nothing like that."

"Then what?" Abby asked.

Steph glanced over her shoulder at Adam, who was leaning over the bow, latching a line to the mooring. "I'm sorry, but I need to go."

"We need to talk," Abby said, wanting answers.

"Yes," Steph agreed, "but not here."

Adam was already in the dinghy, paddling toward shore, his movements exaggerated as if he was rowing against a strong tide or for an audience.

Abby sighed. "How about my place tomorrow morning at nine?"

Steph nodded and turned away.

"Wait. Was he okay out there?" Abby asked, knowing it was an odd question to ask a relative stranger, but she needed confirmation.

Steph gave a resolute shake of the head, and Abby had her answer.

At Tzuco's, Adam went off on a tirade about Hillary Clinton's failings—her careless handling of classified information, her trading access for gifts to her charity, and how she'd had hundreds of fundraisers with only five open to reporters. "How does your old friend David feel about that?" he asked.

At the mention of David, Abby swallowed hard. She needed to hear from him and know his marriage was over. She should have told him about the pregnancy by now, though, to be fair, he hadn't been around.

"The woman's dishonest, and the last thing we need is another political dynasty," her father continued.

Abby knew better than to engage but couldn't help herself. "Have you considered the alternative?"

"Well, I still think Bernie Sanders would make a great president."

"Bernie's out, Dad. Not an option. You know who I'm talking about." Not five minutes at the bar, and her father had already gotten a rise out of her. Where was Joe?

"Only because the Clintons have the DNC in their pocket. Mark my words: Chelsea will be on the ballot in your lifetime."

"Abby, Adam," Joe said, appearing just in time. "What can I get you tonight?"

"Bourbon on the rocks," said Adam.

"Pellegrino, please," said Abby, "lots of lime."

Joe chatted aimlessly as he prepared their drinks, placing a bowl of Spanish peanuts in front of them.

Adam lifted his glass. "To pelagic abundance."

Abby gave Joe an eye roll.

He winked back. "'Pelagic' is, like, your father's pet word."

"Derived from the ancient Greek for 'open sea,' you ignoramus," Adam said affectionately. He took a leisurely sip of bourbon, which settled him visibly, and tossed a handful of peanuts into his mouth. "Now, for a lesson on the subzones."

God, the man loved an audience.

"In descending order, there's the epipelagic, where there's enough light for photosynthesis; the mesopelagic, or twilight zone; the bathypelagic, where things get pitch black; the abyssopelagic, aka the abyss; and finally, the hadopelagic, named for the Greek underworld Hades." Adam smiled broadly. “Expanding your meager vocabulary, my dear fellow, might go down as my life’s great accomplishment.”

“You gotta love this guy,” Joe said to Abby. Then he saluted Adam and turned away.

Abby gathered her thoughts, gazing out upon the busy harbor. The light was changing, dancing and reflecting off the water. “I noticed you had a passenger today,” she said.

“I did at that. A lovely young woman. Stephanie Murphy. We met right here.” He tapped his pointer finger on the bar.

Had Abby mentioned to Steph and Toni that her father was a Tzuco’s regular? She was certain she had.

Adam continued, “She’s a detective, you know. A female Columbo. Now, *that’s* not something you see every day, is it? Anyway, we hit it off.” He leaned in and whispered, “Between you and me, I’m helping her with a missing person’s case.”

What? “Um . . . who’s missing?”

Apparently, her father hadn’t considered this. “I don’t know yet,” he said, brow furrowed. And then he was off chasing his thoughts, describing every whale interaction he’d witnessed that day.

He was talking way, way, way too fast.

“Dad!” Abby said.

Adam looked at her as if she’d slammed a cleaver into a side of raw beef. Abruptly, he stood, patted the front pockets of his jeans, found what he was looking for, and popped it into his mouth, downing it with a swig of bourbon.

What pill had he just taken? His pants hung from his hips and his shoulders seemed narrower than they used to be—he had lost more weight. Abby felt the surge of something protective and had to resist the urge to brush the peanut skins off the front of his shirt. “Should you be taking medication with alcohol, Dad?”

Adam rubbed the bridge of his nose between his finger and thumb. “Don’t start mothering me, Abigail. I know what’s what with my meds.”

“Just expressing a little daughterly concern,” she said, treading lightly.

"How are things going on that front?" So much for her take-no-prisoners approach.

Adam didn't answer.

There was a rush to the bar at 5:00 p.m. when happy hour began, and drinks and food were half-price. In a matter of minutes, the place filled, raucous with the chatter of flamboyantly dressed men. Joe ping-ponged back and forth along the narrow passage, booze on one side, bar on the other, effortlessly wielding shakers, beer taps, and soda guns, making small talk as he served his patrons. Adam was staring blankly into his drink.

"Earth to Dad," Abby said, as she used to when she was thirteen. "Where are you?"

Adam looked suddenly despondent, his mood changing visibly before her eyes. It was as if he was shedding his skin, emptying himself, and leaving behind a hollowed-out shell the shape of his absence, like a dragonfly.

He lowered his head until it touched the bar.

Oh, God. Abby didn't like the look of this.

"Things aren't good, honey," he said morosely. "My idea is slipping from me. Every single day, it's further from my reach."

"Hey now," Abby said. She put a hand on his back and felt his shoulder blade move. "Don't talk like that. You're brilliant. Your idea will resurface."

"That's just it. I think it might have been preposterous from the start."

Abby tried to get him to pull his head off the bar, but he wouldn't budge.

"C'mon, Dad," she cajoled, all thoughts of having a confrontation gone. "You'll have other ideas." She just wanted him to be okay. "Remember your favorite Roosevelt quote: 'Far better it is to dare mighty things'—"

He waved a hand dismissively. "Don't patronize me, Abigail. I'm not in the mood."

Despite herself, Abby felt brokenhearted for him, ready to forgive his bombast and narcissism. So much for not falling into their old cycle.

After a few minutes, Adam lifted his head to stare into his reflection in the mirrored wall behind the liquor bottles. "It's as if we're all just on one long conveyor belt, waiting like chickens to be executed. What's the point, really?"

How had she ignored so many warning signs? Abby's hands moved to her belly. She'd been preoccupied with her own life. This was her fault.

Adam motioned for another drink.

"Dad, I don't think that's a good idea." Abby knew she had to be strong. "You've had enough." She raised a palm as Joe approached, and he stopped. She turned back to her father, keeping her voice even. "We've been here before and we'll get through this. Now, when exactly did your symptoms start?"

Her father lowered his head again.

"I'll call Dr. Peabody first thing in the morning, and we'll go to the clinic."

"Peabody's gone," her father cried. "And not one word to me. Thirty years and the man didn't even bother to call, just shunted me off on some kid."

"Dad, please concentrate. When did this start? What protocol are you on?" This was not her father's normal cycle pattern.

"Seventy. Jesus Christ. How did I ever get this old? Seven, zero. Seven, zero. Seven, zero," Adam repeated, a monk at the meditation gong. "Joe," he barked. "A drink, please."

"Dad—"

"They *do* language, Abby. Is it too much to ask that I be bilingual?"

"What?"

"Last week, I understood. I understood everything they said."

What the hell was he talking about?

"Every last thing." Then, something distracted Adam. Was it Joe, dallying at the far end of the bar? A switch flipped, and her father began to rhythmically tap-tap-tap his glass on the bar for attention, petulant and impatient.

Joe hurried to fill Adam's glass, giving Abby an apologetic look, and then retreated.

Adam gulped down the drink in a few sips and swirled the ice cubes around in the bottom of his glass. If he angled for another, she would put her foot down.

"Your mother's been visiting me," he said.

That caught her off guard.

"You used to see her as a kid, remember?"

Of course Abby remembered.

"Well, she's been showing up for me for the past couple of months. To rehash things. It starts sweet, but soon enough, she insists I tell her the truth. What a thing for a ghost to demand! Then, she disappears." Her father's smile left. "And I'm left wide awake to contemplate my one big mistake and my mind turns into a failure zoetrope, spinning around and around." He shakes his head. "There's no sleep after that."

Abby wondered what her father considered his one big mistake to be. Apparently, his guilt was enough to rouse her mother's ghost. She flagged Joe for the check. "Dad, it's time to go," she said, her rebuke turning into a plea.

Her father's displeasure was instantaneous. If there was one thing that pissed Adam off, it was messing with venerable rituals. He was the one who signaled for the check. His scowl was withering.

"Sorry, sorry. I'm just worried and trying to make a plan." *What happened to taking charge?* Abby steeled herself. "Look, Dad, we've got to get a handle on this. We need to see your new doctor right away."

Joe stood frozen before them, unsure which way to direct the leather check holder.

Abby held out her hand.

Her father cleared his throat, a warning.

Joe handed Adam the folder.

"When last I checked, I was still the father," Adam said, smiling while enunciating each word like he was goddamn King Lear.

Ken

When they were little, Ken and Abby's favorite pastime was creating installations for Charon's large aquarium. They'd change out his habitat every week or so when the smell got rank, taking long walks in the scrub forest together—sometimes all the way down to the beach—to collect moss, bark, pebbles, shells, and whatever else might make for good turtle decor. Together, they'd build elaborate interiors of inverted clam shells, woven twig bridges, moss-covered slopes, and meandering paths of flat pebbles. And always, always, Abby would make a turtle bed—her specialty—decorated with flowers, feathers, and leaves. Charon usually destroyed the whole of it within hours.

When they got home from school in the afternoons, Ken would make them a snack, usually apple slices with peanut butter or cheese and crackers, which they'd munch on while they fed Charon his supper of earthworms and insects. Their father had taught them to drop the food directly into the tank's pond as snapping turtles need water to swallow (something about poorly developed saliva glands). Despite Charon's diminutive size, he attacked his dinner with a savagery that left them breathless, thrashing his slender neck as he swallowed smaller grubs whole, and holding the bigger ones in his beak-like jaws while shredding them with his claws.

Abby clutched her brother during the carnage, clinging to him as if her life depended on it. And Ken loved the feel of her hard, round head under his chin, the tangy smell of salt, shampoo, and wet wood. He loved her so much, he'd like to squeeze her to death. Occasionally, they sat on the denim beanbag in front of Charon's cage, observing the action as if at a movie; but more often, they watched from Ken's twin bed, where his arm would often fall asleep under his sister's weight. He remembered not moving—not budging even when he was uncomfortable, his neck at an odd angle against the wall—for fear of ending the embrace early or calling attention to its strangeness. If they heard their father or Gretchen, they'd wordlessly separate.

As an adult, Ken often wondered if Abby ever thought about these sweet moments. She must. But they'd never once, in all these years, spoken of them.

Ken recalled the day that their father arbitrarily declared that the turtle had been in Ken's room long enough and it was his sister's turn. In hindsight, Ken realized that their stepmother Gretchen had been behind the decision. The woman was a meddler, inserting herself where she didn't belong. At the time, Ken pretended the switch didn't bother him—Abby could have the turtle and the stink that went with him—but inside, he fumed. It wasn't right. He'd found Charon, after all. On the same day that he and his father had tossed his mother's ashes into the pond. The turtle was rightfully his. But the bigger problem with the new arrangement was that Abby's bedroom was right off the kitchen and den, without the benefit of a long hallway with creaky floorboards, warning them when adults were approaching.

Now in Command Central, some thirty years later, Ken tapped a slender chisel into a piece of soft driftwood, slowly shaping it into a dome. He tried to focus on what lay ahead, his father's party, but was awash in kaleidoscopic memories of his mother: her hair falling onto his face as she kissed him good night, the warmth of her torso against him at the wheel of the *Francesca*, her steady voice reading *Where the Wild Things Are*. Ken had always related more to the monsters than Max. He tried—and failed—to remember the line where they begged Max not to leave their island.

Ken spent hours carving the tiny replica of Charon, curlicues of wood decorating his desk, the creature taking shape in his hands. When it was finished, he placed it carefully on the front stoop of his father's model. Ken wasn't sure what had possessed him to add the sentimental figurine to his gift, but not everything needed an explanation. He'd felt moved to do it, so he had.

In the background, *TED Radio Hour* played. Something caught Ken's attention and he ordered Alexa to turn up the volume. Guy Raz was interviewing a linguist about the inadequacy of language to express precise emotion. The expert cited a Mandarin word, *yu yi*, which he defined as "the longing to feel intensely again, as you did when you were a child." The word explained so much, and yet, had no English equivalent. Ken was struck. *Yu yi* was why he'd carved Charon for his father. *Yu yi* was why he could still smell the little-girl tonic of Abby's head and hear the melody of his mother's voice reading bedtime stories.

A knock.

"Come in," he called.

"Ta-da!" An arm entered first, its outstretched palm holding miniature rag rugs, throw pillows, and curtains.

Ken watched the rest of his wife enter his office and saw that his least-favorite tie had been put to good use. "Baby, you're the best."

"I'll remind you of that the next time you're being an asshole," Jenny said cheerily, clearly happy to have pleased him. She placed the textiles near the base of the model, where Ken's new carving caught her attention. She ran a finger across the grooved ridges of its shell. "Ken"—her voice sparkled—"this turtle is amazing!"

"What? Did you think there was room for only one artist in the family?"

Ken had always found the mysterious status bestowed on artists deeply irritating. Yes, talent was a thing, of course, but as far as he was concerned, success always came down to hard work. Concert violinists weren't born able to play the violin; they practiced. The great ones practiced all the time. Had Ken decided on a creative career path, for sure he wouldn't be blending colors on a sandbar in obscurity; he'd be Keith Haring by now. Why? Because Ken worked harder than the next guy. He had determination in spades.

"Of course not," Jenny said.

Ken replaced the chisel and plucked a pair of elegant tweezers from his mother's tool box, so thin they looked designed for a Giacometti sculpture. Holding them carefully, he attached the rug to the floor with tiny brass pins.

"Hard work and the right tools. That's what it takes," Ken said, plucking up the curtains next and affixing them to the wall on either side of the windows. And this was just the model. The real gift—a state-of-the-art condo worth seven figures—was yet to come. Adam Gardner might not know the difference between Wolf and GE appliances, but anyone could appreciate quality. Ken couldn't wait to see the look on his father's face. Just two more days.

Steph

If Steph's years on the force had taught her anything, it was that the direct approach was best. She knew she'd been avoidant with the Gardners, and that was going to stop now. Toni was furious that she hadn't come clean with Adam on the boat, but it wasn't Steph's fault. Adam had spent most of the time singing to the whales. Now, sitting opposite Abby on the sofa, Frida's blonde body curled between them like an oversize pillow, Steph wondered if her half sister might already have an inkling of the truth. It couldn't have escaped her notice that Steph looked just like their father.

"Go on," Abby prodded.

But Steph didn't see recognition on Abby's face, only apprehension, the morning light picking out tiny beads of sweat on her upper lip. The studio was just as messy as it had been the first time she'd visited: dirty dishes stacked on the counter, flip-flops piled by the door, a broom lying on the floor. In Steph's home, everything had its place. "Okay," she said. "Here goes." And she forced the sentence out: "I think I'm your half sister."

As the words landed, Frida nosed her head onto Abby's lap, where Abby started stroking the silky flaps of her ears.

Steph corrected herself. "I *know* I'm your half sister."

Abby's eyes scrolled across Steph's face and body, processing the news in what Steph could only imagine was a forensic anatomy comparison with their father: copper-flecked brown eyes, check; black hair, check; athletic build, check; chin cleft, check.

Steph waited for a reaction—anger or denial—but she saw only confusion and hurt. Abby had had absolutely no idea.

Oh shit. Steph had misread the situation. She was not on the job, in uniform, informing next of kin about a crash. She reached for Abby's arm, but Frida gave a low growl. "I'm sorry for blurting it out that way. Are you okay?"

"Let's walk," said Abby.

•

They left the Arcadia without another word, Frida leading them, single file, along a pine-needled path that meandered through the scrub forest, toward the ocean. Steph chastised herself for her stupidity. Toni had warned her to proceed with care. But, oh no, Steph had blundered ahead as usual, self-righteous in her pursuit of the truth, collateral damage be damned.

Now, staring at Abby's bare feet heel-toeing the ground ahead of them, pale arches exposed with each step, Steph regretted her rash action. Ever since Abby had "caught" Steph with Adam at the dock the previous afternoon, Steph had allowed herself to imagine that this news might somehow be welcome.

They crested a dune and a pristine sweep of beach materialized below them, stretching long in either direction, not a person in sight, just khaki sand and an endless ocean of silver and shadow. Abby snapped her fingers and Frida heeled, allowing herself to be leashed. A distressed bird hopped ahead of them, dragging its wing theatrically. It led them down the beach where it took off effortlessly, apparently having faked the injury to steer them away from its nesting ground. Abby dropped the leash and Frida raced ahead until they arrived at a massive driftwood log, its clump of sea-softened Medusa-like roots half-buried.

They sat, propped against the enormous timber, feet dug into the sand, and watched waves roll in with metronomic consistency. After about five minutes, Abby said, "Okay, I'm ready. Start at the beginning."

"Well, when I was pregnant with Jonah," Steph began hesitantly, "I discovered a medical issue that turned out to be genetic." It felt important that Abby know there'd been a compelling reason behind all this, not the haphazard outcome of a holiday DNA kit. "I investigated my family first and came up empty. No one had it. Then it dawned on me that the carrier must be from outside of the family." Steph sighed. "Long story short, I unwittingly forced my mother's hand. She'd kept the secret from all of us, my father included."

"What's she like, your mom?"

Steph smiled. "Kind. Unassuming. Family-centered. And apparently, a lot more complicated and secretive than I knew."

"Or scared," Abby offered. "Do you have brothers or sisters?"

Steph shook her head. "It was always just the three of us: Mom, Dad, me," she said. "I have lots of aunts and uncles, and a gang of first cousins who were like siblings." But she'd been the odd person out as the only child. "For what it's worth, your father never knew of my existence." Steph hoped that Abby would find some comfort in knowing that her father hadn't lied.

"How old are you?" Abby asked, creating a visor with her hand to look Steph in the eyes.

Yes, there was that. Liar . . . cheater . . . what was the difference? "Same as you, I turned thirty-eight in May."

The wind kicked up, islanding the clouds, and Abby's gaze moved to a trio of stick-legged sandpipers, scurrying along the shoreline, chasing the remnants of waves as they foraged for invisible aquatic creatures. "Those guys are my favorites," she said.

Steph pulled her legs into herself and wrapped her arms around her shins, placing her forehead on her knees and staring at the countless grains of sand beneath her.

"I'm sorry for springing this on you. I was thinking like a cop, not a sister."

Abby didn't respond. She lifted her face to the sun and closed her eyes.

"I had this stupid idea that maybe you already knew," Steph said.

"Well, you look just like him. I mean, I should have been able to figure it out. The resemblance is uncanny. But I didn't put it together." Abby stretched and the sandpipers abruptly took flight, bursts of wing beats followed by short glides, low over the wave line. She rearranged her legs beneath herself to face Steph. "I had no idea. I mean, I grew up believing my parents had a perfect marriage."

Steph felt a stab of guilt. "Was it always just you three—you, Ken, and your dad?" she asked.

"Mostly. My father has an older brother, but they're not close. No cousins. I had a terrific stepmother for a few years. Gretchen." Abby released a handful of sand through the funnel of her fist. "She was a ray of sunshine and made everything bearable for a while. It was just so great to have another woman in the family. But then she left." Another handful of sand. "I stay in touch with her, but we keep it on the down-low."

"Why?" asked Steph.

"Hmm. Let's just say, loyalty is an expectation with the Gardners."

"What about Ken?" Steph asked, having always wanted a big brother. "Are you two close?"

Abby frowned. "Not really, not anymore. We're like enemies who love each other. At least, I love him. I honestly don't know how he feels about me. We used to be close, arguably too close. If you drew a Venn diagram of us as kids, there was barely any part that wasn't overlapping. Between not having a mother and having a"—Abby took a moment to find the word she was looking for—"*complicated* father, sometimes we were all each other had. But now, the truth is, Ken scares me."

Steph flashed to the Ten of Swords and Toni's warning: *Wounded people wound*. "Scares you . . . how?"

Abby picked at a ragged cuticle. "He's just angry. Very angry."

"At . . . ?" Steph prompted.

"Me?" Abby shrugged. "His lot in life?"

"His lot? You?" Steph repeated. "I don't understand. The man has everything. What more could he possibly want?"

"Come on. You know that things are never what they seem. Ken suffered in ways that I didn't as a kid. He'd be the first to tell you. He *really* lost our mother, whereas I never had her. And, of course, deep down he blames me, and I get it." Abby took the cuticle between her teeth and ripped. "Plus, he was bullied at school, if you can believe it."

That was hard for Steph to picture.

"Anyway, I think in some ways he's still that same little boy. I don't know if he ever really got past any of it."

Just then Frida charged toward the water, barking at a couple of seals whose heads had popped up. The ocean was clear enough that even when the seals dove, their silhouettes were visible through the waves. The dog was so happy that her hind section moved independently from her front, bouncing side to side as she barked.

"Steph, I'm curious. What are you hoping to get out of this?" Abby asked.

The question felt like a slap. Did Abby think she was after their money?

"What I mean is, you came to Cape Cod in search of your biological roots . . . What were you hoping to find?"

Before she could answer, Abby rose and proceeded to the water's edge. Steph followed, considering the question. It went back to her childhood sensation of not quite belonging. "I don't know. That missing piece that makes the puzzle whole?"

Abby bent down and picked something up, dropping it into Steph's hand. A nugget of green sea glass perfectly frosted. She turned it over in her fingers; she'd treasure it. But how to answer Abby's question without embarrassing herself? The truth was, she'd imagined it playing out like a Hallmark movie, all soft focus and sappy music. A cold wave slapped her ankles. "The fantasy was that my existence would make as much sense to you as yours did to me," Steph admitted. "Idiotic, but true."

Abby whistled for Frida, who'd raced ahead. "So, why so sneaky?"

Steph considered trotting out the detective excuse. The impulse had been entirely self-protective. "Frankly, you Gardners are more intimidating than you think. I grew up with nurses, teachers, cops, full stop," she said. "I was scared you might not like what you saw." Then she flashed to the image of Adam Gardner keening like a madman on the bow of his boat. "Your father freaked me out yesterday."

"*Our* father," corrected Abby.

Steph studied the water. "So, what exactly is his issue?" To think, she'd come to find answers about one genetic illness only to discover a potentially worse one.

"You've heard of bipolar disorder, right?" Abby asked.

"Of course." Steph had dealt with all sorts on the job.

"Well, then you know how broad the diagnosis is. Obviously, Dad is extremely high functioning," Abby said. "For what it's worth, he hasn't gone off the rails like this in years. Usually, he manages his symptoms well with medication. I'm trying to get to the bottom of what happened this time."

About fifty feet ahead of them, a seal lumbered out of the water, moving caterpillar style onto the beach. Abby whistled again for Frida. The dog heeled immediately and allowed herself to be leashed.

"Good girl," Abby said, giving her a treat. "What's the plan from here, Steph? I'm assuming you're going to tell Ken and my dad?"

The plan had been to come clean after Adam's birthday party. But given what Steph witnessed on his boat, she'd been reconsidering her options. "I'm not sure," she said. "I'm glad *you* know of my existence." That much was true.

Another bulky seal hauled itself onto the sand ahead of them. Steph had never seen seals on the beach before. Out on the sandbars, yes. There, they gathered by the dozens. These two were massive, and she wondered if it was smart to walk between them and the water.

Abby seemed to have the same thought and directed them up the slope of sand, where they made a large semicircle to give the seals space. Frida sniffed the air wildly.

"If what you're looking for is a father figure—" Abby began.

"Oh, I'm not," said Steph. "Not at all. I have a great dad."

Frida stopped in her tracks and let out a rumbling growl.

Abby shushed the dog. "Well, that's good to hear."

Then they saw it, a shadow appearing out of nowhere, becoming visible in the wave like an enormous torpedo, cruising parallel to the shore, two thousand pounds of primordial beast.

"Oh my God," Steph gasped. "Is that—"

"Yes! A great white shark. Sixteen feet easy," Abby said, thrilled. "That's what drove out the seals!" She patted Frida's head. "Good girl. Good girl. Stay. Stay right here." She dropped the leash and took off toward the water.

Steph froze, hands clasped over her chest as if that might slow her racing heart. "Careful," she called.

Abby waved for her to follow, but Steph couldn't budge.

"They haven't had feet for millennia," Abby called back, laughing. "Get over here. This is a once-in-a-lifetime sighting."

"I'm scared," Steph said, feeling absurd.

"There hasn't been a shark-related death in New England since 1936. You're more likely to die from driving on Route 6," Abby said.

Steph would take her chances on the highway, doubting she'd ever swim in the ocean again. But she edged her way down to where Abby stood, ankle deep in water. Side by side, they watched the forked tail move—back and forth, back and forth—leisurely propelling the giant fish along, its dorsal fin cinematically poking up every once in a while. Then, with a single, abrupt thrash, it disappeared, leaving a swirl on the water's surface that vanished in its wake.

Adam

For a good week now, Adam awoke sapped and drained, as exhausted as when he'd gone to bed. His mind was no longer an enchanted loom, weaving tangled dreams and scientific observations into theories. Gone were the pepper-hot stars that guided him through the black night. Outer space now just seemed dark and endless. And the ocean, well, it was just metric tons of salty darkness. The secret of the universe was that there was no secret. It was all meaningless and absurd, and anyone who said differently was a fool.

Still prone, he reached for his iPhone and tapped his humpback playlist, listening incredulously. How had he once heard poetry and love songs? These were grunts, clicks, screeches. Unintelligible mammal sounds. That was it. The product of air reverberating through the larynx and complex systems of sacs near blowholes—closer to burps than speech. Whatever grand thoughts Adam had had about discovering a majestic leviathan culture, well, they were the meanderings of an undisciplined mind.

Adam looked at his clock. It was already 9:00 a.m. and how he felt at this moment was likely the best he'd feel all day. For the next twelve hours—if he could stay awake that long—his concentration and energy would float away, a helium balloon turning into a dot on the horizon. At that bleak thought, Adam swung his legs off the bed and forced himself to a sitting position. He pushed himself up with a grunt and made his way to the kitchen where he dumped the remainder of a bag of coffee into his French press, hoping to push back the fog bank in his head.

Mug in hand, Adam shuffled out to the deck. On his pond, two regal and haughty swans, a cob and a pen, moved listlessly against the dark water, their shapely necks dipping below the surface to harvest aquatic plants. Not even one of their cygnets had survived this season. Adam had heard the alarm squawks of the chicks on four different occasions as they were snatched by some predator, a coyote or raccoon, perhaps even Charon. Four, three, two, one, and then *poof*, all babies gone. So much effort for naught.

He sat in his Adirondack chair for over an hour, a gray anchor of hopelessness pulling him down. Intellectually, Adam knew he'd swung to the opposite pole and into that warped black hole where gravity pulls so hard that light cannot get through. People got depression all wrong. It had nothing to do with feeling sad, and everything to do with feeling nothing. And "depression" just might be the most inadequate word in the English language. How could a word used to describe a sunken hollow on a pillow also encompass this? This soul-destroying state deserved its own word.

Adam rose. He needed to go back to bed before Abby arrived. If he were asleep, there would be no point to her spouting bromides: *You'll feel better soon! We've been here before!*

Gah. Adam was too far gone.

What was the point of any of it? he wondered, depositing his empty mug on top of a pile of dirty dishes in his sink. Filling up gas tanks . . . grinding coffee . . . signing mortgages . . . vowing to love a single person for eternity? It was time to call the game. Adam's moments of greatness were behind him, his scientific discoveries long over. As he passed his office, he closed the door. He didn't want to see all those graphs and charts, evidence of his lunacy.

In his bedroom, he kicked off his slippers and climbed back under the sheets, desperate for the oblivion of sleep. When it didn't come, he thought of the exposed beams that ran the length of the living room ceiling, his father's hunting knife that he kept on his desk, the welcoming porcelain of his bathtub, his beautiful kettle pond. What might it be like to observe the swans from below? All frantic, paddling feet. But these contemplations only made Adam feel worse. Deep down, he knew he didn't have the cojones to off himself. He was *that* pathetic.

Maybe seventy wasn't the end of the world, but it was a vertiginous milestone, a hulking step toward the cliff face of mortality. What did Adam have to show for seven decades on the planet? Would he be leaving it a better place? Would his children? Not particularly. Not at all, in fact. Somehow, he'd even managed to fail to ensure the survival of his family line. After Ken, there was no one to carry on the Gardner name. Adam would be forgotten in a generation or two, his legacy having less impact on the world than a single, life-creating, energy-rich whale fall.

Ken

Ken smiled patiently, nodding along as Jenny guided him across their lawn to review the seating chart for Adam's party. To think, just yesterday Abby had called suggesting they postpone the party. Their father, she told him, was in a "precarious" mental state. When was their father *not* in a precarious mental state? Ken knew he'd been obnoxious when he told her to calm down and stop overreacting, but such were the grooves of their siblinghood. The party plan would not be changing, he informed his sister. He had too much in the way of sunk costs to cancel this late in the game. Abby had zero sense of how the world worked.

Normally, Ken didn't get involved at this level, but he was keen to know the details and figure out the best, most visible spot for his gift. Jenny showed him where the head table would be and where his father would be seated, and Ken squatted to check the view lines, deciding exactly where the high top on which his model would be mounted should go.

"Where are you thinking for the toasts?" he asked.

Jenny stopped in front of the stairs to the deck, her taut thighs visible through the gauze of her sundress. Through the sliding doors behind her, Ken could see the backs of Frannie's and Tessa's heads bobbing above the sofa cushions. The Olympics were on, and he could make out a blur of swimmers porpoising down turquoise lanes on his enormous flat screen.

"Well, I thought the impromptu ones could just be given from the tables. But for you and Abby"—she ascended the steps—"it would be more dramatic from up here."

Yes, Ken liked that idea. "You've already ordered a mic?"

Jenny gave him a look that told him of course she'd ordered a mic; he should know better than to ask. Ken felt a rush of appreciation. She was going to make an exceptional congressional wife.

"What?" she asked.

He met her at the top of the stairs but couldn't find the right words to express the gratitude he felt, and the moment passed. Jenny's eyes darted back down to her clipboard. Ken looked out to where the head table would be and imagined his dad's astonished expression once Ken unveiled his gift. Beyond that, he noticed that the expensive, new, salt-tolerant vegetation he'd planted to reinforce the upper bank of his property was not thriving. He'd need to call his landscaper. Beside him, Jenny reviewed the event flow: an hour of cocktails and hors d'oeuvres on the deck; dinner in the tent; Frannie and Tessa to kick off the program with the song they wrote; then toast and gifts served with cake and champagne.

"Do you want to go first or last?" she asked.

"Last," Ken said, imagining it would be awkward for Abby to follow such an extravagant gift.

Out of his peripheral vision, he saw the girls were now jumping up and down on the sofa. An American must have won the gold. Who? Ken wanted to get inside and find out. He made a circling motion with his hand, impatient for Jenny to move things along.

She scowled. "You asked for this run-through."

"Yeah, well, I think we've covered just about everything," he said. "Make sure the high top for my gift goes here." He tapped his foot on the location where he knew the deck's spotlight would hit. "You can put Abby's easel there."

"Aye-aye, Captain," she said.

Ken made a mental note to pick up a stronger floodlight bulb. He felt Jenny's eyes boring into him. "What?"

"I was just thinking . . . maybe you and Abby could go up on stage together?" She shifted her weight from one foot to the other.

Why would he want to do that?

"You know how nervous she gets speaking in public."

How had the conversation turned into helping Abby?

"Plus, her painting is personal," Jenny continued. "She's likely to feel vulnerable."

Ken dug into his pocket and found his phone, which blinked to life.

"Abby's a big girl," he said and scrolled through some messages. "I've got to get going."

"Hey, I thought I had you until noon," Jenny said, reaching for his arm. "I'd hoped we could have a bit of a talk."

Ken shoved the phone back into his pocket. "About?"

"Well, um. About Abby and the Arcadia."

Not this again. He wasn't in the mood. "No can do. David and I moved up our tee time," he said. "I figured you'd appreciate having me out of your hair sooner."

Jenny crossed her arms. "Ken, I'm serious about having this conversation."

"Sure," he said, already turning away from her and reaching for the sliding door.

"And sooner rather than later," she said to his back. "Some major stuff is going on with Abby, and she needs you."

"Jenny—" A warning. There was a time in his life when he'd have done anything for his sister. But that time was long gone; she'd thrown him aside. Ken slid open the door and was greeted by a wall of cold air. His stomach growled, hollow and empty.

"Please," he heard Jenny say from behind him.

The anger came from nowhere, and Ken shut the slider behind him. *What the fuck?* Jenny was supposed to be on his side.

The girls let out a sudden whoop.

"Did Phelps win the gold?" he asked.

His daughters threw their arms around each other as they jumped up and down.

"No. Simone Manuel!" Tessa screamed, pumping a fist overhead. "An Olympic record!"

Who the hell was Simone Manuel? "What about Phelps?"

Tessa looked at him as if he smelled. "Is it only real for you if the athlete is a dude?"

If there was a shittier time to be a man—let alone a successful, white one—Ken couldn't think of it. He stormed into the kitchen and grabbed two mozzarella sticks out of the fridge. On the counter, Jenny's phone vibrated annoyingly. He touched the screen to shut it up, and saw an alert, a message from Abby. He wondered exactly what this "major stuff" of Abby's was and shoved a cheese stick into his mouth whole. There was only one way to find out. He looked up—the coast was clear—and unlocked Jenny's phone. A grainy image came through that he couldn't make sense of—a bright lampshade shape of striated lines on a background of black—followed by three bouncing ellipses.

Ken waited.

Ur nephew!!!

Out of nowhere, the Maurice Sendak line came to him: *Oh, please don't go—we'll eat you up—we love you so!*

The clubhouse overlooked the golf course, which undulated above Pleasant Bay. Close to shore, sailboats rocked on their moorings, and in the distance, they shot across the open water, white triangles taut with wind. Ken and David sat at the blond bar, where they ordered beers. The two had been golfing together since they were kids, and never once had Ken been so off his game, bogeying hole after hole and chunking the green at least a half dozen times. The truth was, he couldn't concentrate. All he could think about was Abby's sonogram. And that she'd kept it secret from him. He wondered how long Jenny had known.

Their beers arrived, cold and hop bitter.

"To the election and better times ahead," David said, lifting his stein.

Why hadn't Abby told him? Ken felt hurt, a fresh wound atop the old ones. Rejected, blindsided, kept in the dark. He flashed back to the day Abby told him he wasn't allowed in her room anymore. He'd never been able to figure out what had changed to precipitate that verdict: they hadn't fought; Gretchen was finally gone for good; and their father was stable—or stable enough. *Oh, please don't go.*

David cleared his throat, his beer midair.

"Oh, sorry," Ken said, knocking his mug against David's. "Cheers." He took a sip and tried to get his mind off his sister. "So, how about you give me the real scoop on old Hillary. What's she like in person?"

Considering the Republican Party's unelectable nominee, Ken had been forced to wrap his head around the inevitability of a Clinton presidency. But what would that mean for his own congressional campaign? It could be a good thing. By 2018, Americans would likely be disenchanted with their first woman president, dishonest and strident as she was, and Ken could ride the wave of the backlash. Midterm elections seldom went to the president's party.

"Surprisingly likable," David said. "Way more chill than you'd imagine. Super funny. Wicked smart."

Crooked Hillary, *funny*? David must be downing the Kool-Aid by the gallon to believe that. The good news was that even if Madame Clinton was chill and funny, she was incapable of projecting it. Like or hate The Donald, the man had tapped into some live wire of rage residing within every average Joe—it was nothing short of extraordinary.

"How are Rebecca and Peony doing?" Ken asked, pivoting before they got too deep into politics. "I don't think I've laid eyes on them since the Memorial Day party." He hadn't seen that much of David, for that matter. They'd hung out at a couple of the usual summer gatherings, but this was their first one-on-one of the season.

David drew in a breath and blew it through puffed cheeks, placing his hands on either side of his beer. "Rebecca's back in DC." He rapped his knuckles twice on the bar. "We're splitting up. Everything's amicable. Everything's good. We've been moving slowly for Peony's sake, but it's over."

Ken sucked in a deep breath. He hadn't seen this coming. "Sorry to hear it, buddy," he said, slinging an arm across David's shoulder and squeezing. "Sounds tough."

David nodded. "It has been, but it's okay now. It's been brewing for years. The hard part is behind us." David sighed and changed the subject. "How are Jenny and the girls? What's your news?"

Before Ken could answer, the burgers landed, filling his nostrils with the potent aroma of grilled meat—crusted on the outside, juicy on the inside, topped with dripping cheddar, and sandwiched in a ciabatta roll, hearty enough to handle the mess. The rest of the plate was a profusion of pickles, tomato and onion slices, and lettuce leaves. The bartender returned with a large cone of crispy fries and three mini-crocks: mustard, mayo, and ketchup. Ken shoved the burger into his mouth, consuming a quarter of it in a single bite. Why was he so famished?

"Everyone's good," he said, the words muffled over the mouthful. He chased down the bite with a swallow of beer. "Our summer's been a bit dominated by my dad's birthday party, but that'll be in the rearview mirror soon enough."

"He doing okay?" David asked. "I went over to say hello last week and he seemed kind of . . . well, you know, kind of off."

Ken shrugged. "No surprise there." His thoughts returned to Abby. It occurred to him that she might announce her little miracle at his party, once again trying to steal his thunder. "Here's something hot off the presses," he said, not caring that it wasn't his news to share. "Guess who's knocked up?"

"No clue," David said, dipping a fry in mayo.

"My sister."

The fry tumbled down David's front, landing on his lap, three small globs of mayonnaise staining his shirt and shorts.

Ken shook his head like they were in on the same joke. "I know," he said with a chuckle. "I didn't know she was seeing anyone, either."

Jenny

"Momma," Frannie whispered, lifting the pillow that covered Jenny's head. A stab of morning light. "The tent guys are here. What should I tell them?"

"What time is it?" Jenny groaned, consciousness leveling her like a steamroller. She was thirsty and bloated, her wedding band digging into her flesh. She considered asking Frannie what day it was but then remembered that the tent was to be erected the day before the party.

"It's 9:40, sleepyhead," Frannie answered, leaning in to give her a kiss. "Last night was so much fun, Mom. You were hilarious."

The words were not comforting. Jenny's mouth tasted evil, and she turned her head to spare Frannie her hangover halitosis. *Hilarious, how?* She replayed what she could remember from the previous evening. Her first glass of wine, sipped on the deck, had softened the edges of her stupid fight with Ken. The next glass was consumed in the kitchen when it became clear that Ken—petulant man-child that he was—would not be coming home for dinner, or even calling, for that matter. That glass had been the miracle worker; the second one *always* was the miracle worker, sending in the cavalry—endorphins! Come home, don't come home, she didn't care.

But then, Jenny made her usual mistake: chasing the miracle. The third glass was *never* as good as the second. And last night, number three had flipped the switch. She'd downed the rest of the bottle and wanted more. So, Ken didn't feel the need to come home for dinner? Didn't think he owed her a call? Well, screw him! They'd have a blast without him. Anything that their uptight father normally said no to would be A-okay with Momma tonight. Could the girls watch *Orange Is the New*

Black? Absolutely. Eat ice cream on his Le Corbusier lounge chair? *Bon appétit!* Do craft projects in the den? Jenny would get the glue gun.

"It'll be a Gardner girl party," Jenny had said.

Frannie and Tessa were all in, and as soon as they became absorbed in an activity—braiding strips of their father's T-shirts into bracelets with eyes trained on the large flat-screen television—Jenny snuck over to the liquor cabinet, careful not to jangle bottles, to throw back a shot of whatever was nearest.

After that, the memories became sketchy. She recalled teaching the girls to do the merengue, watching for shooting stars flattened on the lawn, and—oh God—had she taken them skinny-dipping? Jenny reached for her hair, stiff and salty. Indeed she had. She hadn't had a blackout since her RISD days, and yet there was no mistaking the light-flickering-on-and-off-in-a-dark-room sensation. What she didn't know was whether she'd lost five minutes or two hours. Her stomach lurched and a cold sweat broke over her.

"Sweetie, tell the tent guys I'll be down in fifteen," Jenny said. A dent in Ken's pillow told her that her husband had made it home after all. "Where's Daddy?"

"Putting stones in the revetment, I think."

He did this before every full moon when the tides were strongest. *Would he ever give up?* "And Tessa?"

"Still asleep."

"Thanks, sweetie," she said and watched Frannie hurry out of the room.

Jenny squeezed her eyes shut, hot tears rolling down into her ears. Had the girls known she was drunk? Jesus Christ, this could never happen again.

Jenny pushed herself gingerly to a sitting position, trying to calculate just how much of her day would be lost to this hangover. She reached for the Advil container that had taken up residency on her bedside table and swallowed three. Then she picked up her iPhone, in the hopes that it would help with the patchy arithmetic of recalling the previous night. Well, here was something: she'd taken 6,847 steps (to where, she had no idea). To her relief, there were no selfies or social media posts. Thank God. And no outgoing calls, though apparently, she'd had two conversations. One with Ken, lasting under a minute. The other with her father, which went on for more than ten. She had no recollection of either. All in all, it could have been worse.

Abby

When Abby arrived at her father's house, it was past noon, and he was still asleep. She studied him through the open bedroom door. Adam lay faceup, legs and arms splayed toward the corners of the mattress, mouth hinged open. He'd definitely lost weight, maybe ten pounds or so, and his face looked skeletal, with sunken eyes and loose skin gathering by his ears. Most disturbingly, every feature that had once made him look distinctly like himself—almond-shaped eyes, sharp nose, and precise jawline—seemed to be dissolving into something generic. Her handsome father was starting to look like every other old person, droopy and flat-cheeked.

As she watched his chest rise and fall, Abby was seized by the terrifying notion that people could hide their entire lives behind a lie. As if the truth was somehow up for discussion. She had a sister. Was it even possible that her father hadn't known? Perhaps Steph's conception had happened during a manic cycle when her father wasn't himself. Small comfort. She could have dozens of half-siblings for all she knew. Abby knew that her father wouldn't be around forever, and when he died, their intense, inexplicable relationship would disappear with him. As would a fundamental way in which she'd known herself: as Adam Gardner's daughter.

Abby tiptoed through the house, seeing it with new eyes. She'd grown up on the myth of happy parents, the story fundamental to her sense of self. Abby was the product of true love. If that had been a lie, what else had been? She pushed open the door to her bedroom, which had remained unchanged since she was a girl. A time capsule. She'd only ever heard one story, straightforward and tragic: life had been idyllic for the Gardners until a fluke embolism killed her mother and changed their course. But that hadn't been the whole story. With the discovery of a half sister, a new plotline had been added. Abby wondered if her mother had known about the betrayal. Didn't all women secretly know? Maybe it wasn't a blood clot that had killed her. Maybe it was heartbreak.

Abby found herself sitting on the floor of her closet, a familiar place. She'd spent hours in here as a child. Doing what? Hiding was what, but from who? Abby felt her heart race as she chased those memories, focusing on a strip of light coming under the door.

Her phone pinged and illuminated. A text from David.

That u at ur dads?

Abby rose, exited the closet, and looked out her window across the weather-beaten deck toward David's family house, barely visible through the thick summer brush. How did he know she was here? As kids in the summer, they used flashlights to signal to each other at night. Three pulses meant the coast was clear. He must have caught a glimpse of her car pulling in.

yup, she wrote back. **when did u get back?**

time for a walk?

gimme 5?

A thumbs-up emoji appeared.

Abby stepped into the bathroom to freshen up before meeting David. It was a mess of toppled-over pill jars and Post-it Notes affixed to the side of the mirror: DARE GREATLY and FUCK THE BEGRUDGERS. *Oh God, her poor father*, she thought, peeling off the notes and tossing them into the trash. She'd deal with the rest of it later. Her reflection startled her. Her skin glowed and her face was fuller. She looked good, beautiful even.

Before she left the house, she looked in on her father again. Still dead to the world. While she felt guilty at the thought, Abby was relieved that her father wouldn't do anything too outlandish at his party. He was so much more manageable when he was depressed.

She met David at their tree, the scrub oak where he'd carved their initials into a heart when she was in the ninth grade.

"Hey," she said.

"Hey," he said back.

Why did she feel shy?

David's eyes bored into her. "So, it's true."

Abby smiled. "What's true?"

"You're pregnant." His eyes glistened with tears. "Is it mine?"

Abby flinched but nodded. *Jenny had told David?* No, she wouldn't.

"Your brother spilled the beans."

So, Jenny had told Ken. Worse.

Then David's arms were around her, and she could feel his sobs move through his body. "Abby. We're having a baby!"

She hadn't expected this reaction and started to cry herself. Was it too much to hope for that perhaps David was finally ready for the type of partnership she'd always wanted? "I'm sorry I didn't tell you sooner," she stammered. "At first, I wasn't sure that I was going to keep it. And then, well, when you said you were splitting up with Rebecca, I didn't want to add to your pressures."

"Shhh. It doesn't matter now." David rocked her back and forth in his arms and she felt his shoulder blades move beneath her hands. Then he stepped back to look her in the eyes. "And for sure it's a boy?" His voice choked with emotion.

Did it matter? Abby smiled back. "That's what my OB seems to think."

And suddenly she was off her feet. David lifted her in his arms. "You're giving me a son!"

Giving him a son?

Then he was kissing her.

"Wait." Abby pushed him back.

"It's okay. Rebecca left for DC last week. It's over. And Peony's off with friends." His fingers were already at work, unbuttoning her shirt, and a moment later, they were half naked, falling into avid, urgent sex, lust streaked with tenderness.

Afterward, Abby laid her head on his chest, feeling soothed by the rhythmic beat of his heart.

"So, what are you thinking about how this will work?" she ventured.

"Don't worry," David said with a laugh. "I know better than to try to make an honest woman of you!"

Abby sighed with relief. That was a start. She'd be entering her last trimester as the presidential campaign would be in its final stretch, David's busiest time. She didn't want him to worry about her, but she also didn't want to have to worry about him and his feelings. This pregnancy had been hers alone until now. "You don't need to change your plans. I've got everything taken care of—I've hired a doula and have Jenny to help with the early days."

"But we'll need to find a home together. It doesn't need to be in DC, of course," he said. "I'm happy to commute from wherever you want to live. Alexandria is a charming town."

Abby lifted her head. She wasn't moving to Virginia.

"You could keep the Arcadia, of course," he said. "And spend as much time there as you want."

"Why, thank you for your permission, David," Abby said, pulling away.

David winced as though he'd been slapped. "You know I didn't mean it that way."

What other way was there? Abby rolled off him, pulled on her shorts, and sat with her back against their tree.

David rolled onto his side, one hand propping up his head. "Abby, please. I didn't mean anything by it. We can work out the details later. We'll make it work. I'm just excited that we're finally going to be together, that's all. I love you."

She placed her palms on the underside of her belly and closed her eyes tightly, trying to ground herself. "I love you, too, David."

"I know there's a lot to think about," David soothed. "We can take things as slowly as you need. Deep breaths."

He didn't just say that.

"In and out. In and out." He inhaled and exhaled as if to show her how it was done.

There was little on earth that Abby liked less than a man instructing her to calm down. "I've got to get going," she said. "Ken and Jenny want my painting tonight. You know those two and their schedules."

David walked her back to her car, holding her hand tentatively. "Abby?" he said.

"Yeah," she answered, not looking at him.

Neither of them said anything else, the dangling question filling the space between them.

Ken

Moonlight streamed into Command Central. Abby's painting, delivered earlier in the day, leaned against the far wall, draped in a pretentious cloth emblazoned with *Little Monster* in stenciled block letters. The canvas was huge, far bigger than Ken had pictured. He scratched his chin. When had Abby's paintings taken on such colossal dimensions? Ken's model would be dwarfed beside it. To think of all the hours he'd spent crafting minute details—hand-carving the shingles, lettering the sign, collecting dime-size stone slivers for the path. He felt embarrassed and foolish. How was it that Abby could still do this to him, return him in an instant to the awkward little boy who missed his mommy?

Ken pushed off his desk and approached the painting, absentmindedly brushing his mother's X-Acto knife back and forth across his thumb, the blade making a soft scratching sound against calloused skin. He did *not* need to feel this way. He was Ken Gardner, for fuck's sake. He owned an apartment on Beacon Hill, waterfront property in Chatham, an artist's studio in North Truro, a forty-foot yawl. He had a stunning and clever wife and two beautiful daughters. When Ken spoke, people listened. He was widely admired and soon would be elected to District 9. And yet, one person still had the power to make him feel small. Abby was like a spring trap around a bare ankle, dragging him back to the past. Only guess what? Ken was capable of gnawing off his own limb. He was ready to cleave himself from his sister and be free of this feeling once and for all.

Two steps brought Ken directly in front of Abby's ostentatiously cloaked painting. *Little Monster*—of all the things to name it. Neither of them had ever liked this pet name of their father's. Ken flipped back the cloth. His breath caught. He'd forgotten how genuinely talented Abby was. The painting was bold and commanded attention. His eyes first landed on a dazzling central image: a pregnant torso with a baby curled inside. The Madonna and child. Was that boy supposed to be him? He moved on to the framing device, which he determined was an eye. Was it his eye or was Abby just demanding that he look? Ken knew there was a message for him in here somewhere, there always was—his sister's cryptic and passive-aggressive way of communicating. The lines kept shifting, making it hard to find purchase. Then his eyes were drawn to an entanglement in the lower-right corner—a snakelike boy coiled around a girl, crushing her. Ken studied the girl's expression, pained like she was being suffocated. He moved on to the boy, whose legs and arms strangled her. There was a blob of paint at the base of Abby's signature that created a kidney-shaped spot on the boy's buttock. Ken touched the birthmark on his backside. Oh my God. She hadn't. She wouldn't dare. But she had. Abby had outed them right on this canvas. A private message. No, a threat.

Pain, exquisite and precise, shot through him. Without meaning to, Ken had pressed the X-Acto knife deep into his thumb. His emotions galloped from betrayal to helplessness, and then morphed into fury. And with a violent thrust, Ken stabbed the knife through the offending image, slashing up and down and up again, leaving a trail of blood from his thumb on the canvas.

He heard a twig snap outside his open window. "Who's there?" he hissed into the night. All was silent.

Jenny

The dress Jenny planned to wear to Adam's party tonight hung on a hook on the closet door of the master bedroom. It was an irreproachable navy linen number, knee-length and sleeveless. She'd slip into it and—*presto!*—Mrs. Ken Gardner, model wife and hostess. But *where* was Jenny in all this? *Be Jennifer Lowell.* That was the advice that her mother had meant to impart, she felt sure of it now. *Be Jennifer Lowell.* And if what Tessa had witnessed the night before—her father destroying her aunt's painting—had taught Jenny anything, it was that behaving like a Stepford wife had done nothing to protect her family. For too long, Jenny had allowed herself to believe that if she behaved like a perfect wife and mother, nothing bad could happen. Well, that was a load of crap. Trauma was meted out randomly.

Jenny needed to figure out how to comfort her daughter. What Tessa had seen could not be unseen, and the worst thing Jenny could do would be to minimize or make excuses for Ken's behavior. Bad stuff was happening—right here under her roof—and Jenny needed to confront it and show Tessa that she was willing to take a stand.

She regarded the navy dress with pursed lips and then she threw open the closet doors and started rifling through the hangers. Where was it? Ah, there, there in the very back. She hadn't thrown it out, after all. She plucked out a vibrant, three-tiered peasant skirt and held it to her waist, regarding herself in the full-length mirror on the inner door. She spun, and the skirt swooshed delightfully. This was exactly the look she was after, bohemian chic. (No one need ever know that she'd paid $450 for it at Barneys.) But what to wear with it? The skirt needed a little oomph, some sex appeal. Soon enough, she found what she was after, a form-fitting top, more corset than shirt. *Oh, yes!* Instead of blow-drying and spraying her hair into its customary dome, Jenny finger-tousled her locks into a windblown beach look. A smudge of kohl on each eye, a smear of Vaseline across her lips, and that was that. She called the girls in.

"Wow, Mom! Beach hair. I love it," Frannie said, smiling approvingly. "Are you and Daddy getting a divorce?"

"Ha, ha," Jenny said.

But Tessa, not even dressed for the party, just gave her mother a blank stare. She was still in shock. And Jenny could understand why, having snuck into Command Central to see the damage for herself. Even knowing what to expect, she was unprepared for the gash and the triangular flap of canvas that revealed gaping blackness behind it.

It was a picture-perfect evening for Adam's party—temperatures in the 70s, breeze enough to dispel bugs, a cloudless sunset would occur at 7:35, and the ultimate party trick: a full moonrise at 7:47. It didn't get any better. Sure, she and Ken still weren't speaking, but they were handling it in the reserved manner of adults, pretending nothing was wrong and stiffly avoiding each other. Ken had no idea that she knew what he'd done, but he'd figure it out soon enough and know where her true allegiances lay. Abby was her best friend, and tonight, Ken was going to find out that the power dynamic in their marriage was shifting.

"Girls, it's time to make magic," Jenny said, retrieving two multipurpose lighters from the utility drawer and placing them in the hands of her daughters. There were dozens of unlit citronella candles decorating the property. "Let there be light!"

Jenny surveyed the house and lawn. Everything was ready: caterers in the kitchen, bartenders at the bar, waiters set to pass appetizers once the guests started to arrive. Through the windows, she watched Ken figuring out precisely where his and Abby's gifts should be placed. What was he expecting would happen when Abby's destroyed painting was revealed?

An urgent craving for a drink arose, and Jenny pictured tequila poured over ice. She loved the crackling sound of ice cubes collapsing and longed for the burn of the alcohol as it hit her throat. Just one. One would do the trick. No. Instead, she put on some jazz, knowing Ken hated it. The sultry tones of Coltrane jostled the tiny bones of Jenny's ears and she swayed, the bottom of her skirt fluttering like a petal in a breeze.

Welcome back, Jenny thought, feeling fiercely alive.

Adam

The sober sound of Mozart's Requiem seeped onto the deck where Adam sat. If there was a more heartbreaking key than D minor, he didn't know it. Even the purple pickerelweed flowers that grew abundantly in the shallow water of his pond looked desolate. While most people lamented Mozart's untimely death—so many masterpieces never composed—Adam felt envy. Wolfgang had died at the height of his powers, immortalized while he was vibrant and relevant. Had Adam been so lucky. Instead, he was destined to decline. This was the ultimate paradox of being human: the longing for vitality in a world ruled by decay.

Oh, how desperately he wanted to get out of going to this party. But when he suggested it to Abby that morning, she told him that he could wallow in self-pity for the next nine months, but not tonight. When had she become so bossy?

A text from Stephanie Murphy: **Happy Birthday, Adam! Looking forward to celebrating with you tonight.**

Unable to muster the energy to respond, Adam placed his phone screen-side down. It was just one night. Even he could get through one night. He read the speech he'd composed—embarrassing dreck. It read more like a Nobel acceptance than a thank-you-for-coming-to-my-party. He scrunched it into a ball. Who did he think he was? Charles Darwin? More like Victor Frankenstein—just another foolish scientist, believing his potential was limitless, only to be felled by an inflated ego.

Adam willed himself to walk back inside and get dressed. Abby would be picking him up at any minute. But after tonight, he promised himself, he would hole up in his cozy nest in the middle of the woods, commune with the birds and critters, and recede in every way from public life. Screw that rage-rage business, Adam would go gentle into that good night.

Ken

T-minus fifteen minutes.

How was Ken going to explain what had happened to Abby's painting? It was all he could think about as he maneuvered the easel to its spot on the deck. Here was an idea: What if, when his sister lifted the covering, he gasped along with everyone else? *Oh no! Whatever could have happened?* But what then? Bit by bit, Ken constructed a story like an eagle building a nest from twigs. He'd acknowledge his part in the calamity. *Yes, this could work,* he thought, nodding to himself. Here's what had happened: he'd been maneuvering Abby's enormous painting out of his office when he'd accidentally banged into the corner of his desk. The painting had been covered—he'd promised not to look! He had no idea any damage had been done. He was so sorry. So very sorry.

Suddenly, Ken had the unpleasant sensation of being watched and spun around. There was Tessa, her eyes boring into him. Sometimes his daughters could seem like young witches.

"Hi, honey," he said.

Tessa stared past him, flicking the trigger of the lighter in her right hand so that the flame shot out and extinguished, again and again.

"What?" he said.

With her middle and pointer fingers, Tessa made a *V* sign beneath her eyes and then pointed at him.

How did parents survive their children's teenage years? If twelve and a half was any indication of what was to come, he wasn't sure he'd make it. The days of arriving home to a sweet chorus of "Daddy, Daddy, Daddy!" were long gone.

Ken smiled at Tessa and returned the gesture: a *V* sign followed by a point. *I see you, too.*

Tessa shook her head.

He'd missed the point. *Again*. Giving their mime game another shot, he raised his shoulders and opened his palms to the sky. *What, then?*

Tessa's look was inscrutable. Frustration, yes, but there was something else. Anger? Not exactly. Then he saw it: pain, confusion, hurt. What was she trying to say? She repeated her original gesture—a *V* beneath her eyes—only this time, instead of pointing at him, she pointed at her aunt's painting. *I see you. I see Abby's painting.*

Before he could follow up, Tessa scampered off, lighting the remainder of the tea candles that ran the length of the deck.

I see you. I see Abby's painting.

Then it hit him. Oh God. Oh no. That twig snap he'd heard was Tessa.

The doorbell chimed, sending Ken back through his house and to the front door, where his father-in-law waited.

"Theo, good to see you," Ken said, gathering himself together. "Come in."

Theo gave him a hearty pat on the back. He was a small man with thinning blond hair and watery blue eyes. "I know it's not *your* birthday, son," he said conspiratorially, "but I trust you're excited about my little surprise?"

What had Ken forgotten? He was so shaken by Tessa's revelation he wasn't thinking straight. "Your surprise . . . ?"

"John Kaufman," Theo said, grinning wildly.

John Kaufman was the national committeeman of the Republican Party of Massachusetts, arguably the most powerful political ally a candidate could get. Ken had been desperate to get in front of the man. He was key to the success of any Republican race in Massachusetts. Over Theo's shoulder, Ken saw the first guests pulling into his long drive. Ken repeated the name. "John Kaufman?"

"Jenny didn't tell you?" Theo's voice was incredulous. "We spoke about it a couple of nights ago. John Kaufman will be my plus-one tonight. I'm afraid he'll arrive late and only be able to stay for thirty minutes, but still . . . you'll have the chance to make an impression."

Ken's breathing became shallow. John Kaufman. The man had been handpicked by Reince Priebus. Was it possible that Jenny was so angry that she would withhold this information? "Tonight. John Kaufman is coming here tonight. To my father's seventieth."

"Don't worry. John knows it's a family party, not a campaign event. Son, this is your lucky break. Do you know how booked his schedule is?"

"Yes, yes, of course," Ken stammered. The timing was far from ideal. There were so many unknowns: The shape his father would arrive in—Abby had tried to warn him. How angry Jenny was—he had to get to her quickly and beg her forgiveness (or at the very least, secure a truce for the evening). And Abby's wrecked painting. How would he play that now that Tessa knew? Sweat prickled on his forehead. Ken swallowed hard.

"Impress John tonight, and money will flow into your campaign like the tide into this harbor."

"Thank you, Theo," Ken said, ushering his father-in-law toward the bar where the off-putting rhythm of jazz was playing. Oh, Jenny was mad, all right. "I'm grateful."

More cars pulled into the driveway. In a matter of minutes, the party would be underway. Ken wondered if he had time to call an emergency family meeting—two minutes in the den to rally the troops. He'd beg if he had to. But the doorbell rang again. Apparently, it was already showtime. He heard Jenny's footsteps on the stairs. Okay, he'd communicate everything with a look: *I'm sorry I didn't call. I'm sorry for being a jerk. I'm sorry about whatever you saw and overheard me doing in that chat room last spring. I'm just so, so, so sorry.* But as he looked up and arranged his face to convey his apologies, Ken barely recognized the woman descending. It was Jenny, but not *his* Jenny. It was some other Jenny—a sexy, windblown, wild-child version of his wife. Ken thought he might pass out.

The Party

Perched atop its small hill, Ken and Jenny's home glowed gold in the late-summer light. Ruby-throated hummingbirds darted from blossom to blossom, gorging in preparation for their long journey ahead, and tissue-thin monarch butterflies teetered over Jenny's prize-winning hydrangeas, whose petals were just starting to antique. August was the Sunday of summer, and in the coming weeks nature would be on the move again—the sun lowering in the sky, seasonal residents pulling their boats, Stage Harbor emptying. Then school would start, clocks would turn back, and the autumn winds would reveal the true shape of the trees.

Abby pulled the Jeep off the driveway near Ken's tidy vegetable plot, adjusting a long, loose duster over her belly. In the garden, the tomato plants were heavy with fruit, and sturdy zucchinis sprang from bright-orange flowers. At the slam of the driver's side door, a rabbit froze like statuary.

Adam slipped out of the passenger side and wordlessly followed his daughter along the sandy perimeter path that allowed them to circumvent a front door entrance. Although he hadn't said much on the drive to Chatham, Adam had pulled himself together for the occasion, looking dapper in a gray linen suit, face freshly shaven. They paused at a small bench near the flat walkway on top of the revetment and gazed out to where the *Francesca*, queen of the harbor, rocked neurotically on her mooring. The tide was going out, tugging boats and their wobbling reflections toward the channel. On the far side of the cut, the Stage Harbor Lighthouse station—a red-trimmed keeper's dwelling and tower—rose from the dunes, postcard-ready.

"It's perfect," Abby said.

"Too precious, if you ask me," Adam said, preferring the unkempt look of the outer Cape. "You know what the French explorer Samuel de Champlain called Chatham?" The question, rhetorical. "Port Fortune!" Adam guffawed. "That man was prescient. This town is rotten with yuppies."

"Dad, no one says 'yuppies' anymore."

"Well, I'm nothing if not blissfully out of touch," Adam replied.

For several minutes, they sat quietly, lost in their thoughts. All around them, water was on the move, streaming from tidal pools and estuaries into the harbor where it drained through the mouth of the inlet and into Nantucket Sound and, from there, swept out into the Atlantic. Water was unstoppable, always on its way to somewhere bigger. Abby wondered if she should tell her father about her pregnancy now, in this private, peaceful moment. That might be nicer than hearing the news along with everyone else. She was at the end of the second trimester and her body had burst into bloom. All she'd need to do was toss off the cardigan.

"Dad—" Abby began, working up her courage.

"Have I ever told you about the migratory paths of our local humpbacks?" Adam interrupted.

Only about ten thousand times, thought Abby, as her father launched into a whirlwind tour of the humpbacks' stomping grounds in the waters off the Greater and Lesser Antilles—Cuba, Puerto Rico, the Virgin Islands—and as far south as Trinidad and Tobago. Abby's news would have to wait.

She took in the convivial party sounds floating down from the deck, now dotted with people in their pastel summer best.

"Ready?" she asked when her father stopped to take a breath. She was asking herself as much as him.

"Not quite," Adam said, clearing his throat. "There's something else I want to tell you." He paused. "I'm so proud of you, Abigail. I know I don't say it enough."

She could tell he was test-driving his talking points for his speech tonight, seeing how they sounded before he presented them. Sure enough, he launched into an ardent monologue of what he'd do differently if he had the chance for a do-over. But make no mistake, the admissions of his shortcomings weren't an apology. Rather, they seemed to raise his stature:

a genius who recognized his deficiencies. Somehow, by acknowledging his mistakes, Adam moved them to the credit side of the ledger. "Darling, as you know, my motto has always been 'Family first.'"

Abby felt heat rising in her body.

"Family has always meant everything to me," Adam said, the words agreeable in his mouth. "You and Ken . . . Jenny and the girls . . . you are the future of the Gardner family."

"Dad—"

But Adam wasn't ready to stop. "And your mother, of course. My dear, sweet Emily—" His voice caught. "Oh, she'd have been proud of you, too."

At the invocation of her mother, Abby put up a hand. She didn't want to hear his bullshit.

"We should get up there," she said and stood and turned toward the house.

On the deck, the party was in full swing.

At the far end was a raw bar where shrimp curled around the rim of a bowl of ice, bite-size chunks of lobster had been pre-skewered with toothpicks, and live shellfish were being shucked and served alongside piquant condiments: cocktail and mignonette sauces, lemon slices, and freshly grated horseradish. Trays of margaritas, champagne, and white and rosé wine circulated. Inside, a full bar was staffed by a clean-cut young man in a tuxedo T-shirt.

Jenny welcomed their guests, injecting party patter as she led them through the house and onto the deck: "What a lovely dress," "Nice to see you again," and "So good of you to come." With each new arrival, the crowd parted and shifted, introductions were made and forgotten, and chitchat resumed.

When Adam and Abby summited the three steps to the deck, a burst of claps and cheers erupted, followed by a spontaneous round of "For He's a Jolly Good Fellow." Adam frowned and waved his hands to silence the group, but the cheers only grew louder.

"What, haven't any of you seen a guy grow old before?"

Laughter.

A blonde waitress rushed over with a tray, aiming a flute of champagne Adam's way.

"Not a chance, sweetheart," Adam said, buoyed by all the attention. "I'll have four fingers of something amber."

More laughter.

Frannie got to him first and kissed his cheek. "Happy birthday, Gramps."

"Ah, Frances!" Adam said, lifting her hand over her head, so she could pirouette underneath. "You look like a perfectly ripe peach."

Frannie blushed and gave a little curtsy.

"When did you decide to skip thirteen and go straight to twenty-one?" he said. "Now, where's that sister of yours?"

"Right here, Gramps," said Tessa, stepping forward. She wore khakis and a blue blazer, hair slicked back against her scalp.

Time had no mercy. A girl one day, a boy the next—Adam could not wrap his head around this new generation and their "fluidity." And yet, question it, and *you* were the jerk.

"So, how does it feel to be a septuagenarian, Gramps?" Tessa asked.

Straight for the jugular, this one.

"Like a shipwreck, kid," he answered truthfully.

"C'mon, Gramps," Frannie cajoled. "It's your birthday!"

Adam sighed. To be so young as to have no idea of your insignificance. "In that case," he said, "I feel terribly, terribly wise. Ask me anything."

At the sight of Abby, Jenny knew she couldn't face this party sober and retreated into the kitchen in search of booze. Already, there was a strange energy to the evening. An edge. She'd been so close to changing back into her navy-blue dress, but when Ken demanded she do so, she'd defiantly refused. Now, she worried about what John Kaufman—a man capable of making or breaking her husband's political future—would think of her. And while she was going down that rabbit hole, what would he think of Tessa, dressed like a boy? In a nod toward damage control, Jenny tossed a gauzy shawl over her shoulders, which only served to make her look more like a flower child. She retrieved a bottle of tequila from under the sink.

The only thing that mattered now was Abby. Abby and her ruined painting. Jenny hoped her fix—skinny strips of gold mylar tape—would hold at least through the night. After that, if Abby ever forgave her, Jenny would work some real *kintsugi* magic on it and repair it permanently. But no matter what, she needed to get to Abby and prepare her. She'd left a half dozen messages on her voicemail but received no response. Jenny poured a shot and threw it back.

"Yowza." The word was followed by a low whistle. David. "I do not believe I've seen this girl for close to twenty years. You look amazing." He hugged her and then pulled back for another look. "To what do we owe this fabulous transformation?"

Jenny searched for a pithy response—"Life's short" or "Full moon"—but nothing came. Instead, she said, "Let's get you a drink," and reached for another shot glass. For David, she found salt and sliced open a lime. Lick. Gulp. Bite.

David threw his back. "I forgot how much I hate doing shots," he said, making a face and pushing the glass away. "Where's the man of the hour?"

Jenny pointed to where Adam held court in the middle of the deck. Her father-in-law didn't so much tell stories as perform them, puffed up like a pigeon in search of a mate. Up or down, the man loved an audience. As she and David made their way onto the deck, she saw Abby.

"Hi, handsome," Abby said to David.

"Abby," Jenny said. "Did you get my messages? We need to talk."

Abby kissed David on the cheek. To Jenny, she said, "Don't you think you've done enough talking already?"

David took a step back.

"What?" Jenny said, confused.

"My pregnancy was *not* your news to share," Abby hissed.

"Um. I think I'll get a glass of wine," David said and sped toward the bar.

"I don't know what you're talking about, Abby. I promise, I haven't said a word to anyone," Jenny said. She knew that once dinner was announced, she'd lose the chance to prepare Abby for what was to come. "I need to talk to you about your painting. It's urgent."

Abby narrowed her eyes. Was Jenny going to try to talk her out of unveiling *Little Monster*? She'd always known that painting the monster would come at a price, but she'd never considered that the price might be this friendship. The sun was starting to dip below the horizon and the sky turned the color of a peach. A gull, wheeling over the shoreline, released a crab from its claws, letting it smash on a rock below. Abby was willing to risk her heart tonight. "We're done here, Jenny," she said and walked away.

Abby saw Steph and Toni hovering near the raw bar awkwardly—they barely knew anyone at this party. Now that the shock of Steph's news had settled slightly, Abby wondered what having a sister in her life might mean. All endings were also beginnings, she told herself and moved toward them.

Tink, tink—the sound of a knife against a glass.

"Welcome, everyone," Ken said. "Thank you all for being here tonight to celebrate my father's birthday. We have a wonderful evening planned, so please head down to the tent and find your seats. The festivities will begin with a song that Frannie and Tessa wrote for the occasion." He glanced at the notecard in his palm. "I am supposed to encourage everyone to sing along with the refrain. The tune is the Beatles' 'Hey Jude.'"

The guests drifted off the deck and onto the lawn, heels sinking into the ground as they circled tables in search of their names. The sun threw its last javelins of gold and the sky passed through violet to become deep indigo. The waitstaff transformed the deck into a stage, placing a standing mic and two stools at the top of the stairs. Frannie and Tessa took their places on the stools. Seated in the wings with her ukulele in hand, Abby hummed a note, which the girls found, and started strumming.

Frannie:

Hey dude, don't make it bad.
Seventy's old, yeah, but you're still kicking.

Remember to accept things you can't change
Then you can slow the clock's tock-ticking.

Tessa:

Hey Gramps, don't be afraid.
But please stop talking about the ol' days.
The minute you see your audience doze,
Then it's time to try a new way.

Frannie:

And anytime you feel your age, hey Gramps, refrain,
Don't carry the world upon your shoulders.
For well you know that it's a fool who plays it cool
As he gets older and older and older.

Tessa:

Hey Gramps, don't let me down.
I know you love your humpback whale friends.
Remember to let them into your heart,
Then you can start to make it better.

Together:

So spout it out and spout it in, hey Gramps, begin.
Soon you'll be talking with your pod friends.
And don't you know that it's just you, hey Gramps, you do,
For humpbacks, they aren't listening.

Hey Gramps, don't make it bad.
Seventy's old, yeah, but you're still kicking.
Remember to accept things you can't change

Then you can slow the clock from

Ticking ticking ticking ticking, ticking, ticking OH!

Na na na na-na-na-na, na-na-na-na, hey Gramps . . .

The guests roared, joining in at the final *na na na na-na-na-na*, cheering "Encore! Encore!" when the song concluded. Frannie and Tessa beamed from the stage.

Then, the tent became unexpectedly silent, all eyes on the head table, where the guest of honor sat motionless. A luminescent arc of pearly moon crested the horizon, and somewhere in the distance, a great horned owl screeched.

Adam pushed himself to a stand.

"Tessa, Frances," he called from the table. "Thank you for that"—a beat passed—"*touching* tribute." Then, disregarding the agreed-upon sequence of toasts and tributes, Adam made his way to the deck like Moses parting the Red Sea.

So much for Jenny's well-orchestrated evening.

On stage, Adam positioned himself between Frannie and Tessa, a hand on each of their shoulders, and projected to his audience. "Please put your hands together for my delightful grandchildren."

The guests clapped.

Frannie and Tessa slid off their stools and made their way back to the head table with Abby following. Behind the guests, the enormous moon climbed out of the water, a watchful silver eye. Once the applause quieted, Adam spoke again, his voice soft and intimate. "As you have just heard, my friends, becoming irrelevant is not for the faint of heart."

At the head table, Jenny's father arched an eyebrow at Ken.

Ken shrugged. What could he do about it?

Nearby, Toni squeezed Steph's knee, Morse code for *I warned you*.

And all the while, the waitstaff lifted and lowered plates, moving through the room with fresh bottles of wine, making sure every glass remained filled.

Abby was mentally rehearsing what she planned to say about her gift when she felt her abdomen tighten and harden, followed by a wave of dull pain. No doubt a Braxton-Hicks contraction. She rocked in her chair, unaware that she'd winced until Jenny, leaning across her father's vacated seat, asked if she was okay. Abby didn't respond. Instead, she tried to catch David's attention, but his eyes were fixed on Adam.

"My friends," Adam continued from above, "it took over four billion years for us to come together tonight. If that isn't special, I don't know what is."

"We can't hear you," someone called.

Adam stepped in front of the mic. "Better?"

There were murmurs of approval.

"As the elder statesman of this little shindig, I have some words of wisdom to offer." Adam paused theatrically. "Homo sapiens have a one hundred percent mortality rate."

"Oh God," whispered Ken.

Beyond Ken, Jenny saw John Kaufman arrive and take his seat. She'd placed him at the only table with a vacancy, which happened to be the "outsider" table, where she put everyone she didn't know well—Betty the barista, Joe from Tzuco's, that nice lesbian couple, some of Adam's scientist friends. Jenny caught Ken's attention, notifying him with a head tilt of the late arrival.

Ken stole a look at Kaufman, who was seated beside the lady couple who'd won Jenny's bouquet at the church auction. The dark-haired one, Steph, noticed him noticing, and gave him a small wave. Tessa was right, she did look familiar.

"One hundred percent, folks," Adam repeated, and the microphone screeched. "And there's nothing any of us can do about it. You don't want to believe that any of this old-person stuff will happen to you, but guess what? It does. One day, you can't recall the lyrics to your favorite tune. Then, the melody goes. Then, the whole damn song." Adam wiggled his fingers at something going bye-bye on an invisible horizon.

The moon, fully out of the water now, hung cool and detached in the night sky, tipping the waves with silver.

"In my case, I was on the brink of the discovery of a lifetime, and then—*poof!*—it was gone." Adam smiled ruefully. "Old age. It's why we humans have the good sense to die."

Silence.

"I used to comfort myself with the knowledge that at least my good name would live on . . . but guess what? Even *that* has eluded me. No grandsons to carry on the Gardner name."

The guests shifted uncomfortably.

Ken glared at his sister. "Do something," he hissed. "If Dad will listen to anyone, it's you."

"So, my friends," Adam continued. "Let's lift our glasses to my demise!"

Abby sprang to her feet. "Do not—I repeat, do not—lift your glasses to that," she shouted, trying to make her voice sound sunny. Having no intention of going this alone, she pulled Ken up by the arm, which set off another dull ache of a contraction, this one lasting a little longer. She tugged him up the three steps to the stage.

Once there, Abby forced a smile. Her contraction had subsided. "Dad, we're here to celebrate your amazing life," she said.

Adam popped the mic off the stand—apparently unwilling to give up the spotlight—forcing Abby to employ her secret weapon early. She shrugged off her long, loose cardigan and revealed a protruding belly in a form-fitting dress onto which she'd painted a red circle with an arrow pointing northeast, the male glyph.

Adam dropped the mic, which crackled on the ground.

The audience cheered, making Abby feel as exposed as a freshly shucked oyster at the first squeeze of lemon.

"Does this mean what I think it means?" Her father's voice quavered. "Abigail, my darling girl, are you giving me a grandson?"

Once again, that word: *giving*. As if babies were gifts women bestowed upon men. Abby bristled: "Well, I'm having a baby in November. And yes, he will be your grandson. But your gift is over there," she said, pointing to the shrouded canvas.

"The Gardner name will continue!" Adam bellowed.

David crossed his arms. This had not been an immaculate conception, after all. He *was* the father, and the baby's last name would be Mandel.

"Umm . . . do we not count as Gardners?" Tessa whispered angrily at her mother.

Ken plucked the mic from the deck and returned it to the stand. Time to take charge—his house, his party. But suddenly, the toast he'd memorized was gone. He scanned the crowd, landing briefly on John Kaufman's appraising eyes. He moved his gaze to the head table, but things were no more welcoming there: Tessa glowered; Jenny was flagging a waiter for a refill, and Frannie made circles with her wrist, suggesting he move things along. Still, the words didn't come.

Abby came to his rescue, speaking into the mic he held. "We're speechless in the face of so much love, aren't we, Ken?"

"Why, yes," he managed.

Abby unfolded the biographical notes her father had written for them, but they were wrong for the occasion. A list of accomplishments wouldn't do. Adam's eyes were still shiny from the news of his grandson.

"How about we just skip straight to our gifts, which are from the heart," she suggested. "Ken, why don't you go first?"

Ken had made it clear he wanted to be last, but he couldn't very well punt for a second time. Below, his father-in-law was whispering furiously into John Kaufman's ear, no doubt making excuses for his subpar performance on stage. He needed to up his game. His eyes landed on that Steph woman from the church auction again. How did she even know his father?

"Ken—?" Abby said.

"Yes, of course," he said. "Thanks." He turned to his father, who was propped on a stool, one foot on a rung, the other planted on the ground. "Dad, you taught me how to sail and fish and survive in the wilderness and gave me an abiding love for the natural world of Cape Cod." Ken glanced at the audience to gauge how he was doing and zeroed in on John Kaufman, who was nodding approvingly. "And while I will never be able to repay you for the gifts you've given me over my lifetime, I think this will be a good start." Ken lifted the covering off his model.

Adam rose to examine his son's gift, illuminated in a bright cone of light. It was an architectural rendering constructed from balsa wood—just like Emily used to make. What a strange little gift.

"Why, thank you, Ken. It's adorable." Adam bent down to have a closer look. There was a miniature sign in front of the building: GARDNER SENIOR LIVING. Adam picked up the sign. Oh, this was rich. Gardner Senior Living. A laugh sputtered out of him like an old water faucet. Addressing the audience, he said, "Of all the buildings I ever thought might someday bear my name—say, a lab at the CCIO or a library at one of my alma maters, Dartmouth or BU—it never once occurred to me that my inaugural building would be a nursing home!"

"It's not a nursing home, Dad," Ken said. "It's a state-of-the-art senior living center."

"Potato, po-tah-to," Adam said and embraced his son. "Ken, I'm touched. And you built this all by yourself?"

His father wasn't getting it and was making Ken look foolish.

"Dad," he said, trying to rein in his irritation. "This isn't the gift. It's a *replica* of the gift."

But Adam wasn't listening. "Folks, my eldest is about to change the face of old people's homes!"

Ken looked at his father incredulously.

"Excellent craftsmanship, son," Adam continued blindly. "I haven't seen a model this elaborate since your mother designed the Arcadia." Adam made a show of admiring the homey touches: a replica of Charon on the stoop, his grandmother's rocking chair, shelves lined with tiny books. *Where on earth would he put this model?* Adam wondered, sure that Ken would expect it to be prominently displayed.

Ken handed his father an envelope. "Open this, please."

Adam stuck a finger under the flap and ripped. Inside, a legal document with his name on it. It seemed to be an investment—shares in Gardner Senior Living. He folded up the paper and returned it to the envelope. Then, the connection shunted into place so forcefully that he felt it physically: Ken had gifted him a condominium in his retirement community. To live in! Adam felt the color drain from his face. He'd move into a nursing home over his dead body. Was this some kind of joke? Was Ken *trying* to humiliate him? But when Adam looked into his son's eyes, he saw an earnest and vulnerable boy. Apparently, Ken thought this was a gift he'd want.

Just get through this night, Adam told himself. He could do that. He'd channel Anthony Hopkins and give an Oscar-worthy performance—*I ate his liver with some fava beans and a nice Chianti.* Tomorrow, he'd set things straight and let Ken know exactly what he thought of the plan to move him into a rest home.

"What a thoughtful gift, Ken," Adam said, smiling tightly. "Thank you."

Thoughtful? That was the best his old man could do? Ken had just given his father a million-dollar gift, one which would make his third act possible. Adam would never have to worry about money again.

Adam did his best to keep his expression neutral. One gift down—two, if you counted his granddaughters' brutal song—and one to go. He turned to face Abby, whose shrouded present now filled his horizon like a thunderhead. It was a painting, that much was obvious. Adam steeled himself for further public humiliation—perhaps it would be an elegant portrait of a withered man floating out to sea.

"Dad," Abby said, taking his hand and feeling unexpectedly nervous. "My gift to you is our family story. To most people, it will just look like a painting, but I hope you will see much more." As she pulled off the covering, Abby kept her eyes on her father for his reaction.

Ken stared straight ahead, his fists balled deep in his pockets, awaiting gasps from the guests who'd be horrified by the ripped and ruined painting. Instead, there was velvet silence. Ken risked a look over his shoulder to where his father stood besotted, both hands covering his heart.

"Oh, Abigail!" Adam said. "I don't have words. It's magnificent." To his guests, he said, "My late wife, Emily, picked out the name 'Abigail' for our daughter. It means 'father's joy,' and nothing could be truer."

Ken had never heard this story before. Did his name mean anything? A small, triumphant smile crossed his sister's face as quickly as a blip on a hospital monitor. Behind her, her painting loomed into focus. There was no flapping triangle of canvas. Was he losing his mind? Then he saw it, glinting in the moonlight: a gold ribbon, a gilded stream, branching across the painting. His wife's doing.

Adam choked up. How had he underestimated his daughter's talents and missed her progression as an artist? He knew she'd springboarded from her sculpture juvenilia, but he hadn't realized how powerful and original her new style was. Finally, his daughter had mastered beauty. The central image, a womb, captivated him to the exclusion of the rest of the painting. His grandson! A boy to carry on the Gardner name. "I will treasure this forever," he told her.

Ken stifled the urge to lift his model over his head and smash it on the ground. He stared at his sister, who was radiant beneath their father's approval. She'd outplayed him on his own turf. He'd like to wipe that sanctimonious smirk off her face once and for all.

"I have a little more to announce," Abby said, emboldened. "*Little Monster* will be featured on the cover of *Art Observer*'s fall issue and, along with other works of mine, will be included in a group exhibit about self-portraiture and identity at the Institute of Contemporary Art in October."

"Go, Aunt Abby!" Tessa shouted from the head table, standing up. Then the rest of the guests followed her lead and pushed back their chairs to give Abby a standing ovation.

Ken fought the urge to walk off the stage without looking back.

Abby beamed and bowed deeply. But as she tried to lift herself, a cramp radiated from her groin. Instinctively, she turned away and as she did, her eyes landed on her painting, where she caught the misplaced shimmers of moonlight streaking this way and that across the canvas. New lines. Ones she hadn't painted. She felt light-headed. Gold channels zigzagged their way across her work. Then it hit her. This was Jenny's doing. But Jenny would never intentionally damage her artwork. But then, who? And just as the answer came to her, an agonizing contraction tore through her, and her knees buckled.

Once on the ground, the deck felt downy soft, like a feather bed in a dark cave. And although there was urgency all around Abby—worried voices and hectic movement—the pain had been transformed into bliss.

Suddenly unburdened by the carapace of her body, Abby floated toward a brilliant light, possibly the moon, and observed herself from above.

"Abby!" Ken's voice near her ear.

"Wake up, Abigail." Her father's. "Someone, call 911."

David and Jenny were beside her now, too, and so were her sweet nieces—all of them on their knees and haunches, looking worried.

Abby wished she could let them know that everything was okay. She wasn't dying. She wasn't even miscarrying. She was just taking a much-needed break.

Abby, Abby, they kept calling.

If only they could float up here with her and see the world as she was seeing it. Then they'd realize how small a sliver of the universe they occupied.

Below, a compact shape burst up the stairs and onto the deck. Her half sister.

"Step back!" Steph said, taking charge.

Who the hell was this woman? Ken wondered. "I've got this," he told her, blocking her with a possessive arm.

"Move back," Steph ordered again, and when he didn't, she shoved him, causing him to lose his balance and fall on his ass. "I've had EMT training."

From where Ken sat, he watched John Kaufman frown and exit the tent. "That's *my* sister," he shouted, scrambling to a more dignified position.

"Mine, too," Steph said, pressing her ear to Abby's chest and listening for breathing. "More space, everyone! Give her more space."

And just like that, Steph had taken control of the situation, and the circle of bodies expanded.

Abby felt pressure on her wrist. Warm hands behind her neck, lifting and tilting her head back. A dry finger probed inside her mouth.

"Airway unobstructed," Steph announced. "Patient is breathing and with a pulse."

Who the hell did she think she was talking to? Ken wondered.

"Towels," she ordered. "I need towels."

Frannie dashed into the house and returned with an armful.

"Abby," Steph said, gently patting Abby's cheeks. "Squeeze my hand if you can hear me."

Not yet, Abby thought. Couldn't she have just five more minutes of this ecstasy? She felt towels, soft and warm, pushed against her crotch.

"Jenny," Steph said. "Hold the towels there with firm pressure. The paramedics should be here soon."

"Got it," Jenny said. "Is she miscarrying?"

Not on my watch, thought Steph. "No. Just keep the pressure steady. She'll be fine."

Abby felt pulled toward the voices. She wanted to let her family know that she was okay but she couldn't. She peeked out through the slit of her eyelids and tried to give a reassuring smile.

Ken saw Abby's glimmer of consciousness.

Jenny: "Hang on, Abs."

David: "I love you, Abby."

Wait. Ken felt a familiar prick of betrayal. What? Was David the father?

Tessa glared at her father and turned away.

Enough, Ken thought, standing up. This was vintage Abby. Her drama would be all anyone would remember of the night. Not his beautiful home. Not the fabulous catering. Not his extraordinary gift. How long would Abby keep up the show? He'd seen her open her eyes and smile even if no one else had. He didn't have to take another minute of it. He was done, he decided, and marched into his house to get his car keys.

"Abby," Steph whispered, continuing to slap her cheeks. "Come on, Abby. Wake up. Your baby needs you."

At the mention of her son, a cylindrical force pulled Abby back into her body. Her eyes fluttered open. Just inches over her face, her sister stared back, eyes glistening with love and relief.

Ken

Ken wasn't sure where he was headed, but he was driving fast, flying over the bumps and curves of Route 28, begging to be pulled over by a cop. When he reached the rotary in Orleans, he slowed down and stayed in the circle, going around and around, figuring out his next move. He could exit and head home to Jenny, smooth things over with her before Abby took her auto-art stunt any further. Jenny loved him, Ken knew this—she'd chosen him, after all. But his wife also loved his sister, who was a master manipulator. Or he could go toward the outer Cape in the direction of the Arcadia. Ken shuddered at the thought of what other damning images he might find there. Why had Abby portrayed their embrace so perversely? What trouble she was brewing. *Women and long-held grudges*. This was ancient history. No one had been hurt. Nothing had gotten out of hand. Okay, maybe the cuddling got a bit intense when his hormones kicked in. He remembered occasionally copping a feel or rubbing up against her. All minor-league stuff. Abby had never protested, so he assumed she liked it. They were just kids experimenting. No big deal.

Ken flicked on his right blinker as the turn back toward Chatham approached. But some invisible force kept him from exiting. He slapped the wheel, thinking about how he'd botched his chance to impress John Kaufman. How embarrassing that Kaufman had witnessed that woman—Steph whatever-her-name-was—shove him aside. Ken was built to take a blow, but Steph had knocked him off balance easily. What was she even doing at his father's birthday party?

Ken's thoughts traveled back to Abby—she'd idolized him when they were kids, trailing after him like a puppy. When she was eight and he was eleven, they'd mushed their pinpricked pointer fingers together and made a blood pact; they'd stand by each other forever. He recalled how safe he felt when they spooned, his sister's warm body curled into the cradle of his, watching Charon devour his meal. He would have done anything for her.

A blast from a car horn chased him out of the circle and the next thing he knew, he was on Route 6, heading toward Provincetown, the opposite direction from home. Decision made. How dare Abby portray his love this way and turn his affection into something degenerate?

"Hey, Siri," Ken called, and his phone illuminated. "What's the derivation of the name 'Abigail'?"

"Here's what I found from nameberry.com," Siri answered robotically. "Abigail comes from the Hebrew name Avigail, and is derived from the Hebrew elements *ab*, meaning 'father,' and *g-y-l*, meaning 'to rejoice.'"

Why had he even bothered to ask? Of course that's what it meant. He asked about his name, Ken, which according to Nameberry meant "handsome," trite in comparison.

Ken's mind kept bouncing, and the next place it landed was on George, wearing that ridiculous mask, preaching the gospel of change. *Careful what you wish for, ol' Georgy-boy*, Ken thought. *Transformation in progress.*

He rolled down the window and hollered into the night air. That felt good. For months, he'd felt agitated, aroused by some gathering of energy, a private storm. And none of his old tricks seemed to help—not visits to the online cuddle room, not a couple of rounds of golf, not even long, solo sails on the *Francesca*. Ken simply couldn't put enough miles between himself and the shore to keep the injustices of his childhood at bay. His rage had slipped past the point of no return and become an unstoppable force.

Ken pulled into Abby's driveway.

Call me if you ever need to talk. That was what George had urged him to do at their last session. *Anytime, day or night.*

"Hey, Siri," Ken said, "call—"

At the incomplete order, Siri prompted, "Who would you like to call?" She repeated the question a few seconds later: "Who would you like to call?"

Even Siri knew better than to ask a third time.

Why should he call George? The Arcadia was his. He owned it. He didn't need anyone's permission to enter. He wasn't breaking any laws. Besides, he had a right to see what Abby was up to. How he wished she would just disappear. She took up way too much of his mental space. With any luck, she and David would be playing house in DC soon.

Ken got out of the car. Although he knew no one was home, he stood in place and listened hard. Nothing but woodsy night sounds. All clear. He circled the Arcadia, noting all the things that Abby neglected to repair—rotting boards, creeping vines, a leaking pipe.

He pushed the front door open and was greeted by the pungent smell of oil paint and turpentine, behind it something familiar and fleeting, a sweet and unidentifiable scent from childhood. Frida ambled over to greet him, all happy grunts and wags. Stupid dog. The studio was a mess, as usual. But had his sister ever been busy. Paintings covered practically every inch of wall space, filled racks, and rested upon easels. There were enough wobbly lines to give a guy vertigo.

The first painting to draw his attention was of a girl in a bathtub, bony knees poking out of the water, a phallic-looking faucet looming over her head. What a twisted imagination Abby had. Ken leaned in to have a closer look, pleased to note that the proportions were all wrong: the bathtub was too small, and the faucet too large. But as he relaxed his eyes the brushstrokes started to dance, creating the sensation that the walls of the tub were closing in on the girl. Oh, now he got it: the confinement, the dick, the powerless girl—this was another patriarchy rant. Men oppressed; women suffered; *yada, yada*. Wasn't it about time to change tunes already?

Then, unbidden, Abby's face emerged on the head of the figure beneath the faucet, and Ken saw genuine fear. What did Abby ever have to fear? He'd been her protector, shielding her from harm. Ken tried to dismiss the look on her face, but his sister's eyes were insistent, forcing him to back away from the painting until his spine met a wall, where he sank to the floor and wedged himself into the corner. From there, Ken squinted and blinked, his gaze traveling from canvas to canvas, taking in the story of their childhood from a different perspective. Abby's version contradicted his memories. Like the painting on the wall to his left: two sets of disembodied legs, his and Abby's, running through the woods. He recalled the times they'd joyfully raced to the beach, him chasing her through the scrub pine forest, allowing her to stay in the lead until they got to the beach when he'd catch her, and they'd tumble down the dune together. But in this painting, one pair of legs seemed menacing and the other bloody from brambles. Hunter and prey. That was simply not how the game went. And what about the painting on the closest easel, where a torso hid under a canoe in their shed, contorting away from a groping arm? It hadn't been like that.

How well is your mask working for you now? George's voice in his head. *Call me anytime.*

Ken covered his face in his hands. How had he gotten it so wrong?

"Siri, call George Kunar."

Steph

Jittery from adrenaline, Steph felt pressure in her throat like she might cry. The last thing Abby had said to her was to please take care of Frida. Then, the ambulance sped off. That must've been more than thirty minutes ago. And yet, she and Toni were waiting for the valet—a kid who looked barely old enough to drive. They were the last in a long line of guests.

"You were amazing, Steph," Toni said. "Do you realize that's the first time I've seen you in action?"

Steph swallowed over the lump.

"You were smoking hot," Toni said.

Steph took in the compliment. It *had* felt good to take charge, especially in front of that group. They might seem superior with their Ph.D.s and fat wallets, but in a crisis, who did they want to call the shots? Not a real estate developer or a marine biologist, that much was for sure. Steph was the only person in the crowd capable of managing a medical emergency.

"Is Abby's baby going to be okay?" Toni asked in a whisper.

Steph suspected placenta previa was the culprit. It was the most common cause of bleeding during late pregnancy. "Everyone is going to be fine."

Their car finally arrived, and Steph palmed the valet five dollars. "Would you mind driving?" she asked Toni.

Toni got behind the wheel and clicked on her seat belt. "What happened up there to make Ken storm off?" she asked as she put the car into gear.

"No idea," Steph responded. "There's something off about that guy."

"And Jenny? Was it me or had she had a bit too much to drink?" Toni asked.

Jenny had been tanked, falling all over herself to apologize for things that weren't her fault. "She was hammered."

"And what about Adam?"

Steph shook her head. She didn't want to talk anymore. Her biological father was oblivious to the chaos he created, and Steph wanted no part of his madness. Even at seventy, Adam was like a kid who threw a lit match over his shoulder and was surprised by the wildfire that followed. Steph thought of her own parents—flawed, yes, but solid, loving, dependable.

Forty minutes later, they turned into Abby's rutted driveway. On the far side of the Arcadia, Steph saw a vehicle tucked behind a tree. She reached across the console and turned off the headlights.

"What?" Toni said, startled.

Steph put a finger to her lips and pointed to the other car. "Stay here," she whispered, stepping out and leaving the door ajar. She crept toward the studio as quietly as possible. Through the picture window, she saw her half brother, sitting on the floor, talking animatedly into his iPhone. At the screen door, Steph cleared her throat to alert him of her presence.

There was something about the way that Ken sprang up and jerked his cell phone away from his ear that made it seem like she'd caught him doing something wrong.

"Who's that?" he demanded.

"It's just me, Steph Murphy. From the party. Sorry to have scared you." She pushed open the door.

"You didn't *scare* me," Ken said. "But what are you doing here?"

"Abby asked me to take Frida for the night. I guess you had the same thought."

Ken pressed the device back to his ear. "George. Hey, sorry. I've got to go." Pause. "Yes. Yes. Okay. I'll see you next week." Another pause. "Yes, *with* Jenny. Absolutely. I'm . . . Thanks, George. Really, I appreciate it." Ken pocketed the phone and scratched his head. "Had I known you were on dog duty, I wouldn't have bothered to come."

Steph nodded, unsure why she was still on high alert.

"Remind me," Ken said. "How is it you know my dad?"

So, he still didn't know. Steph glanced at her phone—the babysitter was expecting them. She smiled at him. "We met at happy hour at Tzuco's a couple of months ago and just hit it off. Fascinating guy," she said. All true. "He even took me on a whale watch."

"Flowers, fine art, whales." He gave a long whistle. "For a cop, you sure have some varied interests."

No surprise that Ken was a snob. "Yes, I imagine I do. Just as varied as, say, a wealthy, golf-playing, aspiring politician."

Ken lifted his hands. "Didn't mean to offend."

Time to go. "So, shall I take Frida or do you want to?"

"I'm not really a dog guy."

"Okay, then," Steph said, snapping the leash onto Frida's collar. "Have a good night," she said and pushed out the door, hurrying toward her car.

"Hey," Ken called to her.

Steph ignored him and kept walking, but she could feel the cogs of his brain set their teeth into something solid.

"I know who you are."

Adam

Adam lay flat on his back on his bed, listening to the pulsating buzz of bugs outside his windows, the sound like a ratcheting sprinkler. Abby and the baby were going to be fine. They'd been admitted for observation and would likely be released sometime the next day. A relief.

Adam pictured what it would be like to have a grandson, his mind leapfrogging over the baby and toddler stages, presenting him with an attentive boy of about seven, an inquisitive lad who reminded Adam of himself at that age. Oh, how he'd enjoy passing knowledge down to this child. He pictured them walking down a sandy beach, the boy's small hand in his, hanging on his every word. In his reverie, they came upon a conch shell in shallow waters just like the one he'd found with his father all those years ago in the Florida Keys, poking through the cerulean ocean like a miniature cathedral.

In the here and now, that conch shell rested on his bedside table, and Adam reached for it. To stare into the spiral of a shell was to see the swirl of a galaxy, the logarithmic spiral of life itself, the intertwined miracle of art and science. He pressed it to the side of his head and listened to its voice, echoing deep time and truth, and imagined the boy—that younger and long-gone version of himself—doing the same. And with the conch against both of their ears, Adam drifted off to the soft happiness of sleep, eavesdropping on an ancient dialogue between mathematics and magic, between life and death.

Abby

Abby blinked rapidly and a faded, striped curtain came into focus. It hung from a metal slider that made a U around her, encircling dozens of acoustically sensitive ceiling tiles, off-white dotted with holes. She was propped up on pillows tucked under her right side, hand resting on a stainless-steel railing. There was a whiteboard on the wall at the foot of the bed, which bore her name, as well as the date, August 19, 2016. She was in a hospital. The last thing she recalled was her consciousness corkscrewing back into her body under the watchful gaze of her half sister.

"Good morning." The voice came from a young man in blue scrubs, who introduced himself as Dr. Simons, a neurology resident. "How are you feeling?"

"Okay, I think." Abby's mouth was dry. "What time is it?"

The doctor checked his watch. "Almost six a.m.," he said. "Rounds start early here. The good news is that all your tests are normal, and you and your baby are both fine." He led Abby through a routine neurological exam, testing her reflexes and assessing her motor coordination, and then asked her to answer some basic questions: *Where are you? What year is it? Who's the president?*

"Cape Cod Hospital. 2016. Barack Obama."

She refrained from adding, *And Hillary is next.*

"You have a condition called placenta previa. In a nutshell, this means your placenta is partially covering the cervical opening. An OB resident will be in shortly to discuss this with you."

Abby flashed to the bumps of her brother's spine rippling under his shirt as he was hunched over her, trying to help. "When I lost consciousness," she told the doctor, "I was still there. I watched it all from above."

The resident typed into his rolling computer, pecking away as he spoke. "That type of perturbation is most likely an inner-ear issue, the result of your fall. Even a small disturbance in your vestibular system can give you that floating sensation."

But Abby could recall what each person had said and where they were positioned around her prone body. "No, it was real."

The doctor nodded dismissively, and Abby felt like Dorothy, waking up in her bed in Kansas, no one understanding that she'd been to Oz.

An hour or so later, Abby heard fingers drumming on the wall.

"Morning," said Steph. A little wave.

"Hey there," Abby said, surprised to see her—visiting hours didn't start until 10:00.

Steph flashed her police badge. "Comes in handy at times like these."

"Badass," Abby said.

Steph nodded.

Abby extended her hand. "Thanks for coming to my rescue last night."

"No problem," Steph said, taking Abby's hand. "How are you and my nephew feeling?"

"We're fine. My placenta doesn't seem to know which end is up," Abby said. "Which means I have to deliver by C-section."

"It's not so bad," Steph said. "It's how Jonah came into the world."

Unexpectedly, Abby choked up. She might not have a mother, but she did have a sister, someone who would be there to give baby advice.

Steph pulled over a hospital chair and straddled it. "Are you up for a talk?"

"About . . . ?"

"All of it, I suppose," Steph said. "I've made some decisions."

A knot of dread settled in Abby's stomach.

Steph cracked her knuckles. "I've decided not to pursue things further."

"By 'things'"—Abby faltered and sucked in her breath—"do you mean me?"

"No. Sorry. Not you," Steph said. "I just don't want to pursue things with the rest of your family. Toni and I stayed up all night discussing it, and it's for the best."

Steph hadn't left much room for debate. "I don't understand," Abby said. "I'm supposed to keep your existence a secret?"

"No, it's not a secret. I don't care who knows about me," Steph said. "In fact, I think your brother already does, in which case your father won't be far behind. What I'm saying is that I don't want to be a part of their lives."

Abby had trouble making sense of these words. Was it possible to just pick the family you wanted?

"Just yours," said Steph.

"But I thought . . ." Abby's voice trailed off. "What changed?"

"Um. Were we not at the same party last night?"

Abby looked at the ceiling and blinked back tears. "Hormones," she said.

Steph let her forehead fall onto her arms, which were folded across the back of the chair.

"Spell it out for me," Abby said.

"Your family is completely fucked up."

Sure they were. Wasn't everyone's? "Isn't yours?"

"No. Not really," Steph said. "I mean, they make mistakes. But I can count on them to always have my back."

Tears rolled down Abby's cheeks.

"Abby, I want for us to be sisters, and for our sons to be cousins," Steph said slowly. "But I don't need two fathers—I have a great one. And your brother? Well, I'm not interested in being around that kind of rage."

Abby felt the familiar urge to defend her brother, an old refrain looping through her head: Ken had had the harder childhood—he'd lost his mother, been bullied, and was misunderstood by their father. And she knew full well that she'd added to his pain by blowing him off, leaving him alone to deal with his hurts, abandoning him without explanation.

She started to protest.

"You told me to spell it out," Steph said.

That was true, she had. Abby closed her eyes and watched the light show behind her eyelids.

Jenny

"It's a pleasure to meet you," George said, shaking Jenny's hand and ushering her and Ken into his office.

Whatever apprehensions Jenny had about a double session of couples therapy—ninety minutes seemed like a very long time—evaporated as she crossed the threshold into this sun-filled office. George Kunar exuded warmth, and his office was calm but not without personality.

"It's nice to meet you, too, Dr. Kunar," Jenny said, admiring the colorful masks on the far wall.

"Please call me George."

"I love your collection, George," she said. "Is that eagle mask Inupiaq?"

"Close. It's Kwakwaka'wakw," he said, nodding. "Do you know much about Native American masks?"

"It's a trick question," Ken warned.

"No, not much," Jenny answered. "I took an overview of indigenous art when I was at RISD. I've always been fascinated by masks."

"RISD, huh?" George said, glancing at Ken. Something unspoken passed between them.

Jenny wondered why Ken had never said more about this adorably hirsute, teddy bear of a man.

"I'm not sure how I forgot that you studied art at RISD," George said. "Were you there at the same time as Ken's sister?"

"Abby and I roomed together our freshman year." *Was it possible Ken hadn't mentioned this?* Jenny looked at him. "Abby introduced us. We're best friends."

George nodded and leaned back in his chair.

Ken mirrored the posture, sinking back on the sofa.

A long silence followed. One that Jenny felt desperate to fill. But where to begin? With what she'd overheard Ken saying in the chat room? With the fiasco that had been her father-in-law's birthday party? Ken's destruction of Abby's painting? Their daughter having witnessed it? Or should she just start with what was bothering her most: Ken's refusal to give the Arcadia to Abby? Jenny exhaled. Maybe ninety minutes wouldn't be enough, after all.

But before she could speak, George broke the silence. "What do you think, Ken? Are you ready?"

Ready? Jenny pivoted toward her husband. The Ken she knew was gone. In his place, a lost-looking boy, vulnerable and scared.

"I'm ready," Ken said softly. He looked up at Jenny with shiny eyes. "I love you, Jenny. I should tell you that more often."

Jenny placed a hand on the base of her throat. She did not like where this was going.

"I haven't been totally honest with you," Ken continued, his voice tightening. "I haven't been totally honest with myself, either." He took a deep breath. "Through therapy, I've uncovered some pretty complicated shit about my relationship with Abby. Stuff that I'd buried. Stuff that's hard to talk about."

Pretty complicated shit. The tips of Jenny's ears grew hot. Her mind raced. Oh, God! It hadn't been a coincidence that he'd called the woman in the chat room *Abby*. She bit down on her cheek.

"Go on," George coaxed. "Jenny has been waiting a long time for this."s

Had she been? Right now, all she wanted was for things to slow down. Bile rose in her throat.

"Are you okay, Jenny?" Ken asked.

"Just keep going, Ken," George said. "Jenny deserves to know the truth."

Did she want the truth? Jenny loved Ken, but even more than that, she loved the life they'd made together. Her children—she had to protect her girls. And what about Abby? Abby was her best friend. Ken's revelation might change that relationship, too.

"Hold on." The words shot out of her mouth. "I need a minute." Jenny was not ready for her world to come crashing down. "Dr. Kunar, a moment alone with my husband, please."

George did as she asked and left the office.

Ken sat rigid, unblinking.

"Before you say anything that can't be unsaid"—Jenny veered into the conversation the way she'd wander down a dark tunnel: with one hand out, feeling her way along—"let's press pause for a moment."

She ran the charm on her necklace back and forth on its chain, feeling herself start to crack. She wished her mother were alive. Her mother would know what to do, how to extract the pain she felt like a splinter from her skin. Might church be a way to move forward without going too far in? She thought of suggesting he talk to their priest. "Are you sure about this?"

Jenny watched her husband consider this get-out-of-jail-free offer. If he were willing to handle things another way, they could just drive home. He could disappear into Command Central and she into a bottle of Sancerre. But even as she imagined this—that magical hit that followed the first sip of wine, chased by a spectacular sunset—she knew it could never work. The only way out was through.

"I'm sure," Ken said softly.

"Okay," Jenny said, leaning toward her husband. "I'm ready."

Ken stared down at his hands, which rested on his knees. Then a tremor passed through his body, landing in his shoulders, which started to heave. "I just . . . I just . . ."

Jenny put her hands to her mouth.

Ken clenched his fists so tightly that his knuckles whitened. He looked at her. "I just loved her so, Jenny. So, so much."

October

Abby

Abby sank into her love seat and touched the cover of the new issue of *Art Observer* reverently—a full-bleed image of her in partial shadow, sitting on a stool beside *Little Monster*, no white edges. She was in sharp focus, staring directly into the camera lens, arms crossed, the painting softly blurred behind her. The headline read: "The Female Gaze." 2016 would be the Year of the Woman after all. Abby flipped to the profile. She hadn't known if Rachel Draper would be able to update the article to include how Jenny had repaired the painting with *kintsugi* after an "undisclosed" accident. Given the magazine's printing deadline, Abby assumed it would be impossible. Yet somehow Rachel had managed to make it happen.

Now, with Frida lying droop-headed at her feet, Abby studied the results: an "after" photo of *Little Monster* highlighting its scars with channels of gold; a small photo of Jenny and her together, taken eons ago near the student gallery at RISD; and an insert about the art of *kintsugi*. As Abby read the piece, it was as if she was reading about someone else. This article lauded a brave artist who used personal narrative to question the social landscape and challenge the existing male-dominated art canon.

Since leaving the hospital nine weeks ago, Abby's pregnancy had been blissfully uneventful. With the diagnosis of placenta previa, her obstetrician scheduled her for a C-section at thirty-eight weeks, which meant the baby would arrive on November 8, Election Day, now just two weeks away. He'd told her to take it easy, which for the most part she had. The exceptions came in unbidden jolts of energy that compelled her to clean and organize the Arcadia. Sometimes Abby would find herself scrubbing bathroom fixtures in the middle of the night or rearranging her paintbrushes by the length of their bristles or handles. Her tubes of oils were organized by color in bins; her windowsills, free of dead bugs; her canvases, stacked on shelves and racks. She'd even culled her various collections of beach treasures—shells, stones, starfish, and sea glass—picking through them and scrubbing the mason jars as she went. In her bedroom, she'd set up a trifold shoji screen to create a separate nursery space, and hand-painted the panels with sea imagery: tentacled octopuses, scallop and nautilus shells, stingrays, starfish, seahorses, and whales. She'd decided to name the baby Reid, her mother's maiden name. Reid Gardner.

Autumn had slipped over the Cape, wedging itself between the solstice and equinox: warm days, cool nights, the occasional storm, but mostly bright blue weather. As Abby's body expanded, her wisteria tree contracted into its winter skeleton of gnarled branches. The milkweed pods had split, and bellows of wind scattered the cottony parachutes, a dark seed passenger in each. Soon, the ground would harden, and Abby would light the first fire of the season and commence the daily practice of moving piled firewood from outside to in. Her artwork had shifted in tandem with the season's change as if to reorient itself to the sun's withdrawal. She was working on a smaller scale, charcoal drawings and collages, anticipating a season of shorter days spent mostly inside, tending to her son and herself.

Tessa burst through the door first, shovel in hand.

"Hey, Aunt Abby," Tessa said. "Where do you want the hole?"

Since Abby had seen her last, her niece had cropped her hair asymmetrically—buzzed so close on one side that her head looked painted.

"Far side of the wisteria tree," Abby answered, snagging Tessa and planting a kiss on the top of her head.

Through the screen door, Jenny and Frannie unloaded bags from the back of their SUV. At today's gathering, there'd be no pink- or blue-frosted cupcakes, no diaper games involving chocolate, no onesie-making station. The time capsule had been the girls' idea, one that Abby loved immediately, envisioning it as a small-scale version of the Voyager's Golden Records, intended to communicate their hopes into the future. The goal was to let Reid know how much he was loved and give him a sense of what the world was like the year he was born.

Frannie got to the door next, arms hooked through the straps of two canvas bags. "Check out the goods, Aunt Abby," she said, resting the satchels on the floor and pulling apart the handles to reveal their contents: newspapers, magazines, an envelope of money and coins in every denomination. There were also pens, paper, card stock, scissors, tape, ribbon, paper clips, glue sticks—everything they could possibly need to create a time capsule.

"How lucky is your baby to be born right now!" Frannie exclaimed.

"How so?" Abby asked.

"Duh," Tessa said. "In two weeks, a woman will be leading the free world. First. Time. Ever. Can you imagine how much better a place the world will be?" *The Future is Female* was emblazoned across her T-shirt.

Oh, to be almost thirteen again, and filled with so much optimism.

"Future Reid is not going to believe how messed up things were in 2016," Frannie said. They'd agreed that he could open the capsule in 2037 on his twenty-first birthday. Frannie burrowed through one of the bags, pulled out the envelope full of money, and fanned the currency. "Not a single woman or person of color on any bill!"

Abby considered the token gestures of the past: Sacagawea, Martha Washington, Susan B. Anthony. At least by 2037, Harriet Tubman's face would have long replaced Jackson's on the $20.

Frannie froze. "Oh. My. God."

"What?" asked Tessa.

"We're going to be thirty-three years old when Reid opens this."

"Thirty-three," Tessa repeated.

"Practically dead," Abby teased, putting an arm around each of their shoulders.

Both girls rolled their eyes.

"One thing is for sure, he's one lucky guy to have you two for cousins," she said. *And Jonah,* she thought. *Jonah will be his cousin, too.*

"Between the three of us, we're going to create one seriously evolved man," Tessa declared.

Frannie nodded. "Let's get digging."

As the girls reached the screen door, they pushed past their mother who was on her way in.

"My word," Jenny said with a gasp. "Abigail Gardner, nesting?"

It was true—the Arcadia had never been tidier. "Didn't you do this when you were pregnant with the girls?"

Jenny shook her head. "Only if you count having the housekeeping service on speed dial."

"Who knew you could farm out maternal instincts," Abby said and smiled.

"I'd have hired a wet nurse if it was an option." Jenny gave Abby a peck on each cheek. "But before you get all cocky and superior, I give it a week after the baby's born for the place to look like its old self again."

But Abby didn't laugh.

"What?" Jenny asked. "Oh, honey. What is it?"

A hard knot formed in Abby's throat. "I'm just scared," she said.

Jenny took Abby's hands. "Of course you are. Being a mom is scary," she said and pulled Abby in for a hug. "Just remember, we're *all* here for you."

Not everyone, Abby thought, looking past her best friend and through the front door to where Jenny's shiny SUV sat empty. Ken hadn't come.

Jenny followed Abby's gaze. "Yes. No. I mean . . . I'm sorry that Ken couldn't make it," she said. "He's got a lot going on."

"Right," Abby said, surprised that despite everything, some part of her wanted him here.

Her father also would be a no-show, but Abby had expected that. Adam wasn't a "baby shower guy." She'd done her best to convince him that this was a birth celebration—not a shower—and that she wanted the men in her life to participate. Adam had sniffed the air and scoffed. "Smells like a shower to me."

David was on the campaign trail and had no choice but to stick by Hillary's side for the duration, right through election night. He'd had to bolt in early October when the *Access Hollywood* pussy-grabbing tape went viral and hadn't been able to break free since. He'd miss his son's birth. On the bright side, Clinton was ahead in the polls with twice the cash and field offices of Trump. She'd bested him in all three debates—even in that one when he'd loomed over her like a gorilla as she was talking. And now—daily, it seemed—new women were stepping forward to accuse Trump of inappropriate behavior.

And after the election? David hoped to land a role with the Clinton administration—his dream job, White House press secretary—while Abby had made it clear she was not leaving the Cape. They'd landed on a wait-and-see arrangement.

Jenny and Abby went up to the deck where they rested mugs of tea on the flat wooden railing, waiting for Toni and Steph to arrive. No matter the season, the sight of the dunes rolling into the ocean always awakened Abby's senses and filled her with awe for the cycle of life. She thought of how the horseshoe crabs emerged from Cape Cod Bay each spring to mate and deposit their eggs; how juvenile sea turtles knew to travel to these waters where crabs and jellyfish were plentiful; how monarch butterflies—each of which lived up to only six weeks—managed to transfer knowledge intergenerationally to complete their year-long migration to and from Mexico.

"Jenny?" Abby ventured, wrapping her hands around her mug of tea. Beside her a squadron of ladybugs huddled together, soaking up the long rays of autumn sun, their split, red shells polished with black polka dots.

"Yes."

"Can we talk about my brother?" Abby hadn't seen or spoken to Ken since their father's party. She'd left messages but received no calls in return. She had so many questions for Jenny. Why had Ken destroyed her painting? How did he feel about their half sister? Had he discussed it with their father? Why wasn't he returning her calls? But the question that left her lips was this: "Is Ken gone from my life for good?"

Jenny shut her eyes.

A ladybug landed on Abby's sleeve, and she felt her heart contract. *Ladybug, ladybug, fly away home, your house is on fire and your children will burn.* She blew the beetle into the breeze.

"I don't know, Abby," Jenny said. "Maybe."

Abby couldn't speak. All the times they'd hid in her closet together, the hours they'd spent collecting twigs for Charon's cage, their beach walks.

"But I'm here," Jenny said. "And I will always, *always* be here. For you and for Reid." The twins' voices wafted up from below over the rhythmic sound of the shovel smacking the earth. "And so will Frannie and Tessa."

Abby tilted her face toward the sun.

"I have something for you," Jenny said and reached into her bag to retrieve a folder. "You'll get the official documents once the baby is born."

Abby took it from her and flipped through documents written in legalese. Long story short, the Arcadia was hers. *Sort of*. Ken had created an irrevocable, generation-skipping trust that deeded the property and dwelling to Reid while allowing Abby lifetime use of it. Leave it to her brother to snatch the world out from under her and present it back to her as a gift.

When Abby looked up again, the low-lying tip of Cape Cod appeared unusually fragile. She could picture a time in the not-too-distant future when the ocean would sweep over Provincetown, sloshing down Commercial Street and devouring everything in its path.

Jenny frowned. "This is what you wanted, isn't it?"

Abby cleared her thoughts with a shake of her head. It was and it wasn't. She'd have preferred to be able to give her home to her son herself. But it was done. Irrevocable meant irrevocable.

"Yes, it's what I wanted. Thank you." Abby knew that Jenny must have fought to make this happen and decided to focus on gratitude. The Arcadia was hers—hers and her son's—and could never be taken away. With it, Abby had everything she needed: a bay full of oysters that she could scoop up with her hands; an ocean teeming with fish; woods bountiful with mushrooms and berries; and, most important, a proverbial room of her own.

Around her, scrub oaks and pines rustled in the breeze, looking like wise old women, faces etched in the bark, branches blown back like hair. Overhead, a red-tailed hawk rose out of the woods, its cinnamon tail feathers splayed like fingers. Abby watched it soar in a sweeping arc.

Then the bird saw something that caused it to freeze and transform into a missile in midair. Down it plunged.

"How are things between you and Ken these days?"

Jenny's eyes stayed locked on the spot where the hawk had dropped. "Okay. Better. We're working hard in therapy."

The hawk rose—a snake wriggling from its talons.

Lunch was a variety of homemade sandwiches and salads that Steph assembled in Abby's small kitchen. The six of them arranged themselves in a circle on the floor, chatting and noshing on their indoor picnic as they clipped and glued articles into the soft scrapbook they were making for the baby. So far, they'd included reviews of *Hamilton*, Beyoncé's new album, *Lemonade*, Jane Mayer's *Dark Money*, and the all-female remake of *Ghostbusters*; obits for David Bowie and Prince; the comeback story of the Chicago Cubs reaching the first World Series in one hundred and eight years; David's coverage of the Clinton campaign, as well as dozens of clippings about the dire state of the world—Zika, Brexit, Russian hacking, the water crisis in Flint, Michigan, global warming, and more. But Tessa insisted they save the best news for last and glued down the recent *New York Times* presidential forecast that Hillary Clinton had a 91 percent chance to win the election on the scrapbook's final page.

Tessa lifted the top piece of bread from her sandwich. "This is, like, the best sandwich ever. What's in it?"

"Yeah, it's really good," Frannie agreed.

"Family secret," Steph replied.

Tessa smiled. "News flash: we're your family."

"Hard to argue that, Steph," agreed Toni.

"Speaking of . . . what should we call you?" asked Frannie. "Aunt Steph?"

"If that feels good to you," Steph said. "I'd love nothing more."

"Works for me," Frannie said.

"Me, too," said Tessa. "So, what's the secret ingredient, *Aunt* Steph?"

"You promise to take it to the grave?"

The twins drew Xs over their hearts.

"Cumin," Steph whispered solemnly. "Just a pinch in the guacamole mayo."

A long silence followed.

"That would be a conversation stopper, Aunt Steph," Frannie whispered.

Jenny frowned but Steph just laughed. "We're family."

"I have another question, Aunt Steph," Tessa said, reaching for a second sandwich. "Did you, like, always know that your dad wasn't your real dad?"

"Tessa!" Jenny gasped.

Steph waved away Jenny's concern. "I don't have a good answer," she replied. "Yes and no. Knowing the truth has made some things make more sense."

"But that could be a hindsight thing," Tessa said.

"I suppose."

"Does any part of you wish you'd never found out? I mean, it must be hard."

"It has been," Steph admitted. "But moments like these make it worth it. I wouldn't want to miss these for anything."

As they continued to work on their project, they took Polaroid snapshots of one another, the camera spitting out white-bordered gray squares, one after the next, until dozens were lined up on Abby's coffee table. David had made the time capsule out of a durable piece of plumbing pipe with fittings on both ends, one removable, the other not. When, at last, they were ready to fill it, Abby placed the photos in first, stacking them neatly on the bottom of the tube. They'd be the last things Reid would discover. Abby's favorite photo was a picture of Jonah with his hands splayed on her belly like tiny starfish, making it look as if he was trying to touch his unborn cousin. A rolled-up issue of *Art Observer* magazine went in next, unfurling to meet the edges of the tube. Inside that, they placed the scrapbook. Then, one by one, they added their gifts, separating items with scrunched-up balls of newspaper: a $25K Treasury bond from Jenny; a blue topaz signet ring that Toni promised would calm the Scorpio in him; Steph's ten favorite recipes, handwritten on index cards and bound with a stainless-steel ring; a minuscule bottle of honeysuckle honey that had taken Frannie and Tessa weeks to collect; a flash drive labeled "The Secret Language of Whales" from Adam. And, at the top, Abby's gift: one treasure from each of her mason jar collections and topped with the best ceramic piece her mother ever left—items that fueled her creatively.

As the sun began to sink, they gathered outside, lowering the sealed time capsule into the hole. They each tossed in a ritual handful of dirt, and then Tessa shoveled in earnest. A few moments later, the vessel was gone, swallowed up by the earth alongside ancient arrowheads and stone tools left by indigenous people. Would it still be here in twenty-one years? Would they all still be here?

Everyone looked at her expectantly. But what was she supposed to say?

She recalled the worlds she used to build from seaweed and shells as she waited on the beach for her father and brother to return from their sailing adventures. And, even as she vowed never to leave her child alone like that, Abby knew that she wouldn't be the person she was today had she not had that solitary time. Like everyone else, she got only one life. The one she was living right now. This life that could only have happened with every experience she'd ever had—that had landed her here, in this perfect moment, alongside these women and two men-in-the-making—Jonah and Reid.

But still, Abby had no words to offer. Time leaped forward, and she saw her future unfold—games of peekaboo and bedtime stories; toy boats and fishing rods; discarded bread crusts; an indigo crayon, its wrapper half gone. Later, there'd be friends, gangly boys who'd abandon their bikes against the side of the house and kick off their sneakers, leaving them in a heap at the door. They'd build forts, play flashlight tag, and rummage through the cupboards for snacks, leaving crumbs on the counter and the faucets dripping. *Pick up, for God's sake!* she'd scold, but they'd know she didn't care. She was *that* mom. The Arcadia was *that* home. Later still, Reid would grow, learn to drive, and come and go as he pleased. He'd ask her advice, bring home partners, and someday, maybe even have children of his own. She might not have her brother—she knew Jenny was right and that Ken might be gone for good—but she would have Reid and the people who surrounded her now, the family she'd created.

And that was something. It was more than something. It was everything.

Acknowledgments

Thanks to my editor, Lauren Wein, who offers brilliant suggestions and always sends the just-right poem when I need it most; my agent, Brettne Bloom, a champion like no other, and my friend, Sarah Rosell, the first and last reader of every page.

For their thoughtful feedback at various stages, thanks to: Erica Bauermeister, Lea Carpenter, Julie Costanzo, Carole DeSanti, Julia Felsenthal, Heather Harpham, Lee Harrington, Lauren Johnson, Michael Korda, Scott Lasser, Stephen Lewis, Katie Machen, Ruth Ozeki, Sara Powers, Joanna Rakoff, Deb Robinson, and Eilene Zimmerman.

For their support, help, and encouragement, thank you to my father, Paul Brodeur (1931-2023); my stepmother, Maggie Simmons; my cousin, Anne Dubbs, and the whole Ryan family—especially Marie, Patrick, Timmy, Lauren, Olivia, and Nick; my friends and champions: Melissa Bank (1960–2022), Rebecca Barber, Marcella Barganz, Kristen Bieler, Alisyn Camerota, Kenna Kay, Pete Rock, Taryn Roeder, George Shafnacker, Jane Simmons, Jessica Vitkus, and the Thunder Moon women, and my colleagues at Aspen Words and the Aspen Institute: Ivy Chalmers, Elliot Gerson, Mallory Kaufman, Madeline Lipton, Elizabeth Nix, Daniel Porterfield, and Caroline Tory.

Thank you to Avid Reader for stewarding this novel into the world. I appreciate the work of Jofie Ferrari-Adler, Amy Guay, Ben Loehnen, Alexandra Primiani, and Meredith Vilarello. Thanks also to Josie Friedman, Jenny Meyer, Jesseca Salky, Will Watkins, and everyone at The Book Group.

Above all, to my husband, Tim, and my children, Madeleine and Liam, for graces innumerable. And to my mother, Malabar Brewster (1931–2022), who I think about and miss every day.

About the Author

ADRIENNE BRODEUR is the author of the memoir *Wild Game*, which was selected as a Best Book of the Year by NPR and the *Washington Post* and is in development as a Netflix film. She founded the literary magazine *Zoetrope: All-Story* with Francis Ford Coppola, and currently serves as executive director of Aspen Words, a literary nonprofit and program of the Aspen Institute. She splits her time between Cambridge and Cape Cod where she lives with her husband and children. *Little Monsters*, a novel, is her most recent work.

Little Monsters

Adrienne Brodeur

This reading group guide for **Little Monsters** *includes an introduction, discussion questions, ideas for enhancing your book club, and a Q&A with author* **Adrienne Brodeur**. *The suggested questions are intended to help your reading group find new and interesting angles and topics for your discussion. We hope that these ideas will enrich your conversation and increase your enjoyment of the book.*

Introduction

Adult siblings Ken and Abby Gardner hold fast to the only family narrative they know: their parents had a happy life together until their mother's untimely death, when Adam, their heroic father, stepped into the role of single parent and gave them an idyllic childhood in the Wellfleet Woods. Now, in the summer before the 2016 election, Ken is a troubled yet high-achieving businessman with his own outwardly flawless family; Abby is a talented, iconoclastic artist with a big secret; and Adam is an aging yet still fiercely ambitious patriarch who opts in to his usually medicated bipolar disorder in the hopes that mania will lead him to one last scientific breakthrough. When Ken and Abby's unknown half sister, Steph, appears on the scene, thorny truths come to light, upending the Gardner family story and detonating long-suppressed emotions. Inspired by the archetypal story of Cain and Abel, *Little Monsters* is a kaleidoscopic, propulsive, and sophisticated drama exquisite with the tension of characters careening in and out of one another's orbits, alternately sharing and withholding secrets from one another and themselves—and with Cape Cod's magnificence and hidden corners elevating every page.

Topics & Questions for Discussion

1. How would you describe Adam, Ken, Abby, Steph, and Jenny? What aspects of their identities create the biggest rifts and points of connection between them? Who most resonates with you?

2. Why do you think Brodeur chose to set *Little Monsters* in the summer of 2016? How does the charged political atmosphere affect the characters' relationships to each other? What would have happened if the novel took place in the summer of 2017, or the summer of 2012?

3. As Abby's best friend and Ken's wife, Jenny is enmeshed in the Gardner family; Steph, on the other hand, is only just introducing herself to the relations she didn't know she had. Compare and contrast Jenny and Steph's arcs as they (re-)calibrate their place in this complicated family.

4. The attitude gap between the men and women of the Gardner clan regarding gender figures prominently in *Little Monsters*. Think back to when this difference results in conflict. Who did you align with in those moments? Did you find the character with whom you did not agree sympathetic in any way?

5. Steph has just had a child, Abby is pregnant, and Emily's premature death—as well as the short-lived stepmothers that succeeded her—shape the remaining Gardners in both subliminal and obvious way. What is the role of motherhood in *Little Monsters*?

6. Cape Cod—its beauty and wildness—is a core piece of the novel's fabric. What were some of your favorite descriptive lines evoking the landscape? Would this book feel different if it was set in New York or California?

7. Ken's therapy sessions and Adam's bipolar disorder are the sites of important emotional momentum in *Little Monsters*. Why do you think Brodeur chose to make mental health—specifically of the male characters—a key element of their respective characterizations?

8. David is a more minor character, despite his intense and long-held connections to both Ken and Abby. What do you think of him, especially as another third point in a relationship triangle in which Ken and Abby find themselves? Do you think he and Abby will end up together in the end, or will they have a less conventional arrangement?

9. Why do you think Brodeur titled the novel *Little Monsters*, yet the name of Abby's painting is the singular "Little Monster"?

10. We learn the contours of Ken and Abby's childhood via flashes of memory—not all of them reliable. Point to some sentences or passages in the beginning of the novel that hint at the siblings' complex dynamic. Having finished the book, how would you characterize what happened between them when they were young? How would you characterize their relationship now—and how do you imagine it will affect the other characters in their life?

Enhance Your Book Club

1. As a group, come up with a list of other pieces of media that deal with entangled family bonds, gender politics, women's friendships, and childhood trauma, and discuss how these selections differ from or are similar to *Little Monsters*.

2. Be like Abby and get crafty! Paint, draw, sketch, or collage using *Little Monsters* as the inspiration—it could be a scene Brodeur explicitly includes in the novel, a memory of one of the characters, an abstract feeling a passage evoked in you, an imagined future for the Gardner family, and beyond. Bonus points if you reference some of the "comps" to which Rachel compares Abby's art when she visits Arcadia in the beginning of the novel.

3. Cast the *Little Monsters* movie or miniseries: Choose your top picks for the main roles, and make a case to the larger group about who would best embody each character.

A Conversation with Adrienne Brodeur

Your memoir *Wild Game* is largely set on Cape Cod and also deals with family secrets. What made you want to explore this territory in fiction?
For those of you who have read *Wild Game*, it will come as no surprise that I'm fascinated by family secrets and that they loom large in my new novel, *Little Monsters*. This obsession was no doubt informed by my own family who were prodigious secret keepers going back for generations. But of course, secret keeping is not unique to my family and makes for great storytelling, which is why it was a delight to invent a fictional family and take a kaleidoscopic look at their buried truths, and at the risks and rewards of confronting them.

As for Cape Cod, I find it an endlessly fascinating landscape. Obviously, it's a place of privilege and class—some people live there, and others summer there. But it's the natural world that most animates me. As soon as I approach the Sagamore Bridge and smell the brackish air, my heart rate slows, and my body relaxes. From its kettle ponds to its sand dunes and cranberry bogs, from its shorebirds to its migrating marine life, there is simply no place that captures my imagination quite like it. Cape Cod is essentially a large and fragile sand bar—a landscape that changes by the season but also by the hour from weather and tide, and one that is destined someday to be swallowed back into the ocean.

What are the difficulties and benefits of writing a novel versus writing a memoir? What was your writing process like?
For better or for worse, you have so much more freedom writing fiction than nonfiction. With memoir, obviously, it takes skill and control to carve a narrative out of the block of stone that is your life, but all the elements are there: you know who the narrator is, and you know the story,

even as you must shape it. With a novel, you start with nothing. You don't even know what material you're working with. Everything—the story, the characters, the point of view, the setting—is up to you.

Writing a book is a bit like holding something delicate and stealthy in your hands—if you hold too tight, you risk crushing it; too loose, and it might get away. *Little Monsters* started with a persistent curiosity about the often-fraught nature of sibling relationships, which led me to reflect upon the biblical story of Cain and Abel. That was the foundation. From there, the process is all about patience and discipline. I wake up around 5 a.m., get a big mug of coffee, go straight to my desk, and write. While it is a cliché, writing a novel is like building a plane as you fly it. I must write to get to know my characters and figure out the narrative. Aside from Adam, the patriarch, who arrived fully developed on page one, it was only through writing that the characters revealed themselves. By the end of the first draft, I knew who they were enough to go back and revise, which of course, is the process: write, edit, repeat.

What interests you about sibling relationships? And what spoke to you about the Biblical tale of Cain and Abel?

Sibling relationships are compelling fodder for a novel simply because it's hard to fathom how people growing up in the same family can experience the world so differently. Also, the relationship is so ripe for both closeness and conflict. I looked to the archetypal story of Cain and Abel, hoping for answers about sibling rivalry, and was left wanting. It is truly a bare-bones story. That said, the tale informed the structure of the book in as much as Cain and Abel made offerings to God, and God favored Abel's gift. In *Little Monsters*, the narrative structure builds toward the patriarch's seventieth birthday where his children present him with gifts of great personal importance and the father favors one child's offering over the other's.

What made you choose to set the events of the book during this particular summer?

I didn't start writing *Little Monsters* until the spring of 2020, but I always knew I would set the book in the months leading up to the 2016 election as I found the uneasy mood of the country riveting. It was a time when you could practically feel the ground shifting beneath your feet, although most people I know, me included, did not correctly anticipate how. I also love the subversive idea that the readers know more about what will happen next than the characters.

There are many reasons people hide their feelings—shame and fear come to mind—and equally as many that determine why some people can stop hiding, while others go deeper underground. I'm no political historian or sociologist, but I feel sure that 2016 was a global inflection point, marking the collapsing of established social orders and creating a perfect storm of sorts, enabling some people to reckon with their history and privilege and forcing others into deeper denial.

What media—books, films, or music—inspired you as you were developing and writing *Little Monsters*?

There is rarely a time that I'm not absorbed in a book, listening as I take walks, or reading before bed. That said, I'm unable to point to a specific book that inspired *Little Monsters*, rather I feel indebted to all writers who've ever ignited my imagination and empathy, as cumulatively, they encouraged me to join the conversation. As for music, I can be very specific—every morning as I sit down to write, I put on headsets and listen to whale songs. There is something so profoundly moving about these ancient-sounding ballads that I'm almost instantly transported into a perfect state of openness to write.

Did you find Ken and Adam's problematic natures difficult to grapple with?

Obviously, there are some truly evil people in the world but for the most part, I think humans are like any other animal—at their most aggressive when they're wounded. Who hasn't said something horrible to someone they love? As a writer, I want to portray the complex gray areas in character. I'm far less interested in heroes and villains than in what's courageous and corrupt in all of us.

Which of the characters in *Little Monsters* did you find easiest to write? Who would you return to in the form of a short story or novella?
That's easy: Adam. Adam popped into my head pretty much fully formed, demanding that he be a point-of-view character. He was sarcastic and funny, and always said things that surprised me. I pretty much just held my hands over the keyboard and let him rip. It's something I've never experienced as a writer before and I hope will happen again! The rest of the characters took their sweet time in revealing themselves on the page, which is more typically the way it works for me. If Adam demanded more time on the page, I certainly wouldn't refuse, but I think Ken's wife, Jenny, is the character who has the most left to say.

What do you hope readers will take away from the novel?
I hope people will find it both entertaining and thought-provoking, of course, but beyond that, I imagine everyone will take away something different based on their personal experience. The unexpected question I took away from the book was that we are all born into families and accept the terms of families without thinking we have a choice. What if you didn't?

Avid Reader Press, an imprint of Simon & Schuster, is built on the idea that the most rewarding publishing has three common denominators: great books, published with intense focus, in true partnership. Thank you to the Avid Reader Press colleagues who collaborated on *Little Monsters*, as well as to the hundreds of professionals in the Simon & Schuster advertising, audio, communications, design, ebook, finance, human resources, legal, marketing, operations, production, sales, supply chain, subsidiary rights, and warehouse departments whose invaluable support and expertise benefit every one of our titles.

Editorial
Lauren Wein, *VP and Editorial Director*
Amy Guay, *Assistant Editor*

Jacket Design
Alison Forner, *Senior Art Director*
Clay Smith, *Senior Designer*
Sydney Newman, *Art Associate*

Marketing
Meredith Vilarello, *VP and Associate Publisher*
Caroline McGregor, *Marketing Manager*
Katya Wiegmann, *Marketing and Publishing Assistant*

Production
Allison Green, *Managing Editor*
Jessica Chin, *Manager Copyediting*
Alicia Brancato, *Production Manager*
Ruth Lee-Mui, *Interior Text Designer*
Yvonne Taylor, *Desktop Compositor*
Ritika Karnik, *Desktop Compositor*
Cait Lamborne, *Ebook Developer*

Publicity
David Kass, *Senior Director of Publicity*
Alexandra Primiani, *Associate Director of Publicity*
Rhina Garcia, *Publicist*

Publisher
Jofie Ferrari-Adler, *VP and Publisher*

Subsidiary Rights
Paul O'Halloran, *VP and Director of Subsidiary Rights*